# BRIEF CANDLE

# BRIEF CANDLE

## MARTIN BORIS

CROWN PUBLISHERS, INC.
*New York*

Copyright © 1990 by Martin Boris

All rights reserved. No part of this book may be reproduced or transmitted in any form or by any means, electronic or mechanical, including photocopying, recording, or by any information storage and retrieval system, without permission in writing from the publisher.

Published by Crown Publishers, Inc., 201 East 50th Street, New York, New York, 10022

CROWN is a trademark of Crown Publishers, Inc.

Manufactured in the United States of America

Library of Congress Cataloging-in-Publication Data

Boris, Martin.
    Brief candle / by Martin Boris.
    I. Title.
    PS3552.07534B75      1990
    813'.54—dc20                        89-27021
                                        CIP

ISBN 0-517-57484-5

10   9   8   7   6   5   4   3   2   1

First Edition

For Margaret Basner


With special thanks to Arthur Pine,
loyal friend, wise counselor, and
agent extraordinaire

# BRIEF CANDLE

# *one*

THOUGH MORE than a year has passed and we've gone through enough turmoil and self-destruction to last a lifetime, I've forgotten nothing of that hot, August Thursday. Not a sight, not a sound, an odor, an emotion—not the tiniest, most insignificant incident. Yet this is as it should be, for to forget even the least tick of time that day is to dishonor her memory.

I know this goes completely against the grain of accepted therapy, not at all what grieving is about, or so I've been told by the experts. But there are really no experts in such matters, only those who've gone through the fire and those who haven't. Survivors alone know about their private purgatory. All the rest is hearsay.

The fragrances that wafted up from the garden that sun-drenched morning came flooding through the Andersen windows of my den, six panes to the frame, eight frames to the room, over the wooden railings of the upstairs porch, through the screen door, invading our bedroom. Roses and honeysuckle and mimosa, tempered by the acrid earthy smell of tomatoes, which I've been raising for years on an unused and neglected portion of the garden that nevertheless receives sunshine the whole day long. Laura called me the only gentleman-farmer in town.

Those mixed fragrances, I remember, were the first to rouse me from sleep, soon followed by the more robust ones of coffee freshly brewing in the kitchen, and scrambled eggs and toast. If I'd have thought of drifting back, the rude clash of silverware changed my mind. I was fully awake and I strained to catch the musical interplay of voices, Laura's and Bobbi's, like a duet of reedy instruments, dominating all other impressions of the morning.

My wife and daughter had gotten up at dawn, as it was their habit and pleasure to go jogging. Like a pair of matched Thoroughbreds, they'd cantered slowly along the winding, leaf-arched, sun-splotched lanes of Woodsburgh, dressed in the same magenta running suits and duck-white Adidas. While I was lost in the dreamless sleep of the untroubled, they'd ticked off their usual five miles measured by the pedometers attached to their right legs.

Laura loved this time of day for more than its pristine beauty. Not only did the exercise prepare her for tennis matches at the club, where she was often winner of the annual trophy, woman's division, but she also got to be jogging partners with Roberta—affectionately tagged Bobbi—our youngest and only remaining child at home, who shared confidences with her mother as they chugged along. Some of which, if they weren't too personal, Laura would share with me.

While shaving, I made a mental note to bring home another tablet of cup soap for my wooden bowl and another cartridge of blades. In the shower I sang aloud and muttered a few mild curses: the lady jocks before me had used all the hot water after their run. Singing, nevertheless, because the night before Laura and I had made love. Very fine love, for as proficient as she was on the court, she was even more so in bed.

It was true, however, that occasionally she had declined my advances. What the hell, I thought, we're both in our late forties, had been lovers for almost thirty years. I certainly couldn't expect her to be the firecracker she'd been when Eisenhower was president. When I had all my hair and didn't wear bifocals. I could easily wait until she was in the mood. There was always tomorrow.

I knew Laura had always been a very sensuous woman beneath her cool and reserved exterior. No one before me had ever penetrated it or her. She's not one of those modern women who can discuss sex in public, or swear like a Marine Corps sergeant the way most of her friends do, deeming themselves totally liberated. She had this agile way of changing the subject whenever X-rated conversation cropped up in mixed company. Not that Laura's a prude. We had three daughters as up-to-date as Gloria Steinem. At the dinner table in our home, we have openly kicked around every subject from pederasty to penis envy—no blushing and no holds barred.

Sex for us had gone from the roaring fires of our youth to a banked flame. From the be-all and end-all to more a form of communication (except when it's very good like that night before). We'd often just lie quietly in our large double bed talking randomly about ourselves, the kids, and the tight little world we'd fashioned in the Five Towns, that gilded ghetto on Long Island's South Shore. Then, perfectly sated, we'd fall asleep almost simultaneously.

I remember dressing in a tan Izod sport shirt, bone-colored slacks, and sneakers, then walking down the steps to the sexagonal-tiled floor of the central hall. I turned left and entered the kitchen. Laura was alone, so I kissed her cheek while my hand slipped under her tennis shorts to squeeze that neat little hemisphere of ass. A not-so-subtle reminder of how good it had been last night.

*[3]*

"You're bad," she said, leaning over the table to remove the remainder of Bobbi's breakfast. Bobbi was in her room upstairs dressing. Of all the family, she was the only one to eat breakfast first, then dress.

"How bad?" I wanted to know.

"I'll tell you later in the dark," she said, imitating Mae West. She served me my orange juice.

"Is that a firm commitment?"

"Firm as your . . . oh, shut up and drink your juice." She laughed.

We heard a stirring above us. Bobbi came down the stairs, herd-of-buffalo fashion, said hullo, good-bye, glanced a kiss off the bald spot in the center of my head, and propelled herself through the screen door. She was wearing her red and white uniform, and I still recall how it blended with the red and white roses climbing up the garage wall. Bobbi served as a candy striper every summer at the local hospital. Mornings from nine A.M. to noon she made beds, did women's hair, shaved the men, read letters from families, wrote replies, fetched, and made herself generally useful in the wards and private rooms at St. Joseph's. Laura and I had often speculated over why a Five Towns princess would want to perform such menial chores. Her sisters had not been so altruistic.

"I don't know why. I just have to," she'd tell Laura as they'd jog. Laura would then tell me and we'd speculate on what it meant for Bobbi's future.

"I hope we don't have another Mother Teresa on our hands," Laura would say.

"There are no Jewish saints," I'd assure her. "Maybe it's only a passing phase."

I finished my second cup of brewed decaf as her '79 Cutlass with its bronchial muffler limped down the cracked shale driveway.

"A dynamo, that girl," said Laura with unabashed pride.

"Hell on wheels," I agreed.

My new Volvo, by contrast, purred like a well-fed tiger, then eased fluidly alongside the house and onto the road. In six minutes

I was at my pharmacy in Cedarhurst, the center village of the Five Towns. Inwood and Lawrence were to the west, Woodmere and Hewlett to the east. Everyone knew, however, that Cedarhurst was the finest jewel in the necklace. It had the best restaurants, the trendiest shops, the most prestigious professional practices in its office buildings.

Cedarhurst Chemists were ideally located on Central Avenue, the main street, between Gordon's Shoes for Women and the Garden Spot, an excellent medium-priced restaurant. The people of the Five Towns love to eat well, dress well, and zealously guard their health, so our three stores were gold mines, agreed Paul Gordon, Andy Thanakos of the Spot, and myself. Not smugly, but with pride and gratitude. We'd been fellow merchants and friends for over two decades as well as three-quarters of the infield of the Cedarhurst Businessmen's Softball Team.

If ever a man was foolish enough to love an inanimate object, it was me, the object being Cedarhurst Chemists. The store was notoriously successful. Every year volume grew at no less than ten percent, excluding inflation. And it had a throbbing vitality, a life of its own, providing a very cozy sanctuary within the invisible walls of our ghetto, as well as the perfect other pole to oscillate between. The house in Woodsburgh—the very woodsy, very exclusive community south of the Five Towns—was, of course, the opposite pole.

My crew had opened the store at nine A.M., half an hour earlier. The air conditioner was humming and already the store had the chill of a wine cellar.

I took it especially slow that August morning, looking for imperfections, for eyesores. I was trying to find something, anything, to convince myself that I was still in touch with the main action, and not distanced by all the paperwork that had become my lot.

It seems funny now, and sad, after all that's happened, how I drew out my entrance that morning and took a slow, eagle-eyed walk down the center of the store, eyes right, eyes left, like Patton reviewing the troops. I stopped opposite the baby department. It needed enlarging, I thought. All those new Orthodox families moving in. I'd seen their women pushing double-seated baby strollers along the Avenue. An infant in one half, a two-year-old in the other, an older child walking at their sides, bellies swollen with a fourth. Women hardly older than Caryn and Sara, my other daughters.

Before I'd gone much farther than midway, I was greeted by Maureen O'Connor, my head cosmetician. A large genuine smile. Maureen was blonder, perkier, and prettier than Doris Day. In the five years she'd been with me, she'd become an expert in the art of making the beautiful women of Cedarhurst even more beautiful. A gilder of lilies.

My manager for a decade, Eric, had also opened the store that morning with Jack Laitner, the second pharmacist, a large burly man of forty or so who sweated profusely in all kinds of weather and thermostat settings and needed a second shave by noon.

Mary Tannenbaum, sixty and ebullient as a corporate CEO, was at the prescription register. Mary's a proficient juggler, taking in prescriptions, ringing up sales, giving out prescriptions, joshing with the customers, eyes peeled to the flow of store traffic.

All greeted me after mainly ignoring my inspection of the store. They'd gotten used to this morning ritual and saw nothing sinister or threatening in it.

Eric had been instrumental in the store's success. He ran a tight ship, never permitted Maureen or Mary or any of the three part-timers to chitchat on the job or read romances when business was slow. It was Eric who'd sold me on installing a computer with three screens long before it had become fashionable.

I bought the whole package: hardware, software, and monthly updates. All the bits and bytes. Now it had a complete dossier on all my regulars, their allergies and other medical problems, what they swallowed to make their days livable, what they took to put them out at night.

"I'm getting started on the Christmas inventory," Eric piped as I'd been about to enter my monk's cell of an office. "The show is next week."

"Already?" I sighed, as though forgetting that the annual gift show was always held in August, and that this year's would be at the Javits Convention Center on Manhattan's West Side. Perhaps

I hadn't wanted to know since it meant rising early on Saturday, forsaking my weekly softball game, and trekking into the City.

I'd grown to hate Manhattan, the clogged roads leading there, its dangerous garbage-strewn streets, the general tawdriness, those enterprising beggars who dashed up at red lights to smear your windshield with old rags, then expected a tip.

Thirty years ago I'd felt part of the City: the Village, and SoHo before it went posh. The Cloisters, MOMA, and the American Museum of Natural History. Laura and I used to meet in Grand Central Station and visit all those places. They were the backdrop of our storybook courtship. Since then, both Manhattan and I had changed, off in different directions. It had gotten shoddy and I'd gone east, to Eden, to a place of safety, contentment, and peace.

I closed my door, prepared to wade through a mound of paperwork. I remember feeling a twinge of longing for Eric's job behind the prescription counter, a sense of alienation in mine behind a desk. No longer did I have much to do with the human aspect of being a pharmacist. Gone forever was the contact I'd spent a lifetime acquiring, perfecting, enjoying: those hushed conversations with female customers, gentling them through menopause, trying to explain away their fibroid tumors, their postpartum depression. Now a thing of the past, the men who'd once confided to me their extramarital adventures and social diseases. Men who'd suffered strokes and heart attacks, poignantly wondering if they'd ever be whole again. The boys who'd purchased their first box of Ramses Rolled, asking shyly if it came with instructions. The girls seeking the counsel they could never get from their mothers about taking the pill for the first time.

My daughters had all worked in the store, but not to increase my bottom line. The real profit was that I enjoyed having them around. I thought it important that they know how their father earned his living. Mothers aren't the only ones with umbilical cords. Caryn, now twenty-four, was fashion conscious, bright, and sharp as a winter's morning. She worked beautifully beside Maureen, despite the fact she was the boss's daughter, had a B.A. in marketing, and was a "Five Towns Girl."

Sara, two years younger than her sister, and now a newlywed as well, was the family scholar, with a degree in chemistry from Ohio State and minors in English and psychology. Like her father, Sara was also an introverted grouch at times. Her contribution to Cedarhurst Chemists was limited to the prescription department. She used to bug Eric and Jack unmercifully about the pharmacodynamics of each drug they repackaged. She'd take home the accompanying inserts and read about chemical structure and mode of function, then quiz them the next day. They were pharmacists, they told her, not chemists. Dispensers, not professors. My love for Sara, I'd often told myself, was part self-love.

Then there was Bobbi. Bobbi drove the delivery truck. Minimum wage plus tips. "I'm hedging my bets just in case college doesn't work out," she'd inform those who wondered what Laura Gerber's daughter was doing behind the wheel of a panel truck, as if toting bedpans wasn't odd enough.

Bobbi was neither her cool, reserved mother nor her bookish father, I remember thinking that day as she prepared her afternoon's work, but a throwback to some unknown, more sociable ancestor. Her face was as lovely as Laura's. Unadorned, full of goodness, and wholesome as a ripe apple. Her figure was mine: rangy, light-boned, narrow-hipped, yet not the least fragile. Bobbi had nailed a basketball hoop, formerly a symbol of adolescent maleness, over the garage when she was twelve, and forced me to shoot baskets with her on the evenings I'd come home early.

Though the hands-down charmer in the family, Bobbi had no boyfriends. She had instead, she was quick to point out, loads of best friends of both sexes, and no easily discernible gender. She recognized only qualities, not genitalia, and she'd bristle when I'd poke gentle fun at the ponytailed boys and girls dressed like hoboes who roamed unchecked through the house.

Though what happened in the store was my domain, Laura always wanted to hear how her working girls were doing. We'd lie in bed at night, connecting to each other across the links of our children. I'd tell her everything. A regular CIA briefing. Then she'd reach out and our fingers would intertwine. I could feel her glowing with pride.

*[8]*

"They're lovely girls," one of us was sure to say, not smugly, but with profound gratitude.

"You know why?" Laura would invariably ask.

"Why?" I'd say, as if I didn't know or couldn't guess.

"Because we were always there for them."

"Sometimes that's no guarantee."

"I know," she'd say so softly that I had to guess her reply.

"It's still a crapshoot, raising kids. Hostages to fortune after all. You know what I mean."

"I know. We're so lucky."

---

I remember the temperature had floated to the middle nineties that August afternoon. There was a necklace of perspiration across Bobbi's forehead and she'd changed from candy stripes to jeans and a white, cotton, man's shirt.

"Deliveries set to go?" she'd asked Jack who had been manning the phones that day.

"Set," Jack had said, a man of few words or no words at all.

"You're half an hour late," I recall reminding Bobbi. As was her habit, she never offered an excuse. "Yes, Pharaoh," she said, then looked up at the ceiling in an exaggerated show of sufferance I wasn't supposed to see.

The truth was, however, that Bobbi had been the best delivery person ever to work in the store. Without consulting a map, she knew every street, lane, road, court, and avenue in the Five Towns. She knew the fastest way to get there. The short cuts, the traffic lights to avoid. From her route, she'd come to be on a first-name basis with every cabdriver, gas-station jockey, cop, and store owner in the area. People she delivered to trusted her instinctively and regularly revealed themselves. Things they would often not tell me, their personal pharmacist for more than twenty years, they told Bobbi.

Some nights she'd come home looking as though she'd lost her best friend. "Such sad stories," she'd say, then burst into tears. Aaron Wellin had inoperable cancer and his son in Loma Linda, California, a Silicon Valley hotshot, had refused to fly home for maybe the last time. And Xavier Todeschi, who used to run the Amoco station on West Broadway, had Alzheimer's. At age fifty-five he had to retire. Will there be a cure soon? she'd asked. In time to save Xavier, her buddy, who'd always come out on the coldest mornings to jump-start her old Cutlass?

When I'd refuse to give her false hopes, she'd look so forlorn that I'd put my arms around her to squeeze away the pain. Her soft shoulders would shake, and I'd feel less than useless, but Bobbi would perk up, smile, and rescue me.

"Where there's life, and good people, there's hope, right?" she'd say, and I'd agree with her.

As Bobbi opened the back door of the storage room, heat flowed in like lava from a volcano. She took the keys and jiggled them as she walked to the truck parked in the municipal lot. I watched from my office as the white Dodge Ram, with blue lettering and a blue mortar and pestle anchored to the roof, edged up to the back door. Bobbi got out and loaded the white delivery bags according to town, street, and promised delivery time. Such quick hands, I recalled thinking. My daughter, the teamster.

"Okay, Pharaoh, I'm off to see the wizard," she shouted, knowing that my door was ajar and I was monitoring her actions. "Back in two hours," she promised.

"Shut the door," I shouted back. "We're losing all that cold."

"Yo," she yelled, slamming the door with spirit.

---

Bobbi didn't come back two hours later, or ever.

Only now, more than a year since that afternoon, and after a thousand attempts, can I say those horrendous words. Only now can they form in my mouth without the taste of ashes. It's taken that long to accept the series of events that followed. Of course there is a level at which I'll never accept what's happened. Never.

I'd just returned from a late lunch with Paul Gordon. Waiting for me and sweating even more profusely than Jack was Joe Pagano, a young darkly handsome Nassau County cop I've known since adolescence.

"Joe. You got a problem?"

"I wish I did," he said, shaking his head. He pointed to my office, where we'd shared many a cup of coffee during his winter-night patrols.

Inside, he ran his hand over a heavy brush mustache. "It's Bobbi," he said.

"What's she done this time? A stop sign? I keep telling her that stop means a *full* stop and not just slow down."

"Jeez, I wish to hell it was that." He halted and took a deep breath. "I'm sorry to tell you this, but she's dead. She was rammed broadside on Woodmere Boulevard by a drunk driver. She died instantly. She wasn't speeding or running stop signs or nothing. Just driving normally. I'm—I'm sorry. I was crazy about that kid."

It was as if he had taken out his revolver and pumped six bullets into my heart. I remember the blinding pain. I remember trying to open my mouth. I remember slumping into my chair. Then I passed out.

*two*

MARK'S RECOLLECTION of
that day is sharp and detailed. Whenever we talk about it, I hear
the same loosely connected series of events building to that moment the policeman asked Mark to come into the office, ending
life as we had known it for more than twenty years. So often has
he repeated it to me these last few months, it's almost as if I was
there that day with him.

Mark's memory of the week that followed is faulty. Mine is
much more distinct, though it shouldn't be with all the Valium I
swallowed, enough to addict many times over. Proof of how different we truly are—different from each other and, it turned out,
different from our own self-conceptions. Whenever I remind

Mark of the funeral and *shiva*—the standard week of mourning—and how he acted and what he said to loved ones and dear friends of a lifetime, he says, "Was that me?" And his face creases in bewilderment.

To distract him, I stroke his cheek or cover the bald spot on his crown with a lock from the side, but he usually persists, and we go on to recite our own thoughts and actions for the fifteen months that followed Bobbi's death. We wonder aloud about the two strangers who emerged from ourselves—terrible, destructive strangers who are no longer but whose actions we can't forget.

Mark called me at the library where I worked as special-projects coordinator. I'd been on the phone arranging for the loan of three pieces of sculpture for our reading garden. The artist was making a score of demands about insurance and protection for his work and proper advertisement in the local paper. I interrupted myself to take Mark's call. "Come home now. Please. Now," he said in a strange, twisted voice.

Oh God, *Daddy,* I thought. He was seventy-eight, and at that age . . . But before I could put down the phone, there was a policeman waiting at the Return Books counter.

He was a dark, handsome boy and bore a distinct resemblance to Keith Hernandez. When I asked him who it was, he said he didn't know. He was just doing a favor for Doc.

I started toward my car.

"You'll get it later," the policeman said, pointing to the patrol car.

A thousand murky scenarios churned in my head as we raced along Broadway. Luckily, my two oldest girls were safe at their jobs, Caryn at Lord & Taylor in Manhattan, Sara at the high school in Valley Stream, a few miles away. Sara was to start teaching science in the fall but had gone in early to acquaint herself with the building and its facilities. With Mark at the store, Bobbi was the most secure.

It could be Mark. I suddenly felt sick. After all, he was a retailer and holdup men do have cars. But Mark wouldn't summon me after a holdup. He's the Rock of Gibraltar, nerves of titanium.

Unless he's been shot. Then, of course, he wouldn't call himself. No, it had to be Daddy.

We turned down Woodmere Boulevard, picked up speed, then cut into Spruce Lane, an exit-only road. Fortunately, no one was coming in the opposite direction. Seconds later we hurtled up the driveway and I opened the car door before we'd fully stopped. I kicked off my shoes and ran barefoot across the grass to the front door.

Mark was in the living room by the window, his face the color of cottage cheese. When he stammered out what had happened, I didn't understand at first. Over and over he said it and gradually the two words combined and registered. Dead. Bobbi. Bobbi dead.

I began to scream. I screamed and screamed like the injured animal I'd suddenly become. I stared horrified into his eyes. He was crying and his face seemed submerged under tears. I pounded his chest and pounded and pounded for a retraction, for the truth, that it had all been a mistake, that it had been someone else's child, not ours.

Mark threw his arms around me, partly in self-defense, pinning my flailing arms to my sides. "No, no, no," I howled, thrashing, struggling to get free. Mark's a powerful man, lithe and athletic, but I was too much for him. His strength gave out, then mine did, too, and we collapsed to our knees. He released my arms. I wound them around his neck and cried, "Bobbi, Bobbi, Bobbi, Bobbi."

Mark opened his mouth but nothing came out. His lips were swollen and parched. I could see the words forming, then getting lost there, dying. His head fell into his hands and he shook all over.

A second wave of realization hit and I began tossing my head from side to side. I half fainted, though I do remember Mark lying next to me on the floor. The floor was parquet and recently polished. I recall the lemony smell, the glitter of its wax surface from the sun through the living-room window. Mark was holding me. We were like two sailors clinging to one another during a storm at sea.

We lay there for I don't know how long. Then through a prism of tears, I looked up and saw my father standing over us as if I'd conjured him up.

For the third time in his life that I'm aware of, my father cried. When my mother died was the first time, then after Caryn was born following twelve hours of labor. Daddy had always been a one-way door as far as emotion is concerned: everything in, nothing out. Now tears were streaming down his weathered face. A small, wiry man, he lifted me up and set me on the couch. Then he helped Mark and sat him next to me.

Daddy joined us. He took me in his arms and leaned back against the couch. "Baby, baby," he said, rubbing my back. "They called me from the store and . . ." His voice trailed off. He smelled of tobacco and sweat and old clothes. "Eau de Grandfather," Caryn had called it, though she adored him despite his musty odor.

For reasons just beginning to make sense, I'd felt more comforted, more secure in my father's arms than I had in Mark's. In my extreme agony, I had become Irving Peres's child again. I'd been one of these rare children, raised entirely by her father. My mother had been sick most of my infancy; I hardly remember her death. Daddy, in real estate at the time, had no fixed work schedule, so he'd been able to drop me off at school every morning and wait for me at the bus every afternoon. He attended all my school plays and volunteered for every outing requiring a parent volunteer. His evenings were spent helping me with homework. We went through public and high school together, two educated for the price of one.

Without relatives or loyalties, we'd become a nation of two. Daddy was there for me when I cried and when I laughed. I never remember being lonely.

Those first few minutes after Daddy arrived were a kind of retreat into the past. I'd been hurt as never before and fell into my father's arms in the foolish hope that he'd make things right again. Mark shuffled across the room and slumped down on the piano bench, as if he were a sack of laundry. The sag of his shoulders, his stooped, old man's walk, and the look of agony in his eyes should have told me to leave my father's arms and go to Mark. I regret not doing that, now. It might have made a difference.

But I was in shock and couldn't help myself, so how was I to help Mark? My father's thin, spindly arms were the haven I badly needed and couldn't possibly desert.

We sat transfixed for about an hour. The room was stifling without air-conditioning but no one made a move to turn it on. The late-afternoon sun had lifted over the eastern walls of yews lining the driveway, bathing the front lawn in sunshine and gilding the living room and all its objects. My father joined Mark on the piano bench, sat with him, an arm around his shoulder. Then suddenly, Daddy rose like a man who remembered he had things to do, and whispered in Mark's ear. Mark nodded and stood up slowly, like a servant reluctant to follow his master.

I knew at once where they were going and what they had to do. I didn't ask to go with them. I didn't want to know or see.

They were about to leave when two cars, a yellow taxi and a tiny blue Acura, sped up the driveway and stopped. The front door was still ajar and I could see Caryn running along the slate path to the veranda. Sara shot across the lawn, the path I'd taken, and beat Caryn to the door. Her face was bathed in perspiration and her short curly hair hung in limp ringlets as though she'd just stepped out of a shower. Nervous blotches crept up her arms and neck. Caryn, her long sable hair in her face, came close behind.

We all joined at the front door, forming a tight knot of five. We remained united until my father broke away. Mark also extricated himself, leaving me and my poor broken children to close ranks. Then they left.

How Mark had been able to go and identify Bobbi still to this day amazes me. The courage. The strength. Whenever I tell him this, he admits, almost with guilt, that he doesn't remember that part either. Especially *that* part. I guess it's better he doesn't.

Two hours later they returned, their faces drawn and tired, their eyes red-rimmed. One of the girls had turned on the air conditioner; otherwise nothing had changed. We were still numb, in shock and often hysterical in turn. When Mark came in I ran to him and held him as if he'd come home from the wars. My need for him had returned and he was once again my beloved husband, my best friend. He held me so tightly, so tenderly, I was sure he'd forgiven my lapse. My father held the girls.

I asked no questions. Their faces, Mark's and Daddy's, provided the most important answer. Yes, it was Bobbi lying in the Nassau County Medical Center morgue.

My father stayed with us in the living room for a few minutes more, then broke away to Mark's den. Above the whimpering of the kids I could hear the lock turn. The only time until that day the lock had been used. Since then, I've heard it turned many times.

While we sat in the deepening darkness, my father was in the den on the phone making the necessary arrangements. With a sense of order he passed on to me, Daddy first drew up a list. To us, a list is a commitment, a contract with ourselves.

I found my father's list later on Mark's desk and have saved it with my cherished memorabilia of that time. Each entry is in the bold scrawl he put on real-estate contracts and letters he'd send to summer camp after he'd finally consented to surrender me to the world. A heavy straight line through each task is his mark of completion.

His first call went to Jules Kaplan of Kaplan Brothers Chapels to arrange for Bobbi's removal from the hospital. Then he spoke to Rabbi Davidson of the Reform temple in town to deliver the eulogy in the chapel and at the grave site.

A third call went to the rental service that sends the mourning benches, the extra chairs, and the other paraphernalia of *shiva.*

A fourth went to Diamond Caterers in Lawrence for the appropriate food and drink for the seven-day mourning period.

Next, my father dialed long distance to Nat Gerber, Mark's father, retired for fifteen years and living in Boca Raton, Florida. Only my father calls it "Rat's Mouth," the literal translation and more fitting to the man, according to Daddy. Irving Peres tolerated Nat Gerber only because they had grandchildren in common. But Daddy knew that Nat had to be called. Nat loved the girls.

Finally, Daddy spoke to Paul and Suzy Gordon, our closest friends. They knew, of course, from the Avenue. To the Gordons, my father gave the onerous task of informing everyone that services were to be held at Kaplan Brothers the next morning at 9:30 A.M. As is the custom, except for the Sabbath and certain holidays, a death before sundown means burial the next day. In the other cases, it's a day later.

Knowing what the call to the Gordons would unleash, my father left Mark's phone off the hook. Then he went to my den at the opposite end of the house and lifted the second phone. Daddy was no stranger to tragedy even if Mark and I were. He'd buried a young wife and two small children, both girls and both less than a year old. He'd lost his parents at an early age, a brother on a Normandy beach during World War II, three sisters in a plane crash, and dozens of friends. Daddy knew all about sudden, inexplicable loss, and his protectiveness all through my early years must have been its result.

While Daddy completed his list, the two newest additions to our family, Warren Costa and Steven Levin, had arrived. Mark turned on the living-room lights as if signaling the entry of strangers to our mourning. We'd welcomed our sons-in-law to the family, Warren two years ago and Steven last May; however, subconsciously, I guess, Mark still considered them visitors.

My father nodded at the two young men, then went around the house opening lights as if in agreement with Mark. They're much alike, those two, which was why Daddy warmed to this first and only lover I'd taken in my youth. They both valued modesty, reticence, and candor, yet each defined a thief differently. With Mark it was in the performance; to Daddy it was getting caught.

———————

Midnight or so, Steven and Warren left to get a change of clothes for themselves and their wives, who were crushed but refused to leave. I couldn't help noticing how tragedy had made men of them. And women of my daughters. They were certain we needed them for support. They were so right.

Daddy left soon after the boys to return early in the morning. He lived close by in Lawrence.

Mark and I made our way up to the bedroom, where we didn't undress but fell on the bed and lay there like broken toys.

After a few minutes I said, "Honey, do you want a Valium? Eric brought some over while you and Daddy were . . . out."

"No," he said in a voice I didn't recognize.

"You're sure?"

"Yes."

"Some tea, then? You haven't eaten."

"Nothing."

"Sure?"

"Yes."

I got up.

"Where are you going?"

"I want to make sure the girls have pillows and sheets on the bed. I'll be back soon."

"Don't hurry," he said. "I'll be all right. Stay with them awhile. They need you."

At first, I believed he was so unselfish in his sorrow, thinking first of the children, sending me out to minister to them. Later, however, after everything went to pieces, I knew that he really wanted to be alone, completely alone. He preferred isolation for mourning Bobbi, to keep her to himself. He'd fobbed me off on Sara and Caryn so that he might hole up like some wounded animal.

Then I remembered, I had an impossible task to do: choosing the burial clothes for Bobbi. My father had taken care of everything but that. "It's the hardest part, Lorri," he'd said before leaving, "and I'd do it if I knew what to pick out."

"No, I'll do it, Daddy," I'd said.

It meant going into her room, and for a moment as I stood on the threshold, I wished I had sent Daddy up to take things from her drawers. Wished it had been somewhere on my father's list.

I turned on her desk lamp—the bright overhead light would have sent me fleeing from her room. I was surprised by the total disarray. Her clothes were strewn about like the aftermath of a hurricane, the bed unmade, Bruce Springsteen tapes scattered across the furniture like stepping-stones in a pond. I cried because the room seemed to imply Bobbi's immediate return and the recurring battle with the Board of Health inspector—me—over this potential health hazard. Listmakers also tend to be cleanliness freaks.

But everything had changed. Irreversibly and forever. I glanced at the poster above her desk. "Don't compromise yourself. It's all you have." An uninitiate's credo but she more or less had lived it. On the three other walls were *Saturday Evening Post* covers and farm scenes and old *Life* magazine covers of Fiorello LaGuardia and Joe DiMaggio, heroes to Bobbi.

Cluttering her room were the souvenirs she'd gathered in seventeen years of peeking into corners and traveling the byways: an odd-shaped, brilliantly speckled rock she'd picked up on the beach during a family outing to Lloyd's Harbor on the North Shore. She must have been six or seven at the time, terribly taken by the rock's unusualness; a feather from a snowy owl she'd once observed in the Lawrence Nature Preserve; a duck egg she'd rescued from a cat at the Woodmere Country Club, which its mother refused to take back.

"If it breaks and gets on the carpeting, it'll never come out," I'd said.

"You worry too much about the ifs," she'd said, a girl of twelve then. "Relax, kiddo."

Now all these objects had, in a few hours, become holy relics I'd treasure even more than Bobbi had and for better reasons.

After moments of hopeless sobbing, I chose Bobbi's favorite white dress. Fingering the hem created in me such a weakness I thought I'd pass out. I almost lunged at her bureau for support. From it, I chose a pair of her panties. It would seem strange handing them panties but no bra. Bobbi was small-breasted like all of us and didn't wear one. Should I include one of mine?

By now, the cumulative effect of all that Valium slowed my forward motion. It felt like walking through water to get to Caryn's old room. I recall praying that I'd have enough tranquilizer in me by midmorning to permit them to take Bobbi and put her in the ground. That I'd be paralyzed to the point where I could abandon her, leave my child who'd once rejected sleep-away camp because she couldn't bear to be separated from us overnight.

Caryn was sitting in her old rocker by the window watching the interplay of moon and clouds. Sufficient light deflected to her so that I could see the streaks of mascara like dried rivulets down her cheeks.

Her old room was now my music studio. I'd pushed her canopied Victorian bed against the wall and carried up from my den the music stand, the reams of sheet music, and my flute. I'd set up shop here overlooking the front lawn with its colorful floral palette: the red and yellow marigolds, the pastel blue four o'clocks, the flowering pear tree, and the cool mimosa under which I used to rock the girls to sleep when they were babies.

For half an hour a day I'd shut out the world to play Alex Wilder or Vivaldi or Mozart. On special days when I'd been particularly able to divorce myself from my surroundings, I'd try composing. Nothing elaborate, just a bit of melody that had come to me in the shower that morning or during lunch or the drive home from the library. A tune that had grown in me like a child and needed birthing.

What Mark would gain from his reading I'd achieve with my music. He had his space and I had mine and we had ours together. And there had been room and love enough for everything. If that had been a fool's paradise, then I wouldn't mind playing the fool again.

"I'm waiting for Warren," Caryn said. "And thinking about all the fine things Bobbi and I shared. Just the two of us. Did you know that she was thinking of taking off a year before college and going to Europe? With just a backpack and a Eurailpass? She didn't know how to tell you and Daddy and was trying it out on me first."

"No, I didn't know that."

"She tried all her ideas out on me, all the dicey ones, since we all know that I'm your clone. Sort of a trial balloon."

"And what did you say?"

"I encouraged her, told her that she was much too close to you and Daddy. And that maybe college wasn't for her. Not at this time, anyway."

"That's surprising. If you were really my clone, you'd have discouraged her, I imagine."

"I guess, then, I'm not really your clone."

I left Caryn by the window. The moon had gone behind a bank of clouds, leaving her face in shadow and mystery. I felt a sharp longing to be with Sara.

At Sara's door I could hear her crying and moaning, as sad a sound as I could imagine. I tapped lightly. "Do you need another pillow?" The room was as black as the inside of a box because of Bobbi's plants. After Sara had married last May she'd turned the room over to Bobbi, who then converted the scholar's retreat into a terrarium. She anchored hooks into the ceiling beams and hung pots and bowls and jars of green stuff at various heights. Spread around the room, some rising to meet the hangings, were bonsai and dwarf orange trees and plants with gorgeous flowers and Latin names.

"My ecosystem," Bobbi had announced, showing off to us.

"Your jungle, you mean," said Mark. "I'm warning you, though, I'll shoot the first snake I see." But when Bobbi stayed at friends for the weekend, it was Mark who watered her plants as diligently as he cared for his tomatoes.

I remained with Sara only a few moments. We sat on the bed holding each other. Wordless, tearless, exhausted. Her breath had a stale odor and I knew that she had been smoking. We'd all worked so hard to get her to kick the habit. Bobbi and Caryn had sent her little anonymous notes about the dangers. Mark quoted statistics. If cigarettes helped now, who was I, loaded with Valium, to object?

I thought about Mark; I crossed the hall again and entered our room.

He lay on his side, away from the door. I lay down next to him. He turned and held me so tightly, I couldn't breathe. Then he relaxed his grip and we lay there, and I was sure the same thoughts were going through both of us: why had this happened and how could we live without Bobbi?

I dozed off for a while or perhaps blacked out. Sometime before sunrise, I woke thinking that Mark was having a heart attack, he was gasping so. He sat up, his hands clutching the light quilt. Then he suddenly let out a long groan and fell back. "It's true, isn't it?"

"Yes," I said. "It's true."

He held my hand until he fell asleep again. I took it away when his breathing resumed its normal pace. Usually when he's asleep there's a peacefulness, a uniformity to his breathing that acts like a sedative to me. It's as though he's cleared a path for me to follow.

Out in the Atlantic, beyond the bedroom window, a pink opalescent dawn came despite my prayer that it wouldn't. Like specters, we rose and floated through the rooms, preparing ourselves for what was to come. Morning had made things worse. The nightmare of yesterday hadn't gone away, but intensified and become today's brutal reality. Daddy arrived and took Bobbi's package of clothes. For breakfast we all had black coffee and blue Valiums.

---

The funeral chapel sat like a frontier fortress on the far end of Hewlett, the easternmost anchor of the Five Towns. A square, solid, windowless building of yellow concrete, it gave the impression of impregnability. I'd been there for the funerals of the parents of friends but had never before noticed the second, recessed part of the structure where the less obvious functions were carried out. Now, seeing that half-hidden portion, I thought only of the strange hands that had touched my child, preparing her. I grew dizzy and nauseated, popped another Valium into my mouth, and bit down hard.

We'd arrived at eight to confer with the rabbi. My father had arrived an hour earlier to prepare the way. He was wearing a dark suit, his Mafia outfit, he called it, taken out of mothballs each time one of his friends or enemies departed.

Mark asked Rabbi Davidson for a short eulogy because he'd known Bobbi only slightly. Daddy agreed, since he thought eulogies were mostly acts of theater designed to squeeze the maximum of tears from an audience. Bobbi would not have approved of her friends and family being milked that way. I agreed.

While Daddy, the girls, and their husbands waited in a small room off the entrance to accept visitors before the actual ceremony, Mark and I slipped into the main chapel. Her coffin was already there, in front, opened.

Fifteen feet from the casket, Mark halted. I thought he was going to collapse. He steadied himself by gripping the back of a row of seats, his free hand unsteady as he motioned for me to go on alone.

Bobbi lay calm and lovely, encased in satin in the dark walnut box my father had chosen. She seemed asleep, as though waiting for me to wake her for our early-morning run through Woodsburgh, at peace with the world and herself.

I leaned in to kiss her lips. They were cold. Face, cold. Hands, cold. My heart cried out for a blanket to cover her. Whoever had prepared Bobbi in that hidden area of the building had done a wonderful job. They'd even refrained from applying makeup. My father must have told them she never wore any.

I looked at Bobbi for a long time. It would have to last forever.

Mark hadn't budged from his position. His eyes had refused to glance at the coffin or at me, fixing instead on the brilliant sunlight filtering in through the multicolored stained windows. He seemed mesmerized by its kaleidoscopic effect.

"Aren't you coming to say good-bye to her?" I said low because I could hardly speak.

"I can't. I'm sorry, I just can't."

"Mark, she's not disfigured. She looks . . . beautiful."

"It doesn't matter. I just can't look at her."

I know I should have gone and uprooted him. Taken him by the hand. But at the time I couldn't leave my place either.

He must have seen the hurt in my eyes. He said, "If I look at her, I might not be able to go through with it."

"But Mark . . ."

He shocked me with the swiftness of his reply, his sudden vehemence. "Don't ask me again," he said stingingly; and to make sure I wouldn't, he darted out of the chapel to find the rest of the family. When I rejoined him in the small anteroom, I touched Mark's face to let him know that though I disapproved of what he'd done in the chapel, I understood.

We received the mourners. They passed by in single file as if we were royalty, to kiss us, to hold us loosely or in gentle bear hugs, in tears or solemn-faced, silently or with hushed commentary. They were our dearest friends, our closest acquaintances, our neighbors, some neither Mark nor I cared for very much and a few we actively disliked. In and out they filed: Mark's staff and customers, and my people from the library and the Five Towns Women's Symphonic Orchestra. Caryn's friends and Sara's. And Bobbi's—a strange but wonderful collection of long-haired boys with the faces of Christ's apostles, or tough-looking young men in studded leather jackets holding motorcycle helmets; and young girls with wild woolly hair and frayed jeans, and fashionably dressed kids from Bobbi's class in school. Volunteer firemen and cops in their best uniforms and the kids who washed the store windows on the Avenue and pumped gas for a living.

We entered the main room and took our places in the first row. The coffin was closed. Later I learned that Mark had requested it, that being the only way he could sit so near. Before the sealing, Caryn and Sara had placed notes inside. They never told me what they'd written. I never had the courage to ask.

Mark was seated to my left and I took his hand. It was cold, cold as Bobbi's. With my other hand I reached for Sara. She took Caryn's. Caryn at once took my father's and together we formed a chain. After a short, direct opening, the rabbi read from Thornton Wilder's *Our Town*. Someone, Sara probably, had told him that Bobbi loved the play, a hymn to the inherent goodness of ordinary people leading ordinary lives. In well-modulated tones he read, " 'Now there are some things we all know, but we don't take'm out and look at'm very often. We all know that *something* is eternal. And it ain't even the stars . . . everybody knows in their bones that *something* is eternal, and that something has to do with human beings. All the greatest people ever lived have been telling us that for five thousand years and yet you'd be surprised how people are always losing hold of it. There's something way down deep that's eternal about every human being.' "

I was moved, of course, but the reading provided me with little comfort. I didn't care much about the eternalness of the human spirit. It had nothing to do with Bobbi and our loss.

Our hands held firm through a recitation of that exquisite portion of Ecclesiastes beginning with, "For everything there is a season." Another of Bobbi's favorites. She knew it because Pete Seeger, her idol of idols, had set it to music.

With this section, I felt more in tune. After all, Bobbi's time on earth had been so short. She'd had little of it to love, none at all to plant or reap.

Tears freely coursed down our cheeks but we refused to break our chain of love to wipe them away. Only Mark was tearless. He hadn't cried since last night. Was he taking something that he was afraid to give us?

Services were concluded with a reading of the Twenty-third Psalm. By its conclusion, most of the crowd was sobbing. For more, I think, than the psalm's profound imagery. "The family of Roberta Gerber," said the rabbi, "has requested that all contributions in her name be sent to MADD, Mothers Against Drunk Driving. They hope that in some small measure this might prevent other such abominations. The seven-day period of mourning will be observed at the home of Mr. and Mrs. Mark Gerber at Twenty-seven Spruce Lane in Woodsburgh." Seated in a long limousine, our lights turned on, we left for the cemetery. In the rearview mirror I could see the cortege behind us.

My father sat between Mark and me, a beaten man. His hands rested on bony knees, sighing, wiping tears from eyes even narrower than their normal peasant slits. I thought, feeling his shoulder against mine, that though Caryn was his favorite by reason of being the first grandchild, he loved Bobbi best. Only she had fought his unceasing largess. Only Bobbi had declined those twenty-dollar bills my father freely dispensed to all his grandchildren when he came for dinner, as if trying to pay for the meal.

"Honestly, Pops, I have more than enough," Bobbi would sweetly say, and firmly push away his hand. My father found other ways to show his love. He'd leave gift certificates from all the stores in town under her pillow like some tooth fairy. Later, when I could bring myself to clear out her room, I found a stack of unused ten- and twenty-dollar certificates for shoes and handbags and waxings and manicures and haircuts piled up in her desk along with old birthday cards and concert programs.

Our procession slowed traffic along the Southern State. Sun worshipers and swimmers were trying to get it all in before Labor Day. Our headlights blazed in the sharp, almost autumnal air, but that meant little to the beach bound. Crawling by, they glowered at us. I wanted to shout to them that they had next week and next summer and a lifetime ahead of them. Bobbi had run out of summers and sunshine. Couldn't they see the headlights? Were they so blind, so selfish?

A few miles into Suffolk, the procession left the highway and took a two-lane strip as treeless as the tundra. We entered the cemetery gates and my heart plummeted as I viewed the vast city of headstones, mausoleums, and flat markers no larger than business envelopes.

The last time I'd been there was in November, with Daddy, on the anniversary of my mother's death. We'd tidied up the large plot and my father had stared at the cocoa brown headstone. "Mine will be to her left. I always slept on the left side of the bed. My will is in the bank vault, by the way. Along with all those pictures of Ulysses S. Grant and Benjamin Franklin."

"Now, you stop that," I'd said, clearing the weeds from the base of the stone. "You take Ulysses and Ben and go on a round-the-world cruise. Haven't you done enough for us? And don't you dare talk to me about death. You have lots of years left."

We each put a pebble on Mama's stone, a religious custom I felt good observing, which the caretakers would remove. When I'd visit again, I'd put on a fresh one. Somehow this give-and-take kept the small ceremony meaningful for me.

"Why is it, Lorri," my father always asked leaving the cemetery, "the grass is greener here? The air sweeter, purer?"

I'd never answer, but I knew why and I thought now, approaching the shady hill, how much sweeter the air would be, how greener the grass with Bobbi a new resident.

An ugly gash had been carved in the earth earlier that morning. A mound of butterscotch-colored dirt on either side glistened with unevaporated dew. At my side Daddy muttered, "I should have been next. First grandparents, then mother and father, then children. It's not right," he said bitterly, a man who usually took the world as it came.

The service this time was in Hebrew. We huddled together, my family, as against a punishing wind, to the recitation of the *Shma,* the declaration of faith in the unity of God. Caryn and Sara, who I thought were totally dehydrated from all their crying, found new wells to tap. My own tears poured as from an open faucet. Daddy dabbed at his eyes with a large yellow handkerchief. Only Mark was tearless, his face a stone carving that had been left out in the elements for a millennium. A twitch in his lower right eyelid was the only sign of life I could see, as though something locked within was sending out distress signals.

Bobbi was to be buried less than five feet from her grandmother and two infant aunts. I heard the opening prayer and went deaf. Then it was over. An orange bulldozer appeared at the foot of the hill, followed by four men in army fatigues carrying rolled-up heavy straps. The rabbi wisely motioned for us to lead the gathering back to the waiting cars so that the men might complete their task, and we wouldn't witness the final act.

Mark walked away so slowly, he became the last one off the plot. I lost him momentarily as the crowd dispersed. When I spied him again, he'd turned around and was heading back to the grave. The men had lowered the coffin with those heavy straps and were waiting for the bulldozer to begin.

At the edge of the grave Mark halted and peered in as if on a roof ledge, considering whether to take the plunge. He teetered dangerously and my heart began to swell and throb. There was a wild, desolate look in his eyes. He bent down and scooped a handful of the soft earth, now powdery and bleached to a light beige by the noonday sun. Mark sifted the soil through his fingers, eliminating the clumps and pebbles, then lightly tossed the strained earth into the hole, trying not to cause a sound or a blemish on the coffin below. His lips trembled, and although I couldn't hear what he said, I knew nevertheless: good-bye Bobbi.

I guided Mark to the waiting limousine. He didn't look back as we drove off. Now that I can think clearly about that morning, I realize a strange irony. In the chapel I was the one saying good-bye at the coffin while Mark had held back, unable to join me. At the grave site it was Mark who couldn't tear himself away, while I stood off to the side. At the two most painful moments in our lives, we weren't side by side. We'd taken opposite positions, at a great distance. We were like performers on a trapeze.

---

The ride home was in total, stony silence. The day had turned windy and cold, so we kept the windows closed. The air in the limo quickly turned stale and smelled of my father's mothballs. Still, no one said a word or made a move for air. The girls sat stupefied, like rush-hour passengers on a train after a day's work. My father seemed to have aged a year for every hour since yesterday. For the first time I noticed liver spots on his hands, quarter-size blotches like coffee stains. When had that happened?

Appearing older as well, Mark seemed to take up less space in his seat by the window. In a ball of himself, he studied the road. In his lap he supported the hand that had held the bit of soil. His fingers were stained but he'd made no effort to wipe them clean.

The limo drove up the driveway and let us out. Daddy helped the girls along the gray slate to the veranda. I took Mark's hand, breaking the spell. "I didn't know we knew so many people. That Bobbi had so many friends."

We were at the front door. Mark whirled and sprang at me as if from ambush. "For most of them it was just a goddamn fashion show. A chance to show their fall finery."

How venomous he sounded. How vicious. I didn't know the man who'd made those remarks. I told myself it was the dark side of grief talking, the agony. Like a sudden summer storm, it would quickly pass.

As it turned out, I was wrong. The storm lasted for quite a long time. To this day it hasn't completely subsided.

# *three*

I'VE NEVER GIVEN much thought to the behind-the-scenes activities of *shiva* or its logistics. In the past, when Laura and I made condolence calls, everything was already in place and functioning—like photosynthesis or space-shuttle shots—accomplished by obscure people you never saw or heard from until needed and never saw again.

We'd arrive, offer our regrets, take a sip of coffee, a bit of cake, remain perhaps half an hour, then leave. I was surprised, therefore, at the change that had taken place in my own house when we returned from the cemetery. Crossing the threshold, I could see that the ornate mirror in the front hall had been covered with a white sheet. Large expanses of material, like painters' dropcloths, hung from the entire left wall of the living room, hiding the smoky full-length mirror that made the room seem enormous. These shrouds would obscure all symbols of vanity so mourners would think only of the newly deceased.

The coverings hadn't been Laura's idea. We were both closet atheists and nonconformists. It had been Irving's idea, as well as the mourning benches stacked in the kitchen. Low cardboard boxes the size of the record storage units I kept in the basement of Cedarhurst Chemists. Sitting on them was also symbolic: low in height, low in spirit.

But the most jarring sight was the elaborate assortment of foods Irving had ordered with one of his phone calls the night before. In the dining room, under the brilliance of the crystal chandelier, covering the entire cherrywood table around which the family had gathered at least once a week, were enough provisions for a banquet.

On one huge circular platter radiated spokes of corned beef, pastrami, tongue, sliced turkey, and roast beef, rare and lean. In its hub, wedges of potato salad, coleslaw, pickles, and sour tomatoes.

A second wagon wheel held Nova Scotia lox, smoked salmon, herring in wine sauce, tuna salad. Heaps of it. Strategically placed on the table were stacks of rye bread, pumpernickel, and whole-wheat squares as high as the two-liter bottles of Coke, Diet Pepsi, and Seven-Up. On the adjacent breakfront were paper plates, plastic utensils, styrene cups, and napkins made of recycled paper.

The spread sickened me. I'd come home to be alone with Laura, the kids, and my thoughts, not to play the good host. I'd steeled myself for a few visitors and a pot of coffee. Instead, a feast had been prepared. Suddenly I hated everything he'd done for us. Like me, Irving should have been contemplating how long it would take for the gleaming handles of her coffin to rust, the oak to crumble, the flesh to melt from her bones. Instead, he'd been concerned with five kinds of cold cuts, four kinds of fish, three kinds of bread. After he'd washed his hands—another archaic tradition—he began at once giving instructions to the rotund Peruvian woman who'd come with the food.

But worse than these abominations was Irving's frame of mind during that week of *shiva*. His unquestioned acceptance of her death. More than a few times I overheard him saying, "What can I tell you? She's gone to a better place. She's with Rachel and the girls. I know it in my heart."

A better place? Better than with us? How could she be alive for him and dead for me? What right did he have to believe in immortality when I couldn't?

---

I followed Laura up the stairs and joined her in the bedroom. Languidly, she stepped out of one shoe, then the other, pulled her dress over her head, let it fall to the floor, then crawled into bed. Fully clothed, I lay down beside her. Our arms wound around one another as though a silent command had been given. We lay motionless, incapable of uttering a single word of anguish or comfort.

Laura did try to speak, but the words came out blurred. I knew she had taken too much Valium. I'd done without anything. I hadn't the desire to shield myself. I wanted the pain acute, unfiltered, potent. To take Bobbi's death straight, I'd thought, would be the measure of my love. Over the year that followed, the reality and force of that pain kept me alive and going. Often, when I'd hit bottom, it was all I had, and as long as I had it I had Bobbi.

After Laura's incoherent mumbling, she cried. Gently, like a mild spring rain, and I let her tears wash over me and into my shirt. I could smell the slightly floral, almost musky odor her body was exuding.

Though I tried, I couldn't match her tears. Some powerful dam inside held them back. I told myself I was beyond tears, beyond sorrow, beyond mourning. If Laura wasn't, I certainly wouldn't hold it against her. As it turned out, I did.

We might have lain there forever if Irving hadn't coughed at the bedroom door, then rapped lightly. "Children," he said in a low, semistern voice, as if we *were* children. "They'll be coming soon to pay their respects."

Laura pressed her eyes into my shirt, drying them. She lifted her head. "Yes, we'll be down soon." Raising her entire body, she left for the bathroom. I heard the water running. I heard her gargling, readying herself.

Laura put on a white dress and flats after some hesitation at her closet door. She came and stood over the bed. I was still irked at being spoken for, as I hadn't intended coming down soon. And it nettled me that she had enough presence of mind to wash her face and perfume her breath, then select the proper attire for the *shiva* callers.

When I didn't follow her lead and Irving's tune, she returned to my side of the bed. "It's something we have to do," she said. I hated being reminded of my obligations like some homework-shunning schoolboy.

She spoke again, emphasizing "have to."

I stirred lethargically, overcoming some powerful force holding me to the bed, and accompanied her downstairs. I was becoming so distorted that I felt a twinge of triumph in not washing my face or dousing my mouth with Listermint.

---

"Sonny, Sonny, Sonny," my father intoned, holding me first with one arm then the other. "I'm sorry, so very sorry about Bobbi. Such a tragedy. Such a loss. I couldn't make it to the chapel. Irving's call last night came too late for even standby. By the time I got here this morning you'd already gone."

From the intensity of the Scotch on his breath, I knew where he'd waited and how long. My father held me and slowly rocked, then let go, but kept one hand on the back of my neck like a hold-and-hit boxer. Laura joined me in the front hall. She offered her cheek to Nat and he kissed it. Then he rocked her as he'd rocked me.

Nat gave up Laura only when he saw Sara and Caryn. They'd been sequestered in Laura's den with their husbands, dreading the certain onslaught of consolers but responding to the sound of their grandfather's voice. Like Laura, they knew that civilities must be observed, especially Caryn. Like me, Sara had been repelled by the dining-room spread, telling her sister, her husband, her brother-in-law that Irving's potlatch had been in poor taste. As far as covering the mirrors . . . positively medieval.

The girls flew against Nat, who swayed back and forth with them in his arms. They loved him without reservation. Of course they'd noticed the great difference in grandfathers, but that never affected their love. I'd always kept my feelings about my father from them.

To his credit, Nat didn't flinch from their hot tears as they fell on his very expensive dark blue suit. He wore a narrow matching tie, and Guerlain's Impériale cologne, which was, for as long as I could remember, part of his aura. Underneath the suit he wore a white-on-white shirt, French-cuffed, with square gold cuff links the size of dice. His black Italian-made shoes were polished to a mirrored surface. Nat could have been a banker except for those gaudy nugget-sized cuff links.

I was surprised. I'd never seen Nat in anything but bright plaids, houndstooth or stripes, the colors in a Crayola crayon box. Shirts and slacks equally as loud. Ties wide as a hand span and decorated with fish or horses. Shoes with tassels. To Nat Gerber, clothes had always been both a statement about himself and a way of attracting attention, of standing out at parties and business conventions.

As always, his full head of pewter gray hair had been freshly cut and carefully groomed, his nails lacquered. He'd been to a barber for his weekly trim, polish, and lube job.

My father hadn't gained a pound or added a facial line since Caryn's wedding two years ago. He'd missed Sara's because he'd been in the Soviet Union at the time with some rich widow who'd picked up the entire tab.

He'd come to the wedding with a ravishing redhead, younger than the bride, a lingerie model. Nat's women were all ages, all types, each as flashy as goldfish. He either supported them or they supported him. He was a great believer in equality between the sexes. As a child, I knew that he cheated on my mother with women who took the lion's share of his earnings as eastern regional manager for Cutty Sark. Mother and I got mouse droppings. Until she died in 1954, a bitter and shrewish result of his maltreatment, we never knew where the next month's rent or this week's groceries were coming from. He wrote enough rubber checks to make a life raft and we had to pay cash for everything. When I'd ask him why—he was earning good money, enough to dress like a movie star and visit the barber once a week—he'd always quote Browning. "A man's reach should exceed his grasp."

At my wedding, he'd said, "You're one lucky son of a bitch, you know. Or maybe you don't." There'd been as much admiration in his voice as begrudgement. "Just like that to fall in so soft. Here I've busted my balls all my life to put a few bucks together—scratched and fought and cut corners where I had to—and you strike gold your first try. And what burns me is that you never meant to! You don't give a rat's tit about what comes with the princess."

I couldn't very well deny that Irving Peres was rich but I hadn't felt guilty about marrying into all that wealth. The truth was, I seldom thought about money and it was, ironically, Nat Gerber's doing. I'd grown up hating all that he stood for and I molded my character into the diametric opposite of him.

The fact of Irving's real-estate holdings was a minor attraction, way down on the list of Laura's qualities. Higher up was her tall, shapely, tiny-breasted figure, her lovely serene face, soft brown shoulder-length hair, and most of all, her self-assured yet shy intelligence: the ultimate aphrodisiac to me.

When a portion of the Peres fortune had been handed us—the house and the store—I accepted them without reservation since I'd married for love. At Caryn's first birthday party when I took Nat on a tour of the house—his insistence—I realized how the fires of envy still burned. We'd strolled from room to room, my father and I, basement to attic, then out to the three-car garage and the back lawn, where we finally came to rest in the new gazebo I'd added.

"I've got to admit, Sonny," he'd said, running his hand along the rough-hewn oak railing of the gazebo. "You're a better man than I, Gunga Din. Though you probably still don't understand what a great deal you got."

"What I got," I said, eager for Laura to call us in to begin the party so that I could get away from him, "is a best friend and a damn good wife. Those priceless things you threw away."

Nat tried to sear me with one of his withering stares, the kind that used to scare the hell out of me before I knew him well.

"What do you know about your mother? What do you really know? She was no saint, Sonny. No woman is. Not even your Laura. Let a few things go bad in your life, then we'll see about friendship."

---

When Nat announced he had to catch the eleven P.M. to Fort Lauderdale, a previous, unshakable commitment, I didn't try to stop him. Laura didn't either. Over the years she'd never warmed to him. Neither of us thought to insist that he call Lauderdale and cancel his commitment.

People began to arrive: the ones I barely noticed in the chapel or at the cemetery and those who couldn't make it or who'd just found out, or the few who came out of curiosity, wondering how the Gerbers lived, that most golden of golden families whose lives had been a modern fairy tale instead of a TV soap.

They trooped in and I couldn't help resenting their pained expressions and automatic words of sorrow, the ones, I'm sorry to say, I'd used myself on occasion. But unlike myself, they didn't dispense their condolences and leave. They gave their stale little offerings, then gravitated toward Irving's spread where they took paper plates, knife and fork, napkin and cup, then went clockwise around the table and made their choices of fish, fowl or red meat, rye or pumpernickel, soda or coffee.

Ready to erupt, I cornered Laura in the hallway between the kitchen and the dining room. She seemed paralyzed from the first round of visitors. She stood there quaking, as though lost, alone, and too scared to ask for directions.

Driven to the edge by my loss, I hissed, "You'd think they hadn't eaten in days." My voice swelled to a stage whisper. "We've got a fucking banquet going on out there."

"Please, Mark," she said, her eyes beseeching me as well. "It's not our way of doing things, but Daddy's been a godsend in all this."

"Don't you dare talk to me about God. There is no God," I snarled. "And if there is one, He's a rotten bastard to do a thing like this to us."

That Friday evening to the following Thursday became one long day of continuous torture, of rising and falling anger, of forcing myself to converse, to gulp black coffee, to nibble at food, to sit among those I've known half my life and find, much to my amazement, they were all total strangers. To usher the last of them to the door each night and trudge wearily up to bed without the slightest hope of sleep. To lie in the dark next to another fellow sufferer for four or five hours, unable to share the ineffable, though we'd shared everything else until that Thursday.

Each morning, sapped from reliving that moment in the store with Joe Pagano, I'd watch Laura force herself from bed and create the miracle of reinventing herself, using only willpower. It's so satisfying to hate the strong. You tell yourself it's not strength but a lack of caring. An insensitivity. In Laura's case neither was true, but at the time I had to believe that her love for Bobbi was far less than mine.

I watched as she'd shower, put on fresh clothes, brush her hair the usual fifty strokes—I'd count them—then go downstairs to prepare the house for the next assault. It was an act hard to follow.

---

During the week, the consolers came and went, the new replacing the old, the old making two and three appearances, expecting Irving's hospitality to remain at a four-star level. And it did. Each day at noon and again at six, a bright, electric orange van would pull up at the kitchen door and a man would emerge and take out two platters as large as truck tires, wrapped in amber cellophane, and hand them to the waiting Irving Peres or the Peruvian girl. The driver would follow behind with fresh utensils and cases of soda and loaves of bread. I tried not to be there when the new provisions arrived. They only fed a flame that needed no fueling.

Sara and Caryn, who had moved in with their husbands for the *shiva,* were our commanding officers. Grandpa Irving was the rest of the army. How a man close to eighty summoned the energy to remain alert and active from noon to nine each day, every minute of the day, was a source of constant wonder. Subsisting on only cigars and seltzer, he wandered unnoticed among the various groups, steering in and out of rooms like a submarine through a convoy, emptying ashtrays, retrieving abandoned soda cups and half-empty food plates, putting out cigarettes, refilling ice buckets, making small talk here and there, issuing orders on the phone to the caterer and to his Peruvian helper.

Late at night, when only the family was left, he'd cap the liquor bottles, wash the swizzle sticks, close off the containers of soda, empty the ice buckets, and reset the ice trays in the refrigerator. Only then would he relight his cigar stub, say good night, and go home. Much as I disapproved of the carnival atmosphere, I had to admire his singleness of purpose, his devotion to us.

---

Those seven days of *shiva* I'm afraid I waged a kind of guerrilla warfare against everyone who came into the house, daring friends of long standing to do or say something so outrageous to my ears that I might decimate them. I wanted to grab them by the throat, male and female, shake them until their fillings loosened, and say, "What the hell are you all jabbering about? Bobbi is dead. Don't you realize that? How can you eat and drink and make small talk as if nothing happened?" I wished similar tragedies in their own houses. I did say I was out of my mind at the time.

My first explosion came late on Tuesday. Jack Laitner and Eric Kornblum, my two pharmacists, showed up about 8:30. As pharmacists do when they get together, they talked shop. Seeing me nearing, they halted discussion. The usual offerings of regret; I'd been hearing it all day. Then Eric handed me an envelope of payroll checks to be signed. He'd be back tomorrow night to pick them up. About to leave, Eric made his blunder. "Well," he said, "time heals all wounds."

Never say that to a grieving parent. Never.

I glowered at Eric, a father of two himself, so nimble behind the prescription department yet so doltish beyond. "I thought you liked Bobbi," I hissed. "Now you want me to forget her, to put on a Band-Aid and go about my business? Is that all she is? A goddamn boil or a blister?"

The poor fellow didn't know what to say. He hung his head like a condemned man before a judge, mortified. He left at once and didn't return the next day for the signed checks. I had to give them to Mary Tannenbaum when she visited on Thursday. When I returned to the store I apologized to Eric, but it did little good. I'd shattered our relationship, and before the year was out, I'd paid dearly for my ill-tempered outburst. He couldn't have known what it was like to lose a child. No one does until it happens, and the truth is time doesn't heal. It forms a scar, at best, over the wound, but beneath the new tissue is the old sore, fresh and raw as ever, festering.

I was even less civil on Wednesday to my dearest friend, Paul Gordon. A few years ago when Paul turned forty, his marriage to Suzy began to flounder. A classic case of middle-age crisis, Paul naturally thought that its cure was other women. Despite our many lunch discussions, he began fooling around with one of his salesgirls, a twenty-seven-year-old divorcée with two children, a high bust, flawless body, and unblemished skin.

Suzy found out and came crying to me for help. I was reluctant to get involved because one wrong move and I could lose both of them. Still, a few right moves and I might save their marriage. Besides, I owed Suzy. She'd run interference for us back in our courting days, by telling Irving that his precious child was spending the weekend with her, not in some motel out in Suffolk making wild love.

Snooping around, I learned that Ms. Flawless Body was also solving problems for Nikos, the volatile Greek waiter at the Garden Spot. I invited the girl for lunch one day, at another restaurant. I spoke to her Dutch-uncle style, hinting that if she didn't cool it with Paul, word might filter back to crazy Nikos that he was being two-timed. The divorcée fiddled with her Dieter's Delight platter of tuna and cottage cheese and left before the no-calories baked apple. She cleared out that weekend for Boston, where, she told Paul, a job managing a very fancy boutique awaited her.

That night at *shiva*, because I think he had nothing to say but felt the need, he offered, "Well, it'll bring the four of you closer together."

Another piece of garbage not to lay on the grieving parent. "Asshole," I said, and he jumped back, startled. "Where the hell have you been all these years? Don't you think we're close enough? Closer than any goddamn family in this whole goddamn county? You think I say to Laura, 'Oh well, Bobbi's gone but we'll close ranks with Sara and Caryn?' What are we, Paul, a fucking army platoon?"

Paul backed away and began searching for Suzy. The Gordons left at once without saying good night. Laura's eyes followed them out the door and down the driveway where the cars were lined up like a railroad train. A sadness infused her face and she looked at me across the room.

Needless to say, I called the next morning and asked to be forgiven. Paul accepted my apology, but as with Eric, our relationship was never the same.

Every night I expected a stern lecture from Laura but got none. I was prepared to counter with her own strange, un-Laura-like conduct. This very private person, it seemed, had gone public, sharing memories of Bobbi with anyone who'd listen. Did she have to tell Jerry Wheinman, the mayor of Woodsburgh, and a Republican, that Bobbi intended taking off a year before going to college? How come I didn't know that? And that Bobbi knew more about car engines than the mechanics at Lawrence Olds?

I confess these were the moments I began questioning my true feelings for Laura even as I admired her grace with friends who had the callousness to laugh under my roof that week. I didn't know that my grief had taken a terrible path. Hers, I know now, was on the road to recovery, while I could only thrash about in my thicket of despair.

The only one I honestly welcomed to my house that week was

Joe Pagano. He came in civilian dress, and at first I didn't recognize him the way some of my customers fail to recognize me without my white jacket.

I greeted him warmly in the hall. Laura tore herself away from Maureen O'Connor, Mary Tannenbaum, and Violet Fleming, the conductor of the Five Towns Women's Symphonic Orchestra, to add her welcome. She also said how grateful she was for the ride home and for later fetching her Saab from the library parking lot.

"No sweat, Mrs. Gerber. We didn't want it vandalized. Seems there's a bunch of kids from Queens running around ripping off foreign cars."

Then, probably realizing that the theft of her hubcaps or the stereo meant nothing compared to losing her child, Joe fell mute. Laura left us and I told him to please help himself to the food and drink. But he was so shy about it that I had to lead him to the table and hand him a plate, knife and fork, napkin and cup.

After Joe had taken a slice of turkey and some coleslaw and a cup of Coke, I asked him into the den and locked the door.

I sat down in my swivel chair at the desk. Joe sat in the captain's chair facing me. He balanced his plate on one armrest, his Coke on the other. He looked straight at me, waiting.

"I'd like to know about the accident."

"What would you like to know?"

"Everything you know."

"Everything I know," he echoed.

I could see that he was ill at ease and suspicious. His policeman's mind at work.

"Oh, don't worry about my doing anything foolish. If I cut the bastard into a thousand pieces and threw each piece to a pack of hungry dogs, it wouldn't bring Bobbi back. I just want to know about her last moments on Earth and the circumstances that ended them." The truth, of course, was that I would have gladly torn her murderer apart but lacked the energy to do so. Grief had sapped all my strength.

I imagine he decided that if I was a queer duck, I wasn't a dangerous one. He stood up, placed his plate on top of my desk but kept the drink in his hand, then sat down again. He was probably afraid of overturning it should he become emotional in the telling. I thought that showed more sensitivity than the entire battalion invading my house.

Joe Pagano licked his lips. "Man's name is Christopher McGuire. Lives in Rockville Centre. Twenty-seven years old. Single. His first offense."

"The vehicle?"

"A seventy-seven Chevy. Blue. Two-door."

"Was he very drunk?"

"Drunk as a skunk."

I waited for more.

"You're sure you want to hear this?"

"Yes."

"Okay." He took a long draw on his Coke. "We got there at two exactly, me and my partner. We saw the Chevy with its nose sticking into the passenger's seat of the van. The driver's door of the van was open and Bobbi was lying on the ground. You're sure I should go on?"

I concentrated on the bookshelves behind Joe. "Sure. Please."

"She was lying there, twisted. I went to her and felt for a pulse. Nothing. Meanwhile my partner called in for an ambulance and some backup. I got a blanket from my car trunk and covered her."

"Thank you."

"Then I checked out the other vehicle while my partner went looking for the driver. He found him wandering around on one of the side streets. Northfield Road. No shoes, weaving like Walter Payton through the secondary. His eyes were all bloodshot. He was incoherent and smelled like a saloon."

"What did he say?"

"Not much, really."

"What?" I insisted.

"That he was drunk, not crazy. That the drugstore van crossed the line and smacked him. Then my partner showed him that the van was in its lane and his car was in the opposite lane, perpendicular to the van."

"And?"

"And then he puts his head down and said he was sorry, that he didn't mean her any harm. He was only trying to pass some old lady in front of him and went around her and smack into Bobbi."

I was getting sicker by the second, pumping Joe for all the details. But I had to know. I just couldn't let those last seconds of her life remain a blank to me. Hearing about them couldn't be any worse than imagining them.

"I tell you, Doc, I wanted to blow his fucking brains out. We put him through the tests, you know. Made him walk a straight line. He flunked. Had him try and touch his nose with his right index finger, then his left. He couldn't even find his face. Meantime the ambulance from NCMC came and the backup patrol car. My partner took McGuire to Central Testing in Mineola for the Breathalyzer and I came to tell you. I wish it had been the other way around."

I was calmer now, lulled somehow by the cold facts of police procedure. My hands formed a triangle and I rested my chin on its apex.

"The dividing line is point-one percent alcohol in the blood. He came up with point seventeen. We arrested him, booked him, and held him overnight in the station house. Next morning he was arraigned in district court. One count vehicular manslaughter, two counts of driving while intoxicated. He posted bond and went home."

"What's next?"

"Oh, he'll get a lawyer, one who specializes in DWI cases. He'll be arraigned in county court. He'll post another bond. He'll get indicted by the Grand Jury. Then he goes to trial."

"Can I attend?"

"It's a public matter."

I nodded. "I guess it's that, too."

---

After Joe left, I found I had something to cling to. I had a name: Christopher McGuire. I had a blue 1977 Chevy, two-door. I had a case to follow. I'd stick with it until the system put him where he belonged and for a long time, until they were satisfied that justice had been done, even if I could never be.

The moment finally came when it was all over, this week of hell. The food platters stopped coming, the last guests had left, the Peruvian girl (had it been the same one all week?) had gathered the mess into six olive-green plastic bags, sealed the tops with plastic-coated wire, and set them outside by the regular garbage pails. Irving gave the house a thorough once-over, then permitted the girl to leave.

I thanked Warren and Stephen for their efforts and devotion and sent them and their wives back to their apartments. The girls kissed and clung to us as if we were sending them out west in covered wagons. Laura and I stood in the doorway as their cars disappeared into the darkness, their taillights the size of quarters, then dimes, then pinpoints of red.

Irving took his daughter's face in his two hands and kissed it. He shook my hand, then changed his mind and embraced me. He walked haltingly to his Silver Cloud and drove away, not putting on his lights until he was well past the house.

"Don't hate my father," said Laura.

"No. I did at first, but he's been a rock, really. We couldn't have managed without him." I couldn't help thinking, however, that we wouldn't have had the hoopla without him, either.

"I'm glad it's over," she said.

Is it? I wanted to ask.

---

We were lying in bed hours later, unable to close our eyes. A rising wind was sighing in the trees. The pines against our bedroom wall scraped the screens like tiny birds trying to get in. I heard the foghorn of some ship close to shore, a dirgelike bleat that paralleled my own weary soul.

The movie projector that had been running in my head for six straight nights, replaying scenes of Bobbi's childhood, suddenly locked on a day about five years ago. We're on the beach, my four women and I. On low, short-legged, peppermint-striped beach chairs. Sporting oiled faces and bodies, and zinc-oxide-coated lips, heads tilted to the sun at the same worshipful angle. Their swimsuits—not mine—are briefer than I feel comfortable with. Their figures slow traffic in both directions along the water's edge.

Very quickly, Bobbi tires of this reptilian activity, this self-indulgence. She gets up smartly, sings out, "You're so vain," as in the song about Warren Beatty, then makes for the water. Later it's her turn to choose the restaurant for dinner. Wendy's—much to the chagrin of Laura and the girls. But Bobbi insists—a rebel, a square peg, even at thirteen years of youth. I couldn't help admiring her stubbornness despite Caryn's claim that roaches rule the kitchen at fast-food joints.

Admire Bobbi, yet fear that if any of them do give us heartaches in the future, it's bound to be her. A disastrous marriage, years of floundering after a foolish career, submergence into a religious cult or some violent radical movement.

Sadly, I'd been correct, but in a way I'd never dreamed.

The film ended and I hurt so badly I had to tell Laura. "She's gone, you know. Bobbi's gone."

"I know."

"I mean she's *dead!* Obliterated. We'll never be able to talk to her again. *Never!* Do you realize that?"

"I guess I will, given the time," she had trouble saying. "Not now, though."

I could feel her side of the bed shake.

"She had such a mischievous smile, like she was about to tell a joke. She was terrible with jokes, you know. Always lousing up the punch line."

"Stop it, Mark, please," she shouted.

"I wish I could, honey," I said, moving back toward her, holding her against me. "I wish I could stop everything."

When she finally ceased to tremble, I asked, "What are we going to do now?"

I gave her enough time to frame an answer, but when I asked again, she was sound asleep. I carefully separated from her and moved to the very edge of my side of the bed, waiting for sleep to rescue me as well.

# *four*

ON SATURDAY I WOKE from a bit-
tersweet dream. We were all together at a small wedding reception
in someone's backyard. The girls were in summer white, tan as
acorns, and magnets for every young man at the party. Mark and
I were with friends, but we could see the girls laughing, enjoying
their popularity but fending off the excess attention. Mark leaned
over and whispered in my ear, "Each of them is more beautiful
than the bride. But they're only copies of you."

Waking with a smile, I saw Mark staring at me, his eyes dulled
from lack of sleep. I saw perplexity in them that I should be
smiling. I waited for him to say something cruel—or sad. Until
this calamity we'd been able to read each other's mind, know the

other's most intimate thoughts, predict our actions. Until now, there was nothing we couldn't say to one another no matter how foolish or petty it might seem to the rest of the world.

Mark continued to fix on me. I felt a vague sense of unease, as though a stranger had been watching me undress. Then he moved to the edge of the bed and stood up. "Want some coffee?"

"Maybe later," I said.

He expressed neither satisfaction or disappointment, wavered for a few seconds, then went into the bathroom.

Throughout my married life, except for the three times in the hospital giving birth and when on vacation, I'd made Mark's breakfast. To me, breakfast together was a commitment to marriage and family. Our morning communion.

That Saturday, when I finally groped my way downstairs, I found Mark had already finished his juice, bran flakes, toast, and coffee. He'd washed the dishes and put them away. I took this not as an act of consideration but as further evidence of rejection. Wasn't he telling me that in certain matters I was no longer needed?

Of course there was no deliberate attempt to hurt me. Mark is incapable of hurting those he loves. The fact is, however, that he did freeze me out of his grieving process. Often during the day we'd pass on the steps or in the hall and he'd inquire how I felt, and I'd hunch my shoulders in a gesture of hopelessness and ask how he felt. He'd pause and ponder as if I'd told him to explain the double helix. Then he'd run his hand over his face, all coated in bristle, muffle his answer, and continue on his way.

With no formal treaty, we divided the house. When I was upstairs, he'd stay down. When I went down for a cup of tea, he'd come up or go out to the garden to putter or pick his tomatoes, buckets of which he brought into the kitchen and left on the table for me to wash and separate into batches for Caryn, Sara, and my father.

We weren't ships that passed in the night as much as caretakers of some large and deserted mansion who met in halls and empty rooms by chance and exercised only a perfunctory politeness.

At night, I could hear him making the rounds below, touching things as if trying to make contact with the memories they contained.

Each day was the same compulsive routine. My hearing grew neurotically acute as I lay in bed, unable to do anything but track him from room to room. Gradually this fine, amiable old house that I'd always loved became a prison, a tomb haunted by the living as well as the dead. Mark and Bobbi, hand in hand, her unseen presence and his barely audible one.

I didn't have to go hunting for Bobbi. I'd only enter her room and an overpowering sense of her would sink into every pore. I'd drop to my knees and remain helpless for what seemed like hours. It got so that I, too, began avoiding her room. Just as Mark did to keep from falling completely to pieces. I wasn't disloyal; I could still sense her vibrant spirit anywhere in the house.

The caring multitude who'd filled my house last week were suddenly gone. When the phone did ring, it was Sara or Caryn checking in. Or my father offering advice. "At least go outside a little. Get some fresh air. You'll make yourself sick and that'll help no one but the doctors."

The call and visit I craved most, outside of family, were Suzy's. I could understand her annoyance with Mark. He'd behaved abominably toward her husband, but Suzy knew me longer than she knew Paul. In many ways more intimately. And she understood me, knowing as early as grade school that my aloofness and snobbery were more a case of extreme shyness. Of not being raised and groomed by a mother. Suzy told me about boys, menstruating, and growing up female.

So where was Suzy when I needed her?

Once Mark tiptoed into the bedroom and, seeing that I was awake, asked, "Who was that kid in the Thanksgiving play? When Bobbi played Priscilla Mullins? He played Miles Standish. Big ears, overbite, copper red hair?"

"Donald Blumenthal. Dr. Blumenthal's son."

"Yes, of course. Donald Blumenthal. Bobbi didn't want to play Priscilla. She had her heart set on Squanto, the Indian."

I thought he'd stay and we'd talk but he turned around and walked away, back to his private sanctuary, condemning me to mine, leaving me to wonder why her death had so fractured us, set us off in opposite directions, walled off one from the other.

Even our sleeping patterns became divergent. He'd come up at night drained from all his meanderings about the house. I'd lie in bed for hours listening to him breathe. The next morning he'd be up and about again, once more to his routine, while I'd fall into a light sleep, dream pleasantly, but wake every few hours to the realization that my child was dead. Every time a fresh cut. Always new blood.

Dinner, our one meal together, I served early, so that if any friends should come by, we'd be ready for them. I made simple meals—salads, scrambled eggs, soup from a can. Mark didn't complain. He hadn't the least notion of what he was eating. When he spoke, I had the impression that his words were coming from a million miles away.

"Another slice of bread?"

"Huh? Oh, no, thank you."

"Is the tuna salad too dry?"

"What?"

"The tuna. Did I put in enough mayonnaise?"

"Mayonnaise? Sure, it's fine."

"Coffee or tea?" I asked him, and waited for the question to travel that great distance.

"Uh, whatever you're having," came the delayed response.

Then I'd rapidly clean up the kitchen and wait in the living room. And wonder how Mark would act if we did get company. Would he be vicious? Cordial? Contrite? Distant? I didn't honestly know and that's what made the week and Mark so unbearable.

He was my friend, my lover, my lifemate. And he was in trouble. We both were. How I wished I wasn't Bobbi's mother so I could save him. How I wished he wasn't her father so he could save me.

What had we done wrong all our married life to create such a lack of communication? If our loving friendship had been a lie and not a paradigm, what chance did Sara and Caryn have? What chance did any couple have?

By Thursday the trickle of condolence cards arriving by mail became a stream. Mark took in the bundle and I found him, much to my horror, sitting in the kitchen with the pile in his lap, tossing the unopened envelopes into a paper bag ten feet away. Some landed in the bag, while most fell on the floor.

I ran to him. "What are you doing?"

"Phonies, hypocrites, two-faced liars," he recited with each toss.

"Mark, stop it. How could you? People are just expressing their feelings."

"Via Hallmark and Norcross?"

"Why not? They're only trying to find the right words."

I took the pile away from him and picked up the cards scattered about the floor around the paper bag. I turned to reprimand him again but he'd gone outside. I saw him making for the gazebo. The cards rescued, I went upstairs to read them.

By Friday, I couldn't stand to be in the house any longer. A week of solitary confinement with Mark was all I could bear.

If forcing myself out of bed each morning had been heroism, then leaving the house was an act worthy of sainthood. Actually, it had become a dire necessity, as I was out of coffee, tuna, and bread, our daily fare for that week.

I stood by the car, unsure as a new colt. I doubted if I had the power to get inside, buckle up, and turn on the engine. I did, though, and felt a sense of relief in fleeing what had become intolerable.

I did my shopping and, to my surprise, felt a small surge of pleasure mingling once again with those I'd lived among all my life.

Not that it was without cost. My stomach churned seeing teenagers, the way some tossed their heads and bounced along the Avenue, their ponytails flicking like lazy whips. I grew weak seeing mothers and daughters together, the fortyish mothers svelte and attractive, their daughters awkward and tentative, two sides of the same Five Towns coin. I couldn't stop myself from recalling all those afternoons when I'd shop, the three girls trailing alongside.

I picked up my groceries and fresh fruit at the usual places. The store owners were so very sorry about Bobbi. I accepted their condolences with averted glances. I preferred to believe that they thought only of what a wholesome sight we'd made passing their stores, and not the business I gave them.

Feeling more positive about the human race, and stronger, I headed back to the car. Down the block, at the corner by the bank, I spied Suzy Gordon. But not until she saw me first. I'm certain that she had because the moment I began hurrying toward her, she turned down the block in the direction of the railroad station. I ran to catch her, the bundles held against my breast.

By the time I reached the corner, Suzy was gone, vanished, as if she'd been only a product of my need. I leaned against a parking meter and cried. All that bravery in leaving the house had vanished.

---

On Saturday morning I returned to the library. I thought if I made it to my office unnoticed, I'd lock the door and do paperwork for as long as I could. Then I'd leave.

Like some wealthy recluse, the Cedarhurst Library was sheltered behind a densely packed rampart of rhododendron and billowy cypresses that hid the low, sprawling graystone building from motorists passing along the Avenue. The structure, however, was one of the vital centers of the Five Towns, for book lovers, as well as those drawn by the programs I'd helped create.

I arrived at ten A.M., parked in the section reserved for staff, and swam against the tide of my own resistance to the employees' entrance. A young man—probably a new employee—held the door open, thus removing the last obstacle against which to test my resolve.

I crossed the main room and was stopped first by Stella, then by Margarite, who left their enclosure to say how happy they were to see me back at work. I was moved. At least they hadn't caught the Suzy Gordon virus.

I continued beyond Reference to my office, and once safely inside, I leaned against the door, weak and panting as though I'd run a few miles. I closed my eyes against the intense throbbing in my head. When I opened them again, I remained in place, surveying the territory I'd called my own for seven years. I thought of how hard I'd fought to win it and the effort since to keep what I'd won.

"A job that pays five dollars an hour? Are you for real?" my father had said. "Why, I can get you double that working for the county. With a better title. With people who'd be thrilled to work with you. Not like that shit, Phil Coolidge."

But I'd insisted on the library. Phil had bitterly fought my appointment and cried politics to Stella. When I came to work that first day, however, he was the first to welcome me. Giving her enough rope, he'd told the librarians.

I half expected that Phil had cleaned out the office, assuming Bobbi's death would end my so-called career. But everything was the same except for two neat plateaus of mail on my desk and the three-inch stack of reading material between them.

My first call of the day was from Mark. "How's it going?" he asked.

"Fine. Better than I expected."

"That's good." Mark cleared his throat, then there was that awful emptiness that had driven me out of the house. "As long as I'm home, can I do something for you? Defrost something from the freezer? Or make a salad?"

"Don't bother, dear," I said, touched and saddened. He was so contrite and helpless in his offer, I wanted to run home and hold him. "I'll pick up some lemon chicken and fried rice from the Chinese restaurant after I drop off the payroll checks."

"That'll be fine," he said. "Are the girls coming tonight?"

"No, I asked them not to. They're exhausted, poor things. They need to spend some time with their husbands."

"You're right," he said, though I could detect disappointment in his voice.

His utter humility destroyed what little energy I'd been able to muster and I sat at the desk waiting for it to build again. Pain came over me in large drenching waves. If only I could drown. If only I could let go and surrender. As Mark had done. Of course he would come back to himself; he was too solid a man to stay down for long. Eventually everything would be fine. I was certain of that.

At my desk, fighting the urge to fling my mail and papers into the trash basket as Mark had done with the condolence cards, I was saved by two phone calls. First Sara, then Caryn, one on the hour, the other on the half hour, as though prearranged.

"It's nice of you to call," I told each one, "but you don't have to take my temperature every thirty minutes."

By noon I'd made a serious dent in the white mountains. One letter, dated a week ago, was from the library's insurance company. It indicated that the three pieces of sculpture I'd asked to have insured would be, from September 1 to November 30. When the artist delivered the goods, I was to inspect each personally for chips and cracks and if there were any to so indicate and have the artist sign, thus exempting the insurance company from any claims.

At one P.M., Phil's secretary, Amelia, called to ask if I wanted a sandwich from the deli. She and Phil were going out. I'd brought some tuna salad, one of Mark's tomatoes, and a thermos of iced tea from home, and politely declined.

Amelia's call reminded me that I had an appetite after all and I spread a paper towel on my desk and opened my lunch bag. If I took lessons, I still would never learn to eat a whole tomato with delicacy and grace. The pulp oozed out and ran down my fingers. I was so engrossed trying to keep from getting soiled that I failed to hear a tap-tapping on the window. The tapping became an urgent rap. I looked up, startled to see a pumpkin smile with hands that wigwagged on either side. A Peeping Tom, I thought at first. He mouthed something that didn't seem obscene so I put down my leaking tomato, went to the window, and lifted it slightly.

"Bruno Coletti. Mr. Coolidge said it was all right to set up my statues in the garden. You're supposed to supervise so that I can't make a phony claim later."

Bruno Coletti had a tidy baldness that contrasted perfectly with his intensely black beard, closely cropped as any lawn in Woods-burgh. He was thin but densely packed, of average height, eyes either hazel or gray—it was hard to tell with his back to the sun.

I told him to stay put and went out the back entrance of the library to the garden. He was walking the perimeter of the small section of land, stopping, judging distances to the back wall of forsythias, to the library entrance, to the sides where beds of blood red chrysanthemums rose waist-high and profuse under the pair of Japanese maples.

Neither hazel nor gray, Bruno Coletti's eyes were lime-colored like a cat's, with apostrophes of brown radiating from the centers. Shamelessly they disrobed me and I wished he'd set up his statues so that I could examine them and send him on his way.

"I was just selecting the new homes for my children," he said. "I have them in the van on the street."

He was about forty and not nearly as bald as he'd seemed at the window. He wore faded blue jeans and a black T-shirt on which was written "Andy Warhol Sucks."

"Your children? Oh, yes. I guess children and statues are both works of creation."

"You smile," he said, though I was certain I hadn't. "I'm not married, so these pieces of stone are truly my flesh and blood. So, like any good father, I worry when they're with strangers."

"They'll be in good hands, Mr. Coletti. Five Towners are properly respectful when it comes to children and art."

The man was draining what little strength I possessed. Oblivious to my loss, he belabored his metaphors. Statues and children, indeed.

"Please call me Bruno," he said. "Since you are going to be foster parent to my offspring."

Little chance of that, I thought. I knew he was flirting. He hadn't been the first to try to seduce me, though at my age I might well be receiving my last overture.

Bruno even moved like a feline, to the street entrance of the library garden. A black Volkswagen was parked at the curb, a larger U-Haul attached to it.

He opened the doors, removed two wide wooden planks, and made a ramp. I peered inside and saw three entities resting like prisoners inside a paddy wagon.

"Do you need help, Mr. Coletti?"

"Bruno. No, thank you. I must do this alone."

Using a felt-lined hand truck, Coletti carefully removed the first piece and wheeled it to its assigned place. He took his time centering it according to the plan he'd worked out previously.

Frankly I was captivated by the statue. A delicate shade of cafe au lait marble, it was a trio of musicians—violinist, clarinetist, and a viola da gamba player—each caught at the precise moment of leaning into each other. I was touched by the way the trio seemed to gain sustenance from each other's presence and performance. The utter humanity of it. Good musicians do that, and Bruno Coletti had noticed. I disliked him more—and less—for his insight.

He continued to position and reposition his piece until satisfied with the effect of the September sun on the marble. Then he gave each musician a fond pat on the shoulder, theatrically, since I was observing him. Coletti: artist, showman, seducer.

The second piece, in gray stone, was an old man in rags asleep on a park bench. The hands in his lap reminded me of my father's—heavily veined and liver-spotted. They were so real that I longed to stroke them but didn't, with Bruno's eyes on me, catlike.

Bruno wheeled the man to the forsythias alongside the redwood reading chair as though supplying companionship for the next alfresco patron. There was humor in this arrangement, a sly juxtaposition of stone and flesh, sleeper and reader.

Bruno had less difficulty negotiating the last statue to its new home. Smaller than the others, it was quickly wheeled into place and set between the maples. When I saw it, I had to turn away. In a pinkish marble that closely approximated skin tones was a mother and two babies so intertwined that I couldn't tell where one began and the others ended. Their embrace was the essence of motherhood, and all I could think was: Damn you, Coletti!

Damn your talent and your perception for transporting me into the past.

I wanted to run back to my room but I refused to be manipulated. "You have very lovely children, Mr. Coletti."

"Bruno," he insisted.

"Bruno. I'm so moved. They're the finest I've seen since Norway. Frogner Park in Oslo. Hundreds of acres of the most lovely family scenes."

Inside Bruno Coletti a delicate crystal seemed to shatter. He shook his head knowingly. "I've never been there but I've seen photos. As a matter of fact, I've never been anywhere. Travel is a luxury I can't afford. Perhaps someday when I'm known." Then he brightened. "It's enough for me that I'm an artist."

I disliked him again for his maudlin self-pity and wished him gone. Rapidly, I checked each statue for damage, knowing I'd find none. He signed the insurance form with a showy flourish of my pen. I folded the paper in thirds while he walked from piece to piece. "Have a nice autumn," he said to each. "Be good little ones and Papa will come for you after Thanksgiving."

I could have said something to him about talking to dead marble but I let it pass. If the world were perfect, art would be anonymous—there'd be no silly Bruno Colettis to contend with.

He shoved the planks into the van, rolled in the hand truck, and padlocked the doors. His work done, he seemed more relaxed. "If you think these are good, you should see the collection in my workshop. A totally different side of Bruno Coletti. Young lovers in the act. Nudes. Of both sexes. Things I don't ordinarily show the public. You'd be impressed."

"Why me?"

"Because you're not the ordinary person. I can tell. An artist can always tell. I've been following your eyes, your windows to the soul. And such lovely windows." Bruno sighed. "I serve cheese, by the way, at my studio. And wine my father makes from anise and dandelion root. How about next Tuesday?"

As much as I disliked his advances, I didn't feel compromised enough to hurt him. He wasn't some lowlife pawing the ground for an hour at a sleazy motel. He was, self-advertised, an artist. But I wasn't that naive about his nonartistic intentions.

"Sounds lovely," I said. "Maybe some weekend if I can bring my daughters. They're both sensitive to art. They're twenty-four and twenty-two."

"Your daughters?" Bruno was weakly amused. "You won't consider coming alone?"

"No," I replied. No elaboration offered.

"Ah, well," he said, rummaging in his pockets for the car keys. "What is not to be is not to be. We artists learn early how to handle rejection."

"You do beautiful work, Bruno," I said, walking him to his car.

"Now, now, Mrs. Gerber. No consolation prizes, please."

"Laura," I said.

"All right, Laura. I'll call every week or ten days—to check on my three *kinder*."

The phone was ringing with a low-keyed persistence when I returned to my office. I knew who it was.

"How's the breadwinner doing?" he asked.

"At my salary level, bread crumbs, you mean."

"You must be exhausted."

"I am. A few more odds and ends to finish up and I'll leave."

"Good. That's very good," he said.

"Do you miss me?"

Mark didn't hesitate. "Yes. Yes, I do."

He wanted me home, but at a distance, at the other end of the seesaw. A strange kind of wanting. Still, I was eager to be with him.

———————

By four I could barely lift myself from the chair. Less than half my mail and memos had been attended to. The three-tiered file bulged with new and old obligations. Next week. Next month— it mattered little at the moment. I was in the trough again, going to pieces again, hurting once more.

I left by the garden entrance, saying good-bye to no one, especially not to Bruno's "children."

I stopped off for the Chinese food and then left the checks at the store with Mary Tannenbaum. When I got home, Mark greeted me with a warm kiss and a tender stroking of my hair.

He'd prepared the table on the patio: place settings, checkerboard tablecloth, a bottle of chilled white wine. I was sure he was at last coming back to himself, to his assistance and mine. We both needed him desperately.

We talked. Our words were congenial and understanding. More than friends, less than lovers, but heading in the right direction. Then, I don't know why, he changed course. He'd run out of steam and lapsed back into the man I didn't know. By meal's end, he and I were suddenly strangers again. He stood up, went inside, and disappeared into his den. I sat until the stars came out and let misery have me.

In my room, I undressed, then stepped into a shower as blisteringly hot as I could tolerate. Numbed by the scalding needles, I screamed as I had that Friday. I screamed for what seemed like an hour, hoping to empty and exhaust myself. I made hard, knotted fists and pounded on the black shower tiles until my arms were too weary to lift. Spent, I slid down the wall and sat on the shower floor, my knees against my chest.

When the numbness wore off, the same old agony took its place, a stabbing so severe I thought I'd injured myself. Not that I cared. I lay alone in bed for hours. Thinking. Trying not to think. Remembering. Trying not to remember. I took half a ten-milligram Valium, then an hour later the other half. But even that dependable friend had deserted me.

I got up and went into my studio. My flute case lay on the straight-back chair, unopened for weeks. I ran my fingers over the sleek cherrywood container and opened the clasps.

It was long past midnight but I felt a powerful urge to play. I reached into the case, removed the three parts, and joined them. I pursed my lips and blew across the embouchure. Nothing came out, the flute unyielding. I tried again, then a third time before the Beatles song "Yesterday" began emerging. There was an unbearable heaviness when I'd finished, so I played the Schubert Nocturne in E-flat. When that dark, moody piece had been absorbed by the walls, I waited for the applause to die down before beginning "Clair de Lune."

I was giving this command performance for Bobbi, all her favorites, as I had entertained my father forty years before. She wasn't here in person but I felt her presence, her approval nonetheless: that clapping in my head.

Tears in great rivers had been running down my face all during the concert, spilling onto the flute. I must stop, I told myself. Salt and water are deadly to the silver hinges. But I couldn't until the last note had faded away.

Still sleep wouldn't come. Mark lay next to me, suspended between this world and the one he'd newly created. Once more I got up. I put on my jogging outfit and stole out of the house, agile as a cat burglar.

At three A.M. the sky was eerily black. The stars had all gone, the moon with them. I started down Spruce, then turned into Bayberry. I kept an even pace. Bayberry into Pond. In the dark, the lanes seemed new and exciting. Pond into Birch, Birch into Keene, Keene into Willow. My chest ached from not jogging for two weeks and I fought the urge to rest. Willow back into Bayberry.

I'd completed my—our—regular route. On the second circuit, I sped up, then switched into automatic pilot, but Bobbi's ghost stayed with me, kept pace, turned when I did. I went faster, hoping she'd fall behind. Think of anything but her, I ordered myself. Review the day. Think of Phil Coolidge and his impersonal welcome. Think of Sara and Caryn's phone calls, angels watching over me. Think of Mark trying to make it out of his personal hell, falling back. Think of that pretentious, overblown Bruno Coletti and his breath-stopping statues.

Better, don't think at all and put everything into running. I increased my pace, redirecting all my energy to lungs, heart, and legs. Faster and faster I ran until I broke through the limits of myself and entered a new world of motion and weightlessness. Freed of my own gravity.

I don't know which lanes I crossed and recrossed over the next few hours. Or how many circles I'd made. But when I turned a corner in that uninterrupted continuum, I was startled by the first powdery blue rays of dawn on the horizon. I slowed, jogged in place, and panted for air. Even more startling was my position: directly in front of my own driveway.

I rested on my haunches and squinted at the pedometer on my ankle. Either the instrument was broken or I'd run ten miles. I was sopping wet. My running suit, weighted with sweat, felt cold and clammy.

I crawled upstairs, undressed, and fell into bed. I slept all through the next day and didn't wake until six o'clock Monday morning.

# *five*

ERIC HAD GROWN a mustache, the thick scrub-brush kind that exuded an implacable fierceness. Jack Laitner had put on a few pounds, swelling his jowls but thinning his five o'clock shadow. The gray in Mary Tannenbaum's hair had turned whiter, and Maureen looked years younger, as though she'd successfully used some of the face treatments she sold her devoted customers.

Otherwise, nothing much had changed at Cedarhurst Chemists. It was my first time back in a month, but I didn't linger at the entrance to do my white-glove number. I felt exposed and vulnerable. There were customers in the store who might come up and offer regrets or make small talk, neither of which I was prepared to handle.

Laura had returned to work two weeks earlier but I'd felt no strong urge to follow her example. When I was ready, I told myself. She'd continued to stop off at the store each Friday for the payroll checks, and for a few blank checks for my own withdrawals.

I'd toyed with the idea of moving my computer screen and printer to the house to set up an office there. Then I'd never have to leave the premises except to make sure the store was still standing.

This thought liberated others. I wouldn't have to go to the bookstore either. I'd ask for a delivery. What the hell, my customers called up for a box of sanitary napkins or a bottle of aspirin. I suddenly remembered deliveries were a thing of the past at Cedarhurst Chemists. I'd given the van to an auto wrecker. Eric had said that it was reparable but I let them haul it away. Even repaired and repainted, it would always be a reminder.

I'd been aiming to make the circle smaller like the old Emmett Kelly routine with the clown and the shrinking beam of light. When the circle dissolved into darkness, maybe I would disappear entirely as well.

From Laura, there wasn't a word of reproach or accusation, or anything else. Only the unsaid hung in the rarefied air between us, absorbing what little oxygen remained. I couldn't stay for long in the same room with her and she couldn't bear me, either. We were excruciatingly civil toward one another, like delegates at a global peace conference.

Every evening I'd enter my own den to continue a project that seemed to have found me: a thorough study of the Civil War. I'd begun with Bruce Catton's eight-volume series, having always meant to tackle the project but never having the time and drive. Now I had the time.

Laura, always an organized and structured person, never varied from her new nightly routine. About ten P.M. she'd go upstairs and shower for fifteen or twenty minutes—a long shower for her—then spend an hour in her studio. I could hear the music filter through the house into my den. This had become her voice, the one I now seldom heard, ranging from the lightness and frivolity of Satie and Poulenc to the structured somberness of Bach and the Winter section of *The Four Seasons*. The program each night varied but Laura's finale, her last sentence, was "Clair de Lune," continuously reminding me that through her music she was trying to communicate with Bobbi and had possibly found the way.

I hadn't Laura's gift or good luck. My only path to Bobbi was through solitude and introspection. So far it hadn't worked. Since I had no other choice, I continued to try.

I told Eric to forget I was back at the store. Not to send in salesmen or call me out for thorny customers. I'd come in strictly for the paperwork.

But that didn't keep him from badgering me before I'd opened a single envelope.

"Listen, boss, I have to know what to do about deliveries."

"I told you last month. We don't do them anymore," I said gruffly.

"That ain't working," he said. The mustache seemed to lend him a new authority or perhaps it had been my absence over the month during which he'd completely run the show. "You can't take away a service without really hurting the business."

"I guess you're right. Suppose you call Cedarhurst Taxi and offer them a flat fee for each delivery. Ask for Josh Cummings. He's been bugging me for years with the idea."

"Good thinking, boss," said Eric, and left. I felt as though I'd put down an attempted mutiny. Suddenly I wanted to flee the store. For the hundredth time, at least, I found myself asking "what if?" What if she hadn't driven the van that day? What if, like most girls in town her age, she'd gone on a teen tour or had visited Israel for the summer, or spent the afternoons at the beach instead of under my thumb? What if, that Friday, one of the stock boys had taken her shift? Had been killed instead? A better scenario? Yes, yes, yes. I'd have gladly traded either of their lives for hers. Mine for hers.

Or, what if she'd taken a different route? Would Christopher McGuire have been there, too, to keep their appointment?

Were any of the "what-ifs" fact instead of tortuous speculation, then Bobbi would have entered her senior year at Hewlett High. We'd be talking college or Europe, the Grand Tour with a knapsack and her unabiding faith in the human race. God, how we'd have worried about her. Would she have the good sense to hide her Star of David while traveling through France and Germany?

Christopher McGuire had relieved us of those fears. Thanks to him, we knew where Bobbi would be—day and night—for the rest of our lives.

---

A month's paperwork awaited me. The mail had been stacked in a sturdy carton on my desk. I turned on the computer, and after a momentary hum it began firing away. Daily reports, weekly reports, the summaries for August and half of September came flowing out over the printer, all the tricks it had been programmed to do, seemed delighted to do, like some kid showing off. Soon there was a carpet of printout sheets halfway across the room. When the machine stopped because it had become current, I turned it off—down boy, good boy—and separated the sheets into organized reports.

I went through the motions of checking my register tapes and daily reports, entering the figures in my ledgers. Volume had declined markedly in the month and there had been cash shortages totaling over five hundred dollars.

As if I cared. I was more interested in using up time than in recording numbers and finding discrepancies. I didn't really care if the first significant drop in business in twenty-five years was a fluke, a trend, or if the shortages at the register were carelessness or theft.

Since I'd called Laura on her first day back, she called me. It was strange to hear the breathy concern in her voice. I'd almost forgotten her basic humanity, with things so tentative at home.

"You don't have to stay all day," said Laura.

"I don't intend to." I detected a desperation in her words, as if she feared my return to the store signaled a kind of irrational, potentially dangerous act. As if I'd decided to drive myself day and night until I dropped. As she seemed to be doing.

"My place here looks like a post office with all the mail piled up. I've got to get to some of it."

"How would you like me to drop in for lunch?" she said, trying to seem spontaneous. "We could have a chef's salad at the Spot. Like the old days."

I declined. "Sorry, too much work. Maybe tomorrow."

"Tomorrow's no good. I have meetings and appointments all day."

I tried to sound disappointed. "We'll make it next week, then. I'll have all of this tamed by then."

Our conversation seemed a parody of the frenetic work lives of two yuppies. The truth was, I had plenty of time but I couldn't stand to be reminded of what it had been like back then, when Laura first went to work.

We'd meet each day at one and Andy would show us to our favorite table under the painting of Greek gods sporting on Mount Olympus. Excitedly, she'd talk and drink her wine at the same time. I'd hardly get a word in. It didn't matter. She was happy, so I was happy.

"It's so electric, Mark, developing, *creating* new programs. You must know that the library has been in a state of suspended animation. But we're moving now, doing things, stirring up the waters."

"You make sure to keep your eye on Phil. He's good with a dagger, from what I hear. Watch your ass."

"I have you for that."

"I don't mean for fondling purposes."

"I'll watch my ass, and my flanks and my back, but I won't make it a consuming preoccupation, Mark. I have work to do."

"Just a word to the wise. You can't do great things with knives sticking out of you."

While she continued, Andy would prepare one of his tureen-size super salads from a sampling of everything in the kitchen. Laura and I would try to eat our way to the bottom of the bowl, happy as illicit lovers at our special table. Was it only seven years ago?

———————

Rapidly, I transformed mail into garbage. By two o'clock I was through. Eric eyed me with mild consternation and some amusement when I told him I was leaving. I'd been away a month and already I was finished for the day. But I couldn't stay in the store another minute. Bobbi's presence filled my office. Starting slowly, like an escaping gas, it grew until I could no longer open an envelope or read a piece of pharmaceutical hype.

She'd always eaten her two slices of pizza and sipped her soda across from me as I'd worked, reading her copy of *Mother Jones* or messing up *The New York Times* crossword puzzle. She'd kept her yogurt in my refrigerator for late-afternoon snacks. Her mark was suddenly everywhere.

I left without saying good-bye and headed for Woodsburgh and some serious walking. The fact that it was raining heavily hardly mattered.

———————

Foul weather would never keep me indoors that autumn. A pelting rain or a biting wind was just the ticket to ponder random events, the folly of trying to build a solid life on shifting tides. I had everything worth having: cars and clothes, jewels and bank accounts, respect and respectability, love and caring and sharing. What I didn't have was experience in handling disaster.

I let the wind numb me, penetrating my clothes and bones, playing a mock-perilous, pneumonia-inviting game to consume the time. But I needed this core in my life. A peg to hang the day on. Proving, at least where the weather was concerned, that I was resilient.

Two wet and blustery hours later, I walked up my driveway, anticipating shelter, a hot cup of coffee, a roaring fire.

The phone: how long had it been ringing? I slogged across the hall to answer it. It was Assistant District Attorney Spotswood.

He called to remind me that next Friday would be the first hearing for the trial.

The week before, he'd introduced himself on the phone, indicating that he'd be handling the McGuire case. The defendant had pleaded innocent and in all likelihood there'd be a jury trial. Spotswood had asked for my thoughts and I said anything less than death by torture would be a miscarriage of justice.

"I fully understand your feelings, Mr. Gerber. But I have to function within the system. And I have faith that the system will eventually provide justice, though it may not be what you have in mind. I want to assure you that I'll go for the maximum in this case. I will not accept any plea bargaining."

"I should hope not. What is the maximum?"

"Two and a third to seven."

"Which means?"

"Which means, if we go to trial and if the jury convicts and if the judge decides to come down hard on McGuire and if McGuire misbehaves in jail, he'll do seven. But that rarely happens, I have to be honest with you."

"*If* the jury convicts?"

"You better know this, Mr. Gerber: juries are dangerous things. I hate juries. You never know *what* they'll do. The defendant comes into court all spiffed up in a three-piece suit. He looks remorseful. Maybe he even cries. His lawyer hammers away at the lack of intent to harm."

"Even though a life has been taken, Mr. Spotswood?" I nearly choked on the words.

"Even though. Peculiarly, many on a jury sympathize with the teary-eyed kid at the defendant's table. Some may have loved ones who drink, and there for the grace of God go they. It's a crapshoot, Mr. Gerber."

I smelled a sellout. "Does that mean a trade's in the works, Mr. Spotswood?"

"No, sir. I said no plea bargaining and I meant it. What I'm telling you is that there are no open-and-shut cases where a jury is concerned. If he's convicted or if he pleads guilty before trial, it's up to the judge as far as sentencing is concerned. That's his domain and he has a wide range of choices. From two and a third to seven, to probation and no time served."

"Probation? I don't believe it."

"That is the law in this state. I'm letting the judge know—and by the way, Judge Cameron is pretty strict on DWIs—that I'll be happy with nothing less than a year and a day of jail time, which means he goes upstate to Dannamora. Believe me, that place is no day at the beach."

"And that's our fine system of justice you have faith in? Three weeks in jail for every year of my daughter's life?"

"Mr. Gerber, that's how it works."

---

The morning of the hearing the roads were slick with leaves, and a thick fog draped the lowest branches of the trees and obscured the houses in Woodsburgh.

Laura and I drove slowly to Mineola, the county seat, listening to Beethoven's *Emperor* on the radio to avoid conversation. Even the prospect of our day in court hadn't made Laura open to me— or maybe she was apprehensive about facing Bobbi's murderer.

It took an hour to go twelve miles. We couldn't find a parking space in any of the five or six municipal lots. I took a chance and parked in a Permit Only slot.

The Criminal Courthouse, which I'd passed a hundred times but never paid much attention to, was square, massive, and imposing, as a place of justice should be. To get beyond the glass entrance doors we had to go through a metal detector booth similar to the ones at airports. Lawyers in front of us turned over their attaché cases for inspection to a policeman in a white shirt, black pants, and large-handled revolver on his hip. The only metal object Laura and I had between us was the car key.

Judge Adolph Cameron's courtroom was long and narrow, but smaller than I'd expected. Calvin Spotswood turned out to be as tall and wide as a running back. He was somewhere between white and mulatto and wore square granny glasses, a medium Afro, and a dark blue business suit that had seen better days.

Under his left arm, like a football, he toted a heavy white folder: the people's case against Christopher McGuire.

I introduced myself and we shook hands. He took Laura's hand, his eyes widening to her good looks. At my request, he pointed out the defendant who was sitting two rows in front of us.

What does a murderer look like? This one had a bloated baby face and puffy cheeks, most likely from too many beers which had killed Bobbi as assuredly as if they had been bullets fired from a gun. He had unruly brown hair and bushy eyebrows beneath which were deeply embedded a pair of bewildered watery gray eyes. Likely, his lawyer had told him to look remorseful and this was the nearest he could come.

The conservative herringbone suit, white dress shirt, and tie he wore were obviously new from the way he fidgeted in his seat and tugged at his collar. He didn't turn around. I'm certain we'd been pointed out as the victim's parents.

I felt Laura turn to stone beside me, glowering with all her might, trying by thought alone to disintegrate him. As for me, I considered reaching across the rows and ripping off his head.

Spotswood leaned into us. "Forget what you're thinking. Or at least put a muzzle on it, Mr. Gerber. You do something rash, he might go free and *you'll* end up doing time. Now *that* would certainly be a miscarriage of justice." Then he left to join the other attorneys in the center of the courtroom.

Next to McGuire sat his mother, who had the same bully face, but was surprisingly attractive. A buxom redhead in a black tailored suit and cherry pink blouse, she could have been an executive secretary or an office manager for a large medical practice. Occasionally she whispered in her son's ear to keep up his spirits— or hers.

The 9:30 hearing began at 10:15 with the entrance of the judge. We rose as ordered by the court clerk, then sat down. Judge Cameron, a former assistant DA, had a broad, stern face the color of boiled lobster, a mottled nose, and jug-handled ears. I wondered if the nose indicated a fondness for the bottle and would that work in the defendant's favor.

*[ 73 ]*

A dapper little man, luxuriantly tailored and meticulously barbered, stood when Christopher McGuire's name was called. Together with his client, they approached the bench, met there by Spotswood. The three made a stunning contrast in dress I found impossible to ignore. The defense attorney was the most resplendent in a rich mocha silk, McGuire a poor second, and Spotswood, my hope for justice, a distant third.

They spoke so low I couldn't catch a single word. Seconds later it was over.

"What happened up there?" I asked Spotswood in the hall where I'd cornered him.

"Nothing, really. An adjournment until December thirtieth. His attorney wants a bunch of things I'll give him and a bunch of things I won't."

"Things? What things? He was drunk. He killed my daughter. He was caught at the scene. How many *things* can there possibly be?"

"Oh, the Breathalyzer results, the policeman's report, skid marks of the tires, if any. Technical data about the vehicles. Look, Mr. Gerber, this is standard procedure. The defendant is entitled to the best defense he can get. Would you want less?"

I didn't offer an immediate reply and he didn't give me the chance to think up one.

"We'll be meeting regularly like this until the trial, if there is a trial. This way, the judge is kept apprised of the case, if there are any new developments."

"For how long?"

"Maybe a year."

"A year? A year of justice delayed." I turned to Laura in disgust.

"That's about average," said Spotswood in a manner designed to cool me down.

Spotswood folded his arms over his broad chest as if to ward me off. "It would probably be better, Mr. Gerber, for you to stay away from these hearings. If anything significant happens, I'll let you know."

"I can't be prevented from coming, can I?"

"Of course not. My suggestion was to save you and Mrs. Gerber from the wear and tear."

"We're so worn and torn now that it won't make much difference. I'll be here if only to stare down the son-of-a-bitch killer. Cause him some stomach churning."

"Suit yourself, Mr. Gerber." Then we shook hands all around and he left.

As we got to the parking lot the sun broke out of its prison of clouds. There was a twenty-five-dollar ticket on my windshield. I stared at it for a few seconds, then calmly tore it into quarters and threw them on the ground.

Without a word, Laura picked up the pieces and put them in her purse.

---

Autumn had come and gone mostly unnoticed. I didn't miss it but I'd grown bored with walking my neighborhood, its houses, their infinite variety, the inventiveness of style, clear evidence of wealth and comfort. It hadn't brought me peace of mind or acceptance of Bobbi's death or respite from memory. Laura was growing more removed, more unreachable by the day. We seldom ate together now. Our daughters, when they came for dinner once a week, provided the only link between us. Neither she nor I went purposely out of our way to avoid one another; we simply gave ourselves to other priorities. She often stayed late at the library for meetings. I'd get lost in my reading between six P.M. and midnight. Not a sound in the house until she opened the front door, then later again when she'd begin her concert. I never heard her play better, with so much depth and passion. Bobbi's death had made her a superb musician.

Then I discovered the Isle of Devon. I'd often seen glimpses of the wooden footbridge leading to it as I drove along the Rockaway Turnpike. Through the corridor of fast-food restaurants, gas stations, and retail stores, I could see tiny waterfront houses which were indistinct dabs of white as I whizzed by.

On a cold, damp, and dreary Tuesday, I drove to the bridge and parked.

It was a dingy, dilapidated structure with gaping holes in the floor through which I could see the bay churning below. To my right was the turnpike, alive with noise, all six lanes fast lanes. To the left were the rears of houses and their docks, most crumbling in decay. A few small boats were tied up at those docks, none very substantial, none, to my untrained eye, very seaworthy.

I crossed over and began walking the streets. They were more constricted than the lanes of Woodsburgh, the houses packed to an urban density. None were copies of one another but almost all were similar in their frailty and need of repair. Many had paint peeling off in large flakes, others needed new walks, the cement cracked and lifted by tree roots.

The main street of the Isle of Devon ran like a belt around the tiny jetty of land. A few cross streets divided the community into blocks. More than half the houses on every block had lawn decorations of abandoned cars resting on rims or elevated on cinder blocks—the gargoyles and stone lions of the not-so-rich.

Within an hour I'd slow-walked the entire spit of land and seen enough fresh sights to warrant a second and third visit. More, if the fascination continued to hold. Until the snows of January, I hoped, when I'd become homebound and so engrossed with the Civil War that I wouldn't mind staying inside.

The only portion of the isle left to explore was the beach that faced the bay. I walked to the end of North Street with an almost childlike eagerness and was immediately captivated by the first house I saw.

"House" was really stretching it in this case. Once it had been a gracious half-brick, half-wood beachfront bungalow. Someone stylish had extended, enclosed, and screened the porch. Above, a sundeck and a bedroom had been added, the windows of which looked out to sea like a man wearing sunglasses.

Since then, the place had gone downhill. The paint on the wood above the brick had blistered to bare wood. Screens that should have been replaced with storm windows by October had gaping holes as though armies of mosquitoes had broken through. An abandoned mini–school bus took up one lawn, a doorless drier the other.

"Tobacco Road," I muttered, then set out to examine the half mile of beach before me.

I was no more than ten feet past this eyesore when I heard a woman's voice. "I wouldn't advise a long stroll," the voice said. Its sharp, mocking quality halted me.

I turned and stared at her. She stood at the edge of the porch leaning nonchalantly against one of the beams holding up the sundeck. She was about thirty-five and shapeless in a huge woolly sweater that came down to her knees and over her faded jeans. Barefoot, toenails painted a garish purple; her long, taffy-brown hair curled about her neck and shoulders. When she continued to lean against the pillar, refusing to explain her remark, I said, "How come?"

Her eyes—her best feature—large and darker than her hair, were full of mischief. "Some of the neighbors up the beach have large dogs that aren't too familiar with the trespass laws. They attack everything that moves on either side of their gates. Most aren't fed on a regular basis."

"The dogs or the neighbors?"

"Both."

"You think I'd be running a risk if I went on ahead?"

"You'd be running, that's for damn sure," she said matter-of-factly. She took a few photographs of me with her eyes, then went back inside the house. After she closed the door, a section of screen fell from its porch frame and clattered to the floor. She didn't come out to pick it up.

I considered the validity of her warning. I decided that she'd seen me look down my nose at her home and craved a little pride-saving. And since it was only three o'clock and too soon to go back to Woodsburgh, I'd push on and risk the dogs of Devon.

The gamble paid off. I enjoyed a fine half hour along the edge of the island without any kind of harassment. The sand was beige, coarse, and clean; the bay spread out before me like a fan.

Many of the houses did have "Beware of Dog" signs posted, but not a single animal appeared, canine or human, to substantiate the woman's warning. Standing on the very tip of the beach where the waves rolled up and died before my sneakers, I shed my troubles and felt at peace. The ground loosened as the waters receded, taking some of the sand out to sea, and I knew I would be back soon, like a cripple to Lourdes.

# *six*

Y NAME IS Nancy Seibert. On August second of last year, I lost two children in the same automobile accident. Hannah, nineteen, and Douglas, twenty-one. Hannah died instantly. Douglas died three days later in the hospital. For almost a year I was a total wreck. I still have days when I can't get out of bed."

The stocky but attractive woman uttering these words with clarity and composure was fiftyish, with bright black eyes and short, curly blond hair, brown at the roots. She stood on a raised platform in a medium-size lecture hall at Molloy College, a small Catholic school in Rockville Centre, a few miles north and east of Woodsburgh. The seats were arranged in semicircular ascending rows as in many college lecture halls and was capable of seating a hundred or more students. There were perhaps thirty people scattered throughout the room.

"Since this is a brand-new group," the woman said, "and our first meeting, I thought we'd introduced ourselves and say a few words."

Nancy Seibert scanned the room, looking hopefully for volunteers. Finding none, she focused on the first couple to her left, a thin, white-haired man with thick black eyebrows, and his wife, a head shorter and fifty pounds heavier.

"I'm Kirk Mason and this is my wife, Amy," he said, tilting in her direction. "On July second, 1985, we lost our daughter, Arlene, through hospital neglect. She was being treated for a brain tumor. They took away her cortisone too quickly and she went into a convulsion and died."

The woman at Kirk Mason's left, exceptionally attractive, about my age and expensively but conservatively dressed, failed to speak on her first attempt. She tried again. "My name is Frances DeVito. My son, David, was killed in a train accident last May." She halted and lowered her head, covering her face with her hand, and began to weep.

Nancy turned her attention to the next couple in the row behind. The man in gray tweed was very distinguished looking, balding nicely, the remaining hair thick and cottony at the sides. "I'm Jaime Martinez and this is my wife, Nina."

She may have been older than her husband and resembled a flamenco dancer: olive skin, olive-pit eyes, long, silky, jet-black hair drawn back severely, pointed nose, sculpted nostrils.

"Our youngest son, Ricky," said Jaime, "was shot to death in the parking lot of a disco on Labor Day. This year. A boy wanted his gold chain and Ricky was too slow giving it up." Martinez put his arm around his wife's shoulder. She buried her head in his chest.

Clockwise, the introductions continued. When one row had been completed, the next began: couples and single parents—mothers only. Each couple consisted of a talker and a nontalker, and I couldn't have predicted which would be which.

I'd been told about this group by Violet Fleming after confessing to her that I'd considered seeing a therapist but had decided against it. I told her that I just couldn't share my private sorrow with a total stranger. Not even Bobbi's death could make me do that. Besides, all salvation comes from within.

We'd finished rehearsals at the high school for our December concert and had gone for coffee, Violet and I. Her idea. My first time back with the Symphony, Violet and the others were amazed at how well I'd played. My solo in *Afternoon of a Faun* brought a look of orgasmic pleasure to her face that embarrassed me. I hadn't been trying to prove anything to Violet. I've never considered myself a *performer*.

We were in Friendly's, talking over brewed decaf. It was past ten but I was in no hurry to get home. "Home" was a large empty house with its resident will-o'-the-wisp and too many painful associations. But I wasn't that taken in by Violet's praise to forget her probable ulterior motive for the compliment and the coffee. She was always on the prowl for new recruits to her Women's Consortium, the prowoman, antimale group she'd built with the same diligence employed in constructing the Symphony.

"Wonderful therapy, music," she'd said. "But if you ever really need someone very fine, a woman who knows and understands the women's problems, I have a phone number."

It was then I told her about the impossibility of my seeing a therapist, though I didn't tell her why.

"But you do need some kind of help. This much I know from personal experience. If you'll bear with me a moment and not retreat behind your barricade, I'll explain."

We'd asked the waitress for refills. Violet, a large disheveled woman with uncombed hair and no sense of femininity, ordered French toast. They were getting ready to close up for the night but accommodated us anyway. I'd never liked Violet as our musical conductor, or considered her a friend. She was much too caustic and critical of her fellow musicians, often crossing the line between criticism and abuse. I appreciated her sympathy during *shiva*. She sent a card and visited twice. When I'd returned to practice, she greeted me like the long-lost friend I've never been.

Violet lit a cigarette and sipped her coffee. "Eleven years ago I lost my son, Harvey. A middle son; they're always the hardest to raise. He was a drug addict and died of an overdose."

"I didn't know that."

"It wasn't common knowledge and Aaron was terribly ashamed of it. And him. But a common occurrence in those days. How would you know about such things in your exalted circle? You and yours were so untouchable then: Suzy Gordon, Roz Fiedler, and the others. The queens of the kingdom. Well, regardless," she said before I could rise to my own defense. "I was a mess. And so was Aaron. We were constantly at each other's throat. Blame, blame, blame. We determined that we needed a therapist but fought over which one. Then we heard about this self-help group in Suffolk and joined out of desperation. I came prepared to belittle but stayed to find a great deal of solace. It surely helped me to survive."

But I was surviving, I was almost ashamed to tell Violet. It was Mark who had problems. We were growing more apart every day, both watching it happen yet unable to do a thing to stop the motion.

Violet gave me the name of the group and told me to read *Newsday*'s activities column for the next meeting.

A week later, when I explained to Mark about the organization and that, as luck would have it, a new one was holding its first meeting next Friday, he said, "Another consciousness-raising kaffeeklatsch? Who needs it?"

"You need it," I said. "I need it."

After some badgering, he gave in. His will wasn't very strong. I'd felt like a shrewish wife commanding him, but it was necessary and it worked.

We drove to the end of a tree-lined, sequestered avenue in Rockville Centre on a dark Friday evening in November. Molloy College reminded me of Vassar, with its compact cluster of medieval-style stone buildings. We were directed to a second-floor lecture hall where a cross hung on the wall above the instructor's desk. I quickly dismissed the religious symbol. Wasn't Jesus also a child taken too soon from loving parents?

The stories—more like haiku poetry in their briefness and pungency—were all different at the beginning, the same in the end. All had lost children of varying ages to one of three major killers: automobiles, cancer, or themselves. I'd known that suicide was a major cause of death in young adults and had always wondered about the kind of parents that let it happen. But the ones here tonight seemed no different than Mark and myself, a little more haggard, if anything, and a lot more guilt-ridden.

We sat high on the right side of the room, and when it came time to introduce ourselves, I was the one to do it. I'd waited for Mark to speak. When he'd hesitated for long, excruciating seconds, I took over. "We're Mark and Laura Gerber. Our daughter, Bobbi, was killed by a drunk driver. She was seventeen on February eleventh."

Nancy Seibert looked pleased, as if she were the teacher and we all had recited well. "So. That breaks the ice," she said, almost chipper. How could she exhibit so much sparkle? I wondered. Two kids dead in the same accident. Two funerals, concurrent mourning periods. One devastation compounding another.

"Now, let me tell you about the Compassionate Friends." She glanced about the room, more than two-thirds empty. "After we all move down and fill in the front rows. It's more cozy this way and we'll get to know one another better. That's the main purpose of our little group. As I'll explain.

"The group started in Coventry, England," said a softer-toned Nancy Seibert, "in 1969, by an Anglican minister. We've grown to over three hundred chapters. We are nondenominational. We do not engage in politics of any kind. We don't get involved in the legislative process. We assess no dues, though we do accept donations for the coffee and cake that follows the formal part of our meeting, which, by the way, is over by nine-thirty. Then we break into smaller groups. You'll find that the smaller groups are the most helpful. Face-to-face. Experience to experience.

"What we offer is understanding and friendship, the kind that can only be offered by other grieving parents. The bereaved helping the bereaved. We understand that each parent must find his or her own way in his and her own time. That there is not a right or wrong way to grieve.

"We don't offer psychotherapy or counseling, but we often seek the cooperation of the professional community. We welcome all races, religions, ethnic and economic groups. Let me stress this," she said, glancing rapidly at the few couples and individuals who—like Frances DeVito—had been unable to speak during introductions. "No one is compelled to talk. If coming to the meetings and just being here is best for you, then by all means come and listen. But be assured that whatever you do or say here is treated as confidential and privileged.

"Nuff said about who and what we are. Let's talk. Anybody care to share anything with us?"

At first, and for long moments, there were no takers. Then slowly, like a white flag raised in surrender, a hand from the left side of the room floated up. It belonged to the female half of a couple whose son had hanged himself.

"He was always an erratic, moody kid, always threatening to take his own life. Only we laughed it off. But the last time he threatened, he went through with it."

She was a large woman, nervous and overweight, with loose pepper-and-salt hair, saucer-shaped eyes, and bad teeth. So many of those at the meeting were overweight, and I knew why. Often, over the past few months, it had taken all my strength to keep from devouring a whole pint of ice cream or burying myself in pasta.

Her husband, a small man with slick black hair, in a leather jacket and workman's boots, sat alongside her, detached and unaffected.

"Everyone tells me," she confessed, "that since it's more than two years I should be over it. Like the statute of limitation on grieving had run out. Your employer gives you two weeks, tops, to clean up your act. Fourteen days and you'd better be bright-eyed and bushy-tailed when you get back. Your family gives you about six months, then they start to shake their heads. A shrink—if you get a sympathetic one—allows you a year. It's been two with me and Ziggy here, but I tell you I still feel like shit most days. I'll have one or two good days, then a whole string of bad ones. The bad days are very bad. The good ones are not that good."

She reached into her purse and pulled out a Kleenex. At the same time, Ziggy handed her his handkerchief. She used both. "The thing is, he committed suicide, so we have this extra dose of guilt to live with. I ask myself every day what I did wrong. What Ziggy did wrong. And I can't honestly come up with an answer. Also, since Chip's death, my father isn't speaking to us, like he *knows* it's our fault. It's not enough I lost my kid. I lost my father as well."

Others divulged their own heartaches and the same inability to cope, the same feelings of uselessness. I took heart in their admissions. I felt slightly better and hoped Mark did, too. Was he listening, really listening, finding strength or at least consolation in numbers?

The subject of religion was raised by the executive of a paper-products company. His sixteen-year-old son, half of twins, had drowned in a boating accident in Mirror Lake three years ago. I'd hoped that religion wouldn't come up for fear that Mark would say something offensive. Most of the Friends were Christian and you don't joke about God with Christians the way you do with Jews, though I'd have thought that losing a child would have severed all connections with the deity—Jew, Christian, or Hottentot.

"Yes, my faith was tested," said the executive. "Then I realized that God doesn't kill his children. We parents do. We pollute the air, the food, the water. We, not God, give them money to buy alcohol and drugs. We allow them cars and boats. *We. Us.* Not God. Never God."

Nancy Seibert stepped down from the desk and sat on the raised platform. "I sure prayed a lot after it happened. What for, I've forgotten. Maybe I just mouthed the words to hold on to my sanity. Or to keep the lines open."

"You were always certain, though, there was someone on the other end," I said, not a question.

"I can't honestly answer that," said Nancy. "Though I must

have at times. All I know is I had to believe my prayers were being heard. Not answered—it was too late for that—just heard."

Oh, to be blessed with blind faith. To see what isn't visible. I've always felt prayer to be the grossest of vanities. To believe that in a world of five billion souls—not to mention the possibility of life on other planets, in other galaxies—one voice could, or deserved to be heard, took an almost childlike self-centeredness.

But this was not the kind of healing dialogue I'd come for, not the sort of wisdom that might help Mark.

From behind us I heard, "I'll tell you something, but I'll bet dollars to donuts you already know it: the feeling of abandonment. Now, Mary and I come from large families. Okay? And we have a large one of our own. But let me tell you, small is better. Or no family at all. They're the ones who really hurt you by staying away after it's all over."

This Compassionate Friend had all the credibility of a banker: ebullient, outspoken, nattily dressed in dark three-piece suit and matching tie. He seemed more bitter than bereaved, as though he'd come to the meeting to grind axes and not to share helpful hints. But as Nancy had said, to each his own method of bereavement. Who was I to criticize: a lost soul who fluted way past midnight and jogged until dawn?

"All of a sudden these relatives began avoiding me as though I had some deadly disease. What had I done? Why was I being punished?" His voice had the ring of false oratory. "My son wasn't a traitor. He wasn't shot by the police for holding up a bank. He was run down by a drunk driver as he walked home from Little League practice. At three in the afternoon." The man's face became florid as though bathed by a sunrise. "They came to the funeral, then they stopped: all my brothers and sisters and their kids. Her sisters and their kids. Like a wall had been erected around us."

I was the next to relate our experiences with friends after *shiva*. I told them first what *shiva* was. Most seemed to know. Then I described Suzy's strange behavior on the streets of Cedarhurst. It wasn't the least strange to them. They all had Suzys who deserted them in their hour of need.

An elderly couple, two tiny wisps of people, silent until now, reinforced this new theme. They'd lost a son, Andrew, an art teacher at Manhasset High School. Dead at forty-three of a massive coronary. "He was loved and respected by all his students, and by the faculty, and by our friends and family," said Sven Gundersen. "But after his funeral, forget it. It was like we were sent to a deserted island."

"We were heartbroken about Andrew," said Margot Gundersen, who could have been Bette Davis's younger sister. "But we were humiliated by all those 'loved ones.' "

"I think I figured it out," said Sven. "Most people are cowards. They don't know what to say to a bereaved parent, so they avoid talking by avoiding us. We live in a society that sweeps death under the rug. We relegate it to some hidden recess in our minds. A youth-oriented society. Except that like in Poe's 'Masque of the Red Death' you can't escape it forever. It comes to all of us eventually."

Mark spoke directly to Sven but everyone in the room heard him. "I suppose in our case, losing a daughter with such a gift for life made all our friends' children seem so vulnerable. Especially those with kids her age. If a girl like Bobbi could be cut down, how safe were their kids? For them, after she was gone, it was a case of out of sight, out of mind, out of danger."

About Suzy, I'm afraid, Mark was sadly on target. Jenny was sixteen, Todd, eighteen. The former idolized Bobbi; the latter had had a kiddie crush on her for years. Bobbi had recruited both into Harry Chapin's World Hunger Crusade. In life, Jen had followed Bobbi everywhere. Suzy must have put poor Jenny under lock and key after the funeral.

What surprised me wasn't Mark's contribution to the discussion—he'd said little until then—but his assessment of Suzy. Why had he never shared it with me? Why hadn't he tried to ease my pain these long months? Realizing her fears, I might have taken the first steps with Suzy.

Closer to ten than nine-thirty, the formal part of the meeting ended. We broke into smaller groups and spoke more intimately about the day-to-day efforts of survival, the techniques of putting one foot in front of the other, the art of slipping past the blues. Reading helps, said Frances DeVito. She recommended Elisabeth Kübler-Ross and *The Bereaved Parent* by Harriet Sarnoff Schiff. I'd read them both.

Arlene's father, the cortisone-death girl, left his group to join ours and offered some tips on Thanksgiving, only a few days away.

"Do things differently—that's the way to get through the holidays. If you had family over before for turkey dinner, go to a restaurant. Not with relatives. They might get antsy with you around, or fawn over you. This way, you don't get sandbagged by a whole avalanche of memories and associations. Start new habits. After all, you're in a new situation."

The subject of religion came up again in our small group. To avoid it, Mark left for the coffee table. A Silex was bubbling merrily on a hot plate on the desk.

"The thing that bothers the heck out of me," said the mother of a seventeen-year-old electrocuted by lightning in Central Park last year, "is I know I'm going to see Peter again. Up there." She cast her eyes at the ceiling. "But with all the billions of people in the universe, how will I be able to find him?"

This sounded very much like my own thoughts on the vanity of prayer: we both questioned God's organizational skills.

Mark had heard the woman, and to keep him from berating her, I replied quickly, "If God is all-knowing and all-powerful enough to have a place for each of us, don't you think He has it arranged so that loved ones can find one another?"

My explanation seemed to satisfy the woman and, in that response, I'd also understood the real value of such gatherings: self-help. I'd be back again.

An hour later Mark motioned for us to go. He placed a five-dollar bill in the wicker basket by the Silex and we left.

We drove home a different way. Some of the houses along the streets of Rockville Centre had already been decorated for Christmas. Plastic Santa Clauses and reindeer were perched atop roofs. Strings of tiny lights outlined bushes, trees, doorframes, and windows, glittering like a view of Manhattan from a jet plane. A few lawn crèches, some of them with the bearded three kings, were illuminated by outdoor spots.

I've always loved the month between Thanksgiving and Christmas: the crispness in the air, the carols, the goodwill on the lips of strangers passing on the street, the overriding theme of world peace, the blatant commercialism as well. Even in my ghetto of glitzy and quiet wealth, people of both religious faiths seemed kinder in December.

The ghostly glow of Mark's dashboard was in stark contrast to the lively decorations on the houses. I tried not to read his face as we traveled. We were halfway home before I had the courage to ask, "Did you get anything out of the meeting?"

"I think so."

"Really?" A small bird of hope perched on my shoulder.

"Not really. I don't know. I'll have to think about it."

What was there to think about? It wasn't an intellectual question. Either you felt better or you didn't.

"Will you go again?"

"Maybe."

Maybe? I could hear the flutter of wings as the bird flew off. "That's not an answer, Mark. That's an evasion."

Mark didn't reply at once and I knew that the door to his mind had slammed shut. The lights in his brain had been turned off. I'd pushed too hard. The first time in weeks we'd been together and he'd felt the need to skirt honest answers. My man of titanium had turned to mercury.

We pulled into the driveway and up the long stretch. The yews along the right side, black in the headlights, stood straight and close as an honor guard.

"I don't think so," he said after a while, so hopelessly that I'd regretted pressuring him.

"Well, we'll be meeting again in a month. You have lots of time to change your mind."

"Maybe," he said, holding out a glimmer of hope. "I wonder. Do you think we're grouped alphabetically or by social-security number?"

"Where?"

"Up in heaven, by you-know-who."

I wanted to strike out at Mark, to defend that sad woman from his ridicule. For a brief moment, I felt at one with her and against him. At least she was searching for a way, while Mark was content to stumble in the dark.

But Mark had gained something after all from the Compassionate Friends meeting. He agreed that we should acknowledge Thanksgiving in a new way, in a different setting. We'd have dinner in Manhattan. Bobbi would have wanted it that way, he said, as if we had to have her approval first. The girls would go to their in-laws.

I carefully planned the day and gave a great deal of thought to the night. We hadn't had sex in three months. I'd missed it and wasn't ashamed to admit it. The man was about to be seduced.

We took the Long Island Railroad into Penn Station. I hadn't taken it in years and had forgotten how unlovely some of the streets of Queens looked: row after uniform row of small boxy houses, bare, lifeless streets with abandoned cars cluttering them; the cars cannibalized to mere frames; the huge complexes of apartment houses with families stuffed twenty stories high into cramped living spaces. And yet there could be great happiness in those cells, I suspected, from the smiling Santas in the windows. Just as there could also be misery in mansions.

Our plan was to get out at Penn Station and walk down to Greenwich Village thirty blocks away. It was to be a pilgrimage of sorts, a kind of trip to the old days when we had visited Washington Square Park to kibitz the chess players and hear the impromptu concerts by street musicians, their guitar cases open to catch the appreciative coins. We'd explore the basement craft shops dealing in copper and Mexican silver, the quaint eating places that held no more than ten diners, the shops that sold books we'd never heard of, though we were both voracious readers, the one-room avant-garde art galleries.

At nineteen, I was in love with the Village, with all varieties of human existence there, with all the possibilities of life spread out before me. Most of all, I was mad about Mark, my tour guide through this wonderland.

We'd met the summer before at Camp Merrimont, the only camp in the east Daddy thought worthy of his princess. I was not a wise-and-worldly nineteen like most girls in Woodmere, but socially backward and terribly shy—a retard, according to Suzy and the other campers at Merrimont. My first week I'd been labeled a loner and a snob. Of course I was both, though I participated in all the inane activities so that Daddy could get his money's worth. I went horseback riding, took tennis lessons, labored diligently in the theater workshop. I was Nora in *A Doll's House,* Portia in *The Merchant of Venice,* and one of the Salvation Army dolls in *Guys and Dolls.*

After dinner, my time was my own. I desperately needed a few hours of being alone to reestablish myself. I'd walk down to the lake—deserted that time of day—sit on the dock with a book, and watch the sun lay down a coat of rust over the still waters. All the boats would be off the lake and in the A-frame boat house for the night. The book was Proust's *Swann's Way,* guaranteed to keep away the dodo-brained busboys and waiters as surely as the cross warded off vampires. My first day at Merrimont I'd seen how the staff—mostly college boys from the Bronx and Brooklyn—preyed on those sheltered nubiles with exclusive addresses in Great Neck, Westchester, and the Five Towns. I'd made it obvious through a kind of clipped snippiness and by lugging around Proust that I wasn't fair game for the smooth-tongued and the muscle-bound. I'd never sneak off after lights-out and lie on a blanket in the boat house with Donny or Barry or Steven the way my roommates did.

Two weeks into July, I was sitting on the dock savoring a particularly graceful Proustian passage. In the middle of the lake I spied a canoe slowly being paddled toward me—toward the boat house to my right, actually. The paddler was in no hurry and I could hear the soft lapping as his paddle cut the calm waters. I returned to my page, completed it, then looked up again. The canoe had come alongside the dock.

A boy leaped out and dragged the canoe onto the tongue-and-groove deck. I'd never noticed him before, since he wasn't among the jackals who'd tried to cut me from the pack of new campers.

"Hello," he said, almost as an afterthought, on his way to the boat house, the canoe suspended above his head.

He was tall and slender, well built but not flagrantly so. His skin was the color of cinnamon from the sun, which had also bleached his hair a sandy blond. He wore it long, at a time when crew cuts were the style.

"Are you a camper here?" I asked, amazed at my boldness.

"No, just one of the peons. I'm Mark Gerber, steward of the lake and all its vessels."

"I'm Laura Peres, Mr. Steward, and I'd like to learn to canoe. Would you teach me?" Not very subtle for a girl who toted Proust.

"I'm off duty," he said. "But be here before five tomorrow and I'll see if I can squeeze you in."

"There are too many people during regular hours. I'm uncomfortable in crowds."

He stood there, the canoe held with one hand over his head like an umbrella, considering my reply, analyzing it. In the canoe's shadow he seemed even darker, handsomer. He looked at my face without scanning the rest of my body.

I closed the book. He lowered the canoe to the dock floor. "Stay here while I get a life preserver."

"I can swim," I said to his back as he made for the boat house.

"Camp rules," he replied over his shoulder.

He sat in the bow of the canoe, calling out instructions. I sat in the rear, trying to follow them. I could see the fine shape of his head, the way the wings of his shoulder blades rose and fell as he paddled. His ears, I noticed, were tiny and shaped like seashells. Their lobes were attached to his skull instead of hanging loose.

One week and six canoeing lessons later, we became lovers. Not in his cabin or the boat house after midnight where five or six couples could always be heard moaning and panting, but on a khaki blanket on the sandy shore across the lake, in such shelter and privacy that I never minded removing all my clothes and fully expressing myself.

Saturday mornings in the fall, after I'd returned to Vassar and Mark to Brooklyn College of Pharmacy, we'd meet at Grand Central Station. I'd come by railroad and he'd take the Coney Island BMT from Brighton Beach. We'd meet at the main newsstand, hug and kiss, then walk down to the Village, stopping every block to kiss in the cool autumn sunshine, pausing to glance in store windows at our reflection and tell each other what a fine couple we made. We'd felt so free and clever and Bohemian, drunk on the heady brew of one another.

Later in the early evening, crammed with a day's experiences, we'd go to Seventh Street, where Delman Feldman lived. Delman was a friend of Mark's from pharmacy school and had this very rococo three-room apartment in an old mud-colored brownstone that he didn't use on weekends. He gave Mark the key and his blessings.

Every Saturday that fall and winter, we made love in Delman's huge round pink bed with such ardor that we spent most of Sunday getting our strength back. Between rounds of glorious sex we'd spin glorious plans about our future.

These thoughts raced through my mind as the train sped toward the station.

---

The day was cool and windless with a kindly sun. I felt a sudden surge of vitality retracing our steps. Mark caught my enthusiasm as we hopped off the escalator at the entrance to Penn and linked arms.

Unfortunately Thomas Wolfe had been correct. The Village we returned to was no longer the charming, idyllic backdrop of our courtship. The streets seemed squalid, the brownstones all leached of their quaintness. Washington Square Park seemed taken over by winos and drug pushers.

Memories should never be tampered with, I thought. Never used to solve current problems. Mark seemed to take it in stride, as if he'd known all along not to have expected time to stand still for us. We chucked the Village and walked east to Second Avenue. He perked up at its ethnic diversity. This was the East Village. The site of onion-domed Ukrainian churches, Italian bakeries, and Bangladesh cafés.

Mark said, "Can you believe it? This was once the jumping-off spot for the sons and daughters of immigrants on their way to fame and fortune. The Jewish theater district was here, and kosher dairy restaurants where you could even get hamburgers made of vegetables, and pea soup so thick you could stand a fork in it." Since we had no fond memories of Second Avenue, we felt no sense of loss at its transformation.

On Houston Street, in an alley between two tenements, a group of old men were playing boccie. We were captivated by the robustness of their Sicilian dialect and the stink of their strong cigars.

"They all look and smell like Daddy," I said. Mark enjoyed the comparison, grunting his agreement. I hadn't been disheartened by the small amount of conversation from him during the day. I was content merely to be alone with him, to link arms or hold hands. We stood and watched as the wooden balls sped down the dirt-packed court, collided, then flew off with a resounding thwack.

Mark grinned as the men gathered around the balls and argued over who'd won. Finally, I thought, he's getting back to himself. I could feel it. He was remembering how it had been just the two of us back then, in our brand-new world of infinite possibilities and limitless dreams.

On Delancey Street, we had to fight our way through streets filled with shoppers. Holiday or not, it was business as usual on the Lower East Side, once Jewish, now Puerto Rican.

I stopped at an outdoor display of scarves. Mark helped pick out one for Caryn, a royal blue, one for Sara with a Mexican theme, and one for myself in rich forest green. I'd thought only in units of three instead of four, my usual purchase number. This saddened me terribly. Next month I should be sending out greeting cards—with Bobbi's name missing. I decided not to send out cards at all.

If Mark noticed the sadness in my face, he said nothing. While I paid for the scarves, he turned his attention to the Williamsburg Bridge a block away. Had he been counting the scarves, I wondered?

Where we got the strength, I'll never know, but we walked to Chinatown, two miles away, to an unassuming place on East Broadway under the Manhattan Bridge.

We ordered our favorite dishes: ten-ingredient fried rice for both of us, chicken and cashews for Mark, baby shrimp and pea pods for me. Then we feasted like barbarians. I was so happy that his appetite had returned. We washed down all that heavenly food with pots of delicately perfumed tea. There was nothing left to take home.

"It's not exactly a Thanksgiving feast," said Mark morosely as we cracked open and ate the fortune cookies without reading our fortunes. "I enjoyed it, though, very much."

"Let's call it a lovely dinner together and leave it at that," I said.

We took a taxi back to Penn and caught the 5:28 home. On the train we held hands again. I sketched out our night together.

We wouldn't used our own bed. We'd go downstairs to the basement, to the hide-a-bed. Once undressed, I'd get under the heavy Irish quilt. If he demanded the tiny light in the boiler room to faintly outline our bodies, I'd agree, but I'd tell him that it would only speed up my climax.

From the Woodmere station to our home, I continued this delicious scenario. I hoped to reach new heights in our lovemaking, to establish new habits, like pouring fine old wine into new bottles.

In the house, Mark began to climb the stairs.

"Let's sleep in the basement tonight," I said, leaving no doubt of my intentions.

Mark stared at me as if I'd asked him to urinate in public. "Why?"

"I'd like to make love."

His mouth dropped open. "Forget it," he snapped.

"Why?"

"Why? How can you ask such a question?" Then he continued up the steps.

I followed a few moments later, went to my studio, and opened my flute case.

## *seven*

I'D ONCE READ that in early spring sea gulls along the Atlantic band together and head for breeding grounds by the shores of inland lakes, or on secluded islands up and down the coast. There, a frenzied orgy of mating takes place. A bacchanalia among the birds. In the winter, however, they're quite peevish and drift aimlessly alone or in small bickering flocks, waiting, I imagined, for the weather to change and the bird-fun to begin.

From my vantage point on the Isle of Devon, I followed an erratic gull's flight to where land, sea, and sky met, until it had become a flyspeck on an otherwise flawless horizon.

An innocuous white sun was doling out precious little warmth against the stiff ocean breezes, but I decided to take my walk anyway. Two weeks had passed since my last visit. An early December snowstorm and my increasing involvement in the Civil War had convinced me to stay indoors. In addition, I was getting busier in the store with Christmas rapidly approaching. What had once been an exciting time for me, now had all the zip of an open can of soda.

Walking the beach in winter, pushing against the hammer blows of wind, rewarded me with a numbness that was my Valium, my therapy, my kaddish. It had protected me from accepting Bobbi's death. Laura had made that great leap, I know, and was rapidly achieving a sort of state of grace. Totally functional again. Getting on with her life. She'd gained the wisdom to accept what she couldn't change and I hated her for it.

I was happy to be on the beach again, where the landscape barely changes in winter. There are no trees to grow bare, no grass to turn yellow, no flowers to wither. Yet to the inveterate beach bum like me, there are noticeable alterations. The sun comes in at a lower angle and paints the sand, sky, and water in more subtle tones. In summer, the bay can be a heart-piercing blue; its winter color is a muddy brown. The sand in winter seems darker, more mottled instead of blinding white; the air feels thicker, filled with sea spray that slows the light, diffracting and dispersing it, creating the illusion of texture. When the gull I was watching had become less than a smudge, I shifted interest to that eyesore, the first house on the beach, the one with torn screens and the slovenly woman.

There were storm windows now protecting the house, but only in the front frames and on the outer door facing the bay. The sides still held screens. I wondered at the logic of whomever had made the changes. It was like putting on one shoe, building half a bridge, locking only a single door against a burglar.

The discarded drier and the abandoned school bus still stood guard over this valueless treasure. Both were crusted with a thin layer of hardened snow, which was speckled liberally with the excrement of roosting birds.

Another concession to winter were curtains on the second-story windows: red and velvety, probably hung to conserve heat.

As I was about to push off, the inner door opened. The same woman came out. She crossed the porch, opened the storm door, and stood on the top step. She was wearing the same knee-length rumpled sweater, the same faded jeans. The same loose, serpentine hair. The same look of ironic amusement. This time, however, she had on sneakers: old-fashioned, low-cut Keds. The kind I was sure had been discontinued in favor of the more fashionable Adidas, Nikes, and Reboks.

She leaned against the doorframe, her hands thrust deep into the pockets of the sweater. A cigarette dangled from the right corner of her mouth. "You're back again," she said mockingly. "I thought you might be sick. Or maybe those dogs had swallowed you whole. There was a time a few weeks ago when I could set my watch by your coming and going. Time of arrival—three-fifteen. Time of departure—four-twenty."

"I've been busy," I said, wondering why I'd felt the need to explain.

"That's good," she shot back across the length of the walkway. I felt awkward shouting, so I advanced halfway to the storm door. She greeted the move by tossing her cigarette toward the minibus where it landed in a snow pocket and sputtered out.

"I also thought you might have had your fill of our little Brigadoon by the sea."

"No, I don't get bored easily." Up close, she wasn't unattractive, but I couldn't tell much about her figure because of the bulky sweater. She had the indifferent messiness of a woman who'd just gotten out of bed or who has the day off to laze about the house. Bobbi or Sara had that unbuttoned look when they'd spend the weekend at home studying for exams, but never Caryn or Laura, for whom the first order of business was to make themselves presentable.

Her hair, still wet from an earlier washing, was a decent, though not lustrous, shade of brown shot through with strands of gray. The gray, more than the drab, stuck in my mind. Women in my town, at the first sign of graying, went running to the beauty parlor to cure themselves of it.

Now that I was closer, I could see a fine-boned, squarish face in perfect harmony with a small chiseled nose that could serve as model for rhinoplasty, and large, intelligent—though I guessed merciless—eyes. A front tooth had rebelled against the solid wall of white in her mouth. Twisted, discolored, chipped at the edge, it took something away from the overall effect.

She viewed me half comically, half suspiciously. "No, I didn't think you were the bored type. If you were, once around would have been your limit."

I moved slowly up the walk, as one approaches a skittish animal. She didn't flinch. She didn't try to look elsewhere. "I'm Mark Gerber," I said.

"Virginia Healy," she returned. We didn't shake hands.

She was about forty, give or take a few years. Her lips were like drawstrings across her mouth and I concentrated on that part of her face. I've always mistrusted eyes. Eyes can be made to lie since everyone looked there for the real self. But mouths gave you away most of the time and hers indicated that she'd been around the block a few times, the strolls not always along rose-strewn paths.

"There are no vicious dogs on the beach," I said.

She smiled. "I know." The maverick tooth didn't take much away.

"Then why did you say it?"

"To test your reaction. I'm always testing people. It keeps them on their toes."

"Not everybody likes to be tested."

"That's their problem. It didn't seem to bother you."

"I was busy trying to solve some of my own problems at the time."

"And did you?"

"They don't have solutions," I said.

"Now that's refreshing: a man who not only admits to having problems, but confesses he doesn't have the answers."

Virginia Healy shifted her weight. She'd been leaning on one foot like the gull in the bay. When she switched to the other, she ran her fingers through her hair, thickening it, trapping some of the weak sunlight.

"Listen," she said, "this is monumentally dumb, standing out here in the cold, shooting the shit. Would you like a cup of coffee before you start up the beach? Instant, that is."

"Is there any other kind?"

"Now, that's coffee and nothing else."

"Coffee and nothing else would suit me fine." I made a move up the steps.

Virginia barred the way. "Nothing else includes that insoluble problem of yours."

"It's *my* problem. It doesn't get any lighter sharing it."

"Come in then, Gerber."

I followed her across the porch. Snow had gathered at both sides beneath the screens, filtered to fine powder by the mesh. It lay in drifts resembling mountain ranges.

I entered a small center hall that led at once to a flight of steps and a room left and right. She led the way through the room on the left, which was unlike any living room I'd ever been in before.

A lozenge-shaped maroon mohair couch and two matching chairs were the centerpieces, so old and in need of reupholstering that it would have been cheaper to buy new. An iodine-colored pianola piano took up the inner wall. Scattered—flung, more accurately—around the room in no discernible pattern were a few tables spanning a century in style, from round-bellied skirted to low, square coffee, blond Swedish to cherrywood. On them, enough knickknacks to make a garage sale worthwhile. On each end of the pianola, a brass hurricane lamp stood, the genuine article, in wide use before the invention of the electric light bulb.

The large threadbare Persian rug covering the floor had long ago given up its pattern. In three piles under the front windows were stacked old copies of the *Saturday Evening Post, National Geographic,* and back issues of *The New York Times Book Review* section, ragged at the corners and yellow with age.

The walls were papered in vertiginous splotches of amber and sienna. On one of them hung photographs in crude wooden frames, aged to a somber sepia. Dour-faced men from the turn of the century stood with their hands in their jackets towering over women who seemed more possessions than wives.

Across the hall I caught a glimpse of the other room. I could see an old Emerson radio, horseshoe-shaped, from which its original owners must have heard Franklin Roosevelt's Fireside Chats, and a massive Stromberg-Carlson television that brought Uncle Miltie and Ed Sullivan to the Isle of Devon.

"It's my home, Gerber, whatever else it may seem to you," she said, watching me slowly revolve around the room and reading my thoughts.

"To tell the truth, Virginia, this is all cultural shock to me. But I like it. Sort of."

"You wouldn't be patronizing me, would you, Gerber? I can take disdain easier than I can take being patronized. I'm very big on honesty. It's one of my worst faults."

"Mine too. A kind of cowardice. I'd rather tell the truth flat out than have to face my conscience later. I have a wicked conscience."

Her kitchen proved to be an even greater jolt to someone used to operating-room cleanliness around food. The room took up the width of the entire house, all windows on the sides and outer wall, a square black Formica table and two wrought-iron chairs at one end. The appliances consisted of a green stove, pitted and scarred from years of spills and boil-overs, and a refrigerator with a beehive compressor on top. Magnets dotted the door, serving scraps of self-reminders, short poems, and a scribbled-on calendar from a kosher butcher.

A few dishes protruded out of a sinkful of sudsy water. One held the remains of a spaghetti dinner; another, evidence of chocolate cake. Above the sink, the knob of a cabinet was missing, and a sheet-metal screw was in its place.

Virginia motioned for me to sit down at the table. I opened my coat and eased into a chair. The table was covered with the remains of breakfast: a bowl of cereal, an eviscerated half grapefruit, a picked-over cupcake, and a glass stein of what looked like coffee. Overhead, only one tube of a three-row neon fixture showed life.

While the water boiled, Virginia cleaned off the table with a wet dishrag.

"Would it help matters if I admitted I was a slob and get that behind us?" she asked, tossing the dishrag into the sink.

"I'm middle class but not judgmental."

"That's a moronic oxymoron," she said.

"I'm a quilt of many colors."

"I suspected as much," she said, glancing up and down me. "Sneakers and a sheepskin coat."

"One is for comfort, the other for warmth," I replied, enjoying the fencing.

Virginia took two fresh steins from the cabinet with the sheet-metal screw and spooned instant coffee into each.

"Sugar's all I have."

"Sugar'll be fine," I said, though it wasn't.

I looked out the window into the backyard. It was a bare rectangle of virgin snow bounded by a haphazard perimeter of wooden stakes that had long since discarded the pretense of being a fence. Through wide gaps and missing members, I could see where the bay cut in to become an inlet, not twenty feet from the end of Virginia's property. A beached trawler lay against the opposite bank of the inlet, a blue cabin stuck up from her center. A flotilla of ducks glided by effortlessly, their phosphorescent teal heads flicking from side to side like boxers eluding short jabs.

A jet coming into Kennedy Airport flew low enough to erase what Virginia was saying. After it had passed, she repeated herself. "You'll have to take powdered milk. I'm not home much, and when I am I don't go in for shopping. Milk turns to yogurt before I can use it."

I stirred my coffee, trying to comprehend what kind of woman would invite a stranger into her home on the strength of a few traded words—hers not overly friendly. I could be a rapist, a pervert, or a thief, though ten seconds in her house would discourage even the most inexperienced crook.

"So," she said finally. "Do I go first or do you?"

"Autobiography?"

"You don't see a chessboard in front of us, do you?"

I smiled, thinking she'd watched too many Glenda Jackson movies or perhaps she couldn't tolerate slow-wittedness. "As I've said, I'm Mark Gerber. I live in Woodsburgh. I own a pharmacy on Central Avenue in Cedarhurst. Married. Two daughters; three until last August. She was killed by a drunk driver."

Virginia didn't offer condolences and I liked her for that: she didn't know me or Bobbi. Instead, she dug into her sweater and came up with a soft pack of Marlboros and a disposable lighter. She tapped the base of the pack, then put her lips around the cigarette that stood tallest and drew it out. She leaned into the orange fingertip of flame from the lighter and inhaled deeply. When she'd filled her lungs, she took the cigarette from her mouth and set it on the edge of the table, glowing tip out. Twin jets of blue smoke issued from her nostrils.

The entire operation took less than ten seconds. I've always hated cigarettes and regarded the whole business of smoking as a foolish waste of time, money, and health. But the way Virginia did it was the most captivating piece of theater I'd seen in years.

I continued. "I'm close to fifty. I've lived well and decently most of my life. No complaints. Until a few months ago. I'm Jewish but I don't spend much time at it. I don't drink, smoke, gamble, or womanize. The older I get, the less material things I need."

She listened as though to music, trying, I imagine, to pick out the false notes. She took a short sip of her coffee and a long drag on her cigarette. The kitchen gradually began filling with gray haze. She got up, removed a seashell from the water-filled sink, dried it, then tapped the inch-long ash into its well. A concession to me, I assumed. Alone, she'd probably let the damn ash drop to the floor.

Virginia fastened on the end of my nose after searching my face for a focal point. She toyed with her cigarette but didn't smoke it. "I'm a waitress at the Arden Diner on the turnpike. The night shift. Five until midnight. The pace is more hectic than days but the money's better. I'm forty-two, part English, part Scotch, part Irish, part Iroquois, and the rest unidentifiable impurities. About the Iroquois, I've only my grandmother's word. But she's a hopeless romantic and may be lying. Regardless, that makes me a mongrel of sorts and you know that a mongrel can run rings around any Thoroughbred on the track."

"I'll keep it in mind next time I bet on a dog race."

Virginia didn't think that funny or even worthy of comment. She took a drag on her cigarette, then stabbed it to death in the seashell. Magically, her crooked tooth grew less noticeable the longer she spoke.

"I'm Catholic the way you're Jewish. I've been married three times—to men I've never learned to hate, only to rise above—and divorced twice. Mr. Healy took off some years ago for parts unknown, leaving me with his house and all its contents. Not a word since. I drink. I smoke. I put a few bucks into Lotto every week. About the only thing we have in common is I'm not a womanizer either."

"I knew there had to be something."

This brought the hint of a smile to her lips.

"I wasn't a waitress all my life. I once taught English in a Bronx high school, about fifteen years ago, when schoolteaching was an honorable but low-paying profession. But the City was going broke and they had to lighten the load or sink. It was the best thing that ever happened to me: getting sacked. The money is much better waiting tables and I don't have to toady to a bunch of dumb parents or brown-nose the pols on the local school board."

What, I wondered, did she do with the better money she made waitressing? She certainly didn't spend a lot on furniture or groceries.

Next time at bat I told her about my penchant for reading history; that I hated foreign cars until I bought one, but loved foreign films and French singers like Edith Piaf, Gilbert Becaud, and Chevalier in his youth; that I thought Reagan and his bunch were the worst captain and crew since the Grant administration; that I loved the Kennedys despite the scandals, the Beatles despite their popularity, PBS despite its constant begging for money; that I watched no mainstream TV, only skimmed the newspapers, and enjoyed the company of few.

From her, I discovered that she abhorred all politicians, right, left, and directionless; adored country music except for Willie Nelson, who sang as if half-asleep; loved Irish soda bread, beer, whiskey, music, setters, woolens, and short stories, especially those of Edna O'Brien and Frank O'Connor. "But I hate their men. Undependable—they make the worst husbands. I should know. All three of mine were micks."

Half an hour disappeared in the fog of her messy kitchen. I finished my coffee but she didn't offer a refill. I knew it was time to leave. "Thank you for the instant and the conversation," I said, zipping up my sheepskin.

She answered with a shrug of her shoulders.

"Well, to my rounds." I walked back through the living room.

"Remember about those hungry dogs," she called out as I made it across the porch and down the steps.

"I'm ready for them," I said so that she wouldn't have the last word.

The day had turned cloudy, the sky a thin opalescent blue, the sea gray as a tombstone. I hiked up my collar and started out. I wanted to turn around to see if she was standing in the doorway, but that might have been asking for trouble.

I walked slowly along the sand, my eyes tearing in the cold, irritated by all that tobacco smoke. My sheepskin reeked of it. When I came to the end of the beach where the sand stopped and the marshes and cattails took over, I found my favorite cinder block to sit on.

The month since Thanksgiving had been uneventful. I'd gone to court again, this time alone. At the last minute Laura had decided to stay home.

Christopher McGuire and his mother sat in the same seats as before, wearing the same suits. Assistant DA Spotswood wore the same serviceable blue suit and told me again of his determination to nail the bastard to the cross. Only McGuire's attorney had on something new, a midnight blue pinstripe as splendid as the one worn by my father during *shiva*.

The three men stood before the same florid-faced judge and heard the case adjourned until the end of January. I felt as though Judge Cameron had already imposed sentence—the Chinese water torture—but on me, the water drip, drip, dripping on my head.

The next night, Laura attended the second meeting of the Compassionate Friends. She asked me to go with her but I declined. A waste of time, I told her. I was being honest, not trying to get back at her for skipping the fifteen-minute session in court. She didn't badger or threaten, but served dinner and left. I did the dishes and some reading.

When she returned from Molloy later that evening, she glowed so radiantly that I wondered if she'd been with a lover. Not that I could blame her. Thanksgiving Day in Manhattan had ended disastrously and I was sorry I'd failed and humiliated her that evening. A few times the next day I thought of trying to explain how I felt, but couldn't. I'd rationalized my inability by telling myself that she should have understood.

One event had touched me deeply. Paul and Suzy had split up, Suzy moving out, taking the kids with her. My attempts to solve Paul's midlife crisis had only delayed the inevitable.

I'd tried to restore our own relationship after I returned to the store. He'd been badly shaken by my abysmal behavior and rightly so. He'd accepted my apology and taken my outstretched hand after I'd sought him out in his store, but I knew he was only going through the motions, anxious to be rid of me.

If Paul Gordon had been my best friend, he was so by default. I'd never had many friends as a child. Nat would ridicule anyone I brought home, finding something unkind to say about my latest buddy. He taught me to trust no one and suspect all, and though I've shaken off most of his influence, a lot still remains.

I'd admired Suzy a great deal before she married, so I liked Paul by extension. At first we had little in common, then I bought Cedarhurst Chemists. He was already established on the Avenue and introduced me to his fellow businessmen. In the spring, he harassed me into trying out for the softball team; was thrilled when I beat out Harry Blumberg, the local optometrist, for the coveted position of shortstop.

Except for those points of intersection, Paul and I were as different from one another as an Australian bushman is from a Southern Baptist minister. I'm a social reactionary despite my other inclinations; Paul is slavishly trendy. He'd been taken with est, Marriage Encounter, sensitivity courses at the high school, an evening of Torah with Rabbi Davidson, Friday-night bowling, macrobiotic cooking, and the Peace Movement after it had become popular. He had a pool table in his den, scuba gear in his closet, a CB radio in his BMW, a darkroom in his basement full of photographic equipment, and gold chains around his neck.

Last year, when Paul acquired a mistress as well, I wondered what had taken him so long. The ultimate plaything for a man who took such pride in self-indulgence. But I'd hoped, along with turning fifty, he'd gained some wisdom when he let her go, that he'd realized the long-range contentment with a fine woman like Suzy.

Evidently not, as it soon turned out. Paul stopped me in the parking lot one afternoon late in November as I was leaving for Devon. "I'd like to buy you lunch," he said so humbly that I scrapped the walk at once, though it had been a highly polished morning and I'd yearned for a few hours on the beach.

Inside the restaurant, Paul fidgeted in his seat like a hyperactive child. "I'm in love," he blurted out after we'd ordered. "Ass over heels in love. With Louise."

"Louise who?" I suddenly realized why he had wanted to have lunch with me.

"Louise Lau," he added, exasperatedly, as if she were someone we'd known all our lives.

I must have had a bewildered expression on my face because Paul said, "I can't believe you. Louise—the hostess at Danny Po's. You'd only see her once a week when we'd go to dinner. Mark, she's a customer in your store, for God's sake. We've been having an affair since September. Suzy found out and left me.

She took the kids, the bankbooks, the key to the vault, and the dog. God, she was such an awful bitch—Suzy, not the dog. The dog's okay."

"I'm sorry to hear that, Paul."

"Don't be sorry. Be happy for me—that's why I'm telling you. I'm in love for the first time and I want you, my very best friend, to know it."

Suddenly I'd been rehabilitated like one of those commissars Stalin had executed in the 1930's. "But Jenny and Todd. This must hurt them like all hell. Not to mention Suzy. I'd hoped that after I'd gotten rid of what's-her-name—"

"Polly Caruso."

"—after she left, everything would be great between you two again."

Paul lowered his triangle of sandwich and wiped his mouth with a napkin. "First of all, it was never *great* between us. Suzy's a spoiled, lazy, Five Towns queen. A good mother, okay, but a lousy lover. As far as Jenny and Todd are concerned, they're adults, past being casualties."

Paul finished his Diet Pepsi and motioned to the waiter for another.

"My kids have their whole lives ahead of them. I have most of mine behind me. I'm fucking fifty-three, Mark. Maybe I have fifteen good years left. Maybe." He paused and glanced around for his drink. "With Louise, they could be great years, fantastic years. You had to have noticed. Louise has a gorgeous figure. No tits, but you can't have everything."

"Where's Suzy and the kids and the dog gone?"

"What?" Paul's roaring engine had become derailed. He stared at me with disbelief as if I'd asked him how much he was paying for home heating oil.

"Oh. They moved into the Dorsett in Lawrence where your father-in-law lives. Don't think for a minute Queenie would settle for some welfare motel or apply for food stamps, not with this golden goose to pluck. She'll end up with most of the family fortune, if I know her."

"Louise Lau," I thought I said to myself. I recalled the hostess at Danny Po's. I didn't think she was that attractive. But then I didn't think Suzy was a chronic complainer or inept in bed.

Paul had heard me. "I love her," he'd said with firm conviction.

"Last time it was also love," I reminded him. "You cried like a baby when Polly left. Then, you couldn't thank me enough when you and Suzy got back together."

"I still feel grateful. If you hadn't sent Polly packing, I might never have known Louise."

"Thanks a lot," I said. I wondered if there was still time for an abbreviated walk.

Paul ordered a third drink and began regaling me with the Eastern attitudes toward sex and how Louise, who'd moved in with him, had molded herself into an instrument of pleasure for his benefit alone.

I got up to leave. Paul grabbed the check. "You've got a penis for a brain," I said, risking another rift in our friendship. Risking very little, actually, since he'd asked me to lunch solely to talk about Louise.

He only smiled. "It's about time I started thinking with it. But what would a goody-goody like you know about yearning and desire and frustrations? You and Laura—the Ken and Barbie of the Five Towns. Except for Bobbi, that is."

I was so lost in thought recalling that unpleasant lunch with Paul that I hadn't felt the rain, so cold and chilling it was almost sleet. I was drenched before I'd gotten off the cinder block.

I ran all the way to Virginia's house and sought refuge under her porch.

As I stood there, soaked and shivering, Virginia opened the door and came out. She was wearing a black raincoat and white thick-soled shoes, and carried a collapsible pink umbrella under her arm, a dash of very red lipstick across her thin mouth.

"I'm going to wait on the porch until it lightens up," I said.

"It may rain like this all night. Want an umbrella?"

"If you don't mind."

"I'd offer you a lift to wherever you're parked but I don't own a car."

"How do you go to work?"

"By bicycle. I have a ten-speed locked in the bus."

"I'll return the umbrella tomorrow."

"No hurry. I have loads of them. Come in and help yourself."

In the hall, she opened the closet and pointed. "You'd be amazed at how many customers leave these things behind at the diner. Some are pretty expensive."

I chose a standard British businessman's model from a shelf above a rack of sweaters, parkas, and raincoats.

"Jesus, you're soaked," she said, staring at the small puddle accumulating at my feet. She examined her watch. "How about another cup of coffee? With the rain, they won't need me this early."

"Great," I said.

She removed her raincoat and threw it over the railing leading upstairs. She was costumed in a light pink waitress's uniform that was completely out of character. I could see that I'd been all wrong about her lack of a figure. She was a bit thin, but had an extra helping of breasts, if they were her own. And decent legs—straight and shapely and not at all waitress-muscled.

In the kitchen, she heated another pot of water and threw me a clean dish towel to wipe my face and dry my hair. After doing both, I went to hand it back. We were close together in that small space between the sink and stove. She turned to face me and I noticed a scar under her left cheek, a thin half-moon that tilted downward. I wondered if one of those Irish husbands had left a memento. Then, for no reason that made sense, I leaned over and kissed the scar.

Virginia hesitated for a moment, reading my eyes, then put her arms around my neck and kissed my lips. I felt her breasts unyielding against me, fuller than I had imagined.

"You look silly wearing my lipstick," she said.

"Then I'll give it back to you." I kissed her harder than she'd kissed me. My hands cupped her face to do it, slipping down her shoulders to her sides, along her hips, joining fingertips at her buttocks, pressing them into me. I began unbuttoning her uniform.

"I do all my lovemaking in bed."

"Sounds wonderful to me," I said.

She led the way up the stairs, which announced us by creaking loudly. I should have thought of AIDS, herpes, or at least infidelity, one step behind her. But I was enthralled by how her body swayed from side to side as she negotiated the stairs. Five, six, seven steps up and we were at her bedroom door.

The room reminded me of a pioneer's cabin: low and sloped and sparsely furnished, with a box spring and mattress, one chair, one dresser without mirror, one sliding-door closet, four walls with nothing on them. A red, oval, hooked rug covered only the center of the floor. And those red curtains.

The bed was unmade, its billowy blue and white blanket in a ball at the foot. A yellow terrycloth bathrobe was slung over the chair, its sash on the floor beneath it.

The saving grace of this untidy room was the melodious sounds of rain on the roof. Instantly, I grew hard. I hadn't had an erection for months, not even lying next to Laura's nude body, which I'm sure she'd deliberately unsheathed to arouse me.

So quickly that I hadn't time to ogle her, Virginia undressed, got into bed, and pulled the blanket to her chin. "Come in, the water's fine," she said, amused by the bulge in my corduroys.

I was so anxious to be inside Virginia that I didn't bother with the necessary preliminaries. My brain, my entire being lay between my legs while I lay between hers. My hands—ten busy fingers—dug beneath her body, raising it to me like some huge cup I was about to drink from. Unnecessary, as she arched her hips to meet my penetration. I'd never felt such a strong pair of legs. They grasped me like pliers. Her arms bound me from above. Foreplay at this moment would have only been a cruel, delaying action.

I forgot about the fifty years of who I was and what I'd worked so hard to become. We danced the oldest dance of man and woman in little more time than it took to take off our clothes. I detonated inside her. It was like a dam bursting, and my needs were such that I didn't care if she'd been satisfied or not. I'm afraid that in my loss of control I pounded Virginia with all the uncompromising force of a pile driver. She never uttered a word of complaint. When I was done and lay on her, deadweight and sweaty, she kept on pumping for a short while, then let out a great cry of pleasure and, digging her nails into my back, climaxed. First it felt like a cloudburst, then a warm bath.

We remained locked together for what seemed like an hour. Darkness was leaking into the room and over me, while I lay in the bower of her flesh, the rain beating against the roof.

Before separating, I kissed her lips, an apology of sorts for my clumsiness. They tasted of coffee and cigarettes, but that didn't detract from the pleasant afterlust I was luxuriating in.

"I never doubted for a second I'd sleep with you," she said contemplatively. "Since seeing you that first time—giving the house the once-over. But I didn't think you'd be so violent, so ...untender. My God, doesn't she feed you at home?"

"It's been a long time and I got carried away. Sorry."

"Lord, I feel as though I've been mugged," she said, stretching across me to get at the cigarettes in the uniform on the floor. She lit up, took a heavy drag, and with her free hand played with the matted hair on my chest.

I had my first real chance to inspect her body. She was indeed thin, but a tiny waistline had given fine contrast to her hips. Her breasts were fuller than a thin woman's should be, with large pink nipples like the toes of a newborn baby. A very tight, firm body, I decided, with not a square inch of useless skin, as though the result of careful, economical design and constant upkeep. Long, coltish legs, adequate ass. If she'd been abused or overworked in bed by any of her husbands, I could find no trace of it.

We lay side by side, eye to eye, nipples aligned, hips only inches apart. She held her cigarette aloft like a torch, a barely visible corkscrew of smoke rising from it. "Violence has its place in the bedroom, Gerber, but I didn't think *you* were capable of it, from the Five Towns and all."

"Some of it has to do with you. You're very attractive. I didn't think so at first. I thought you were too skinny."

"Too skinny for what?"

"For sex, for one thing."

Virginia laughed and turned on her back. She gazed at the

ceiling, silently smoking. I watched, captivated. Then, as though an alarm had gone off, she sat up, opened a window behind her, and tossed the cigarette into the backyard.

The curve of her thigh in my face excited me again. I pulled her down on top of me. This time I made very slow love to her.

Virginia appreciated my meticulous attention to every part of her body, my leisurely exploration of all its cavities and altitudes, and said so. When we were done, there was total darkness in the room and I could no longer see her face. The rain kept coming in spasms across the roof like an army of cossacks.

"Now, that was much better, Gerber," she said. "Worth having you in for a cup of coffee. I guess, then, I'm not."

"Not what?"

"Not too skinny for lovemaking, or screwing, which is the case in point."

"Sometimes it's wonderful to be wrong."

"You know," she said after we'd dressed and were ready to leave. "It has occurred to me, when you came on the porch and saw me leaving for work, you could have suggested we walk together under my umbrella to your car, then you could have driven me to the diner. It was the most obvious choice. Instead, you waited me out until I asked you in and offered you an umbrella, then that second cup of coffee. Like you were angling all the while for that second cup of coffee and where it led to."

"I guess *I* was testing *you*. You don't own the patent. Maybe I also knew that I'd sleep with you sooner or later and wanted it sooner."

"That's pretty good maneuvering, Gerber, for someone who isn't particularly street smart," she said, inserting her arm through mine so we could use one umbrella. "Now let's go to your car and you drive me to work the way you should have before you got yourself into this ridiculous mess."

# eight

A PILE OF MESSAGES awaited on my library desk. Frances DeVito, my new friend from the Compassionate Friends, had called. I dialed her at home. She wondered if we could have lunch today, sorry about the short notice. Today was out, I told her. How about tomorrow? We arranged to meet at an out-of-the-way Greek restaurant in Mineola.

Mark had refused to go with me to the last Compassionate Friends meeting. He said it was no place for him; he wasn't ready to share and gained nothing from others' experiences. Mark had always been a loner and not even the loss of his beloved Bobbi could change that. That second meeting at Molloy meant so much to me. New members showed up, while a few from the last time were absent. "They'll be back," said Nancy Seibert confidently. "Bereavement's a rocky, twisting road. There's a lot of falling into ditches. A lot of backpedaling."

Frances and I had found each other after the formal part of the meeting, two kindred souls drawn by the same perception that we had more in common than the loss of a child. She was much improved over the previous month when she could hardly speak her own name. We took our coffees and pound cake to the highest tier of the lecture hall and, without fear of being labeled snobs, sat for an hour and chatted.

She'd grown up on the North Shore of Long Island, in Sands Point, a community every bit as wealthy as Woodsburgh. Her father was a world-class cardiac surgeon, her mother an assistant professor of art history at Hofstra.

"I guess we were not terribly typical: upper-class Northern Italian–Americans. I grew up with four brothers and sisters—two and two—harmonious and happy in our mansion on the Sound. We were terrible overachievers. My brothers are also heart surgeons. One sister runs an alcohol-treatment center in Detroit. The other practices pediatric medicine at Albert Einstein. Both girls are married to doctors. Some weekends at our house we have more MDs than most hospitals.

"I was the family disappointment. Only a master's in hospital administration. My first marriage, to the owner of a fleet of taxicabs, was a disaster. Luckily, it didn't last long. My second marriage, a very good one, was to my father's partner, a man twenty years older than me. A darling man. I'd loved him all my life without knowing it. We were so happy when David was born. Carl had been a widower for years.

"When David died, I felt as if someone had turned out the lights in a brightly lit room. Carl, who knows death intimately, has been a tower of strength to me."

We compared lives, loves, and losses that night, and cried without self-consciousness. We agreed that we were very much alike despite our dissimilar upbringings, even in the clothes we wore. We dressed expensively but sparingly, unlike most women in our economic brackets. We spent little time haunting the department stores and specialty shops. "My daughter, Sara, once calculated that by not becoming a clothes horse I'd saved about five thousand hours. I could have earned a Ph.D. with the time I'd saved avoiding Loehmann's and Bloomie's."

Frances laughed a nice, open laugh. In it, I could imagine her childhood, the house on the Sound rocking with activity. I fleetingly envied the atmosphere, fiercely competitive though it must have been.

We'd left, promising to get together again. But the reason we couldn't have lunch today was I already had promised the time to Caryn. She was to be in Garden City, preparing for an assistant buyer's sale.

We met at a small pub called the Bluebird because Caryn first met Warren there. What the Spot had been to Mark and me, the Bluebird was to them.

Caryn looked breathtaking in a smartly tailored pearl-gray business suit, flouncy blouse that hid her small bust, and red patent-leather high heels. She wore only a trace of lipstick and a hint of eye makeup, having learned long ago that less was more. Her hair had been shortened and styled in a feather cut that framed her face to perfection, giving her a gamin look. On her finger, a thin wedding band, no other rings, bracelets, bangles, beads, or pearls. She could have been a letter carrier's daughter from Queens.

I was very pleased with her and said so. When the waitress said, "Mother and daughter. That's plain to see," I puffed like a peacock.

"How's Daddy coming along?" were her first words, fret lines furrowing her brow. She'd visited at least once a week with Warren, and Mark had done his best to act civil. He'd fooled Warren but Caryn knew better. "I'm worried. He'd be talking to us, then suddenly he'd take leave of his body and drift off to someplace else. It's weird, Mom. For twenty or thirty seconds, I'd be talking to a statue."

"I know. With me, it's longer than twenty or thirty seconds. It's hours. Days."

"He'll come back," she'd said. "He's our rock. I guess he knows we need him now more than ever."

I don't know what he knows, I thought. "Of course he will," I said. "In time."

We sat and talked for the best part of an hour. More friend to friend than mother/daughter. We tried to keep the conversation upbeat, two high-wire acts, knowing what we knew, suffering the same loss. In her efforts, I recognized one of my own gifts: the ability to swim against the tide. It had been in Caryn all this time, in reserve until needed. She confessed small secrets to me: Warren was wonderful but too dependent on his father. And living in a Manhattan high rise had all the ambience of a white-collar prison. And her mother-in-law was pressing her to have a baby, holding over Caryn's head a rapidly ticking biological clock. All of which, Caryn said assuredly, she took in stride.

"Warren and I are going to wait. To conceive now would be wrong because I'd be doing it for the wrong reason. I don't want to become pregnant to take my mind off Bobbi. When I do, it'll be because we both want a baby for the baby's sake." Caryn pushed away an empty dish. "We don't now."

Clasping her hand, I smiled. "I thought you were already working on it. Those dark circles under your eyes."

"Lack of sleep. Nightmares."

"The same ones I'm having."

A light film coated Caryn's eyes. "I see her sometimes. When I'm alone in my office. Or when I get up at night to go to the bathroom. I talk to her. She answers me. She asks me questions. I find myself looking forward to those moments."

"She's with me, too, most of the time," I said, suddenly unable to finish my lunch.

On the sidewalk outside the Bluebird, Caryn kissed me and we embraced seconds longer than usual. "Hang in, old girl," she said. "Things will get better. I promise."

She'd learned that from my father. From him, it seemed the words had gone directly to Divine Providence and things usually got better. I wasn't at all certain Caryn could work the same magic.

There is no name for that moment in a family's history when the child begins advising the parent. That delicate shift in authority. The moment can be traumatic or gentle, depending on the actors in the drama. In my case, in Caryn's competent hands, it wore butterfly wings and felt as light as a child's kiss. And I knew that years from now Caryn would become a most understanding mother to me, perhaps the one I never had, as well as mother to her own brood.

During the drive home I remembered a cool Saturday in May about five years ago when Caryn was a junior in college. Dusk was beginning to turn my den a rosy shade of blue. Upstairs, Caryn was dressing to go out with Warren; downstairs, I was struggling my way through Cynthia Ozick. We were alone in the house. In stockinged feet, Caryn appeared before me, asking for help with the diamond earrings we'd given her for her twentieth birthday.

"Warren and I have been going out for nearly a year," she said.

Inside I panicked. I thought she was going to ask permission to quit school and get married. Some of her friends had already landed husbands and considered marriage the ultimate career. Warren had graduated from Wharton and was set in his father's business. Caryn wasn't. I wanted her to finish, have a career, be self-sufficient.

"And he's asked me to sleep with him." Our eyes met, mingled, separated. "I want to. Very much."

I stabbed blindly for the hole in her earlobe, frankly amazed that she hadn't already done so. She was twenty, healthy, the object of much ardent pursuit by the handsomest young men. She wasn't a cave dweller where relationships were concerned.

"Is it love or lust?" I foolishly asked.

"Both," she answered without hesitation.

"Are you asking my permission?"

"Yes," also delivered without delay.

I wanted to hug Caryn for her honesty and trust. "You have my permission and sort of my blessings. But be careful. Be very careful."

"I will. I promise."

She lingered leaving the room, her earrings in place and glowing hotly in the setting sun. I read her mind. "Do you want your father's permission, too?"

"Yes."

"You'll get it, but you won't get his blessings, I'll tell you now. Shall I ask him for you?"

"Would you?"

I told Mark that night after our own lovemaking, and as I'd guessed, he didn't object. Not strenuously. I'd explained that Caryn and Warren considered themselves united in spirit and were only waiting for her to graduate before making it legal. I offered us twenty years before as examples. I used the word "hypocritical" a few times. He consented.

---

When I returned to work, Bruno Coletti was sitting in the reference room near my office. A stack of magazines on the table opposite him indicated either he was a fast reader or had been waiting a long time.

"You're late," he declared.

"I don't punch a time clock," I threw back at him.

"Forgive me," he said, broken. "I didn't intend it as criticism. I thought it might be a convenient way to start a dialogue."

"It's not," I replied before he could put a period to his sentence.

"Well then, suppose I back up and start over again. Good afternoon, Laura. You look lovely."

"An improvement, Bruno. You're lucky I'm not one of those who distrust flattery."

"But all women enjoy hearing it, true or not. In your case this is a statement of fact, not a bit of puffery."

"I didn't say I *liked* flattery, only that I don't distrust it."

He rose, put the magazines back in their racks, and accompanied me to my office. "And how are the children?"

It took a few seconds to realize he was talking about his and not mine.

"I know I promised to call every so often, but I've been away."

"They're fine. Excellent. Every morning I take out my magnifying glass and inspect for damages."

"You don't go with an aficionado's eye?"

"Mmm, that too. They've been well received. Quite a few other aficionados have asked about buying them. I have some names and addresses in my office."

"Bless you."

In the office, he took a seat while I went through his folder for the list of potential buyers and the insurance-company release form he had to sign. He thanked me and we went out to the garden, Bruno two steps behind like a Chinese wife.

———————

Actually I'd spent more than a little time in the garden last fall, admiring his work. Before I'd had the strength and courage to go out for lunch, I'd sit there holding unspoken discourses with the statues. The trio had brought me joy, for there was only joy in that area of my life. The mother and children had invoked the bittersweetness there'd been in having, raising, loving, and losing part of me dearer than myself.

I told Bruno none of this as we went from statue to statue looking for chips, cracks, and signs of vandalism. He would surely use it to his advantage. But I did regret my flash of pique a few minutes earlier. I wanted to apologize, but that, too, might be misunderstood.

I couldn't help but notice Bruno as we inspected together. He wore a black turtleneck sweater and tight-fitting, tan jeans. Small sections of his beard had turned a bright silver, as if he'd taken a camel's-hair brush and dabbed it. He was much more attractive than I remembered.

Another U-Haul was parked by the back entrance. Between statues, Bruno said he'd been away in Mexico studying Mayan art in the Yucatán with native artisans for whom the twentieth century was only a rumor. The jets that flew high overhead were thought of as the gods of their ancient myths, said Bruno, who'd listened to those myths while working with a pottery maker in Chichén Itzá using tools over two hundred years old.

The very dense and the very dangerous never give up. "I would still like you to see my studio," said Bruno. We were kneeling at the time, head to head at the base of the trio, four critical eyes searching for damages. "I've done some Mayan-style fertility figures you might appreciate."

"You can see that, too, in my eyes, can you, Bruno?" I scoffed. I remembered his amateurish line about "windows of the soul." I stood up from my ridiculous position.

"No, this time it's your body telling me. Body language is a universal tongue. You need no translator to understand it."

"The answer is still a very definite no."

Bruno sighed. "Such a waste."

"I beg your pardon." I was beginning to fume.

"No offense intended. I call it as I see it, sense it. Your body language cries out that you are pining away. Underutilized. Ignored."

"Are you quite finished?"

"There is more if you care to listen."

"I mean with the statues."

"Oh, yes. It's done. I'm satisfied."

I handed him the release to sign. Unperturbed, humming an air from *Nabucco,* he scrawled his signature beneath mine and twice as large.

"Please close the gate when you leave," I said, spinning around on the frozen ground and walking away. When I was back in my office and safe from his eyes, it occurred to me that the garden would look pitifully bare without the visitors I'd come to love.

---

Violet Fleming raised the baton over her head like a saber. She stood straight as a Buckingham Palace guard, eyes closed as if to blot out her surroundings. The orchestra grew hushed. The last bit of gossip between Margarite Thane and Elaine Himmel—first and second violinists—died midsentence. The mindless flights of fancy on the tuba by Bonnie Schick faded away like dreams. Even Didi Kantrowitz, who regularly dined with Donald Trump and Harrison Golden, submitted to the conductor's gesture to get ready, and poised her harp. A second later, Violet brought the baton down with swift masculine force. "The Rakossi March" was off and running.

Despite the threat of snow in the air and in the evening forecast, all members of the Five Town Women's Symphonic Orchestra had shown up at the high school for the final rehearsal before the annual Christmas concert. It was by now a tedious drag for most of them. They'd been drilled and redrilled by Violet until the juice had been squeezed from the music and the enthusiasm from the musicians.

"There is such a thing as too much rehearsal," I told Violet when she'd called at the library just as Bruno was driving off.

"Not for the professional," Violet had said.

After "The Rakossi," we entered the warm sunshine of the Brahms "Academic Festival Overture." I loved the piece, the way it conjured up images of old European university towns, cobblestone streets, ivy-covered walls.

After the last notes died away, we were interrupted by the sound, then echo, of enthusiastic applause. A solo performance from the darkness of the auditorium. Violet turned and bowed to the single listener, low and gracious. I peered into the darkness. Our conductor had made it a standing order that no one was ever to be admitted to rehearsal. It was, after all, the place to make our mistakes and learn from them.

Rossini's "La Gaza Ladra" was next. I had a great deal to do in the piece and enthusiastically threw myself into it. My thoughts were of outdoor concerts on the Piazza San Marco, the Bridge of Sighs, La Scala, warm Venetian nights in a gondola, gondoliers dressed in red-striped undershirts, wearing silly Buster Brown hats.

There was the sound of applause again after the piece had ended. Then just as we were about to begin Copland's *Appalachian Spring,* some passerby opened the auditorium door. A shaft of yellow light, like an arrow, fell across the back rows. It grazed the face of a man, illuminating only the lower jaw and the beard that covered it.

I knew at once it was Bruno. Who had told him about the

rehearsal? Why? Bruno was not here as a music lover, I suspected. I tried to ignore his shadow presence since it couldn't help but affect my playing.

As luck would have it, our final number was Debussy's *Afternoon of a Faun,* complete with flute solos. I gave myself to the lush piece and was soon sucked into its eroticism, weaving through the green glades and sunlight evoked by the strings and woodwinds. Somehow the image of Bruno merged with the figure of the faun. I poured myself into the music, becoming less me and more the tiny silver instrument. The flute and the faun were all there was in the forest, in the world. I played as I hadn't played in months, as if I had to prove to Bruno that I, too, was an artist.

"That was magnificent," said Violet, tapping her baton on the podium. The players began packing their instruments, eager to get home.

"Better than magnificent," said Bruno, joining Violet at the podium. "I was moved," he said. Those were my very words to him on seeing his statues for the first time. I knew he'd chosen them with care.

"What are you doing here?" I asked pointedly.

"Mea culpa," from Violet, though not at all chagrined to have broken her own rule. "Bruno and I are old friends. He's planning another piece with a musical theme. After that exquisite trio in the library garden, I could hardly refuse him."

A message I couldn't decipher flashed between Bruno and Violet, then she left and I was standing alone with him. I began to pack up my flute. "I wasn't just tossing fragrant bouquets at you, Laura. You handled those solos like Galway. Better. I'm impressed. Let me tell you how impressed. Let me ask your advice about the new work I have in mind."

"Do I have a choice?" I asked resignedly.

"Friendly's is still open."

"I guess it wouldn't do any harm to listen."

Since it was to be a creative meeting and not a rendezvous, I didn't object to Friendly's, where I was well known.

Perhaps to disarm me, Bruno said when we were seated, "My idea is to do a flutist. Or is it flautist?"

"Flutist."

"Thank you. A flutist who is definitely *not* you. I chose that instrument because it's small and I haven't the funds for anything as massive as the trio. A man perhaps. Mediterranean. With long Medusa-like hair. The look I'm after is one of total rapture, of being intertwined with the flute and the music. The look I saw on your face for a brief moment during the Debussy."

An excited Bruno was a hand-flailing Bruno. The longer he spoke of his project, the freer those hands became. They manipulated the air in Friendly's. The fingers were tapered, the skin smooth and waxy with thin blue veins that branched into thinner capillaries. They were not what I'd expected of hands that held mallet and chisel and attacked stone.

"And you," he said after I'd returned from the ladies' room where I'd gone to see if my lipstick had smeared or my mascara had run. "What drives you to such heights of perfection in your music?"

I held back, wondering if Bruno was deliberately baiting a trap, urging me on to open my life to him. Had Violet told him about Bobbi? Should I?

"It's not the creative urge, if you must know. I need to be involved in things that take me outside myself." His eyes were fearless probes. "I lost a daughter in August. I'm trying desperately to survive her."

"Ah," said Bruno. "That explains so much." He didn't elaborate. His hands came to rest on the table very close to mine, and although he didn't touch them, it felt as though he had. At once, I withdrew my hands and held my teacup, absorbing its warmth.

Slowly, testing the water, I revealed to him a little about Bobbi. Then, a bit more, what her loss had done to me, the spiritual damage. I told Bruno more than I'd told Frances DeVito. Frances had merely listened; Bruno asked questions that were scalpels cutting through the fat and gristle to get at the source of my pain.

I was frank. I was honest. I left myself vulnerable, I'm afraid, but he didn't take advantage of me. God, did I open the flood-gates. When I looked up at the clock above the open grill, it was past eleven.

From that moment, Bruno had changed. He no longer came directly at me, dangerous and breathing fire. He *listened*—such a lost art—and sighed when I described the blessing Bobbi had been. And when I'd finished telling Bruno everything I'd dared, I found I wasn't a depleted, talked-out shell. I felt better, the way Freud said one would be.

A subdued, thoughtful Bruno took over. He talked about his family. "Very Sicilian. Poor and large. All the men in my house work with their hands. My brother Pietro is a mason. Bernardo lays bricks for a living. Joseph works for Sanitation. My sisters have all become stereotypical Italian mothers: overweight, over-emotional, with noticeable mustaches.

"Mom and Pop are still alive. They have a house in the ne-glected section of Inwood, near Rockaway Turnpike. Mom goes to church three times a week for religion and bingo. Pop has his friends, his homemade vino, and his tomatoes. What religion is to Mom, raising tomatoes is to Pop."

"I know someone like that," I said.

"We fight on Sundays when we get together. Joe and Bernie are pro–Ollie North, Pietro and I are not. Jocelyn and Marie are pro-choice—surprisingly, for ladies with mustaches—while Mom and Lydia believe everything the pope says, even though he's Polish. The windows rattle. The neighbors complain. Pop is the only one with no opinions. The meek shall inherit the earth, he claims, because the strong will kill each other fighting for it."

"I like your father."

"He'd like you. You must meet him."

"Well, maybe later—one antiwar person to another."

Just as Bruno had changed in the two hours we sat over tea, so did I. Until Friendly's, I'd always talked *at* him, never to him, his sexual aggressiveness the major reason. But once he'd ended his assault, I found an almost feminine sensitivity in him, a fear-lessness in letting his feelings show. When I'd told him how I'd suffered entering Bobbi's room that first time to prepare her burial clothes, a perfect tear welled in each of Bruno's eyes and remained suspended there. He'd tried not to blink, but when he did, each tear made a slow descent down his cheeks. I was so touched.

I stopped short of telling him about Mark. That would have been an open invitation to disaster. It was time to go home.

---

Outside, the ground was covered with a light film of snow, though the clouds were breaking and scudding across the charcoal sky. Bruno said, "I was right about you, after all. You are an unfulfilled woman." He bent over and just grazed my lips. His beard felt as soft as mink. I saw the smoke of his breath in the frigid night air. Over his right shoulder, the moon was the color of those odd patches of his beard.

He left first. I waited for a semblance of sanity to return. The lights in Friendly's began closing one by one like actors leaving a stage.

I got in my car and drove off, thinking about Mark. Had I left him something to eat? He'd probably manage. He'd been doing nicely without me for months.

## nine

HE DIDN'T HAVE A heart attack and he didn't have a stroke. It wasn't even close."

"Then what was it, Rudy?"

"Indigestion, most likely. Maybe a touch of angina. He *is* seventy-eight, you know. With seventy-eight-year-old plumbing and wiring. It's not uncommon for a man his age, with a fairly good heart, to feel a bit of a pinch now and then. So let's call it a warning, okay? Anyway, he's coming in on Friday for a cardiogram and blood work. Then we'll know for sure. In the meantime, give him some Nitro 1/150 and twenty-milligram Inderal t.i.d."

"Should I tell Laura?" I asked Rudy Frank, Dr. Rudolph

Frank, the overworked, overweight, chain-smoking general practitioner who'd taken care of Irving, the five of us, and many Five Towners in his forty years of service. He carefully considered my nonprofessional question.

"No, I wouldn't. Not yet. Let's wait for the tests. No sense in scaring her needlessly after what's happened to you two. You know, I can't remember when he was in for a checkup. The last year Mickey Mantle played for the Yanks, I think."

"Tell him I'll be over in an hour with the prescriptions."

"Tell him yourself, Mark. He wants to talk to you and I'm late. Zelda has tickets for *Les Misérables* and if we miss the first act, I'll be *Misérables* myself."

"False alarm," sang Irving in my car. "Like the man said, a little indigestion. But he sure charges for the real thing. On your way over, pick up a couple of Garcia y Vegas and the *Daily News.*"

"Like hell I will." I was thinking of his seventy-eight-year-old heart.

"What? You don't want me to know what's happening in the world? You got something against Jimmy Breslin?"

---

Jack prepared the two prescriptions while I resumed a sparring match with Eric that Dr. Frank's phone call had temporarily suspended. Since Christmas, Eric had been trying to maneuver me into a fight and this time he'd succeeded.

Since Bobbi's death, he'd grown testy and combative. He'd magnified every small problem in the store to crisis proportions. His big complaint was the lack of solid leadership from me. I was responsible for the drop in business, 9.1 percent in January, according to the computer. He must have been thinking of his bonus, which was based on growth.

Nevertheless, what Eric said was true. I'd grown terribly lax. I hadn't even the courage to face the fact that someone was stealing from me—a hundred or so a week—and that the thief was most likely Eric. He was the only one on duty every day the register was short. I simply couldn't risk losing him, because that meant working his shift until a replacement could be found. The thought of spending all those hours in the store depressed me, so I wrote off the money as part of the cost of doing business.

This time Eric cornered me. "I've put up with Mary Tannenbaum much too long." We were seated, the desk between us. His index finger stabbed the air. "She comes in late half the time. She gives out the wrong change. Hands out the wrong prescriptions. And while we're on the subject, there's Maureen. Last week one day I caught her making personal calls ten times. *Ten times!*"

"I told her she could."

"You didn't tell me."

"Her daughter's been sick. She was checking to make sure the kid took her medicine."

"I told her she'd have to pay for the calls."

"Tell her you changed your mind."

"Tell her yourself."

"It would be better coming from you. It's part of your job."

"Not anymore it isn't."

I felt the jaws of the trap snap shut, saw a momentary flush of victory on Eric's face. "I'm giving you two weeks' notice. Find yourself another patsy."

Patsy? That shook me as much as Eric's notice. I'd taken him, inexperienced and rough-edged, right after graduation. Paid him pharmacist's wages though a year passed before he'd earned it. Lent him, interest free and on a handshake, the down payment on his house. Never charged a dime for all his own purchases.

We took a short break to regroup, and I saw triumph change to relief within Eric: a deflating of his chest and an unclenching of his jaw as a fluted column of air escaped his lips. He'd bided his time, goaded me into a fight I could only lose, then applied the coup de grace, ungracefully.

"Sorry it had to be this way," he said, examining his nails. "But it's been coming for a long while."

"What's a long while?"

"Since before . . . since last spring. I've outgrown Cedarhurst Chemists, Mark. It's time to move on. Maybe strike out on my own."

I made a mental note to go over last spring's readouts, perhaps pick up the trail of larceny if it wasn't too cold by now. Eric was the computer expert. He'd probably rigged the damn machine so I'd never find a thing.

"Where will you go?" I asked, still seeking clues to the missing money. "You're making almost fifty thousand dollars a year and another ten in bonuses."

"Oh, I have plans," he said, coyly, vaguely.

"Something I could help you with? This isn't a nickel-and-dime business, you know. It takes big bucks for even the smallest operation."

"No thanks," he said so firmly that I was now convinced he'd been milking me, that I'd already helped him enough. But what stuck in my mind like a steel splinter was that I had only two weeks of freedom left before descending into the coal mine.

---

My father-in-law had a three-room apartment in the Dorsett, where Lawrence ended and the Queens County line began. The luxury six-story building had been put up five years ago by his old real-estate buddy, Harry Espinosa, who'd succeeded in bringing upper East Side elegance to the Five Towns against the wishes of most of its residents, who preferred the low profile of the suburbs with its unobstructed view of sunrises and sunsets and the vast unbroken ocean of air above their one-family homes.

I took the elevator to the top floor. Irving greeted me at his door barefoot, wearing broad-striped pajamas.

"How come only one lock on the door?" I asked. A year ago he'd promised to add a Medico, as there'd been a rash of burglaries in the building.

"I decided not to." I threw my coat across the leather-and-wood Norwegian couch in his living room and handed him the *Daily News* and a trio of cigars. "It would be like advertising. A burglar takes one look at my fancy lock and figures I got diamonds in the mattress. He comes in through the window. This way, he sees one nothing Segal and knows I haven't a thing worth stealing."

"It makes sense," I said, then gave him the two prescriptions and told him how to take them. His distrusting eyes suggested that I'd been wasting my time. He had no intention of relying on medication. He'd never even break the seals on the bottles.

Irving insisted I share a bottle of seltzer with him. That I shouldn't just drop and run since I hadn't been to the apartment in years. I stayed, figuring he had a few important things to tell me.

He squirted out two glasses of seltzer from an old-fashioned sea-green siphon bottle that was now considered a collector's item. He laced his with Bardinet brandy while I took mine straight. I genuinely liked my father-in-law despite his lapse in good taste during *shiva*. He was self-effacing and direct, and when he told a joke, it was usually at his own expense. He never spoke about his wealth or influence in the county. Between us, there'd never been long discussions. A word was often enough. A shrug of shoulders, the lifting of an eyebrow.

"First thing, you're not to tell Laura. Rudy says it was a warning, and for sixty bucks I believe him. Laura finds out and presto, I've got me a warden. She'll be dropping in day and night. Cramping my style. I like my privacy, know what I mean?"

I caught his foxy grandpa look but honestly didn't know what he'd meant. He let it simmer while I sipped my drink, thinking that his apartment smelled like the smoking cars on the Long Island Railroad. The walls, an eggshell white when he first moved in, were more the color of a urine specimen, from the the Garcia y Vegas savored in the five years he'd lived here.

"You don't know what I mean," he concluded from my confused look. "What I'm saying is sometimes a lady friend'll stay over, and I don't need a 'hello, I'm here' at a crucial moment. I'm an old man. I need a warm body some nights."

Then Irving spoke at length, and lyrically, about his daughter, which was the real reason I'd been asked to stay. The warning had frightened Irving more than he'd let on.

"Very early I knew she was different. Special. Able to do nicely by her lonesome. We were living in the place on Veeder in Hewlett Bay Park. A regular haunted house on a hill, it seemed, with all those wild bushes surrounding the place and the raspberry stalks hanging over into the road and the great big untrimmed lawns. The house itself was a drafty old hulk with two porches, ten rooms, and four fireplaces.

"When Rachel died, we were too entrenched in the house to move. Especially Laura. Maybe it was wrong to keep her cooped up like that, but I knew that inside those walls she was safe and happy. In each of the empty bedrooms Laura created a different make-believe world. She and her friend Suzy. She lives right here on the third floor, you know, since she left Paul."

"I know."

"Where did she get those ideas from?" continued Irving, who'd spoken more to me during this visit than ever before. "From books and from her own head. One room was the Colonial Room. She and Suzy'd make costumes and dress up like Martha Washington and talk about their brave husbands who were off somewhere fighting the British. The Sun Room on the third floor was their Chekhov room. They'd dress up and act like Russian women from the czar's time. Another room, they were two of King Solomon's wives. A Mexican Room, a farmhouse in Iowa, Dr. Schweitzer's place in the Congo. I forget all the rest. All I know is Suzy couldn't wait to be with Laura so they could play their costume games."

Tilting his head against the couch, Irving admired the perfect smoke rings he blew. I thought of Virginia and her obsession with tobacco, how blowing gauzy donuts seemed to give them both a sense of accomplishment. Soon I'd be with her again.

"But what I'd like you to understand is, even if there'd been no Suzy, Laura would have done just fine all alone. She's one of those people who survive because she's got great inner resources. I used to think that all her pretending was useless, but it's what's kept her going. She's got a highly developed inside world to pull from."

I agreed with Irving by not answering. Well, I thought, he's told me how strong his daughter is. Now his mind's at rest.

Irving wasn't finished. "When Bobbi died, I wanted to run and hide. I couldn't. I was needed, so I stayed as long as I could help.

Then, when it was over, I saw what was happening to you and Laura. I got so frustrated, not being able to do something, that I ran off to Florida for a month."

"I didn't know that."

"I stayed only two weeks. Florida's terrible. Full of old people. Ambulances day and night. Medical clinics on every corner. The state symbol should be the prune.

"When I got back, I saw things had only gotten worse. Two enemies under the same roof. The kids told me, not Laura. She'd never say a word. It's not you and it's not her. You're both first-rate people. What I'm trying to say is, have patience and work it out. In case what I had wasn't just a warning, I want to tell Bobbi that you two are the same as before, except for her. I'd hate to go thinking the best marriage I ever saw was down the tubes."

I patted Irving's knee assuringly. "Just a couple of potholes. We'll work them out."

"Good. Glad to hear it." We stood up, Irving first, sort of dismissing me. He put his arm around my shoulder and walked me to the door. "Remember, not a word about Rudy being here."

"Not even half a word."

I left the building without visiting Suzy. I was on my way to the Isle of Devon and Virginia.

———————

"I'm no cook, so if you're expecting a gourmet meal, you're in for a disappointment."

"I've eaten enough gourmet meals in my life," I told her.

"Not that it'll be peanut-butter-and-jelly sandwiches. After all, I work in a good joint. I know what decent food is, even if I can't be bothered learning how to prepare it. The bill of fare will consist of lobster salad on a bed of leafy green lettuce, garnished with wedges of fresh tomatoes, crispy stalks of celery, and shavings of baby carrots for color. As side dishes, we offer fresh coleslaw and German-style potato salad. I hope, being of the Hebrew persuasion, you have no objection to potato salad à la Heinie?"

"Two things German I approve of: Black Forest cake and potato salad. And their music—the three B's."

This almost silly conversation had taken place a week earlier when she'd invited me to lunch. We'd been sitting in my car in front of the Arden Diner an hour after we'd had our first concurrent climax and we were feeling smug and sassy about it.

"I'll bring the wine," I'd told her. "A good Greek retsina."

"One of the things the Greeks do well," she said. "Not that I'm so worldly. You're my first *pharmacist,* as a matter of fact."

"And how do you find us?"

She'd made a wavy motion with her hand. "An acquired taste. Which, by the way, I'm acquiring."

"So glad you are. We can become addictive, I've been told."

"Listen wise guy. So far I've avoided getting hooked on liquor, drugs, and Irishmen. I'll bear up nicely if and when you decide to do your exploring in another part of the county."

"I don't care for the way this dialogue is going," I said. She was so quick to counterpunch, I'd thought. Even though I hadn't thrown a first blow.

Virginia had unhooked her seat belt. "Neither do I, but facts must be faced. Facts are a great insurance policy against getting hurt. See you next week."

She'd opened the door, got out, and walked toward the diner with those athletic strides, indicating that she was already on the job. I'd sat there until all the cars shooting by on the turnpike had their lights on and the snow in the diner's parking lot shone in anemic blue white. A sadness came over me as fast as the change from dusk to evening. I had to hold out for a week instead of a day or two. She was leaving town for a few days—where, she didn't say.

I don't remember now, almost a year later, if the lobster salad was tart or rubbery. If the tomatoes were fresh or frozen, the potato salad German or that acetic mush from the supermarket. That we made marvelous love after eating is all that remains in my mind of the late-winter afternoon. Not just the sexual calisthenics. Lying in her arms, there'd been a total suspension of thought. In fact, I experienced the gift of complete amnesia the moment I entered that run-down bungalow. In it, I had no past, no hint of memory to torment me. The fifty years imprinted on my brain was removed like the writing that disappears from a child's Magic Slate when the flap is lifted.

If I'd used my mind at all, it was to learn Virginia. I found that the gentler I became with her in bed, the more passionate she grew, as if consideration and patience were her favorite stimulants. With these polishing cloths, she became a superb gem whose shine increased with each application. After a month, I found myself astride a tiger I had no intention of dismounting. The guilt I should have felt had also been lifted from the Magic Slate.

Not surprisingly, I knew how Paul must have felt breaking free of Suzy, uniting with a woman from outside his normal sphere. If I'd felt morally superior to him, I had a good reason. My world had gone to pieces in August, a more valid reason than an unsatisfied libido. My defection was the meat of tragedy; his was the poke in the ribs of low comedy. Or so I'd thought then.

We were extremely good to each other that day she invited me to lunch. Each exquisitely tortured the other, staving off climax almost beyond endurance. Mine, when it was finally permitted, came with the force of revelation, to the sound of heavenly harps.

The one wish I couldn't grant myself was to remain in bed with Virginia all night, to see morning on her face. She had to go to work and I had a home elsewhere. So I lay with her an hour longer, knowing a new kind of regret, tasting the salt on her skin, and on her lips, the fresh oranges we'd had for dessert.

Virginia lit a cigarette, her first that afternoon. The flash of the match in the darkening room broke the spell. "Time to make the donuts," she said, rising, walking naked to the bathroom to shower. I lay in shadows, watching her dry her hair with a large white bath towel, then dress. After all the mayhem we'd performed together, it was like theater to see her transformed into that street-wise, no-nonsense food jockey she'd soon become.

I dressed, wondering if it was common sense or experience that she never wore perfume: safer for the man returning home to an inquisitive wife. But her past was none of my business. Who and how many were of no concern except there was a fresh catalog of sex-related diseases that could wipe out whole civilizations. Frankly, I didn't care. She brought me profound peace, this Lorelei, worth any price.

---

I returned home at six, surprised to find Laura already there. It was a Wednesday, her writer's workshop night. She wasn't scheduled to be home until ten.

The kitchen was lit only by night light, indicating that if I wanted dinner I'd have to make it myself.

"Oh, you're home," she said, startled, as though I'd caught her in a shameful act. She was on the steps going upstairs. She'd already changed into a running suit, though she did little of that exercise anymore.

Laura didn't ask where I'd been or if I'd eaten and I didn't offer an itinerary. She continued up the steps, then seconds later came down, carrying a small square carton in her hands, taped and tied.

I blocked her way. "What are you doing?"

"Housecleaning," she answered, and still I wouldn't let her by me. "Room cleaning," she tried.

"Whose?" I asked, my stomach churning.

"Bobbi's."

"Why?"

"Because I have to, Mark. Because she isn't here anymore and there's no use pretending she's away at college and we're keeping things status quo until she comes home."

I still wouldn't let her down the stairs. She made no effort to push by me. It became a contest of wills. Hers gave out first. She placed the carton on a step, sat down beside it, put her knees together, then her arms around them.

I expected her to cry, but she didn't. I might have forgiven her if she had, but I'm not sure of that. She sat there, calmly waiting for me to make the next move.

"What are you going to do with everything?"

She looked up at me, shading her eyes as if I were the sun. "I'm giving them to the Salvation Army. In Hempstead. Not in town. I couldn't stand seeing anyone here walking around in her clothes."

"You didn't have to do it so soon. You could have waited awhile longer."

"It's the middle of February, Mark. It should have been done sooner. It's taken me all this time to find the strength. I won't become one of those parents who make a shrine of their kid's room and leave everything just as it was. It's wrong. Wrong for Bobbi, wrong for us."

"Us?" I shouted. "Speak for yourself. You never asked me." I hated her very much at this moment because she was so levelheaded, despite everything. I hated myself, too, because I couldn't be like her and anything I might say would sound foolish and weak. So I did the only decent thing and let her continue.

I went upstairs and stood at Bobbi's open door. All the lights in her room were blazing as if to drive out the last traces of her spirit. I felt helpless, unmanned. All the strength I'd gained in Virginia's house was gone.

As with everything Laura did, the project had been carefully planned and perfectly executed: flattened cartons lay stacked near Bobbi's dresser. Larger cartons were piled near her closet for the suits and coats. The desktop was cleared, a roll of masking tape, a pair of scissors, and a ball of twine taking the place of Bobbi's usual mess.

Three drawers of the dresser had been emptied. Five filled cartons, double-taped, double-strung, and knotted in the center were waiting to be taken downstairs. The walls had been stripped of their posters and pictures, tiny holes visible where the nails had been taken out.

"You didn't ask me," I said feebly when she came in the room.

"You would have said no." She picked up a carton and came to me. The box served as a buffer between us. "Do you think this is easy for me? Everything I handle has a history. It's like sticking my hand in fire to touch her things." She balanced the carton on one knee and scratched her nose. "But they're only material objects. What's important about Bobbi I have in my heart. Forever."

Again I despised her. My weakness was made worse by her strength. I stood mesmerized in the room, incapable of standing in her way but unwilling to help. When she began clearing out the closet, I retreated to my den. For the next hour I could hear her packing the cartons, hauling them downstairs to the kitchen, and occasionally whimpering at the bottom of the landing.

When she was done and the sounds had died and their echoes had diminished in my brain, it took at least two hours, a large Scotch, and three aspirins before I could open the last volume of my Civil War undertaking. Well after midnight, I closed the book, poured another large Scotch, and entered the kitchen. There must have been twenty superbly packed cartons stacked by the back door, ready to be taken away.

I let the last of the liquor well up on my tongue before swallowing it, feeling the sting as it descended.

In Bobbi's room, I saw a thorough job had been done. Only the holes in the wall from the pictures and posters gave any indication that anyone had lived here. Tomorrow, without a doubt, Laura would patch up the holes and paint over them. Not a trace of Bobbi would remain except for photographs and memories. But photographs are stilted and false, and memory is unreliable, altering with time. Bobbi was slipping away from me and I couldn't bear the thought. Laura took a sleeping pill before coming to bed. I lay there tossing and turning, unable to sleep, plagued by the same demons I'd gone to Virginia to escape. Time dragged by.

The sleeping pill proved short-term and Laura lifted herself on one elbow. She squinted at the luminous dial of the clock ten feet away on the TV table. Then fell back. No, it wasn't daybreak.

"That scene over her clothes was so typical of you," I heard her say. At first I thought she'd been talking in her sleep. "You're an ostrich, Mark. A fraud. Unrealistic, cowardly, incapable of facing the world. You like Woodsburgh and this community only because you've been able to burrow into its ticking and hide. To escape. Not grow and become a part of it. It has all the elements to keep out most people, but that's one of the things you like best. Not the people inside—the bright, clever, decent people who live here. Even your attitude toward money. You don't worship it, you don't despise it, you sometimes don't even acknowledge it. All it is to you is a moat around your castle. And you've been so lucky with money. And with your children. The girls never gave you one second of trouble until now, so you could pursue your pleasures with a clear conscience."

I made no effort to defend myself. Never in our marriage had I heard such caustic, basic criticism. She'd taken the parts of me I thought she'd admired and inverted them into serious faults.

"You never loved me, not really, Mark. Only what I represented—the stability, the security, a means to an end. The freedom to withdraw from the world once you'd done your duty as you saw it. Oh, how I know you. I've known all along but never let it surface. And the terrible thing is we would have been fine if Bobbi hadn't died. The basic flaw would never have been exposed. Never tested. We would have lived the rest of our lives this way, blissfully sailing into old age, adoring grandparents, never knowing how ill-suited we'd been for each other. Without my ever telling you how I felt."

There was no way now, short of violence, to shut her up. At that moment, I realized there was no hate like the hate love becomes when it goes bad.

"You break easily and stay broken," she went on, her voice tempered steel. "I've broken, too, Mark, but I'm coming back. Because I have to. There's Sara and Caryn. And my father. I'm part of a community. Dying is no solution for what ails us. Living is no cure but it *is* a way, the only way. Maybe if I'd spoken to you years ago about how I felt, you might have changed and we'd have something to salvage. Now, it's much too late."

I'd been badly wounded by what she'd said, but I know people build up anger that must be discharged. Usually it's the closest one who must bear the brunt—that's what friends are really for. And I could have taken more but then she said, "It was that total selfishness of yours that killed Bobbi. You wanted each of them to see firsthand how you earned a living. To be appreciated as a provider so you could justify your ivory tower. If it wasn't for that self-centeredness, she wouldn't have been in the delivery van. She'd be alive and I wouldn't be dying inside from giving away all her things. You killed her, you bastard, as surely as if you'd been that drunken driver."

"Don't you think I know that," I said. "That it's been eating at me day and night? I hate you for reminding me, but I hate myself worse knowing it's true! You can't hurt me any more than I've hurt myself!"

Laura fell silent after that.

It was all over between us. The next step had to be mine.

In the morning, after a strangely refreshing six hours of sleep, I rose with purpose. I took a long, slow walk around the place, gave my den a loving once-over, went upstairs, packed two suit-cases, and moved out.

# *ten*

I FIRST SAVORED my new freedom on Saturday. Mark had walked out Thursday morning, but with two days of overlong meetings, and my normal work load, there was little time to consider myself, much less myself-minus-Mark.

I half expected to find him back home on Friday, though it wouldn't have been a welcome surprise. He did return that day, but only to pick up some additional clothes. His personal records, awards, trophies, and books he'd left behind. Wherever he'd gone, he'd gone practically naked, as though trying to start over fresh. If he'd left two months earlier, I'd have been crushed: first my child, then my husband. But in that short span I'd learned a few things, one of which was my own strength.

Saturday morning I awoke and lay in bed for a deliciously wasteful half hour. Not a thought in my head, no regret about Mark leaving. And, I have to admit, not a thought either about Bobbi.

Lazy as a cat, I stretched, got up, and walked totally nude to the tub and filled it with scalding water. I added a few drops of the Shalimar bath oil Caryn had left behind but which I'd never used. Like a launched ship, I slid into the tub and gave myself to the water. My pores opened and out flowed all those years of stale air, stagnation, and pent-up resentment. When I did think of Mark, it was only metaphorically: he was a nerve-dead tooth that had been removed from my mouth. The space left would quickly fill itself.

I didn't leave my bath until the last drop of water had swirled down the drain. Not once did I calculate the time wasted waiting for the tub to empty.

I lingered over breakfast, precisely slicing a banana into a bowl of cereal, each slice a uniform half-inch thick and covering the bowl like tiles on a roof. With my coffee I took two slices of toast, evenly browned and lathered thickly with sugarless grape jelly. Then a second cup all by itself. An entire hour for doing what usually took fifteen minutes. This, I thought, was how Suzy and most of her friends began their day and one of the reasons men bitched about their wives.

The only serious feeling I permitted myself was nostalgia. Not since childhood had I felt so wonderfully whole, not owing any part of me to anyone. I'd always shared a man's roof. At long last, I was under my own.

I didn't tell the girls, not yet, though the urge to do so was strong. Eventually they'd have to know, but I wanted some room before being inundated with their concern. I needed freedom from their love as well, that first weekend. I'd been a good mother for a quarter of a century. I was entitled to a few days of selfish indulgence; some time off for good behavior.

Luckily, Sara and Stephen were in Palm Beach for the week, visiting Stephen's great-aunt. Caryn and Warren were taking courses at the 92nd Street Y that had begun the previous weekend and would involve three more. When Caryn phoned that morning, I told her things were going well, to relieve her guilt. She'd gushed, describing her courses. "They're walking tours of the City, actually. We've already seen Jewish Williamsburg, home of the Satmars. They wear enormous full-length black coats and beaver hats and curls down the sides of their heads. *Payas,* they're called. We've visited a *mikva* and a synagogue where the men sit on one side and the women on the other.

"And next week it's a tour of SoHo. Would you like to join us, you and Daddy?"

"Not really, sweetheart. We've made other plans," I told her, which was true in the general sense.

The next day I gave myself to the Sunday *Times.* All five pounds of it. What had begun Saturday evening as a light drizzle became a steady rain by Sunday morning, and continued for hours. I got a fire going and spent the entire day in jeans and a red, long-sleeve sweatshirt Mark had left behind. Unshowered, uncombed, without a dab of makeup.

Sunday at home with no one but me. I loved it.

In back of my mind, I knew that Bruno would call the way an epileptic knows an attack is coming and animals can sense an impending earthquake. He'd called the library at least once a day since the new year. Each time with questions about the flute, fluters, and fluting. On Friday, however, his questions were more personal and tinged with concern. "How are you feeling?" he asked at least three times in the conversation. He knew. Somehow he knew.

The phone rang as I began an article in the "Week in Review" about federal efforts to control the drug problem.

"Hi," he said.

"Hi," I replied, like one of my kids ten years ago when the phone never stopped ringing.

"Are you alone?"

"No, I'm here with all the news that's fit to print."

"The *Times*. Then you're as good as alone. Would you like company?"

"No, I wouldn't," I said, unwilling to cut short my parole. He'd never called me at home. Very definitely, he knew. Who'd told him? Violet? That woman had ears everywhere, a whole army of loyal fanatics, former battered wives and maltreated women, the walking wounded of the marital wars. Her office at the Women's Consortium must look like the Situation Room at the Pentagon.

"Then how about a movie tonight? Something light and frothy and without the least social significance. It's called *Moonstruck* and it's playing in town."

The first half of the offer tempted me, but the "in town" part was a kind of aplomb I wasn't ready for. I wasn't brazen enough to flaunt a new man before the community, not this soon. Nothing had been formally settled between Mark and myself. The note he left when he'd come back for the rest of his clothes said, "When you get a lawyer, have him call Jason Fiedler. I'll be using Jason but I told him not to start anything unless you do. Please tell the girls first, then I'll talk to them."

Reading the note at the time, I thought how typically feckless of him to leave that job for me. Months later, of course, it made good sense. He was doing me a favor, allowing me to bat first. Then, I'd been so confused and bitter that everything he said and did seemed cowardly.

"Is it playing somewhere else?" I asked.

"Yes, as a matter of fact it is. At the Eightplex next to Green Acres. Or is it the Twelveplex? They expand overnight, it seems."

I tried to discourage him for my conscience's sake. "I really don't feel like getting dressed and going out on a rainy—"

"Come as you are."

"As I am . . . hmmm," I said, staring critically at myself in the hall mirror. As I was, I looked fine, like a graduate student on her way to the library. "What time's the movie?"

I insisted on separate cars, and Bruno met me at seven inside the huge complex, tickets in hand. He seemed ill at ease, bobbing up and down, looking for me in the ocean of young people who were milling about the refreshment booth, buying bushel baskets of hot buttered popcorn and liters of soda. We walked down a long white corridor where paintings for sale hung on the walls. Bruno glanced scornfully at the canvases, then moved rapidly along. The room showing our film was nearly empty and I felt better about being with Bruno.

*Moonstruck* concerned a charming Italian-American widow with the bloom and juice of youth still apparent, and her wacky family of lovable eccentrics. A feel-good movie with a feather-light, mock-wise attitude toward adultery and broken vows. A fantasy considering how most people, especially Italians, view such matters. But Bruno and I had a few laughs, and the ninety minutes flew by.

After an eternity in the rain trying to find our cars among the thousands behind the theater, we met again at a diner in Lynbrook under the Long Island Railroad. He'd arrived first and was waiting for me in the parking lot with an umbrella. He opened my door, offered his hand, and led me to the diner entrance.

We were seated and Bruno said, "They're caricatures, you see. Unlike any Italians I've ever known, and I've known plenty— from spidery Sicilians to the very waspish blue-eyed blonds of Milan and Florence."

"But there was some truth in the characters, some universality."

Bruno cocked his head like a bird listening for a worm. "Where?"

"In Danny Aiello's inept courtship and his inability to break free of Mama even though she lived in Sicily and he lived in Brooklyn Heights. In the loneliness of the young widow. In the communication problem between Cher's mother and father. That's all very human. Some couples grow closer living together and some grow apart for the same reason."

"Well, maybe," he conceded. "I don't know. I'm not a central family member, only a peripheral one. I see my folks two or three times a month at most."

Bruno, I couldn't help noticing, had been the epitome of tact all evening. Not once did he attempt to close in, no space invader.

Not a word about Mark or my personal life. By his inaction, he was serving notice that he was in no hurry. And I enjoyed his company, his nonincursiveness, his pampering me as I'd enjoyed pampering myself that first weekend. With Mark, I opened my own car door and got out unaided, as though I weren't his wife but a business partner, which I'd become over the years, becoming along the way, less of a lover, companion, and friend.

I'm not naive. I know that a husband, even the best of them, is hardly competition to a lover. A husband has suffered all your pettiness, seen your undisguised face, put up with your moods, your unshaven legs, your sniffles, cramps, and all the unpretty things about you. A lover sees only the carefully honed product in best light. But even adjusting for the disparity in roles, Mark fared no better, Bruno no worse.

We ate mushroom omelets and drained pot after pot of tea. We told each other the stories of our lives, truer than the ones we'd told before, that night in Friendly's. Feeling my way slowly, as though stranded behind enemy lines, I told Bruno about my marriage. The early part: the babies, the fuss, the fun. At the end I said, "But that's over with. Finished. We've separated."

"I know that."

"And that's why I'm here with you."

"I know that, too."

"That sounds awful. What I mean is *because* I'm separated, I can be here with you. Not that he's gone and you're next."

"I know *exactly* what you mean."

Of course he did.

Bruno's second layer of truth was revealed when he told of being thrown out of the house at seventeen for wanting to become a sculptor. "'I don't want a bum in the family,' Pop had raged. 'We never had bums. Only hardworking honest men. Artists, they're a dime a dozen,' said Pop. 'But I'm going to be a good artist,' I told him. 'Oh, a good artist,' he said. 'That kind's a dollar a dozen.' My mother, the matriarch of the family, didn't say a word. You see, Italian mothers don't care what their sons become as long as they remain sons. It's the father who carries on about position and occupation."

For a first date, we more than scratched the veneer of ourselves. But not so ruthlessly as to destroy the airy weightlessness of the *Moonstruck* mood.

---

"I had a wonderful time," I said to Bruno on my veranda where he'd insisted on coming after the diner. Only the glow of the globe light on top of the address pole and the pair of imitation hurricane lamps bracketing the front door illuminated the darkness. The rain had slowed to a thin mist resembling swarms of small insects in the outdoor light. It was ten minutes after one, earlier than any of my girls had ever come home from their dates.

"It's a big house," said Bruno, estimating its size from the long veranda and its succession of flowerpots across the length and suspended from the plank ceiling.

I guess my response should have been, would you like to come in and see the rest? I wasn't biting. "Just the right size," I said. Once, I added to myself. I thanked him for the evening and the conversation, both of which I thoroughly enjoyed, I told him.

"Enough to do it again? Soon?"

"I guess so."

He leaned across the no-man's-land that had separated us all evening and kissed me. A peck so harmless that I never felt his beard. I inserted my key in the door, then punched the series of numbers into the alarm system to keep the local police from coming. One-nine-six-two: the year we'd gotten married. Mark and I had immortalized our wedding date in the security code.

As soon as his car had been sucked into the night, I sat on the couch in the living room and cried. Guilt in huge tidal waves came over me. I'd laughed that evening, actually laughed in the empty theater. I'd felt young and gay and had a good time. Now I sat sobbing, with the lights off, begging Bobbi's forgiveness. She was dead and I'd been carrying on like some mindless twit. Date, indeed. Maybe Mark wasn't wrong for implying a kind of callousness on my part.

I changed into running clothes, and though the roads were wet and rain filled the winter's crop of potholes, I ran for more than an hour. Harder than I'd ever run before, if that were possible. To punish myself. To risk—perhaps even welcome—the possible scrapes and bruises for my transgression. To remind myself I hadn't forgotten my child and never would.

---

Monday morning, entering the library, I knew at once that my separation was widely known. It was written in bold letters across the faces of my coworkers. Separately, each asked how I felt and offered injured expressions as if learning I was terminal. All day they kept popping into the office. "Tea? Coffee? A diet soda?"

At my desk, I was immediately bombarded with phone calls from the local real-estate brokers. Would I be interested perhaps in selling my house? Like vultures who smelled carrion, they were zeroing in for the dismemberment of the corpse.

But a good part of my guilt was gone, swept out to sea with all the rain. At noon, Bruno called.

The same brilliant exchange of hi's.

"Would you like to take a drive out to Sag Harbor one day this week? I have to buy some marble there for *The Flutist*. I'd love company. It's a quaint old town that's managed to stay hidden from the yuppies and the developers. It has a whaling museum, a windmill with the likeness of John Steinbeck over the entrance, and a world-class restaurant called the American Hotel."

"No, thank you," I said. My reply was the result of much internal strife. The winner was that part of me that said "too soon."

"Maybe next week," I told him. But I didn't want Bruno going away empty-handed. "Would you consider going to a bereavement meeting? It's not at all a downer."

"I'd love to. When?"

"This Friday night."

"You mean I have to wait five long days to see you again?"

"No, Bruno, five regular days. They're the same size as all the others."

"Maybe for you."

After I arrived home that evening and threw some fish sticks on the microwave carousel, Trish Weiner walked the quarter mile between our homes in her miniskirt and spiked heels to offer consolation and advice. Long on the advice.

She hadn't been the least helpful after *shiva*. "I'm just not a mourning person," she'd said. Her expertise was in other areas. "Listen, hon," she said, sharing my fish sticks. "Listen to Mama Trish. When you're ready to get back into the race, give me a holler. I know some real hunks would go gaga over you. An honest-to-God classy lady."

"That's not the kind of running I do best," I said.

"Maybe you should. It'll sure keep you young and alive. Besides, you scare the hell out of me sometimes, flying by the house at two A.M. when Ken and I are making bed music. All you get from that kind of exercise are leg muscles and floppy tits."

Late Wednesday afternoon Violet called. Could she see me at home some evening?

Violet came to the house carrying a tan calfskin briefcase, as if she were selling insurance. She expressed sympathy and support. "I know about you and Mark. Everyone in town does and we're behind you all the way. Do you have a lawyer?" Violet looked at me as if I was a hit-and-run victim, sprawled out on the ground.

"No."

Shock. Dismay. "You haven't? Well, I'll get one for you. I have a nice young woman, a former Consortium alumnus, who works for us. Her fees are low to our people and she doesn't take any guff from judges. She'll make mincemeat of Mark and his attorney. When she's finished, your ex will be lucky if he has money for a miniburger at McDonald's."

"I'll consider it," I said, dismissing the attorney, the Consortium's backing, and Violet out of hand.

"Consider this as well," she said, opening her briefcase and removing half a dozen brochures. "You've been discarded like an old shoe. You are now in a state of limbo. Helpless. Unprotected. We've helped hundreds of women in the county." Violet spread the brochures on the coffee table like a winning hand at gin rummy. "Time is short. At this very moment, Mark and his attorney are probably scurrying around burying his assets like a dog with a bag of bones. We can dig them up if you say the word."

I didn't say the word, and Violet went on, unstoppable. "Besides legal service, we offer moral support. And reeducation about a woman's role in present society. We hold forums and seminars. We give parties. We're always searching for new members who'll spread the word. Laura, we can't afford to lose the gains of the past two decades. We're presently being attacked from all sides; in the Supreme Court, the White House, both houses of Congress. We must keep our gains and forge ahead."

I thought of the St. Crispin's Day speech in *Henry V*—we band of brothers—then served Violet coffee and apple-crumb cake to sidetrack her proselytizing. It was enough I put up with her in the orchestra. I didn't intend becoming part of her Cripples' Crusade. I'd fight my battles on my own, against my own.

Facing a stone wall, Violet gave up. All she wrung from me was a tepid promise to review her literature. When she had gone, I carried the pamphlets to the kitchen, put them in the empty cake box, and tossed both into the garbage. The gospel may have been good, but I just couldn't tolerate its prophet.

As I knew it must happen, my father came to me, looking for an explanation. He invited himself for a late dinner. The time didn't matter; he had plenty of it.

We sat in the kitchen and ate broiled veal chops, baked potatoes, and creamed spinach, our all-time favorites. He said little during the meal but I could see a load of unanswered questions in his almost Oriental eyes. He wouldn't look into mine.

After the table had been cleared, he lit a fresh cigar. This one was long and slim, encased in a pewter-colored container, like a small rocket. The cigar's aroma nullified forty years of my life. We were back in the house on Veeder. He'd come home from the shopping center he was building, tired and cranky. I'd served him supper and now he was ready to be entertained. Hypnotized by my snake-charming flute, he'd usually say, "A good meal, a good cigar, a good child, and a good piece of music. I'm a rich man," were his words to me.

I didn't feel much like a good child at this moment but one

who was about to be scolded. I brought my father a bottle of Scotch from the bar, the one we kept for him alone. Coming from the living room, I almost made a detour upstairs for the flute. Maybe I could snake-charm that look of reproach from his face.

He poured his usual quarter teacupful and took it all at once. He shook his head sadly. "Smart people like you and Mark. That's how you work out your problem? I'm disappointed. Mostly in you, Lorri. A woman makes the marriage. Men like Mark and me, we want so little. We have to be practically driven away with a stick to leave home."

My father poured another Scotch, as large as the one before, and drank it quickly. He got up and left without a kiss or a word. I sat in the kitchen for hours, too diminished by his words to move from my chair.

I didn't run that evening nor did I retire to my room to play. Instead, I went up to the attic and came down with a carton of things between Mark and me I'd once held dear, items I'd wanted to leave undisturbed whatever happened to us. All those letters he'd sent me in between our weekends in the Village. The greeting cards from the very beginning. After the first few years of marriage, he'd stopped sending birthday, anniversary, and Mother's Day cards. "What for? I'm here in person to share the occasion with you."

I'd started a fire earlier, hoping we'd sit in the living room after dinner and I could tell Daddy what really went on between Mark and me, and he would offer his wisdom and kindness. I sat on the floor next to the andirons and opened the carton. The fire had about gone out. I got it going again with a kindling of those ancient cards and letters. The fire blazed up a solid yellow and fanned across the entire well of fireplace.

An envelope fell out of the pile, its flap turned in, its glued seams beginning to come loose. I read the letter inside, dated June 2, 1956. It was a recommendation to pharmacy school from a doctor in Sheepshead Bay.

"Mark Gerber is a very unusual person. He is honest to a fault, hardworking beyond the necessity for it, intelligent, thoughtful, reserved, but totally human. Frankly, I wanted him for medicine but it seems the young man has other plans. So it is with regret and pleasure that I recommend him to you." The letter was signed by Dr. Anton Harkavi, M.D.

I became angry. Both my father and the doctor had been taken in by this person, boy and man. Indirectly, they were both accusing me of ruining our marriage. I wanted to shout to them that I'd lived with Mark Gerber more than half my life. Whose judgment could possibly be better than mine?

In the flames, I saw only that sour look on my father's face, and I took the letter and offered it to the fire. The edges turned brown but the letter refused to burn. I tossed it into the fireplace and watched it ignite. I waited until it became gray carbon, then white ash.

That week Bruno buzzed the library so often I gave him my direct number so he wouldn't have to go through the main desk. We spoke about nothing in particular, and through that about our new relationship.

"The more I think about Cher dumping her fiancé for his younger brother, who was younger than her, the truer the movie becomes, the more honest," he'd said, calling me at home one night during the week, beginning his conversation with a movie critique.

"Honesty is overrated," I said, returning his serve. "What I found hard to accept was the short time span between their first meeting and the hop into bed. Ten minutes of posturing, then they were horizontal. That's awful, even for the late eighties."

We were doing our own posturing, talking movies, meaning ourselves. Yes, I was at least seven years older than Bruno. And Bruno *had* been rushing me into the hay. We weren't characters in a film where everything was neatly resolved in under two hours. We were characters in life, where, most times, nothing is ever resolved.

--------

Bruno's car crawled up the driveway at ten minutes to six. I could see it from the living-room window where I sat at the piano, plunking out a melody that had come to me at work. When I opened the door, he wasn't there. I went around to the back where the shale fanned out between the garage and the house.

He was standing with his back to me, looking out at the lawn and its centerpiece, the gazebo, all white and gauzy in the widening dusk. "Lovely, just lovely," he said low, as if to himself.

There was still a thin bank of intense blue on the far horizon, and against it I could see something in Bruno's hand. A single long-stemmed red rose, not quite opened, as if its petals were holding a precious object. A dozen would have been excessive. One was exactly right.

I made a fuss over the rose to keep from kissing him, then went back into the house for a vase and some water. I came out with my coat. Patiently, unquestioningly, Bruno waited for me on the veranda. A less sensitive man might have followed me in, as if the flower had been some sort of entrance fee.

I told him to put his car in the garage, we'd take mine. Fine, it didn't matter to him, he said. I liked that. Whenever we went out together, Mark insisted on taking his car and driving. The reason—he loved to drive, he said. It had nothing to do with dominance or my ability behind the wheel. With everything coming clear, I thought about such quirks in Mark, weaving them into not very attractive patterns.

He pressed the automatic garage-door opener and drove his Volks into Bobbi's old spot. He hesitated before entering my car. The spaciousness of the garage seemed to enthrall him, large as a bungalow. It might have been the pegboard wall of Mark's gardening tools, the strategic waste-free arrangement of them, or the steel fixture containing the tomato plant food, his heavy gloves, and the climbing stakes.

We ate a good dinner at a restaurant near the college. A spinach salad for me, filet of sole for Bruno. I insisted on paying, since the evening was my idea. He didn't balk, though he asked to be allowed to leave the tip.

We arrived in plenty of time and I introduced Bruno to my extended family as a good friend. They accepted him without question or upturned eyebrows, though they'd met Mark, and knew he was my husband. I was certain they would. These new friends understood that relationships for people like us shifted radically.

For never having lost a loved one—a blessing Bruno readily acknowledged—he was remarkably sympathetic. And aware. This was not wholly unexpected. After all, he was an artist—sensitive, perceptive, empathetic. An insider as to the human heart.

Once the meeting began, Bruno immediately became its center, its driving force. He took the lead away from Nancy Seibert, who seemed happy to concede it.

"I still can't function more than fifty percent," said Sam Barkeley, the paper-products executive whose son had drowned in Mirror Lake. "I'm tired when I get up in the morning. Tired all day. Tired at night. Then I sleep for ten to twelve hours and wake up tired again."

Bruno told him, "What you're experiencing is a form of escapism. A shift in focus to be with your son. Forgive an outsider for saying this, but it's terribly wrong to try and join him in the world of dreams. It's not the right place for such a reunion and it's not your time to be with him. He'd be the first to say so. You must honor his life by living your own. You have to show how precious it is by using every minute wisely, not wasting time by trying to find him."

To Sven and Margot who'd lost their teacher-son, then were shunned by loved ones, Bruno said, "So what have you lost? Really lost? Those who deserted you in your hour of need?" Bruno shook his head. "You've lost nothing. You still have the best friend you'll ever have: yourselves. Cultivate each other. Do things together selfishly. Take long walks. Go on vacation to some new exotic place if you have the means. To a small fishing village in Portugal, for example. Live above a store or the local tavern. Watch the men go out to sea every morning." Bruno took my hand and intermeshed our fingers. "Your world's been destroyed. Go out and build a new one."

I never dreamed that a man who spent so much time alone exploring inner space could be so forceful and dynamic. Bruno electrified the gathering, and after the formal part was over they came clustering around him, vying for his attention, questioning him as they'd never questioned Nancy who was a twice-cursed expert in grieving. Bruno had exhibited the charisma of an evangelical preacher and I wondered how many other sides there were to him.

I had to take my guest by the hand and break through his circle of admirers to get to Frances.

"Who *is* he?" she asked after Bruno had been reengulfed by a determined group of questioners.

"A friend."

"And Mark?"

"He moved out two weeks ago."

"Oh, I'm terribly sorry."

"Don't be. I'm not. It was inevitable. I know that now."

Frances and I moved far from the din around Bruno. He'd been expanding on artists of the past who sublimated their tragedies into creative works: Van Gogh, Eugene O'Neill, Mahler, and Rodin. His oysters-and-pearls theme.

"We were once at that stage, Carl and I," said Frances. "A few years after we got married. But we worked it out. We spent a weekend at Montauk Point in the late fall. No one but us in the entire motel. We talked all weekend over a few bottles of Chablis. No holds barred. Day and night. Everything came out in the wash: his fears about being able to satisfy me, mine about raising a family where the father could be the grandfather. Other things as well." Frances touched my arm. "To make a long story short, we worked it out."

"I could never get Mark to open up. We could spend a year on Mars and drink up a wine cellar. He considers it unmanly to say everything you feel. He distrusts emotion and so did I once. But I've changed and he's stood still. His emotions have turned to acid and corroded him inside. What's left is only an empty shell."

"And he just up and walked out?"

"No, I pushed him. I said some terribly cruel and truthful things about him and he accepted them. When I came home from work the next day, he was gone."

"Where?"

"I don't honestly know."

"To another woman?"

"I doubt it. He's not the type for affairs."

Frances kept her ears open to me, but her eyes were on the small crowd around Bruno.

"He's certainly a marked contrast to your husband," said Frances. "The little I saw or heard from him that first time."

"Helen Keller could see that," I said, taking Frances's words as all compliment. "But I'm not leaping into anything. Not without a parachute or a landing place. After all, I've been married twenty-five years, in love with my husband most of the time. It's hard switching affections and allegiances. Ways of doing things."

We rejoined Bruno and I was able to extract him from an involved discussion of Bishop Pike and messages from beyond the grave with a new member, a man who insisted he spoke daily with his grown daughter who'd died years ago in a hunting accident.

I left a five-dollar bill in the wicker basket by the coffee machine and we went for tea to the same diner we'd gone to after the movie. We took the same table. Bruno insisted.

"Well, you certainly made a hit at the meeting," I told him.

"I did, didn't I?" he said, pleased with himself. He held up his hand as though taking the pledge of allegiance. "I swear I wasn't trying to win them over to impress you."

"You did both."

Bruno poised the creamer over his tea but didn't pour. "You're a remarkable woman," he said.

"Why?" I asked, flirting with my image in the very flattering mirror behind him.

"To leave yourself that vulnerable, a very private person like yourself."

"*Your* inference, Bruno. Not at all my intention. All I said was you impressed me. I said that months ago about your statues. In the library garden. You didn't think it was remarkable then."

"That was then. This is now. Then, you were talking about my work. You're talking about me now, and though we're often one—my work and I—there's quite a difference."

"That's an awful cliché, Bruno," I said, trying to change the course. Secretly, I admitted to myself that things had definitely changed between us, so slowly and subtly that where and when the winds had shifted was a mystery to me. The day he'd come to reclaim his "family"? In Friendly's after the rehearsal? Or just after the movie? Regardless, there were fresh breezes blowing through my life, and I hadn't a clue to where they'd take me. All my life I'd known where I was going. Certainty, like honesty, was also overrated. I could see that now.

The shaky part of the evening lay dead ahead: saying good night to Bruno. He must have been thinking the same thing, for he ordered nothing with the tea and drank two cups in quick succession, as if he had a train to catch. My face, I noticed in the mirror, wore a grim expression, like that of a soldier going into battle. Bruno's reflected total tranquillity, the face he might wear polishing a newly completed statue.

Fifteen minutes later, we were back in the garage and he was first out of the Saab. I could hear his firm, solid steps on the cement floor as he came round to open my door, each step sending spasms along my colon.

At the front door, it was my choice to kiss him and send him home with the expectation of more the next time, or invite him in and suffer (or enjoy) the consequences.

Bruno took the decision out of my hands by moving quick-step into the hall. "I love big old houses," he said. "Please show me around and I'll leave."

So naive and inexperienced was I that I believed him. Or wanted to. I turned on the living-room lights. Like a magnet to iron filings, Bruno made straight for the walls. He didn't care much for my paintings. "Too tame, too mainstream for my tastes."

Since Mark hadn't stripped his den of those objects lending it a kind of Victorian ambience, I didn't hesitate showing Bruno in. He ran his fingers over the burnished cherrywood rolltop desk.

His eyes glowed. "I'd give a gallon of blood for something like this." Those eyes narrowed in disapproval, reading some of the titles in Mark's bookcase. A forerunner of a sneer curled his upper lip. "Not a work of fiction in the lot. Was he a man of much imagination?"

"He's not dead," I reminded Bruno. "Departed but not deceased." It was the first time Bruno had mentioned my husband. Until now, he'd been content to listen to my intimations about Mark, happy to let me carry the ball. Bruno was getting too confident, too sure of himself. Strangely, I felt the need to defend Mark. "As for his imagination, he considered most books of history to be more stimulating than some of our best novels. Mark is not a dull man."

Believe me, I knew what Bruno was trying to do, and it was not very clever attempting it in this room. The den was so thoroughly Mark that I would often talk aloud to him—depositing his mail on the rolltop or emptying his wastebasket—even though he was elsewhere. Bruno should have been smarter than to try and win me by denigrating Mark. That, I could do very skillfully by myself. But I wouldn't act the vindictive wife, not in front of Bruno, not in front of anyone. I decided then, in Mark's sanctum, that if it came to a divorce, it would be a clean one. Devoid of recrimination and backbiting. I wouldn't become one of Violet's avenging angels.

With trepidation, I entered my den and let Bruno explore its panoply of photographs and family awards. Bruno sensed my mood and acted as if visiting a holy place. All the while I knew he was gauging my reaction to his reactions. Yet even in his charade, I could glean a true affection for what he saw, and a sincere comprehension of what I'd possessed and lost. Bruno had the capacity to plumb the height and depth and width of my wounded soul.

"The kitchen, please," said Bruno. "Being Italian, I love kitchens."

Unlike Gaul, my kitchen is divided into two parts: a cooking area and an eating area. The latter juts out from the back of the house and is walled on three sides by multisegmented glass windows. Eating there was often like eating outdoors.

Bruno didn't stay long in the kitchen. After a few seconds, he went out on the patio. "Does the backyard light up?" he asked.

I switched on the outdoor lighting. The gazebo that Bruno had seen only in fog, shone like a beacon. The back lawn spread out like a small landing field. Surrounding it, rising to the sky, were the outlines of the trees and tall shrubs that had always given me the feeling of safe harbor.

Bruno whistled. "A veritable Eden."

I shut the spots, then the kitchen lights. On the first step on the staircase, I froze. My feet waited for instruction. After a while, I led the way up, expecting Bruno's hands to be all over me, the start of foreplay. If he touched my thigh or ass, would I say stop or don't? It would have been the sheerest hypocrisy, since I was leading him and not being hauled kicking and screaming like Scarlett O'Hara.

A perfect gentleman, Bruno kept our space unviolated.

"My music room," I said, opening the door.

He entered, went to its middle, and began slowly turning clockwise. His rotation took in the aquamarine walls, the busts of Mozart and Beethoven on the shelves supporting my music folders and tapes, the canopied bed Caryn had left behind, the deliberately puritanical chair, and the music stand holding open the part of Stravinsky's *Petrushka* I was learning for the spring concert.

"A fine room," he said. "It has unity and purpose and artistic integrity."

"Yes," I said.

In Sara's old room were the pots and plants that Mark had faithfully looked after. He'd made it his sacred duty to trim, prune, water, and fertilize the terrarium Bobbi had grown from shoots and seed. His own business he'd ignored, his wife and daughters he'd neglected, his health he'd disregarded, but the twenty-odd pieces of vegetation he kept in tiptop condition. I tried to continue their care after he'd moved out, but I knew nothing about growing things that weren't children.

"And whose garden is this?"—from Bruno with a wide sweep of his hand.

"Bobbi's."

"A bit shaggy. Could use some work."

"I know it," I said, but didn't ask for his help.

I avoided showing Bruno her room. I stood by the door but was unable to turn the knob.

"Don't. It's not necessary."

I shook my head, agreeing. I'd forgotten how much I told him about Bobbi. From his few words, it had obviously been enough. He let me stand facing the door until I was composed enough to turn around. I walked by him to the master bedroom that no longer had a master. "And this is where I sleep."

Bruno didn't waste five seconds on the exquisite French Provincial bedroom set that had stood up so well for over twenty years of sleep, lovemaking, and conceiving children. He kissed me lightly on the lips, testing, then harder when I responded. His arms changed from a loose embrace to a hungry-lover hold.

A trail of clothes led from the door to the bed. I thought there'd be more resistance in me, that I would make him earn my surrender. Not so. I folded after the first shot had been fired. Willingly, as if it had been my idea all along.

I'll have no orgasm, I promised myself. Penetration was not really infidelity, nor was lying with him in my half of the bed. I wouldn't, but he could enjoy himself to the limit. My reward would be the bliss of being held, caressed, understood. It would be more than enough.

Bruno was no amateur and, very quickly, I gave up the pretense of noninvolvement. He made love to me and I made love to him, and when it was over, I wondered why I'd resisted for so long. Like any normal, healthy woman, I had no regrets. Not a one. I hadn't even asked Bobbi's permission to enjoy myself. Mark never even entered my mind.

"Do I have to go home tonight?" he asked poignantly, pleadingly, after we'd squeezed the last few drops of pleasure from each other. He was lying on his back in Mark's half of the bed, looking up at the ceiling.

"No."

"No one coming in later tonight or tomorrow morning who might embarrass you?"

I thought of Bobbi, how she inhabited all my dreams, all my waking moments until very recently. "Not a living soul," I said.

"Then good night, sweet lady."

---

Half an hour before sunrise, I nudged Bruno. His eyes opened wide as if controlled by a switch.

"Hold me, Bruno. Not for sex."

He came to my side of the bed. "I'd like that, Laura."

"Are we officially lovers?" I added.

"I'll send out the announcement cards first thing in the morning," said Bruno.

"Because if we are, and we're going to spend time together, be prepared for a lot of down days. For a long time."

"I understand," he said, giving me an extra-hard hug. "You'll see how well I understand."

"When that happens, don't try and reason with me or placate me, or try to change my mood. Just be patient and sweet and let it pass. It *will* pass."

"Of course."

"Am I asking too much?"

"You're not asking enough."

"It won't be easy."

"If I wanted easy, I'd answer the personals and have a different lady every week."

"What *do* you want?"

"What I have."

All the right answers. They filled the dark, cold places inside me with warmth and light. I was drowsy by then and fell back to sleep. I didn't awaken until Bruno's hands and lips and beard were insisting I join him in doing what men and women together did best.

## eleven

I T WAS AN unusually cold April day with all the stark, unflinching quality of a lithograph. The black sea at the far rim brightened to a slate gray toward shore; the sky had the dinginess of two-day-old snow in Manhattan, and the beach was as white as cold ashes. I stood at the living-room window estimating how long it would be before the rain arrived. When it came, it would remain longer as puddles and small pools than in Woodsburgh, without the trees to act as umbrellas and the shrubs to do the work of sponges.

Virginia had left early that morning, as one of the girls at the diner had called in sick. When I told her on Thursday that I'd like to do a few minor repairs about the house, she shrugged her shoulders indifferently. Maybe she'd watch me or maybe she'd go visit friends, she said. Neither alternative, she indicated by the flatness in her voice, would add much zest to her life.

There was so much to do. I decided to start with a complete caulking job on the doors and windows because at night, making love to Virginia, I'd feel the stiff jets of air off the ocean. They would filter through the cracks in the bedroom windows and strike me like cold steel daggers in my most vulnerable and active parts. My performance would be sorely affected. And during the evenings, as I went over the daily sheets and invoices from the store, the house would rattle and the same malevolent gusts would lift and fling my papers over a living room that needed no extra disarray.

During the week, I went to the hardware store in Cedarhurst and bought an assortment of tools, a caulking gun, and a dozen cartridges of white caulking compound.

Viewing my handyman's arsenal, Virginia smiled but said nothing. She had to have been thinking that I intended to stay awhile.

I began at the back kitchen window, standing on a not-too-secure chair. The first cartridge I wasted. The second one I was able to use more productively. Gradually I got the hang of it, becoming adept in doing what the average homeowner did without conscious effort. I finished all the downstairs windows, and front and back door, in two fast-fleeing hours.

The only acknowledgment from Virginia that morning had been to make sure I was dressed warmly. She gave me her old sweater, the one I'd first seen her in, and a wrinkled Marine Corps field hat "to keep the wind from blowing away your brains."

My growing expertise allowed me to work and to consider this new life I'd stumbled into. It hadn't been a straight line from the house in Woodsburgh to the bungalow in Devon. After I'd left Laura, I registered in a motel near Kennedy Airport a few miles from the turnpike toward Manhattan. The motel was a pay-by-the-hour joint offering mirrored ceilings, water beds, and closed-circuit TV showing actors doing what everyone else on either side and above me was attempting, with all that moaning and groaning, thumping and shaking.

I got little sleep and no rest.

Broaching the subject with Virginia was difficult. When I laid it out in short sentences, she stared at me, terribly serious.

"You want to move in here?"

"Yes."

"Right now?"

"Yesterday, preferably. Today if possible."

"For how long?"

"Until one of us cries uncle."

"Or just cries."

Virginia had seemed more amused than taken aback by my urgent request, but agreed at once. I was happy to pack again and leave the motel.

The next day we had a little powwow about ground rules. Virginia's idea. She wanted everything out on the table. No guesswork, no playing it by ear, no bruised feelings later.

"I'm soft as chocolate pudding and just as easy to take, Gerber. As long as I trust you and you don't burn the place down. As long as you're up-front and say what you mean and mean what you say. If you make certain allowances for lack of comfort and you're not too possessive and you look after yourself for most of the fundamentals most of the time, we can make a go of it."

I agreed to her terms, the conditions of my unwritten lease. I tried adding a few of my own riders, though in no position to negotiate. "I won't question where you go and what you do. We're both free agents, but you'll find I don't go out much at night. If I do, it's to a movie, not to pick up women. And another thing— I'm no deadbeat. I insist on paying my share."

"Of what?"

"Food. Utilities. Rent."

"Hold on, big spender," she said, her hands raised as if to catch a basketball. "If you want to buy a few steaks, bring home a pizza now and then, or some Chinese takeout—by all means. We go out to eat, you pay for it. We go to a bar, pick up the tab. But as to rent and utilities—nothing doing. You're no boarder here; you're my guest. As far as rent's concerned, I own the place. I think I mentioned that. It's sort of a gift from the long-gone Mr. Healy. There's no mortgage. The damn fool bought the house for all cash. And the taxes are small potatoes."

"I could take care of those small potatoes."

"Not on your life, Gerber. You do that and you may get the notion you have some proprietary rights around here. Do us both a favor and leave it my way. We'll get along jim-dandy if you do."

Smart kid, I thought. Her way, I could be kicked out at any time. Dispossessed. She had me over a barrel but I couldn't blame her for being cautious.

The meals we ate at home were skimpy. She only prepared hastily assembled salads. Any hot meals served were the ones I cooked. When Virginia cleaned house, it was with sporadic lethargy and little enthusiasm. Most of the time I walked over and around things.

But the nights. Oh, the nights. What really mattered to me was the wealth of passion we each brought to bed and the ecstasy of spending it on one another. And afterward we could tolerate our vast differences and still have a few laughs. Those laughs, that tolerance, would last until the next time in bed.

Some nights, busy weekends at the diner especially, she'd be almost too much to handle. I'd be totally washed out after a day in the store and a full working schedule now that Eric had left for greener pastures. I'd come home with an attaché case bulging with bills to go over, that being the only form of reading I could or wanted to do now. By eleven, I'd put away my bookkeeping, take a shower, and climb into bed.

Sometime later I'd wake up to the shower running and know Virginia was home. A bath towel wrapped around her head, resembling some ancient priestess, she'd crawl in next to me, then exercise hands and mouth to revive the dead.

"C'mon, love," she'd say in the pitch black, with the roar of the ocean as background like some Greek chorus. "Service me. I've been serving the public for the past nine hours and now I want some service, too."

Those hands, that mouth, her body over mine, was all it took for this Lazarus. I was soon inside her and my weariness would fall away as though it were a heavy coat I'd shed.

"Do anything you want and I'll respond," she'd say, lifting her head from my neck, chest, belly. "Make me work. I want to be sore and aching in the morning."

I'd go crazy. In all our years together, Laura had never initiated lovemaking. She'd curtsy nicely, but first I had to bow. How exciting it was that Virginia had no shame or shyness in asking for what she wanted. More so since I was the object of her lust; the pursued. If I'd stirred a tiger in Virginia, she'd created a sexual Frankenstein of me.

Later—it was usually close to three A.M.—after a final burst of activity more intense than anything I'd heard at the motel, she'd say, "Listen to my heart, Gerber. It's about to explode. I'm sure I'm being recorded on a seismograph at some university."

I'd move down and put my ear to her heart. I'd hear the rapid pounding of a muffled hammer. I'd place my lips over her heart and the vibrations would tingle my entire face.

And so, I thought, getting ready to go up on the porch and tackle the bedroom windows and the failing posts, I'd gone down a few rungs of the social ladder in the six weeks. I'd left the calm serenity of a backwater pool for the swift white currents of struggle. I'd entered the lower-middle-class world of never having quite enough money to cover the essentials, of scrimping, of overdue bills. Virginia's mail was mostly credit-card billings and second notices.

At the store, things had also changed for me. To each of my customers, Eric had sent a printed, hand-signed invitation. He invited them to stop in and say hello at his new location in the shopping center a mile away and take advantage of the discount policy he was bringing to the Five Towns.

I had to fight for my survival by offering weekly specials, extra discounts, triple-coupon days. Filling prescriptions for half my usual fee. Staying open later. Working behind the prescription counter sixty to seventy hours a week. Paying bills with money I didn't have. Trying to trim the fat from expenses without drawing blood.

All the while I continued sending Laura her weekly check, the same amount as when I was doing well. I didn't want her to think I was one of those lowlifes who take advantage of a separation to shirk their obligations.

So in a way, Virginia's refusal to take my money was an unexpected bonus and a blessing. I couldn't afford to feed the kitty when barely enough remained at week's end to feed myself.

By now, I was a real hotshot, working the gun with one hand, tamping the caulking into place with the index finger of the other. With all that brain matter unencumbered, I couldn't help thinking about the other times I spent with Virginia, those hours away from her tiny but adequate bed. For much of it, we idled at a saloon at the east end of the Isle of Devon. O'Hara's was one of those retail establishments that didn't attract customers by using the latest techniques of modern advertising. No happy hour. No ladies' night. No two-for-one giveaways. Very much the way Cedarhurst Chemists used to be before Eric had opted for entrepreneurship.

I was introduced to Timmy O'Hara, the third-generation proprietor, chief bartender, and Virginia's good friend. I guessed more than a good friend by the way Timmy greeted her: a short kiss, then a long embrace. He was a big barrel of a man with a full head of impossibly blond wavy hair, a thick mustache, and sideburns that covered the sides of his face.

As Virginia's escort, I was welcomed to O'Hara's. But not with open arms that first night, a day after moving in with her. More with hushed voices and suspicious stares from the men and women drinking in place or at the booths and tables. I haven't come to steal your children, I wanted to shout at them. I was content, however, to be with Virginia, and noticed how much more attractive she was than the other women there, how saloon lighting agreed with her complexion and turned her eyes a warmer brown, made her smile saucier, her movements more lithe.

By my third visit to O'Hara's, I was no longer a stranger, but I still felt out of place, like a vegetarian at a butchers' convention. In my entire existence, I'd spent no more than a total of two to three hours in bars. I was one of those people who only drank at bar mitzvahs and weddings and only when the liquor was disguised to taste good. But in the warm sodality of O'Hara's, at a table with Virginia and her friends, I dropped my reserve and my prejudices and hoisted more than a few. Soon I was one of them, mimicking their thought modes and even their pattern of speech.

The man to my right, Dennis Casey, worked in the fire marshal's office in Jamaica. His hair was flaming red, his hands and arms covered with tattoos. A flattened nose and broken teeth indicated he was not a person to trifle with.

Baseball was Casey's hobby, the Yankees his specialty. Once I'd been a loyal fanatic and knew, for example, all the trivia surrounding Joe Dimaggio's fifty-six-game hitting streak.

Virginia sat at my left hand, caressing my foot under the table with her toes, delighted I had so much to contribute to the table talk. This weird alien was suddenly speaking fluent baseballese with her people.

Dennis didn't accept me on faith or Virginia's say-so. He challenged me to recite all the Yankee firstbasemen after Lou Gehrig. I began dropping names. "Babe Dahlgren, Johnny Sturm, Buddy Hassett, Nick Etten . . . Where should I stop?"

"Go on," said Dennis, like a detective hoping the suspect will give himself away.

"George McQuinn, Tommy Henrich, when he couldn't handle right field anymore, Johnny Mize, Joe Collins . . ."

Soon Virginia grew bored and left to mingle with old friends. I was left alone with Dennis. Through him, I soon learned that bar talk never proceeds in a straight line from subject to subject. Rather, it's circular, going round and round, never beginning, never ending, like the Hindu conception of life. We jumped from the torching of apartment houses in the South Bronx, to the death penalty for drug pushers, to the severity of the past winter, to how the Bronx used to be, to Japanese beer versus American, to the House That Ruth Built, then, after a few other twists and turns, to Yankee legends past and near past.

At some point during the dialogue I mentioned to Dennis that I played shortstop for my softball team. He was at least three beers ahead of me but as sober as the victim of an IRS audit.

"No shit," was his surprised reply. "Shortstop? You could be a grandfather, for chrissake."

I insisted that softball was my game, shortstop my position.

"We got a softball team. The Devon Devils. I'm the manager. We had a good shortstop last year. But he moved out to Bayshore."

"Got a good one this year?"

"No, but we'll come up with someone soon."

"How about me?" I asked, then wondered who the ventriloquist was.

Dennis Casey didn't wonder. He looked directly at me and said, "Maybe you could be assistant manager. Help out with the scheduling, the equipment, the etcetera."

"Shortstop," the ventriloquist said.

"How about right field? We could move Jimmy Ryan from right to short. It's quiet out in right. Get yourself a nice suntan."

"Shortstop," I insisted, enunciating the word slowly as if to prove to myself that it was me speaking.

"Be at the ballfield behind the firehouse at eight Sunday morning. We'll give it a go. Man who knows all that stuff about Babe Dahlgren and Johnny Sturm deserves a shot at it."

Neither Virginia nor I was in any condition to drive home that night. We left the car in O'Hara's lot and borrowed his daughter's bicycle. It was an old, one-speed dinosaur with balloon tires, heavy frame, and a red reflector in the back from which a bushy beaver tail hung.

Virginia straddled the back rack, put her arms around my waist, and dug her chin in the angle between my neck and shoulder. "Home, James," she said, and we took off.

That night was as dark as the void before creation but I could feel her warm cheek against mine as we picked our way carefully through the streets. At that hour, there was no traffic. I began singing "Brennan on the Moors" the way the Clancy Brothers did it.

"I didn't know you couldn't sing," said Virginia, increasing her hold on my waist.

It wasn't until I was back home, ready for sleep, after wonderfully servicing my mistress, that it hit me. I'd been in the company of men much like the one who'd killed Bobbi, enjoying myself more or less. Perhaps Christopher McGuire was a member of his own neighborhood drinking society, a place like O'Hara's. Perhaps he'd had a few cold ones that afternoon and no bicycle to keep him from behind the wheel. It didn't matter. He could have called a cab, the son of a bitch.

Sleepily, Virginia said, "You don't have to accommodate those lushes, you know. I don't. I come from them, I drink with them sometimes, but I'm not *of* them. And what's more important, neither are you. You don't have to perform any heroic deeds, either, to win my favor. I'm won, Gerber. You're my guy."

Nevertheless, eight sharp that Sunday morning, I dug my fielder's mitt and sneakers from the trunk of my car and walked down to Fireman's Field. And got the job. I had more years than most two Devils combined, but I moved with some speed and grace to dig grounders out of the dirt. I flew up into the early spring heavens to pull down a certain double and made an off-balance throw to first that would have pleased Billy Martin. At the plate, I actually sent the center fielder against the firehouse wall to yank down one of my fly balls.

The bedroom windows done, I began working on the railing posts. After every rain, the living-room front wall would bleed, and small puddles would accumulate beneath the windows. In time, I was afraid, the porch would rot away and fall into the junk below. The same thought never bothered Virginia. "I can't worry about small things like that," she'd said, leaving the impression of larger ones on her mind. What they were, maybe she'd tell me, maybe she wouldn't. I wasn't going to pry.

With surgeon's precision, I dug out the dry rot around each post, filling the cavity formed with caulking compound. Neatly, professionally. I was so engrossed with the project that I failed to see a car drive by, stop, then back up.

I heard a voice and looked up, thinking perhaps it was coming out of the sky or from my imagination. Then I looked down between the porch railings. It was Sara. My Sara. What the hell was she doing here?

I stood up, my knees aching from all that bending, and saw my daughter in the shades of gray and green and righteous anger. Two were her favorite colors. The third was entirely new.

"Well," she said. "I'd never recognize you."

On the way down the ladder, one particular hour between us came back to me. Laura had broken the news to them on a Friday. She'd called them together and soberly explained that we'd come to a parting of the ways. Irreconcilable differences. Maybe divorce—she just didn't know at the time.

Early on Saturday, Sara came to the store for my side of the story. We went for a drive along the back roads near the ocean. I parked on the grass and we entered the Lawrence Nature Preserve, a few acres of land the town had set aside to remain forever wild.

"Where are you living?" she asked as we strolled over the ground soft with centuries of mulched leaves, under trees whose naked branches formed complex webbings over our heads.

"Not far from here," I said. "It's not Woodsburgh, but it's not bad."

Assured that I had a roof overhead, Sara said, "You know, it's so ironic. All her life Bobbi was such a unifying factor at home. Caryn was Mom and I was you, but she was a blend of both. And now her death has caused all this. I wonder if it would have worked out the same way if Caryn or I had been killed."

I stopped, held out my hand, and splayed my fingers. "Which do you think is my favorite? Which do you think I'd be most willing to give up?"

Sara didn't answer.

"If something had happened to you or Caryn, I'd behave the same way. Your mother would behave the same way. What happened between us afterward was long overdue. I see that now."

"Mom didn't go into the details and she didn't try and dump all the blame on you, but I'm sure there's enough to go around. I lived with you guys for twenty years. I know you inside out. You're unbelievably great people but you're not a snap to live with. Those unspoken standards, that devotion to excellence. It nearly drove me nuts sometimes."

Sara sat on a fallen log near the water. I joined her. She lay her head on my shoulder and I took her hand. We sat quietly for a long time while I contemplated the terrible things people do to each other, especially people who love one another.

"Do you see any light at the end of the tunnel?" she asked hopefully. "Any chance of you two getting back together again?"

"I don't even see the tunnel, baby." We sat awhile longer, watching a mother duck steer her new family of ducklings around the cul-de-sac, teaching them the fundamentals of duckness. When we got up to leave, I felt old and weary.

And now Sara stood in Virginia's yard like some avenging angel, looking for answers.

She jerked her head at the last second when I tried to kiss her. I grazed her earlobe.

"Well," she said, panning the drier, the minibus, the bungalow, and finally myself. "I don't believe it."

"Come inside. No sense talking out here."

Sara concentrated all her disbelief on me, my cast-off sweater, the Marine Corps hat, my unshaven face. Has he flipped his lid? I read in the invisible bubble over her head.

She stomped through the hall and living room, denying them even the courtesy of her disdain. In the kitchen, I saw in her upturned nose what was once my own attitude that first time. What she didn't see was the mess. Since moving in, I'd added a measure of cleanliness and order that didn't bother Virginia, as long as I wasn't preachy or made it an obsession.

I instantly forgave Sara her how-could-you-live-this-way attitude and made us some tea. She eyed the cup suspiciously, as though it contained anthrax virus, then took an abbreviated sip. Chilled from all that outdoor work, I greedily drank from mine.

"I don't know what the hell's gotten into both of you," she scolded. "You living here in shantytown with some shanty Irish tootsie. Mom living in our house—*our house*—with her artist-boyfriend."

"Who told you about Virginia? That she was shanty Irish? And what's this about your mother?"

"Violet told me. She said this Virginia person has slept in more beds than George Washington. Violet says that sleeping with her is more an act of faith than an act of love. And as far as Mom's concerned, she's really gone bonkers. This Bruno character is some local sculptor who's moved in and set up shop in our garage. He's a real Svengali, I hear, from the art teacher in my school."

I couldn't believe Sara was talking about the same woman. Laura had never as much as looked at another man. All these years, it seemed, I'd been living with a dormant volcano—ivory and ice covering a center of fire. She was playing host to some parasite. We both were, since I sent her a fat check every week. But I refused to feign the cuckolded husband for Sara or myself. I was doing to Virginia what this Bruno was doing to her. Looking at Sara slowly stewing, I had to turn my gaze to the water where a tug slowly crept along the channel.

She was seated at the small table expecting her scornful words to shake me to my senses. I leaned over the space separating us, but didn't try to touch her. "I'm no more than human, Sara, despite what you may have thought. I've found someone who treats me that way. Virginia is a fine person, a good person, a warm person. She may not be a Five Towns lady but that shouldn't condemn her to the stake, should it?"

It was an honest question, probably the most important one I'd ever asked her. But she heard it rhetorically, if at all. "Caryn and I feel humiliated by the two of you. They joke about the Gerbers in town, in the stores, in the library, at school. You're more dessert to them than the Weiners ever were. At least Ken stayed home and had his heart attack while Paula was running off with her guitar player."

"I think it was a banjo," I said to deflate her.

"We've accepted that our parents have separated and maybe there'll be a divorce and we'll be like all our friends in town. What we can't swallow is our mother, who was the closest thing to perfection, is shacking up with some bald, puny leech, while our father, our god of gods, our shining idol, is taking up with someone obviously so beneath him."

I lost my temper with Sara, the first time ever. "Don't you pull that superior shit on me, you little snot. What do you know about her—what she is or isn't? Beyond the crap spread by ninnies who know nothing of life outside their diamond-studded dung heap? You, of all people. She's good and decent and kind and just fine for me."

Virginia suddenly appeared in the kitchen as if all the heated talk had created her.

"Salutations," she said to me but looking inquiringly at Sara. "I'm home early because I must have caught what Diane has and I feel like shit. If I'm interfering with anything, I'll go away for a while."

"Don't go anywhere," I said commandingly, pinning Virginia where she stood.

"Let me see. I know who you are. You're Sara."

Sara rose from the table and moved closer to Virginia in a friendly way that made me cautious. "Correct," she said in Laura's voice, the one she used with the gardener, with Eric, with tradespeople on the Avenue. "And who are you?"

"I'm Virginia," said Virginia, as sweet sounding as I'd ever heard her.

"And what do you do?" Ironic, haughty, contemptuous, Sara was totally devoid of the simple decency she'd always shown meeting strangers for the first time.

"I wait on tables. And when I'm not waiting on tables, I live with your father, I sleep with him and he sleeps with me and we have a grand old time almost every night," she said, not altering her sweetness a calorie. "I would say we fuck like crazy every chance we get, but that might shock your delicate ears. You might even get a poor first impression of me, and we wouldn't want that to happen, would we."

"No, absolutely not," said perfectly composed Sara. "I'm sure you wouldn't want to destroy my illusion that you're really Anastasia hiding out from Bolshevik assassins, or some well-known writer doing research for a book on how the underprivileged are making do in Reagan's America."

I watched the mongoose-cobra scene too fascinated to intrude.

"I'm sure you must have dozens of illusions that need to be shattered," said Virginia. "But who and what I am are not among

*[177]*

them. You know exactly, precisely, who and what, and you knew it long before you met me. Is there something else you'd like to learn about your father and me. How many times a night? In what positions? Some of the things I do to keep him well and happy?"

"He had someone for that," said Sara.

"Quite obviously she wasn't doing her job very well if your father's happy as a pig in shit here in this sty."

"And here he can stay, as far as I'm concerned." Slowly, imperceptibly, Sara had edged to within three feet of Virginia and I was afraid more than words would fly between them if she moved closer. It was time I become more than a discussed subject. "Sara, you've said what you came to say, now go home." I was thoroughly ashamed of her.

Sara took unhurried, measured steps through the kitchen, past the living room, the hall, and out the door. Measured and slow, to demonstrate that she wasn't beating a hasty retreat but leaving the field of combat with honor.

Her tires screeched and I could smell burning rubber as she backed the car onto Virginia's lawn, shifted into drive, and sped off.

---

I made Virginia a fresh pot of tea, gave her two tablespoons of Donnatal, and put her to bed. Not a word passed between us about Sara, her visit, her sharp tongue. Virginia was just too sick to talk.

The cracks in the porch floor took another hour to finish. Through the drawn curtains I checked on Virginia every few minutes. She lay on her side in blue pajamas, the blanket thrown off. She seemed so small and helpless, her face becalmed by the Donnatal, her left arm curled around a stomach that probably still ached. Her hand, I noticed in the gray light of the bedroom, kept opening and closing like that of a person giving blood. Was she reliving her spat with Sara, getting ready to slug my child? What would I have done then?

Long after I'd fallen asleep that night, I was awakened by something wet against my nose. I'd been dreaming of Spain, the

Mediterranean, where I'd spent my honeymoon. I opened my eyes and felt Virginia's tongue circling my lips.

"We didn't form a fast friendship, that's for sure," she said. She smelled of toothpaste, so I knew she'd been up before, preparing herself. "The kid was snotty, so I was snotty. I won't take abuse from anyone, Gerber."

"I don't expect you to."

Virginia moved into my arms. "I'm not apologizing for anything, mind you, but it would have been nice had it gone the other way."

"She was entirely wrong," I said, removing her pajamas, first the bottom, which was easy, then the top with her help. I held myself back from entering her. "I'm the one who should be offering an apology."

"Right now I'd prefer you offer me something more tangible."

We made love as if it were the last time, and though she'd been sick, she was more passionate than I'd ever known her. The climax was a combination of Fourth of July fireworks and the "1812 Overture."

"Either that's what a good fight does to me or you're getting damn fucking good, Gerber. Literally."

"She was never like that," I told Virginia after she'd put her pajamas back on, leaving the top open just in case. "I guess tragedy doesn't always bring out the best in us."

"Don't be so quick to judge the kid," said Virginia. "She's made of pretty good stuff: coming to a strange house, standing up to her adored father, going toe to toe with me, trading insults. Give her a chance to get over the culture shock and maybe you'll be surprised. Maybe you'll find a real piece of work under all that privilege and prejudice."

"From your mouth to God's ear."

"I never heard that expression before. It's kind of cute."

"I never used it before."

"There you go. We've had an exchange of customs. I've shown you a bit of Irish saloon life and you've taught me some of your people's idioms. Tit for tat."

"Speaking of tits," I said. . . .

# *twelve*

SZENT GYORGYI, the Nobel laureate in Medicine, once said that he wanted to see what everyone else has seen but think what no one else has thought. Bruno took this step in another direction. "I want to see what others see—but differently, in a new way, a fresh way that brings out some part of the truth ordinarily hidden from the rest. I want to be a Jeremiah, a Christ, a Tolstoy, a Robert Frost. But I don't want total acceptance, for down that path lies mediocrity. I want the best of both artistic worlds—the popular and the avant-garde. I think I probably want too much."

Bruno introduced me to an undiscovered universe on a day in early April warm enough to be called summerlike. We were sitting in the kitchen enjoying a late breakfast. It was 10:30, my first weekday morning in home in months. At Bruno's urging, I cut back to a more civilized schedule, the one I'd been originally hired for. Phil Coolidge was so effusively gracious about my decision that at first I thought he meant it. Reality soon set in and I knew he saw it as a decline in my competitiveness. I'd come to my senses about trying to take his job away and was now content as second banana.

I'd also stopped going to the meetings of the Compassionate Friends. Bruno had become my compassionate friend, all I needed. I saw less and less of Frances DeVito, Bruno taking her place as well, filling all the voids in my once-wretched life.

" 'Let there be light,' were the first words spoken by the Lord when he was new to the job," said Bruno. "Artists ever since have been mining that mother lode."

I stopped buttering the bottom half of my English muffin to hear Bruno better. Then put it down as he took my hand and led me out onto the patio. Earlier that morning, the gardener had come for his first cleanup visit of the season. All the detritus of winter had been gathered and hauled away. The bushes had been trimmed and the soil turned over, releasing its seminal odors. Lime had been sprinkled on, to sweeten the ground. Inhaling, I felt almost virginal, as if I, too, had undergone rebirth.

"Pure, undeflected light is wonderful," Bruno said. "*Feel* it entering your body, cleaning your soul."

Before I could *feel* anything, he whisked me down the patio steps and across the lawn to the southeast corner of the backyard under an integrated family of pine, poplar, and maple trees.

Sunlight fought its way through the maze of leaf, branch, and pine needle, striking Bruno and me from many directions.

"Feel the difference now," he said. "Forget the change in temperature and concentrate on the changes in light patterns. It's the difference between simplicity and complexity, the pure and the worldly, an instrument and an entire orchestra."

Still holding my hand, Bruno raised it to his lips and kissed each fingertip. "We artists are rewarded in ways even the most successful businessman and professional are not. We're blessed with special vision and permanently pregnant with ideas, if we don't throw it all away on alcohol, drugs, or foolishness. If we don't surrender to the world's view that everyone must take home a weekly paycheck. God, I love your backyard."

A breeze wafted by, stirring the branches, and the light pattern changed. Some maze exits opened, while others closed, creating different patchworks of sun and shade all about us. I saw the shift and thrilled to it.

Bruno had taught me to see again, for the first time.

A week later he set up shop in the garage. He asked, of course. Of course I consented.

First Bruno removed the paisley shades from the windows and washed the glass. Then he stripped the pegboard of all Mark's gardening tools and cleared off the metal fixture. Everything he put into two cartons and stored them in the basement. The pegboard hooks were rearranged to accommodate his own tools.

On the steel fixture, he placed a few old plaid workshirts, a pair of worn jeans, sanding paper of all grades, steel wool, a pile of polishing cloths, and a one-pound jar of Vaseline.

The pegboard now held mallets and chisels in perhaps ten sizes and shapes, in wood, in metal, and combinations of both. On a section of plywood nailed to a vertical beam, he hung four sketches of *The Flutist* in poses from pure uninhibited joy to a self-conscious seriousness. In the center of the garage, speared on three sides by shafts of light from the sparkling-clean windows, stood a square of black marble that could have been an Egyptian obelisk or a Stonehenge slab. Barely discernible were the raised arm of a man, and the beginnings of a head. The man seemed to be struggling to free himself from the marble, as though he were neck-deep in quicksand.

I guess I could have dwelt on how quickly, how thoroughly Mark's last vestiges had been gathered up and condensed into two insignificant cartons, then placed out of sight between the emergency basement pump and the sixteen-millimeter movie projector. I could have thought it ironic that in taking in Bruno, I had evicted both our cars from the garage. Instead, I marveled at how transformed the garage had become, how useful. An artist's studio.

In addition to the garage, I gave Bruno use of the garden. There'd be no more parties or Sunday meals in the gazebo. No more jungle of tomato plants by the garage wall. I had the gardener turn over the soil and plant flowers for this summer instead of vegetables. I never really cared for tomatoes.

Between the house and the gazebo, Bruno set up a wooden platform. One Saturday morning, using a hand truck, he hauled the just-begun block of marble from the garage, across the lawn to the platform where he planted it with the same sense of purpose as Neil Armstrong planting the Stars and Stripes on the moon. "Now to work," said Bruno determinedly.

His daily work schedule was maddingly inflexible. Daily— weekends as well—he'd rise early and shower. A bit of Italian opera would escape through the glass shower door and fill the bedroom, then seep down to the kitchen where I'd be preparing a ranch hand's breakfast of juice, bacon and eggs, pancakes, toast, and gallons of black coffee, while overhead Bruno darted from Rudolfo to Otello to Lieutenant Pinkerton. "I don't stop for lunch," he'd told me at the start, "or coffee or snacks, so I need plenty of fuel for the engine."

In the garage, he'd strip to the waist and coat his face, head and body, and even his beard, with Vaseline to blunt the marble chips that would flint off under his mallet and chisel. Bruno was quite careful about injuring himself. "Self-inflicted wounds are for the likes of Van Gogh, not for this less masochistic fellow. All for art doesn't include drawing blood and risking infection."

He protected his eyes with plastic goggles that gave him the look of a World War I aviator, and wore a white cloth hat, the kind they gave away free at the hardware store with a decent-size order of paint.

Slowly, ever so slowly, the head of *The Flutist* began emerging, born under Bruno's sure and skillful hands. First he'd asked my advice about the sketches in the garage. They were of a man of dubious nationality. Either a Latin or a Semite, from the thick meaty nose and angular face. The head, thrown back ecstatically in one of the sketches, was all wrong. "He's never going to get notes out of the flute at that angle."

"If you will," he said, handing me a fresh sheet of paper and a soft lead pencil. I did what I could, then in a few quick strokes he made the necessary changes in his own sketch.

Of course the rest of *The Flutist* was beyond my knowledge: how he stood, the thickly muscled legs, the narrow waist and bulging torso. "My idea here is to demonstrate that none of this masculinity is lost in his choice of musical instrument. There are, you know, running backs who do ballet, and baseball players who crochet while warming the bench."

"And women who pump iron and arrest criminals."

"My point precisely. The fudging of those once immutable barriers between the sexes."

"You sound like Violet Fleming," I said.

"She has some good points."

"So does a porcupine. In neither case do I intend to get too close."

Once Bruno began his day's work, he left the world completely. But when I came to see *The Flutist* and not its maker, he was very good about it. He'd stop, lay down his tools, remove his aviator glasses, and chat. Only for a few minutes. I realized then that even if Bruno had refused to stop, and ignored me, I wouldn't have been offended. I wasn't entitled to intrude upon his concentration. I didn't own him just because we loved one another and he was living in my house, working on my grounds. Love isn't possession, though that was its equation in my neck of the woods.

When the dark, or weariness, overtook him, he'd shower again, eat dinner, and be back in my world again, rightfully mine, and a different set of rules would apply.

We'd spend the evening in the living room before the fire, talking about the kinds of things lovers talk about, read messages in the flames, entering each other's forbidden zones. Revealing our secret selves, we submitted them as hostages and prayed they would be treated well.

Neither I nor Mark had loved one another enough, trusted enough, to go that far. We'd halted at our peripheries and remained there all our married lives.

Later in bed, Bruno and I would give voice and action to those feelings liberated by the flames and the taking of hostages. Then, possession and love were part of the same process.

By the first of May, the first Sunday of the month, Bruno had a rough draft of *The Flutist*. He called me over to elicit an opinion.

I was on the patio, in a daring new bikini, working on the Before the Beach series for the library, a two-hour Wednesday morning summer program of subjects as light and fluffy as French pastry.

I came to view the sculpture with a glass of spring water in each hand.

"Nice bikini," said Bruno, though he said that every time I put one on or took it off. "Nice," he repeated, running his thumb from my shoulder to my breast to my navel. I shuddered with desire.

"It's coming along beautifully," I told him.

He fed off the compliment. "Yes, yes, I like it, too."

Drinks in hand, we circled the work. "It's going to be the best thing I've ever done. Thanks to you and the environment you've provided. I love being here. I love the way it makes me feel about my work, seeing it come to life in this magnificent setting." He began caressing me again with his thumb. "I love you."

Again I shuddered, this time not erotically. The Vaseline had blunted all the marble chips except one. A tiny fragment had pierced the protective layer and drew a spot of blood on his forehead. He held still while I removed the splinter. A small well of blood took its place, spreading out, then drying up after I applied pressure with my index finger. It reminded me that he was so very mortal, so terribly fragile, that we all were. As if I had to be reminded.

"You're not nervous about this afternoon, are you?" he asked.

"A little."

"They're Sicilians, I know. But they don't eat human flesh. Not when I lived there anyway." He smiled wanly.

"Do you really want to go? I mean at this time. I don't know if I'm ready for . . . other people yet."

"Nonsense," said Bruno vigorously. "They're dying to meet you. I've whetted their appetites for weeks. Figuratively, I mean. My brothers think I've dreamed you up to torment them about their ugly wives. My sisters are sure I'm on drugs."

When I failed to reply, Bruno said, in a voice better suited for dealing with children, "There's nothing and no one to hide from, Laura."

Braced and buoyed, I said, "Give me another hour to finish my work." I meant another hour to gather strength and composure.

Bruno picked up his mallet and chisel and I returned to my library homework. In less than the agreed-upon hour, I had my program in place. All that remained were the phone calls to the speakers, confirming date and time. I laughed to myself, closing my attaché case: Phil Coolidge might not be as relieved that I'd returned to my original thirty-hour schedule if the program was well attended and well received. He might conclude that I was, indeed, after his job. Let the toad sweat.

---

They were standing there awhile—I don't know for how long—like job seekers waiting to be interviewed. Or perhaps they'd been shocked to see Bruno pounding away in the backyard, the turf they'd played on, entertained on, and considered hallowed ground. More likely it was my bikini, flimsier than I—or they—had ever worn.

Meeting Sara and Caryn's perplexed stares, I considered dashing inside for a robe. If I couldn't hide Bruno, I could at least cover myself. But that would have been an admission of guilt, and as Bruno had pointed out not an hour before, we had nothing to hide. Except, perhaps, my nakedness.

"Why are you standing there like statues?" I said. Wrong simile. "Come up here and let me see you. It's been weeks."

Two, to be exact. Phone calls galore, but no visits. Caryn had a perfectly good excuse: those walking tours of the City. Sara had none.

They advanced cautiously up the steps of the patio. Both kept their heads rigid, pretending there was no backyard and no Bruno in it, seventy feet away.

I decided not to call him over for an introduction. That would have been most awkward, even though he and I were about to visit *his* people. Different situation. Better timing.

They stood on the patio, Sara's eyes glued to the skimpiness of my bra, Caryn's to the tiny triangle of material below my waist. Both came and kissed me as though they weren't sure they should, light insulting kisses I could have done without.

"Come inside," I said, to put a wall between them and Bruno. His back was to us. A light wind was bringing in the sounds of his mallet and an aria from *Rigoletto*.

I threw on a robe from the downstairs bathroom, feeling as though I'd donned a suit of armor. "Something to drink?" I asked. "Iced tea? It'll only take a few seconds."

"No," they replied in unison, as though they'd worked out procedure beforehand.

"Am I to be given a lecture, a reprimand, or made to wear a big scarlet A around my neck?" I asked.

"Oh, Mother," Sara said. "Stop talking nonsense."

"Am I?"

"Yes, and acting that way, too," said Caryn, the sterner of this visiting morals squad. She stared out the window at Bruno as if to draw attention to exhibit A. "We are beside ourselves with embarrassment. You are behaving *so* badly, *so* carelessly, so *recklessly* that I can't tell you what it's doing to us."

"Oh, I'm sure you can. And will," I told her.

"And what it's doing to Grandpa," chimed in Sara, once her sister had read the indictment.

"He hasn't said a word to me."

"He can't, he's so mortified," said Sara.

"Nevertheless," said Caryn, "we have to tell you how we feel."

"By all means do," I said, quite coolheadedly. They'd been

standing around the kitchen table waiting for me to sit down first, as if it were my house alone and never theirs. It was at this moment that I first felt for certain the terrible gap that had grown between us.

The girls peered at each other, confused as to what to do next, like actors who'd forgotten their lines. They remained standing. I sat down.

Sara said, "We're hurt. We're angry. We're embarrassed."

"You said that already. The embarrassed part," I told her.

Seeing that I'd neutralized Sara with little effort, Caryn said, "We're absolutely amazed that after so many years of married life, being who you are, that you'd do this monstrous thing to us." Without dropping a stitch, she went on. "It's one thing to leave a husband but something else to immediately take up with another man, and still another to take up with a *younger* man, then offer him your *residence,* your *garage,* your *grounds.* Who do you think you are, Mother, George Sand? Or one of the Medicis?"

"Or Gloria Swanson in *Sunset Boulevard?*" tacked on Sara, an inveterate movie buff, if only to keep in the running.

Mission accomplished. They'd gotten it off their chests, my two witch-hunters. For the next few minutes they repeated themselves with embellishments. I let them go on, saying nothing so as not to give them more fuel for their fires, wondering at the same time how long they would keep going in circles.

I thought once spent they'd leave, tails between their legs. Caryn was ready, I know, after that horrid little speech, but Sara, who'd never been a leader or a follower, stepped forward and took over. She told me about Mark and his new girlfriend (Mark?) whom she described as a suburban street fighter, younger than me by at least ten years, but as worked over as an exhausted coal mine.

Who would have believed that Mark had made the leap, only to fall into a swamp?

It hurt Sara, I know, to dish out this final unkindness. Caryn, on the other hand, seemed triumphant, as if by saving the best for last she could break me. My lovely, brilliantly sophisticated child, was, after all, only a shallow, unfeeling, arrogant snob, and a sad caricature of all those loathsome images the words "Five Town Lady" evoked in our worse detractors.

"Well, you two inquisitors have judged me and God knows what the sentence will be. Quite frankly, I don't care. I don't intend heeling because you think people are talking or because your picture of me is all covered with mud. Fuck them one and all. And the two of you, as well, if this is all I can expect after twenty years of love and patience and giving." I pointed a finger at each of them. They backed away slightly, as if my finger were a loaded pistol. "You both have husbands. Men who care for you. Cherish you. I don't. That is, I didn't before Bruno. Are you shocked? Good. You two worthless shits need a rude awakening. Your noble father may have been great in the image department but he sure lacked substance. He was cold, insensitive, and distant. Now, you chew on that for a while. As for me, I'm over twenty-one, and no longer your combination of Mother Teresa and a Greek goddess. If you can't accept that, then it's your problem, not mine."

Burned and reddened by my heat, they mumbled good-bye, backed off, and left, first Sara, then Caryn, who was so filled with repressed anger that she blew past her sister and beat her to the car.

Leaving the driveway in reverse, Sara wove a crooked path. I prayed she wouldn't drive home in the same disorganized manner. She might do to some unlucky family what had been done to us.

Well, I thought, after I'd called Bruno to come in and shower, I'd survived that. Now I was truly ready to take on his family. Or the devil. Whatever they'd prepared, I could handle it.

---

The bells of a church nearby announced my arrival. I'd never visited that part of Inwood before, though I'd often passed through, wondering about the lower-middle-class neighborhood of modest homes and immaculate lawns, if they were much different than ours. I suspected not. Television, not democracy, had been the great equalizer. We'd all been conditioned by "Dynasty," the Academy Award ceremonies, the late-evening news.

"Be it ever so humble, here we are," said Bruno. We stopped in front of a low, flat, lime-green meandering ranch, partially enveloped in shrubbery. Vines of white roses just beginning to bloom wound through a logwood fence. A dirt path led up to the front door, then veered right to the backyard.

If the house had seemed plain and modest from the front, the back was quite the opposite. Occupying much more space than the house, the backyard was a well-landscaped, richly dense Garden of Eden. A perimeter of apple trees, walnut, cherry, plum, and pear gave way to a wide band of tulips and daffodils. Trellises crisscrossed a good section of the back garden and supported serpentine grapevines already in early light green leaf. The large center portion, reserved for vegetables, had been sectioned off and recently planted. It glowed opulent and pudding-brown in early-afternoon sunshine.

One night after sex, when Bruno was most reflective, he said that the backyard has been his father's mistress, his sanctuary, his consolation when life took its bad bounces. When spirits sagged, he'd retreat there for reward and restoration. "But most of all, the backyard was Papa's refuge from Mama, who, to this day, still blames him for all the world's ills. They have this dance they do. Mama attacks; Papa goes into exile. The separation is what has kept them together all these years. That, and Mama's Catholicism. Pop is pure pagan, though he doesn't know the meaning of the word. He worships nature, prays to rain gods, and performs strange fertility rites in his little shack behind the grapevines. At least *his* gods produce. You ought to see those eggplants, the grapes, the corn."

A small burly man with thick white wild hair and pencil-point eyes burning hotly behind wire-frame glasses, greeted Bruno by kissing him on the lips. He then approached me. I didn't know how to respond. Gaetano Coletti solved my dilemma by taking my hand in both of his and pumping lightly. "Welcome, welcome," he said, bowing and scraping like the Japanese.

He led me to a gathering in the center of a group of small stunted trees. A long table made of construction horses and plywood rectangles had been joined together and covered with white damask tablecloths. Perhaps twenty smiling faces—adults and children—turned my way and heartily waved hello.

Bruno's mother came between us, carrying a large oval aluminum pan brimming with homemade veal and peppers. Steam rose from the pan, but I could see an unrelenting hardness in Carmella Coletti's face, a face still beautiful, with perfect features, though she was shapeless and overweight.

"I thought maybe the queen of England was coming," she said in slightly accented tones. "From Bruno's description. It's nice to see you're just another human being." She set the pan on the table and went inside the house for more.

I have a talent for remembering faces and the names that go with them. That Sunday afternoon it was put to the test. While Bruno and I circled the table, he introduced me to everyone— even to his nieces and nephews, of whom there were many, each perfectly mannered and scrubbed until they shone for the occasion. What made identification a horror was the great resemblance of all Bruno's brothers to their father.

The oldest Bruno—Pietro—was clean-shaven and bald as Telly Savalas. He, Teresa, and their three children lived in Valley Stream, northeast of the Five Towns. Adam, their middle son, had Sara as his science teacher.

Bernardo was the heaviest Coletti male, with a full head of blue-black hair, droopy eyes, and a gap from two missing fingers on his left hand. He was a widower with a bevy of children.

The youngest Coletti, Joseph, was obviously the family pet. Though recently married to a nurse, who was on duty this Sunday and couldn't be here, he considered himself a ladies' man. His hair was gorgeously styled; he wore an expensive jacket and contrasting slacks; he smelled of a cloying cologne that preceded him wherever he went. Joseph tried flirting with me, but I pretended not to notice.

In some spirit of evenhandedness, all the Coletti women resembled their mother—as my girls resembled me.

My sitting down had been the signal to start eating. The long, jerry-built table sagged under the weight of salad bowls the size of footbaths, and huge tureens of broad-noodle lasagna and plates of gnocci, veal and peppers, and platters of lasciviously bloated sausage. Placed every few feet along the table were trays of long, seeded Italian bread and bright green pitchers of Gaetano-made wine.

I was amazed at how the women scurried about the food, filling plates and catering to their husbands. At home, I'd never filled Mark's plate or poured his drink. Neither had anyone else I knew. It was so subservient. I refused to do as much for Bruno, but he didn't expect me to. He filled his own plate and poured his own wine. First, however, he served me, for reasons other than the tribal rules of dominance: I was a stranger and he was a very kind man.

Gaetano tried to make my visit a pleasant one. He took my hand. "Laura's a very fine name. Very Italian. Petrarch was an Italian artist and he had his Laura. I'm sure you know that."

With a keen ear for treachery, Carmella Coletti heard this and threw her husband a stare that could have floored an elephant. I imagined that after everyone had left, she would give him a bellyful about consorting with the enemy. Gaetano would probably hike out to his shack and spend a week there contemplating his misfortunes.

For the next hour, food, wine, and talk freely traversed the table. Of course I indulged in all three, not to insult Carmella's cooking, Gaetano's grapes, and Bruno's faith in my ability to deal with any situation. None of the many questions I answered came from Bruno's mother. I'm sure that without asking a single one, she had all the answers she needed. As my daughter had earlier that day.

Through it all, Bruno never left my side, favoring neither me nor them. He held my hand under the table, every so often squeezing large doses of courage into me. His foot, caressing mine, took the edge off his mother's obvious hostility.

Dessert was fresh fruit and whipped cream—which doomed

me to a month of tuna and cottage cheese—then espresso. Bruno whispered to me, "You're in for a treat, I think."

"This has all been a treat," I whispered back, trying not to seem patronizing.

"The pièce de résistance," said Bruno, leaning back against his chair, allowing his sisters to clear off the dishes.

I followed his eyes to a place beneath the first trellis, under a canopy of grape leaves, filled with emerald-tinted air, where Gaetano and the two older Coletti men had gathered. From somewhere, they'd conjured up a clarinet, a violin, and a viola da gamba.

Gaetano forced a few notes from the clarinet. Pietro tightened a string on his violin. Bernardo sat down on a chair and plucked a descending chord on the viola da gamba held firmly between his knees. It was Bruno's sculpture come to life, except the faces of the Colettis were not the faces on the work that had remained in the library garden all fall.

Without an introduction, they began with a Vivaldi trio full of zest and chugging. It was as I had imagined, seeing Bruno's sculpture for the first time. The same heavenly music, the same weaving and bobbing of the musicians as they stressed certain notes and conveyed their interdependence.

So engrossed was I in the pieces that followed, I failed to notice Bruno's absence. I did see him return with my flute case.

"Oh, no," I said. "Please, Bruno, I can't."

"I'm afraid you'll have to. They've been practicing for weeks. I told them you played Drigo's 'Serenade' like an angel."

"Like a beginner," I said.

"So who do you think we are?" said Pietro, coming to escort me under the trellis. "The Guarneri? Maybe I'm as good as Isaac Stern, but those two . . ."

I laughed, then hesitated. All twenty-odd guests applauded. "Wait until I *earn* it," I told them.

Having accepted their applause and their hospitality, I was obligated, trapped. I opened the case, assembled the flute, and blew a nervous puff of air over the embouchure. Braver than I, the instrument responded forcefully.

And, bless Bruno, the "Serenade" proved to be the perfect encore to end the beautiful little concert under the grape leaves. He knew just what piece in my repertoire to choose, just as he'd taken the trouble to learn so many other things about me.

Their applause was even greater when I'd finished. I begged off a second number. Bruno agreed, telling his family, "Now, now. We've imposed enough on our guest."

He came to me as I was disassembling the flute and removed a cherry blossom that had blown into my hair as I'd played. There were tears in Bruno's eyes. "This has to be the most beautiful moment of my life. Only God could have written so perfect a script."

"I'm glad I came," I said. With a breast full of anguish, I thought of my own family earlier that day, what was left of it. The harsh criticism, their bitter withdrawal. The sight of Sara's car wobbling out of the driveway.

In perfect scripts there are no anticlimaxes. There was one that afternoon in ours. The women gathered together in a clump under the fruit trees to talk children. The men, Bruno among them, were off in their own huddle by the small shed at the end of the trellis. The children formed the third point of the triangle by regrouping themselves around a Monopoly board.

By default or design, I was left alone with Carmella Coletti. We were inside her very adequate kitchen. She was wrapping leftovers in aluminum foil, small individual portions.

"My husband's lunch," Carmella explained. "He takes it with him out there every morning. To his 'office.' The little building in the back. He doesn't like to come into the house until nighttime. It breaks his concentration, he says. On what? The olive trees? The grapes? The zucchini?" She shook her head. "You'd think he was an artist. Like his son."

She asked if I wanted a cup of coffee, just the two of us. I didn't but I took one anyway.

"Maybe you think I was kinda cold to you all afternoon," she said, filling my cup first. "If I was, it's because I liked you at once and I don't want you to get hurt. As you can see, we're simple people. All except Bruno. He's complicated. Too complicated for me to figure out, and I'm his mother. I'm telling you all this because you're a nice lady, a fine lady. Be careful with him. He's a taker. A user. He's my son and all that, but I gotta warn you. That much I know about him."

"That may be, Mrs. Coletti. But he's also a giver."

Carmella closed her eyes. "Whatever he may give you, Laura, I don't think you need it. You seem to have everything a woman could want."

"Appearances can be deceptive," I said.

"That's exactly what I'm telling you about Bruno."

———————

We didn't get out of the car at once. We were parked facing the backyard and *The Flutist.* In the cool early evening, the figure looked strangely alive, as though he'd come out of the forest to play for us.

"So, do I stay or go?" he asked.

"Stay, of course. Whatever gave you such an idea?"

"Oh, first the visit from your daughters this morning. I pretended not to notice but I knew what they were here for. If it's going to cause friction and pain, I'll go. You know that."

"What's life without friction and pain?"

"But I'd feel terrible if I thought I was the cause."

"You're not, Bruno. They are. And the pain is not from *what* they said this morning. It's from knowing the way they really are. I raised them. I molded them."

"If you're enjoying self-flagellation, go right ahead. My father may be unsophisticated and unschooled, but he doesn't blame anyone for me but me. He's learned to accept his children as they are. That's why we've become such good friends."

"Yes, you're probably right, and someday I'll believe it. But for now, it's so hard to bear."

"Then let's share it."

"No, that can't be done. I'll be all right, though. I told you that a while ago, at the beginning."

"Then I was certain you'd want me to leave after that tête-à-tête with Mama."

"Oh that."

"Yes, that. I love her immensely, but she can really dish out the poison. Used to be I'd bring around a friend, then the next day I'd lose her. It took me a while to realize that Mama was doing this terrible number on her. Had the poor lass convinced I was some sort of bloodsucker. It really took a heavy toll on my personal life until I stopped bringing around my friends. Somehow I thought by now she'd learned to control herself."

"I'm a big girl, Bruno. I can make my own decisions, and one of them is not to believe malicious gossip even when it comes from the horse's mouth. I love you. You love me. Nothing else matters."

"Those last three lines are the sum and substance of every great love story," said Bruno.

---

Against my better judgment, I paid a visit to the Women's Consortium. Through all my woes, Violet had been there, if not as a steadfast friend, then as an interested observer. Often the only one. For her own selfish reasons, no doubt, but I was adult enough not to question motives that closely.

Truthfully, what moved me in her direction was the growing sense of isolation I was beginning to feel since that Sunday the girls had tried to save me from a life of dissolution. Bruno had been wonderfully supportive, but he wasn't a mother. Violet was a mother of three boys—not the same as girls—but maybe she had some useful words of advice. Maybe at this level, she could help me after all.

The building on Sunrise Highway was large, one-level, and made of bright red brick. It resembled the small stores and insurance offices that flanked the highway out to the Hamptons.

Inside, encased in protective Lucite, a cherubic woman with short gray hair and half glasses smiled when I told her who I was. She pressed a button on her switchboard and repeated my name.

Violet appeared from the first of a galley of offices that bordered a wide corridor. She came out and seized my hand as if afraid I might run off. "So, the mountain comes to Muhammad," she said, throwing the receptionist a knowing glance.

Before I could get around to my reason for coming, Violet demanded I take the tour of the premises. We started at the end offices. She knocked on each door, each labeled with its service and who dispensed it. Immediately after, she walked in, and I was introduced to patient and counselor, though I felt uncomfortable interrupting something that personal. Violet thought nothing of breaking in, trying hard to show me the scope of her accomplishments.

"We have waiting lists now, and a shortage of good counselors and therapists. We're looking for more professionals and paras who we can afford to pay close to what they're worth. Laura, you'd be a natural here with us, as my executive assistant. Needless to say, the services you'll need during the divorce will be gratis. Professional courtesy."

"I haven't gotten around to that stage," I was almost ashamed to tell Violet.

"Still haven't? You've got to strike while the iron's hot. When Mark's both eager and confused. If you let him grow comfortable in his new circumstances, with his new waitress-lover, he'll be much less inclined to come to terms. You see, without your telling me, I know what's happening in your life. You were paying a pretty stiff management fee to have others run it for you, more than any woman can afford. But you've taken the first step and broken the pattern of slavish indenture."

"Violet, I was never a slave or his servant. And Mark was no brute, only an impossible man to live with. We've both escaped our ruts. He's happy. I'm happy."

Violet, I could tell, found that hard to accept. We continued down the hall, in and out of rooms labeled Family Services, Employment Opportunities, Drug and Alcohol Abuse, Family Planning, and Legal Counseling. Most of the clients we barged in on were in tears or close to it. I thought of Violet as the ringmaster of a small circus. I shouldn't have. All those services were essential, even if I didn't feel Violet was the one to oversee them.

We entered her office, a large room as unkempt as Violet. Papers of all sorts were piled helter-skelter on her messy, coffee-stained, cigarette-burned desk, on bookshelves, stacked in corners on the floor, spilling over like landslides. She could certainly use an organizer, though I was not the one.

On the walls were paintings of women, fully clothed and vaguely familiar. The phone began ringing before we'd taken seats. That day—all week—the Women's Consortium had been agog over their star client, Martha Haymarket. She'd been a garden variety housewife who catapulted to fame by stabbing her husband 128 times with an ice pick. Mostly in the lower part of his body. After thirty-six years of the most horrendous abuse.

"We've gotten a lawyer—our very best—to defend her. In fact, lawyers from all over the country have been calling, offering their services pro bono. Women's groups from as far away as Alaska have kept Mrs. Carbonari very busy at the switchboard."

Violet leaned back in her chair in a loose, almost masculine manner. "I can remember not that long ago, if the phone rang five times in the day, that was a busy day. We'd gotten the building as a gift from the widow of a partner in Lehmann Brothers. A closet women's libber. Last month we turned down an offer of half a mil from a group of Japanese investors. For ten years we scrimped and saved, badgered and bartered until now we're more than self-sustaining. And not a cent have we taken from Albany or Washington. So, Laura, if you decide to join us, you'll be signing on with a very solid, upstanding organization."

In the short time left, I tried to divert the lyrically waxing Violet to the subject of children. She refused to be moved. "We've done wonderful things here, my little family and I. We've built a community, a network, a refuge. Our alchemists have changed hopeless wrecks into independent human beings. We've taught women never to rely on a man, even the best of them, even a man like Bruno Coletti. For the hand that caresses can never be the hand that liberates."

My eyes wandered to the bookshelf and the small marble

horse almost buried beneath the avalanche of papers, journals, and newsletters. I got up from my seat and took it off the shelf.

"It's a Coletti," said Violet. "If you haven't noticed, all the rooms have paintings and small statuettes like the horse, all done by him. He's sold quite a few to clients who asked about them. We've never promoted his work actively, even though he was the one founding father of TWC, among all the founding mothers. He's worked with us since on all sorts of projects."

There was nothing wrong with that, as far as I could see. He was doing good deeds—whatever they were—and trying to earn a living.

I tried for the last time to corner Violet, finally succeeding. Violet had her philosophy of children all mapped out. "They're fine—in their time, in their place. But once they're adults, you've done your work and you must walk away. Regardless. You can't keep trying to edit a book that's already printed." Violet ran her hand over her unattractive face, rumpling it even more than her desk, her room. "I raised my boys as best I could, gave them what the limitations of my ignorance and incompetence allowed. Then I stepped aside. One died, one went to California, and the third is living in Mexico among Chinese immigrants and the drug trade. None writes, calls, or shows the tiniest interest. I gave up on them, wrote them out of my concern. Now I live for myself and my interests. That's the ultimate liberation for women, you know: freedom from children."

I left worse than when I'd arrived. Violet and the Women's Consortium had nothing to offer me and I had nothing to offer them. Did I really have to be told that she and Bruno were such old friends? Did I need to see a woman *that* liberated, *that* child-free?

# *thirteen*

IRGINIA JUST picked herself up and left. No explanation, no apology for deserting me for the weekend, no suggestion that I come along with her. I'd quit the store early that Friday afternoon with the intention of dinner out and a movie. She was dying to see *My Life As a Dog*, a lovely little foreign import.

I found her in the bedroom zipping up a blue canvas overnight bag, dressed in a white blouse, tan skirt, and tan high heel shoes, looking as prim and proper as the schoolteacher she once was. Outside a cab waited, its motor running.

"Take care of things, Gerber. I'll see you Sunday night." She pursed her lips and blew me a kiss rather than smear her lipstick. I stood there nodding. Letting it happen.

Then she was gone. It was the third time she'd done that. Once in March, once in April, and now. I'd said nothing while she came and went like a spy.

Each time, I'd shrugged off her absence, speculation increasing as to where she'd gone, noticing in myself at the same time a growing sense of loneliness, an empty feeling. I'd missed her.

When she'd return late Sunday night, she'd bring with her from that mysterious place a moodiness, an irritability you could spoon with a ladle.

One of the things that bothered me on the two previous occasions was why she never asked to be picked up at the airport or bus terminal. I worked Fridays, so she had reason to call a cab, but Sundays I was always free. Sundays were usually together time for us.

But we had our noninterference pact and, possibly because of it, were getting along so fabulously that I decided to avoid the issue altogether.

It was, however, the worst of times for Virginia to be away. Eighteen years ago, on the same weekend in May, Bobbi had been conceived. I'd dreaded the anniversary of sorts, hoping to block it out with a full schedule of activities centering around Virginia: dining out all three nights, that foreign film, my Sunday ball game, puttering around the house, and extensive lovemaking.

After Virginia left, the house grew unbearably empty and dark, as though she'd taken every sign of life with her, the very air I breathed. I sat in that garage sale of a living room, in the shedding mohair chair, wondering if I'd made any recovery at all since Bobbi's death, if I could long so for a woman I'd known only a few months. I'd stopped taking work home from the store, so there was nothing for me to do. I hadn't opened a book since the Civil War anthology.

Every year, the Five Towns United Way celebrated itself and its accomplishments with a dinner-dance. The Red Feather Ball was held at the club, as were most of the social events that filled the calendars of Five Towners and kept the clothes shops busy year round. Once Bobbi had called out to me from the *Nassau Herald*—the local newspaper—ten separate high-gloss happenings for the month. She'd punctuated each announcement with the cry of "dinner-dance," simulating the frozen smiles of its participants as the cameras blinked and the Magicubes popped. "How do they get any work done with all that partying?" Bobbi had asked.

Little did my daughter know that the Red Feather Ball had been the stimulus for her conception.

That evening, Laura was exceptionally lovely in her powder blue, off-the-shoulder gown, the one that emphasized the fine lines of her neck and upper torso. Her hair was up and I could smell just a hint of fragrance surrounding her.

Though she was only a minor official in the United Way, the other guests treated her with great deference as we whirled around the floor. The orchestra played a popular love song and I mouthed the lyrics in her ear.

Laura smiled and waved with equal sincerity to friends, acquaintances, and enemies. She knew how beautiful she was that night and could be wonderfully magnanimous.

Smiling, waving, she whispered to me, "My, my. The Brodskys aren't here. I heard they've separated. The Delmans too. So many good marriages dying. Everyone's wondering who's next. Mark, it's like a horrible game of Ten Little Indians."

After the standard roast-beef dinner, while the orchestra rested, I retreated to the bar. Laura found me alone, munching on a celery stalk, swishing a Tom Collins. My tolerance for such affairs had peaked and she knew just where I'd be holed up, the mood I'd be in.

"Poor Mark. If there's no one to discuss the Grant administration with, or the Pyramids, you're miserable."

"Not so, honey. I'll talk about almost anything if it's not dull or asinine. Take Aaron Fleming over there, in his denim suit, his rings, his gold chains and medallion. All the idiot wants to talk about is his golf score and the fine young ass he's screwing. Awfully brazen of him—there were half a dozen of us there. Didn't he think it would get back to Violet?"

"It's a game they play, Mark. There's no 'fine young ass' in his life. Violet knows it, I know it, and so does the whole town."

The musicians returned to their instruments, and this time they did Cole Porter. As we glided to "I've Got You Under My Skin," I could feel Laura dissolving, entering my pores, filling me.

"Of course you're right about this whole business being a terrible bore. And a waste of money."

"Then let's go home and make love," I said.

"Later. We have to stay. Honestly, Mark. All this hype goes with the territory and we really do some good with the money we raise. Besides, these are the very folks who patronize Cedarhurst Chemists. Smile at Violet Fleming, dear. I know you can't stand her but she's raised a fortune for local charities and the community. And hold the smile a few seconds longer because we're everyone's image of what's right with being attractive, faithful, and solvent."

"Are you fertile tonight?" I asked, uncertain, because the progesterone shots she was getting from the specialist had skewed her entire system.

"Very, I think. At least that's the way I feel," she said seductively.

"Let's leave right now."

"Right now?"

"I may not be able to hold out until we get home."

Laura considered my situation for another few seconds as the orchestra began "Night and Day." "Get my wrap and meet me at the front door in sixty seconds."

Nine months less than two weeks later, Bobbi was born.

———————

To speed evening into night, I prepared a large tuna salad with preparations worthy of a master chef. Hoping it would take a few hours to prepare, eat casually, and clean up after. My menu consisted of meticulously diced celery, feather-light carrot shavings, microchips of green pepper, and geometrically perfect apple squares thoroughly blended in the tuna with diet mayonnaise and decoratively cupped in florets of lettuce leaves, then topped with tomato wheels. Toast, a beverage of orange juice, seltzer, and a dash of vermouth. It was a masterpiece of creative time-wasting.

After the last dish had been washed and put away, the garbage disposed of, I tried Friday-night TV and found it to be an even sparser wasteland than Newton Minow had once described.

I could have gone to O'Hara's and hoisted a few with Timmy and Dennis and talked Yankee baseball and Irish politics. I was now accepted there, and it would have killed a few lengthy hours. But not without Virginia, who made such visits endurable.

Or I could have gone to a movie. But the sad truth was I'd come to depend on her more than I should have. More than I'd ever depended on Laura. It couldn't possibly be that she alone made the world tolerable for me. In half a century I'd never depended on anyone but myself for that.

I got through Friday night thanks to the hectic pace during the day. I was relearning the retail business and it hadn't escaped me that regardless of outcome, Eric had done me a great service. His leaving had shaken my staid, unreal business world to its foundations. Not as violently as Bobbi's death had, but still, a minor tremor. Before he'd left, my life at Cedarhurst Chemists had been a smooth sail on calm waters in a luxury ocean liner. I'd managed to avoid the shoals and rocks consistent with running a business. And now, when other retailers my age were planning retirement or taking in younger partners, I was starting over. It could be quite an adventure.

My new manager, Chuck Eisenberg, was proving to be efficient, aggressive, and patient with customers. A good man. I arranged to leave him in charge and take off Saturday. To spend time with Virginia. Who was now God knows where.

---

Saturday morning began much like the fourth day of creation: a cloudless Prussian blue firmament of heaven, a friendly sun, the sense of a spankingly clean Earth.

Everything inside the house was now in working order. No leaky faucets, no clogged drains or faulty windows. I turned my newly learned talents outdoors to the backyard and its intermittent fence that had been nagging me for weeks. How would she feel if I branched out and took over the thirty-by-forty plot behind the house? If I refenced and tilled the land?

I took the chance. The fence hadn't been cared for in years. Over the winter, a few more slats had loosened and hung at rakish angles from the horizontal rails, subject to every stray dog, malicious child, or gust of wind.

At the lumber yard I spent a hundred dollars for slats, new round posts, and creosote to make the post ends unappetizing to termites and carpenter ants. By ten A.M. I was back at the bungalow removing the broken pieces, ripping up the insect-ridden posts. They came out easily, resembling stumps of rotten teeth.

Robert Frost was right about good fences making good neighbors. I was no more than two hours into this labor of love when a dignified-appearing gentleman in a straw hat and Bermuda shorts appeared at my side. A whimsical Maker had drilled two tiny holes in his head for a pair of cold, steel-blue eyes, then slapped on ears that stood at right angles to his head, and added an undefined mass of silly putty for a nose.

"Morning," I said, acknowledging his interest.

"Morning," he said in return.

"Mark Gerber."

"John Tierney."

Solemnly we shook hands. Then he turned his scrutiny to my fence work. Gave it his utmost attention. I leaned on the shovel I'd bought to dig out the old posts and turn the soil for my garden. He leaned on the cane he carried in his right hand. I had the giddy impression that we were a song-and-dance team about to go into a snappy routine.

"You work too fast and too steady to be a workman, so you must live here."

"I do."

"Virginia's new fella. I heard about you over at the firehouse. Heard you're not too bad a ball player for a guy your age. Why the devil anyone at any age would want to fry on a hot, dusty ball field is something I can't figure out. But if you're with Virginia, I guess that explains it."

I gave him my best shit-eating grin. We talked. Rather, he did, an expert, I soon learned, in chatter, gossip, and those petty concerns that mark the truly idle, the quotidian requisites I'd never mastered.

I edged my way back to work. John Tierney didn't seem to mind my efforts while he spoke. In his ramblings he treated me to a history of the bungalow.

"First owner was some kind of Broadway director. Right before the Depression. I was a rookie cop back then, pounding a beat on Staten Island. Nice man; sort of gay. Only back then we called them 'fags.'

"He lost it to the bank in '33. They turned around and sold it for taxes to a schoolteacher. Civil servants were the only ones earning steady wages then. When he died, his widow sold it to a World War II veteran and his German bride, then went to live in Arizona. Bad move. Never live with your children. They treat their dogs better. The Carlinskis stayed about ten years, then moved back to Germany to live with her folks.

"The Costellos brought the place in 'fifty-seven or 'fifty-eight. Nice people. Italians. They had no kids. Never home. Owned a 7-Eleven in Elmhurst. Then Mike Healy bought it from them in the middle seventies. Strange character. He worked in a bank. Rode a motorcycle to and from work in downtown Brooklyn. He married Virginia, a mismatch if I ever saw one. I went to the wedding. Nice affair. Catered. Unlimited liquor. They lived fine for a while, give or take a few screaming matches. Then one day, seven, eight years ago, he just took off. I expect Virginia must have told you. She's a pretty honest kid."

"Yes, she did," I said, daubing the tapered point of a new post with cresote, inhaling the odor and liking it. John Tierney didn't seem to care if I was listening or not.

"I guess it was the kid that made him do it."

"The kid?"

"Yeah, Lawrence. The one she goes upstate to see."

"Oh, that kid."

"Totally disabled—that's pretty hard for parents to live with. Especially Mike Healy. Such a big and healthy guy. Guess he couldn't handle it, his kid being that way."

I continued to work, though I wanted to be rid of John Tierney. I needed the room to digest this new element. Not a mention of the boy in all our time together. Not even a photograph of him in the entire house.

"And now it's you and Virginia," he said. I could feel his beady blue eyes trying to pry information from me for his chronicle. "Hope it works out," he said, with the indifference of one convinced it would not, "you look like a nice fella."

After he left, I worked mechanically on the fence, the joy of manual labor sucked out of me. I broke for lunch, then finished painting the final slat just as the afternoon turned cold and cloudy, the bay beyond the road black and choppy.

That night, the house grew even lonelier, more tomblike. This new side to Virginia had put her even further away from me. Through a long, hot shower I considered the man who'd taken French leave at her moment of greatest need—if that was the true story and not some warped version, a product of rumor and hearsay.

None of the food she'd left tempted me. I had to get out for a few hours. I ended up at a fish restaurant on Sunrise we'd never visited, and ordered a salad, baked shrimp in a basket, and coffee. I finished quickly and drove to Tim's place.

For a Saturday night there wasn't much doing. Tim at once buttonholed me with his complaints. "VCRs. They've taken away the night trade. People would rather stay at home in front of that damned box and watch other people fornicate and kill one another instead of enjoying some decent conversation and a few pints."

"That's the truth," I said, and sipped the beer Timmy drew me without my asking.

Dennis Casey joined us before I could wangle any information from O'Hara. He bought the next round of beers, I bought the one after, and the house stood for the one after that.

Growing groggy, I patiently waited for the question that would eventually have to come. I endured an eternity of pseudo-psychiatry, crypto-philosophy, misinformation, and just plain horseshit from both men and from myself. Finally, circling the room with his eyes, toting up the singles, couples, and the assorted groups of Saturday nighters, Dennis said, "Where's that ball-busting woman of yours?"

"She's gone upstate," I said.

"Oh yeah. To see Lawrence," said O'Hara.

"To see Lawrence," I agreed. "Too bad about the kid," I said, offering them a foundation to build on.

But the subject of Virginia's son went by, never to return on the carousel. Unlike John Tierney, my two drinking companions refused to elaborate on her misfortune. They hadn't come to this refuge to dwell on misery. Only fun talk here.

I hung around a little while longer, then said good night to all that knew me. Bleary-eyed, slurred-tongued, Tim said, "Tomorrow at noon. By the firehouse. Get a good night's sleep, Mark-O. We've got ourselves a tough one this week."

---

In the morning light, the fence looked all white and shiny and whole. The flat, scrawny acreage it enclosed, however, could have been the barren steppes of central Asia. And so to work.

I decided not to put all of it under cultivation since I wasn't that experienced. I'd grown only one crop in my entire life. Maybe I was talented in tomatoes and nothing else.

The back half seemed the most promising. I diagrammed it first on paper: six plots, beginning on the right. The first top right for giant tomatoes, then below it bell peppers. The two center sections for peas and beans. On the left, one part for corn, one for potatoes. Plenty of border between the crops for pathways and irrigation hoses.

I spent the morning breaking through the thick layers of crabgrass to turn the soil beneath. The sun felt like analgesic balm on my bare back and shoulders. Sweat poured off my forehead and from under my neck. Pools of it welled in the small of my back, then ran down into my jockey shorts.

The soil itself was sandy and not very arable. I'd have to water and fertilize constantly, to do for the backyard what the Israelis had done for the Negev. The unearthed rocks I piled by the kitchen door. The beginnings of an outdoor barbecue fireplace. We farmers wasted nothing.

By eleven I was done and done in. The second half of the plot had been transformed into a plowed field ready for planting. Next Sunday I'd finish up, maybe involve Virginia in the enterprise. We could farm together like pioneers.

---

A ten-car procession of ball players, wives, sweethearts, and admirers made its way down Rockaway Turnpike, along Peninsula Boulevard, across Merrick Road, then to a high-school ball field that was the home of the Valley Stream Tigers, the league champs. They were waiting for us—the team and their fans who'd filled to capacity the four tiers to the left and right of home plate.

They seemed invincible, those Tigers in their orange and blue uniforms, brawny burnished giants of men who swung two and three bats together as though they were flyswatters.

We began infield practice and were instantly booed. I scanned the hostile crowd for Sara. She taught at the school and I hoped she might be there. I hadn't seen her since that confrontation in Virginia's kitchen months ago. On the telephone she'd been cold and formal, declining my repeated invitations to lunch. Mostly yeses and no's, leaving me with a sour taste in my mouth. Sara, Sara, I thought, picking Tim's warm-up grounders out of the dirt and firing them to Dennis at first. What's to become of us? Where was that inquisitive, pesty child who'd once wanted to know everything but now refused to hear a single word of explanation about what had happened to her father. His changed existence. His new life.

As we warmed up, I could feel the crowd's enmity come across on the same gentle breezes that brought us the smells of the vendors' hot dogs. Uniformly unruly. Jeeringly partisan. The guillotine spectators during the French Revolution must have been like these Tigers' fans.

On the mound, Dr. Bill Feely had been a doubtful starter for our side. A first-year resident at St. Joseph's, Dr. Bill had finished his thirty-six-hour shift at four A.M., and forty winks later had been pushed from bed by Dennis's sister with whom he was living farther up the beach.

A decent gloveman at second, Amos Peters seldom hit the ball out of the infield. Which didn't bother Amos in the least. He was in his thirties—the oldest man on the team before my arrival—and a top-notch auto mechanic for Sears out in Hicksville. I covered shortstop, doing my level best, earning my keep, according to Dennis, who wasn't about to have any player around solely for companionship.

Paul Giovanelli was at third. He owned a small tire store in Bayside and was married to Dennis's other sister. The outfield was patrolled by the three Ryan brothers—James, John, and Joseph. The Unholy Trinity, Tim called them. All three were redheads, simple of mind, slow of foot, but rollicking good fun off the field and on.

The first few innings went along uneventfully for both sides with mostly ground balls aimed straight at our gloves and a few lazy shag flies the Ryans ate up. In the center field Joe attempted to enliven things by dancing a jig under his two putouts, then bobbing the balls three or four times before securing them.

Seventh inning, the score tied two all. Jimmy Ryan began our half with a cannon shot that caromed off the third baseman's knee into left field. Dennis moved him to second with a long fly ball deep to center. In the on-deck circle, I swung two bats, the blood of a teenager parading up my veins. Behind our bench, the women of Devon who didn't know me and shied away at O'Hara's even with Virginia by my side, began chanting my name: "Mark-O. Mark-O."

The first pitch I fouled off: too eager. The next two were high and wide. The Tiger catcher didn't think so, grumbling under his breath about the old man the Devils had scraped the bottom of the barrel to find.

The next pitch had the catcher's face on it and I punished him severely. The ball sailed over the third baseman's head, scoring Jimmy, who hopped around the bag as if on a pogo stick.

Our bench and my newfound admirers went wild. They were small voices in that large crowd, but to my ears it sounded like the roar of the ocean.

Amos Peters and Timmy ended this most glorious inning by striking out. I passed the catcher on the way to the bench to get my glove. He said almost happily, "You're dead meat, pal."

"What was I supposed to do, *pal?* Have a heart attack at the plate?"

"Something like that," he said, deadpan.

Bill tossed hitless ball for the next two innings, as did the Tiger pitcher. Then, in the bottom of the ninth, the young doctor faltered. He allowed a two-out double to the catcher, my nemesis.

The cleanup hitter stepped to the plate, a giant pillar of a man, six-foot-six, two hundred and fifty pounds of reinforced concrete.

At second, Amos tugged at his right ear: the sign to the catcher for a pickoff play. Tim flashed the sign back to Billy, who wheeled around and threw to the bag.

The runner was completely fooled and found himself stranded between second and third, as disoriented as a baby bird that had fallen out of the nest.

We began to run down: second to third, third to second, second to shortstop. The gap narrowed, the trapped man making shorter and shorter dashes between bases. Then, like the cornered animal he'd become, he grew vicious and deadly. My being the man with the ball only made matters worse. He lowered his head and charged me. I gripped the ball to tag him but I couldn't properly prepare myself. He hit me broadside. I went down hard.

I was out for at least ten seconds, to hear Timmy and the boys tell it. My first words—the gospel according to O'Hara—were, "Did I get him?"

I don't remember that. I do recall opening my eyes, seeing first a blur of concerned faces, then closer up, clearly, Virginia's lovely eyes inches from mine. She was sitting on the ground, in the base path, in her tan skirt and white blouse, holding my head, stroking my face. There was a small blue bottle of smelling salts in her other hand. She'd finished waving it under my nose.

"How do you feel, slugger?" she asked.

"You mean sluggee," I said. "God, it's good to see you again. I missed you."

"Well, that big son of a bitch didn't miss you."

"Is the game over?"

"Oh, shut up, stupid. I'm gone a couple of hours and look what you get yourself into," she said, helping me to stand.

Dennis on one side, Tim on the other, Virginia carrying my glove, I was helped off the field. The catcher, brushing himself off, came up to me. "Didn't mean to knock the wind out of you," he said. "Meant to cripple you."

"Fuck off, creep," Virginia told him, suddenly aroused. She'd been subdued and reserved, perhaps frightened by seeing me out cold. Now she seemed capable of tearing him apart with her bare hands. I didn't mind taking the hit for that lovely show of concern.

Virginia waved Tim and Dennis off and took me to the car. She drove home, slowing every few minutes to check on my eyes, touch my forehead, make sure I wasn't bleeding from the ears or mouth.

When we were in front of the bungalow, she turned nasty. "Idiot. Asshole. Getting yourself banged up that way. For a stupid *game.*"

"Okay, okay, you're right," I said, not to get her off my back but so I might shut her mouth in order to kiss it. I was so damned happy to see her again. She was all dusty from the ball field, her blouse soiled and stained from holding my head.

I did manage to kiss her in the car, but it was cold porridge I tasted, not warm lips.

"You're home early," I said, trying to take her overnight bag from her as we walked up the path to the house. She refused to release it.

"How observant," she spat out. "I guess that bastard didn't scramble all your eggs."

"Anything bad happen?"

"Nope," said Virginia with utter finality.

And that was all she said for the longest while. She showered, and when she came down I took mine. A Chinese takeout delivery arrived and we ate supper in awesome silence, as though we were Benedictine monks. Now and then Virginia checked me for signs of concussion.

When we were finished eating and at the sink, cleaning up, I took her hand. "Listen, if it bothers you that much, I won't play ball anymore. We'll go over to O'Hara's later and I'll tender my resignation."

"You're a real dummy, Gerber. Do you know that?" she said, pushing me away. "Come outside a minute."

I followed her out the kitchen door. She strode with tigerish ferocity.

The white fence looked even better in fading light, uniform and even. The posts gleamed like the minarets on a mosque. The soil I'd turned over seemed alive, fertile.

"What are you doing to my backyard?" she asked. Her vocal cords must have been as tight as bowstrings to emit that strident a tone.

"Cultivating it."

"I think maybe you've gone too far. I think maybe you should stop this cultivating nonsense."

"What do you mean too far? I only did half the yard."

"You know goddamned well what I mean. This fixing up. This improving. This saddling me with obligation. When you leave, who's going to do all the weeding, the watering, the . . . whatever you do to make the stuff grow?"

"I don't plan on leaving, not for a long time. Maybe even forever. I like it here, Virginia. I love it here. I—"

"Don't go any further, okay? I don't want any promises or crap like that. I told you so before. This business with the yard is a kind of promise."

"Only for one season, Virginia. Don't you think we're going to last until fall? Don't you want to?"

She waited until her breathing had become more regular. I waited, too. Her move.

"All right, Gerber. You can go ahead with your victory garden, but if you should decide to take off next month or the month after, I'm going to let everything rot on the vine. Understand? I won't come out here and weed and water or help myself to your veggies. I won't. I'm not kidding. I'll open the gate and let the rabbits and raccoons in. I'll tell the neighbors to help themselves."

"It won't happen, Virginia, but if it does, then it's all right with me."

"You'll have nothing to say about it." She was almost shouting. "It's my house. My land. My whatever-the-hell you intend growing."

Inwardly, I grinned. "Corn and peas, beans and tomatoes, peppers and potatoes."

"Well, I don't want to know about any of it, even if you are around. I don't want to be obligated to you in any way."

"It's not the same thing as paying rent, Virginia."

"Oh, shut up. This conversation's boring the shit out of me."

"I didn't start it," I said. I braced for her next line—she was good at next lines—but it never came. It lay there between us like some dead animal. It remained at my feet even after she'd stomped into the house and slammed the back door.

---

We lay in bed, faceup, side by side, reading the ceiling. The lights were out, the curtains drawn against a full moon. We couldn't see a thing, which gave us a kind of anonymity and freedom.

I said, "Why don't you tell me where you go every month?"

"Why don't you mind your own business?"

"Your neighbors seem to know. John Tierney told me without my asking or hinting."

"John Tierney is an old busybody. I don't live with John Tierney. I don't sleep with John Tierney. What he knows or doesn't know can't hurt me."

I sighed. "We're back to that again. Tell me, how can I be anything to you, anything at all, if I don't know the basics? We just can't live together and make love night after night and not confess things. You know almost everything about me, but you don't want me to know anything about you. Except that you've had three husbands, you work at the Arden, and you're tougher than shoe leather. Well, the truth is I know a lot more than you think."

"Oh? Like what?"

"Like you're afraid of closeness. You're afraid to tell me about Lawrence because then I might feel sorry for you and hang around for the wrong reason. Or just maybe sharing Lawrence with me would be sharing too much of yourself. Invulnerability is great for castles and armadillos, but lousy for people."

"Stop it," she said softly. "I've had a rough day and I don't care to fight anymore."

"That's fine with me, only I won't leave this thing between us hanging in midair." I stopped. Waited. "Now, tell me why you're home early. It wasn't to see me play ball and make a punching bag of myself."

She moved away from me, to the wall, and waited a long while.

"Lawrence was born ten years ago severely handicapped. Blind, deaf, brain-damaged. I don't know why. There was no cause the doctors could isolate. But Mike blamed me anyway. The dissolute life I'd led before he'd married me. He was a strange man, so quick to blame, a perfectionist. He couldn't bear the thought that something he had a hand in was less than perfect. He even accused me of becoming pregnant by another man.

"After it became obvious about Lawrence, Mr. Healy took off on his motorcycle. Bag and baggage. I haven't seen him since. I guess I could have gone on welfare, let the state take care of Lawrence, but you know the third-rate care he'd get under Medicaid. It was better all around to put him in a good facility and pay my way. There's this fine hospital near Albany that handles such cases. Five hundred a week, but it's worth it. The newest techniques, the best doctors, the most caring staff. One weekend a month I go up and stay at a motel for two days. Try and keep a line open. Only every month there's less and less communication, if that's what Lawrence and I have. Sometimes he doesn't seem to know I'm there. Then, this morning, he threw a fit over nothing and I was told to leave, maybe come back next month.

They'd let me know. My child, and they'd let me know when I could see him again."

I reached for her hand. It was coming to meet mine. She moved against me and lay in my arms. Sex would have been all wrong, so I just held her.

"Are you sure you're all right?" she asked. "You took some wallop. You were really out. I got there just as you were beginning the rundown."

"Out like a light."

"You don't feel dizzy or lightheaded?"

"Not from that bum on the field. From you. That drubbing you gave me after dinner."

"You deserved it."

"Did you mean to cripple me, too?"

"Oh, Gerber, you're really trying my patience."

We lay that way, asexually, for some time longer. She stirred and changed position, over me this time, which tested my restraint to the full.

"Make love to me," she said. "Make it long. Don't just fuck me, Gerber."

Afterward, we still couldn't fall asleep. We couldn't talk much either, remaining in the recessed wells of ourselves.

"Won't you even try the tomatoes?" I said. "I grow very good tomatoes."

Virginia groaned. "When I'm ready. Without your asking. Okay?"

"Okay."

"Want to talk some more? Not about vegetables."

"If you like. But I've got to get up early and go to work. You, on the other hand, can loll in bed all morning."

"I don't *loll*. Five Towns women *loll*. I rest up, conserve my strength for the workday ahead. I'm a very hardworking kid. I'm also a goddamned bitch, aren't I, Gerber?"

"I've known worse, kiddo. But none better. Does that make sense to you?"

"Kinda, sort of. See you in the morning."

# *fourteen*

O<small>N THE DAY</small> before Memorial Day, my father died in his sleep. Alone and peacefully, I hope, although the latter is only wishful thinking. We'd grown more than a little estranged since Mark left and Bruno moved in. Daddy had refused to set foot in the house with Bruno there. He never came to dinner anymore or dropped by for coffee on Sunday nights. We'd meet once in a while at a local restaurant and vainly try to carry on a conversation. I thought, given time, he'd eventually come around. As it turned out, he had no time left.

My father had no pain, either, according to Rudy Frank, who pronounced him dead. "A heart attack, like some thief in the night, stole him away," said the good and gentle doctor, knowing my fondness for poetic imagery. Rudy could also say this safely to me because he'd taken care of all of us all our lives. He'd given us our yearly checkups and pronounced both my daughters physically fit for marriage, danced with each at their weddings, and found the proper specialist when I was having difficulty conceiving Bobbi.

I'd gotten a phone call from Israel Rodriguez, the building superintendent at the Dorsett, on Memorial Day. The day before Bruno and I had been to Port Jefferson and taken the ferry ride across the Sound to Bridgeport, Connecticut. It had been a lovely day on the water, and in the evening we'd eaten in a little out-of-the-way German restaurant that had photos on its walls of Berlin theater notables from the twenties: Max Reinhardt, Peter Lorre, von Sternberg.

Mr. Rodriguez called to tell me he'd had an appointment to change a faucet washer in Daddy's kitchen that morning, but there'd been no response to his repeated knocking. The Sunday *News* was still sitting on the doorstep.

I called Rudy and asked him to meet us there, then Bruno and I hurried over with the spare set of keys. We found my father in bed, lying on his right side, curled up like a dried leaf, one hand under his head, the other on his thigh, as I'd seen him a thousand times before. His eyes were closed, his face as placid as after I'd played him to sleep with my flute. I'd like to think that at the end my father was listening to the music inside his head.

Like Bobbi, my father had left without saying good-bye, and in his case so much more. "That's the down side of going quickly," said Rudy, who arrived a few minutes after we did, but couldn't do a thing for him. "Look at it this way: he didn't die from Alzheimer's, he didn't have cancer or a stroke, or any of those humiliating diseases. He was himself until the end. Believe me, Laura, I've seen people leave this earth under conditions I wouldn't wish on my worst enemy. Irving Peres went out a class act."

We were in the kitchen when he said this, waiting for the ambulance. On Irving's refrigerator were photographs of the entire family, whole, as if nothing had happened to us.

Perhaps under different circumstances I might have agreed with Rudy. But there'd been so much unfinished business between my father and myself. So much I had to explain to him, whether he wanted to listen or not. I'd been determined to make him understand that I hadn't suddenly become loose and irresponsible. Sex had little to do with it. The problem had started forty years ago and it wasn't Mark's fault or mine.

I could only hope that beneath the surface of my father's current displeasure with me lay a bedrock of solid faith, and if I couldn't have his blessings with Bruno, I might at least gain his forgiveness and eventually a kind of acceptance. Removed to the neutral territory of restaurants, however, he wouldn't even allow me to begin an explanation. All he wanted to hear about was his grandchildren, as though I was merely a source of information like his *Daily News*.

The girls took my father's death very badly. When we'd gotten home, I called them at once. They were there within the hour. We embraced long and tearfully at the front door. By dying, my father had wiped out all the hard feelings between us. They hadn't been to the house since the beginning of the month when they'd found Bruno in the backyard and me in my bikini.

It had been a most trying time to meet Bruno, but meet him they did. Formally, coldly on their part, in the kitchen, where he'd paced nervously, like an about-to-be father in a hospital waiting room, a teacup in his hand to steady him. Under the circumstances, I couldn't expect more. For his part, Bruno acted very correctly, remaining farther from me than usual, after a while asking the girls and their husbands if he could help in any way and would they like something to drink, as though he were a servant.

The rest of the day we sat around, confined to my den reminiscing about Irving. The bamboo blinds were drawn, but through the cracks we could see rain beginning to fall, hear it beat on the windowpanes like padded feet.

For hours, the girls went on about their wonderful "gramps," reciting those stories of his funny habits that had made him so endearing. I joined in, repeating what Rudy Frank had said about the indignities of old age he'd avoided and how he'd departed in typical Irving Peres style. "Gramps was a man of grace all his life and he left life gracefully," I said. I was beginning to believe Rudy.

My daughters were not overtly rude to Bruno. They just had nothing to say to him. In their eyes, he hardly existed. And, wisely, Bruno didn't try to interject himself into our recollections. He remained out of our immediate sphere, near the door, but close enough to make eye contact with me and send what support he could. I felt so much better with Bruno close by.

In my own house, composed and stronger by early evening, I thought I could see to all the details of Daddy's funeral. There was no one else. I couldn't ask Mark, though he would have helped had I called him. And Bruno wouldn't know where to begin. When I dialed the funeral director at Kaplan Brothers and began to falter, Warren asked if he could take over.

"Yes. Yes, I'd appreciate that. Thank you. You have carte blanche, but please make everything as simple as possible. The kind of funeral he wouldn't be ashamed of."

I gave Warren my phone book and Daddy's desktop phone book and left matters in his hands. He whispered a few words to his wife, then asked Steven to follow. They went into Mark's den across the house and shut the door.

With this shift, Bruno became an even more remote figure as the girls and I closed ranks and continued our own personal memorial to Irving. Soon Bruno left the room and I heard the kitchen door close, then saw the light go on in the garage. Bruno was almost finished with *The Flutist*. It stood grandly, heroically, in the backyard against all forms of weather, with only its legs to be freed from the block of stone. Bruno had started sketching a new subject in the garage. A surprise, he'd said. He'd left us to go to work on it, standing at an old wooden podium under a sixty-watt bulb, transported to his other world and not fazed a bit by my clannish, remote daughters.

When I reconsider the funeral today, I'm not too distressed at the small attendance at the chapel. Irving would have wanted to leave the world in the same anonymous manner he'd lived his life.

Sleepy-eyed and yawning, looking bored, Nat Gerber had been able, this time, to attend the last rites for his old enemy. He couldn't make the funeral of the granddaughter he said he loved to distraction, but he was here. To me, this said volumes about the perverse Gerber character.

Before services and before the gathering in the anteroom, Mark had come to me. Alone. He'd had the good sense to leave his girlfriend at home, though if he'd brought her along, what could I do? Wasn't Bruno here with me?

"I'm sorry, Laura," he said, meaning it. "I cared very much about Irving. He was the best man I've ever known."

"Thank you, Mark. He always said the same about you. In spite of everything."

Again Rabbi Davidson gave the eulogy as he had for Bobbi. In a short ceremony, he extolled "a man who'd made an outstanding name for himself in his community. A loyal son of Israel, a loving husband and father who single-handedly raised a daughter when his wife had died all too young. Husband, father, grandfather, businessman, volunteer, patriarch: he bore all these offices exceptionally well. He always gave more than he received."

This time the rabbi got it right. As he spoke, I searched my mind, trying to recall the husband portion of the eulogy. Sadly, I could only speculate on the nature of his love, only guess at what kind of husband he'd been. I remember very little of my mother, except that she was always ill. A scrap, an image, comes to me at odd times, a fleeting moment in my dreams that vanishes before I can solidify it in my mind or write it down. I recall the Boardwalk in Coney Island. Hot dogs at Nathan's. Lobsters at Lundy's. A ride out into the country, horses galloping wildly around a white-fenced track on a hot summer's day, their coats shiny with sweat, flecks of foam on their pink-purple muzzles. Not much of an early childhood to cherish and draw upon. It must be that a benevolent hand had wiped the slate clean. Otherwise, I might have spent years on a psychiatrist's couch coming to terms with my paltry inheritance of memories. I might have even learned to hate my father for his smothering ways, his inability to communicate, instead of loving him, understanding the terrible injury he'd received and his need to shelter me.

Oh, it's going to be so lonely and so hard without him, I thought, not bothering to hold back the tears, not ashamed to let everyone, including Bruno, see me weep. Why should love cost so much? I asked myself again. It was an old question by now.

On either side of me, Caryn and Sara continued to take my father's death very badly. Unlike most kids their ages, they'd never considered grandparents to be doddering fools, objects of ridicule or scorn or condescension. Perhaps because Irving had never spoken down to them. He treated his grandchildren as intelligent human beings, equals—even if they weren't. At worst, he was teased a bit, especially when his generosity got out of hand.

"I *have* a good stereo, Gramps," Sara had told him on her seventeenth birthday. We'd had a small celebration—the family, a few close friends bearing low-key gifts. They well knew Sara's Spartan tastes. After the birthday cake, my father toted in four huge crates containing the quality of stereo equipment usually found in professional recording studios.

Sara had been embarrassed by the boxes that filled the room like city high rises.

"I got a fantastic buy on it," Irving offered as excuse. An obvious lie, since we all knew he never shopped for bargains. "Put it away for your apartment after you get out of college."

"Stop encouraging her, Daddy," I told him when we were alone. "It'll happen soon enough without your help. And don't use that awful excuse to dote on her that way."

"If it gives me pleasure and it doesn't harm their characters, why not?"

"Because it'll only keep them from getting married. How can any young man compete with all you've given them?"

My father had his answer ready. "It didn't stop you from getting a nice guy."

"Oh, well," I said in all ignorance. "There aren't many like Mark. I may own the last decent man in captivity."

"They broke the mold?"

"There was no mold for Mark. He was handmade."

And the *Titanic* was unsinkable, the country would never survive without Franklin Delano Roosevelt, and there'd always be a Cary Grant. Famous myopic utterances.

The rabbi's words continued to echo faintly in a room only partially filled with mourners. Without Valium this time, with a kind of detached objectivity, I noticed Mark and his father sitting together in the back row by themselves, almost like outcasts. Mark was getting to look like Nat, both of them handsome, leather-tanned, and rangy, like ex-ranchers turned politicians. Both men had an air of rejuvenation about them, of sexual readiness. Nat had always exuded that quality; I was afraid to be alone with him. Now the son was unconsciously imitating the father. And the terrible thing about Mark recycled was that I could understand how a younger woman might fall madly in love with him. Especially if she'd had a hard life and had been misused by men.

Our family, once the tightest of circles, formed a triangle around the grave. Mark at the apex with the rabbi. Bruno and myself at one foot, the girls and their husbands, at the other.

Listening to those all-too-familiar words, I scanned Bobbi's new headstone, unveiled only recently. Her plot had been properly tended to, the grass trimmed and as thick and green as my mother's.

With even fewer mourners present than in the chapel, my father was laid to rest to the left of Rachel, where he'd always wanted to be.

Mark tossed in the first shovelful of earth after the rabbi. I watched, numb but wondering what life might have been like had my mother lived, borne more children, grown gray and wrinkled, a hands-on grandmother. Brothers and sisters would have radically altered all our lives, our destinies. I might not have gone to that summer camp and met Mark, had his children—these children—lost one of them, found Bruno, had my life turned completely around. Idle speculation, and dangerous, too. Bruno said it best when I told him my thoughts that evening.

"You'll only debilitate yourself thinking about fate, luck, and chance. We live out the lives we're given. We work with the materials at hand, do the best we can, and not wonder if we could have done better if things were different. Or else we self-destruct."

The hardest part of Irving's funeral was the moment services ended and the coffin was consigned to the earth. Until then, my father was among us in a way, an even quieter presence, yet still hovering over my children and me. But once Mark added his portion of earth, I knew my father was gone forever. I felt a loneliness so deep and so wide I thought I would never get over it. Through my tears I could see the gravediggers lumber toward us to complete their work.

We were in the roadway between the blocks and sections of the cemetery. The rabbi and the other mourners had left. Only the family remained. Mark and his father came to me, Mark to say good-bye, Nat to say hello and offer his condolences.

"The man was a legend," said Nat, his white summer suit gray from the rain. "We won't see his like again."

I let Nat kiss me, then he took both girls around at once, his standard hugging act.

Mark stepped forward and introduced himself to Bruno, who'd maintained a low profile all during the burial. I'd dreaded this meeting. I wasn't sure how I'd feel seeing them together. After all, Bruno was inches shorter, bald, not as initially handsome. I was afraid I might fall into the trap of seeing both men through my daughters' eyes.

Bruno stood up very well, offering his hand in return to Mark. They shook briefly.

Caryn didn't miss a second of it, though locked together with her sister in Nat's arms. She broke the hold and came to me. At first I thought she'd come to kiss her father. She hadn't seen him in months and had ignored him all during services. But she walked by Mark as though he wasn't there.

"This is all your fault," she said, her low heels planted firmly on the macadam road.

Sara heard it and came to join her sister, her ally against me. Mark stepped back a pace and stared bewildered at his eldest daughter. Left in the lurch, Nat's arms were open wide, as if he was unaware that what they'd been holding was gone. Only Bruno remained the same, off to one side, not part of the drama.

"You killed him, you know," elaborated Caryn, as if elaboration was necessary. She whirled and faced Mark. "Both of you. With all your nonsense and carrying on."

Her voice was so high-pitched and strident that the birds in the oaks lining the cemetery road grew frightened and flew off. I wished I could join them.

Sara had lined up alongside her sister. Her hair had frizzed in the dampness of the day, covering her perfectly round head like a nest of snakes. She said, "He expected us to stick together when Bobbi died. To become even closer. Was that so much to ask? Was that so much to expect from decent, intelligent people? And when he saw all this weakness and stupidity, it killed him."

"*You* killed him," corrected Caryn, scorching us equally with her eyes.

"Both of you," said Sara. "Murderers."

Caryn raised the sound level. "We hate you both."

Sara: "We don't want to have anything to do with either of you."

Caryn: "Ever."

Like disobedient children being disciplined, Mark and I stood there and took their accusations. Nat turned his back, walked away, and stood in the road as if waiting for a bus. Bruno took it all in from his vantage point. If my father's grave hadn't been filled, I would have leaped into it.

Then the girls left, and with them their in-laws, who'd been waiting in the second limo all the while. The Costas and the Levins must have been appalled at what an unsavory situation their sons had married into.

When they had gone, Mark said, "They'll hate themselves later for what they said. In the end, they'll suffer more than we will because of it. Don't be too hard on them when they try and apologize." He turned to go. "I'll be there tomorrow night for *shiva*. Nat and I both."

Then he left, too. Bruno and I were alone. I told him to wait inside the empty limo, I'd only be a few moments.

I went back to my father's grave. The gravediggers had finished and were disappearing into the fog, as in some weird gothic tale, the shovels over their shoulders.

The grave was smoothed and tamped down. Already, pools of water from a week of rain were rising from it, reflecting the leaves of the trees overhead. A bird, returned now that the girls had gone, drank at the water's edge.

"I'm sorry, Daddy," I said to the flattened ground. "That they behaved so badly. That they weren't kinder, more understanding. That Mark and I made a mess of things. You were disappointed in me and so was I with them. Oh well, maybe Mark is right. Maybe they'll make amends."

Another bird joined the first, and within seconds there was a handful drinking from the water.

"In the remote possibility that there is a soul and yours is about to go to a better place, I want you to tell my mother when you meet her that I love her. And when you see Bobbi again, tell her that I love her, too, and miss her, and so do her sisters and her father. They're really good people but very troubled. And please, not to fret over what's happened. When the time comes, of course, I'll tell her myself."

---

"They turned on me, Bruno, like wild animals."

"It was an ugly sight. I felt so helpless."

"They just tore into us. Blindly. Viciously."

"Terrible. I ached for you."

"My children. My babies."

"Just terrible."

"I bore them. I raised them. They were my life."

"You're tired. Come to bed. I'll give you a good back rub."

"A life's work wasted."

"I could speak to them for you."

"One minute you're cleaning their ears with a Q-Tip, the next they're tearing you to shreds."

"Let me make you some tea."

"Abandoned. They've abandoned me, Bruno. The girls. Bobbi. Mark. My father. In their own way. Each of them."

"That's something I'll never do, Laura. I'll never leave you, darling. Never. Never. Never."

# *fifteen*

K ENNEDY AIRPORT, especially active after the Memorial Day weekend, was like an overturned anthill of incoming tourists, outgoing students on summer vacation, businessmen commuting, babies crying—one being breast-fed—tearful departures, and joyful reunions. I sat in the Delta lounge reading the *Times* for the second time as I waited for Nat's plane, which arrived forty minutes late because of heavy showers over Atlanta and the increased air traffic.

We were undecided about a handshake or an embrace, and settled for grins, first his, showing some new dental work, then mine, a reluctant imitation.

Waiting one floor below at the baggage carousel, we talked in harmless generalties: the Island in summer was only a slight improvement over Dante's Inferno. The food on airplanes sucked. The sky above Kennedy could use traffic cops.

Nat wore a cranberry sport shirt, yellow slacks, and new white sneakers. Somehow, on him, it all seemed vaguely appropriate. He was tan and healthy and I suppose I should have been grateful for that. To the casual eavesdropper, we could have been any two people waiting for luggage from the inanities we offered one another, except that more than ever we looked like father and son.

By nine A.M. we were out of the airport and on Rockaway Turnpike. I headed straight for the chapel in Hewlett. "Nice car," my father said.

"A Volvo," I told him, as if he were blind and couldn't see for himself.

"Not much on pizzazz but a good, safe set of wheels. Dependable."

"Like its owner," I said.

"Lots of traffic," he said, indicating the southbound lane where we moved at a slow pace. "Maybe they'll all going out to Kaplan Brothers to pay their last respects. Irving was a powerful guy. Lots of people owed him favors."

"I guess so," I agreed. When he'd called the night before (how did he get Virginia's number?) and said he might stay a few days this time, I knew I was in for an ordeal. Virginia had taken the call in the kitchen while we were dismantling a bucket of Colonel Sanders. She got up to leave so that I might have some privacy, but I motioned her to stay. She heard my half of the conversation and mouthed that it would be all right with her to put Nat up in the second bedroom. It was unused since Lawrence had left. I vigorously nodded no.

"The motel near the airport is close enough," I told her later. "You don't know who you're inviting into your house. He'll drive you crazy."

"I invited you, didn't I? That didn't work out too badly."

"We're not the same. He's all vinegar and venom and spite."

"A seventy-five-year-old man?"

"You'll see for yourself. We're having dinner tomorrow night, the three of us. Can you take the night off?"

"I wouldn't miss it for the world."

Earlier that day, Warren had called with the sad news. Virginia came and sat opposite me on the couch. She'd been seated at the pianola while invisible fingers played "Ramona." We'd both sung along, knowing the words and not at all surprised about it. In a little while Bill Feely—the Devils' star pitcher and my new friend—and his fiancée were coming over for a backyard barbecue. I'd built a stone grill from all the rocks unearthed making a garden and we were to initiate it together.

I told her about Irving and asked if she cared to attend the funeral.

Virginia didn't have to think it over. "What for? I don't go to the funerals of people I don't know. I don't even go to the funerals of people I *do* know. I hate the damn things."

I knew she'd refuse, but I had to ask. I didn't want her to think I was ashamed of her in any way. I also didn't want her to think I intended showing her off, younger woman and all. Her refusal had solved a few problems and avoided others.

As though he were a prospective buyer taking a test spin, Nat continued to examine the Volvo. He glanced up at the sun roof and nodded admiringly. My taste in cars had always been conservative, utilitarian, and though the Volvo was no teenager's dreamboat, it was a radical change for me. Nat probably thought I was having a midlife crisis.

"He was sort of a Cardinal Richelieu, a Colonel House," continued my father, pecking away at me.

I let the description hang suspended, hoping it would fall of its sheer stupidity. Irving Peres was beyond sarcasm or whatever my father was aiming toward in his Byzantine way. Irving was a sweet old man who'd lived his allotted time with decency and honor. As far as I knew, he'd never hurt a soul. Nat couldn't come close to such an epitaph.

Without me to spar with, Nat grew restless. His fingers scissored and unscissored. He fiddled with the dashboard knobs and pushbuttons. Then he sat back in his seat and took note of the changes on the turnpike since last August. There was a new Greek takeout where the Ford agency had been. Nat had predicted its demise. "Jews don't buy Fords. They remember that old bastard Henry and *The Protocols of Zion*." A carpet-outlet warehouse had closed, its windows replaced by plywood panels to discourage vandalism. "They sold lousy carpet anyway," said Nat.

I made a left at Peninsula Boulevard and turned on my wipers to get rid of a thin layer of mist beginning to form. This time Nat came directly at Laura instead of going through her father.

"She couldn't take it. She just couldn't take it."

"What are you talking about?"

"You know what I'm talking about. Your wife, her royal highness. How she fell apart after Bobbi. Went to pieces like she was made of glass, then threw you out in the street to make room for that painter."

I didn't know where to begin to ungarble the mess. As usual, Nat had shoved an assortment of facts, half-truths, and no-truths through his meat grinder and come up with an unrecognizable glob of sausage. He knew that Laura and I had separated, that I was living elsewhere, that she had a resident lover. An open-and-shut case for him, though I'm certain Sara and Caryn had helped connect the dots.

"As usual, you got it all wrong," I said without emotion.

Nat wasn't listening. "Rich girls: they're that way, you know. Sooner or later it shows. Things happen. It gets too hot, they get out of the kitchen. I hate to say I told you so, but I told you so. It was at one of the kids' birthday parties. Caryn's, if I'm not mistaken. I remember you sounding off about what a good old buddy you had in Laura. I said just you wait and see until things get a little hairy and we'll learn what kind of a buddy you have. Well, things got pretty hairy last summer and she caved in. Do you remember we talked in the backyard by the gazebo? You were so proud of that gazebo. You paid for the damn thing yourself."

I kept my composure. "You don't know what you're talking about," I said. Nat was very far from the truth. It was I who'd shattered and Laura who'd gotten a hold on herself. The princess rose while the commoner had fallen, a reversal my father would never understand.

"Don't I?" said Nat. "Just because I live in sunny Florida, in the elephants' graveyard, doesn't mean I checked my brains at the border. I knew she'd come apart like a toy after Christmas. I know she's gone gaga over this pint-size artiste. Believe me, Sonny, I've seen lots of middle-aged women and younger man. I've been in the Italian's shoes a few times myself. Years ago I knew it was too good to be true: the princess, the fairy godfather, the castle in the suburbs, the gold mine of a business that the king gave you."

"You shouldn't listen to what the girls tell you about what happened to us. Or did you slap it together yourself in that warped mind of yours?"

"Still with your head in the clouds after all these years," Nat tsked-tsked a few times. "Still don't know about women. At twenty-three it's understandable. At fifty it's a joke."

I turned the corner on Broadway and pulled into the parking lot at Kaplan Brothers. Not more than ten cars, including the hearse, were there. Had I screwed up Warren's instructions?

When we were finally seated in a back row, over the rabbi's eulogy, Nat whispered, "There's nobody here. What happened to all his high-and-mighty politician friends and the movers and shakers in the construction game? How quickly they forget when you're of no use to them."

At the cemetery, listening to the rabbi again, I couldn't help wondering if Irving had been with one of his warm bodies when his heart had given out. If he'd sailed off that way, guns blazing. I cried, recalling my promise to work things out with Laura. People do die of broken hearts, and if sex with a lady friend hadn't done it, most likely Laura and I had.

When my daughters fell on us so atrociously at the close of the funeral, I wasn't shocked. In their hysterical accusations, they'd been more correct than my father in his cold and calculating sniping. I wasn't shocked, but I was shaken, and hurt for Laura. She needed their love, their approval, more than I. She drew from it like water from a well. We loved our children equally and gave love in equal amounts, but I guess Laura was the most dependent on reciprocity.

I tried to take the sting from my daughters' words for Laura's sake. What I'd said to her at the cemetery, I'd meant. Chagrined and begging forgiveness, they would come back to her. Of course Laura wouldn't hesitate to accept them. She'd open her arms at once. The circle would re-form stronger than ever. And even if never included again, I'd feel better knowing they were reunited. It must surely happen. If I could be on speaking terms with Nat after all he'd done to me, they'd close the wound with Laura. They'd think of Bobbi and forget everything else. They were the best of children.

I thought about the man who'd been with Laura in the chapel and at the cemetery, whose hand I had shaken in goodwill. Though I'd heard all kinds of unsavory stories about Bruno Coletti from Maureen, whose position as cosmetician gave her an inside line on all town gossip, he didn't seem a bad sort. Not the suave manipulator of vulnerable women as Maureen claimed.

All my life I've lived near the ocean and felt nourished by it. I grew up in Sheepshead Bay on Brooklyn's south coast, facing the Atlantic where the boats would line up each morning at 6:30 for the fishermen and their gear. Fifty or more to a vessel, they'd go out for the day with their rods and reels and bait cans and beer coolers. Leave the old world behind. The concept thrilled me.

Weekends I'd get up at six, pack a tuna sandwich and an apple, and hurry to the piers, hoping some fisherman would be looking for a sturdy kid to take along to cut up the bait, clean the catch, or uncap the Shaeffers. No one ever did, and I'd spend the day on the docks smelling the salt and the sea and looking for ships on the horizon, imagining their home bases, their ports of call. I'd eat my lunch by ten, throwing the bread crusts to the circling gulls and pigeons, and the apple core into the bay, where it would be picked clean by the fish, then sink to the bottom.

By one or two in the afternoon, the boats would return and I'd earn a few dollars helping the fishermen gut their fish. With the first five dollars I bought a black and gold volume of *The Romances of Herman Melville,* published in 1931.

In the world of Samoa and the Indies, there was no room for thoughts of a mother who had her own personal world as well, transported there not by the printed page, but by phenobarbital and Seconal. My mother abused drugs all her life, though her death certificate read natural causes.

Back then, I was Sonny Gerber, a name my father had pinned on me, I think, to keep me forever childlike and unthreatening. I was usually left to fend for myself. I grew up alone, happily solitary, a great walker of the streets of Sheepshead Bay, where I decided that most of the trouble in the world was caused by those who can't be alone with themselves. They must rush out and form groups, societies, organizations, committees, political parties. They argue, fight, and kill each other to prove their points. If they were content with themselves, they wouldn't have to prove a thing. World history in a single paragraph, and from a fourteen-year-old savant.

At home, I'd try to sail through the domestic storms. When my mother was well enough, she'd stand up to Nat. He claimed he gave her all the money she could possibly need. She'd swear she never received it. "Either you spent it on phenos and Seconal or you lost it." "I did not. I definitely did not. You are lying to justify making paupers of us. Look at the boy, will you? He hasn't had a pair of pants in over a year. Would I neglect him?"

If there was somehow a shortage of money for the table, for rent and clothes, you'd never know it looking at Nat, always a fashion plate. He was, after all, he'd remind my mother, a top salesman. Appearances were important. He couldn't make the money he did make, the money my mother could never account for, if he didn't dress the part.

By the time I was sixteen I'd come to realize that my father was sleeping with other women. I could hardly disregard my mother's allusions. Wistfully, she'd said to me, "If you were a girl, I'd give you a good piece of advice. Never marry a handsome man or one you love too much. If he's faithful, you wonder for how long. You become mistrustful of every attractive neighbor, of the girls in the shops on the avenue. If he's not, it's a life of making excuses to yourself. Either way it's hell."

My mother died in 1955, a month before I was to graduate from high school. Her heart, was all I was told by Nat and our family physician, Dr. Harkavi. Nat grieved the standard one week, then returned to work. I left immediately after graduation for the Adirondacks and my new job at Camp Merrimont. My third year there—I was in charge of the lake and its boats by then—I met Laura. Until the day we married, she refused to believe there were fathers like mine. "In Dickens, yes, but in real-life Jewish-American homes? Really, Mark, you exaggerate something fierce."

She finally believed me at our wedding, when she gave Nat the third dance. The first was mine, the second her father's.

"You know, Laura," my father—an excellent dancer—said as he whirled her around the dance floor. "If this were the Middle Ages, I'd be entitled to exercise the right of the first night. It was standard practice then."

Laura told me she was mortified but recovered quickly. "These aren't the Middle Ages and besides Mark has already exercised that right. A long time ago and often."

"The boy has more spunk than I figured," Nat said. "And I think we're going to get along just fine, you and I."

"As long as you remember who I am and who you are, and believe me, Mr. Gerber, I know exactly who you are."

"Has my son been filling your pretty little ears with his fantasies? He's got some really weird notions about me."

"They didn't mean a thing, Mr. Gerber, until this dance. Until you made your pass."

"Call me Nat, for God's sake, child, and it wasn't a pass. It was only chitchat. Believe me, if I'd made a pass, there'd be no doubt of it in either of our minds."

―――――――――

At the motel, the same one I'd stayed in the first few nights last February, I helped Nat with his luggage. The chambermaid was about finished with the room. There was the scent of pine air freshener, probably to mask the heated activities of the previous occupants.

"I'll be back for you at seven," I told him.

"Dinner for three, right?"

"For three."

Nat nodded vigorously.

It was then I knew Irving's death was only part of the reason he'd flown in from Florida. Meeting Virginia was the other part.

---

I got to Hempstead in plenty of time for the hearing. The week before, Laura had dropped off at the store a letter from the Department of Motor Vehicles. Addressed to both of us, it began, "In the matter of Christopher John McGuire: YOU ARE HEREBY ADVISED that a hearing will be held pursuant to Section 510 of the Vehicle and Traffic Law of New York State to investigate a fatal accident that occurred on August 27, 1987, at Nassau County and to determine whether or not any registration, license and/or driving privileges should be suspended or revoked for said respondent.

"YOUR PERSONAL APPEARANCE IS OPTIONAL at this hearing."

Optional as far as they were concerned. Mandatory for me. I immediately called Assistant DA Spotswood—Cal. We were on a first-name basis by now, since I'd seen him in court once a month for more than half a year. Each month Cal would call and I'd take the day off to sit in court and hear the defense attorney ask for more time and more evidence to inspect. Each time, he'd come in a different suit and I'd wonder if his real purpose in all these delays was to protect his client or show us his total wardrobe. Cal always wore his sturdy dark blues, McGuire his one court uniform. Each time, I had less and less faith in the justice system.

"This is the story," said Cal. "McGuire's license has been suspended—that's the law in this case. The state is now trying to revoke it as well. His attorney will fight tooth and nail not to let that happen, since revocation is a pretty damning fact should you decide on a civil suit. Also, the hearing gives the defense attorney a pretty good shot at the witnesses I've lined up. He has the right to question them and he'll then determine who he can manipulate at the trial and who he can't. Since this isn't a court of law, only a hearing, I won't be there. Frankly, I don't think you should be there either."

I went alone. Even if Irving hadn't recently been buried, I don't think Laura would have gone. It was all part of her getting on with life.

The hearing room at the Motor Vehicle Bureau was located at the rear of the main service area where hundreds of motorists stood in long lines renewing their expiring licenses and returning old plates.

A very young secretary asked my name and I had to shout it because her portable was blaring out rock music. I was told to go to Room Two.

The room was large, airy, brightly lit, and made cooler by the Art Expo winter scenes on its white walls. Around a square table sat McGuire, his attorney in gray sharkskin, Police Officer Joe Pagano, two men I took to be the witnesses, a court stenographer, and what looked like a college freshman in a black suit, red tie, and horn-rim glasses. The nameplate in front of him read: Judge Justin Petrofsky.

I sat at the back of the room in the observers' row, six seats from Christopher's mother. She was wearing a tight, tan safari suit and a knitted top that hung like a half curtain across her bosom. After all these months, I still despised her son and would have blown his head off given the chance.

Through the walls, from the reception desk, came the hoarse, raspy groans of Joe Cocker and "You Are So Beautiful."

Judge Petrofsky opened the hearing by stating that this was not a criminal proceeding but a hearing. Nevertheless, he swore in McGuire, Joe Pagano, and the two witnesses. Then he asked Joe and the witnesses to wait outside. He'd call them in later, one at a time, to give testimony. He turned to McGuire. "In your own words, tell me what happened the afternoon of August twenty-seventh."

At once, the defense attorney objected, invoking the Fifth Amendment.

"Your client certainly has the right to avoid self-incrimination," the judge said sharply. "But I must tell you that I will take his refusal to testify into account when I make my final decision. A different set of rules applies here."

But from that point on it all went downhill. I was forced to sit helpless while the defense attorney tried to trick the witnesses and Joe into stating that Bobbi had contributed to her own death by failing to get out of McGuire's way. Even though McGuire was declared legally drunk by the Breathalyzer. Even though the first witness—a toy salesman of forty with a clear recollection of the crash—swore that McGuire had been traveling far over the speed limit and in the opposite lane. Even though the eighteen-year-old second witness, with a Mohawk haircut and a silver ring in his left lobe, testified that McGuire had shot around him and crossed the yellow line into Bobbi's path.

Defense attorneys in the City and in Nassau had recently won two cases similar in nature. In each, a young woman had been strangled by a young man during sex. Vicious, brutal killings in which the defense attorneys attempted to implicate the dead girls: accidental death as a result of rough sex. The unfortunate young men had been goaded into violence by overpassionate lovers.

And here was this shameless imitator trying to prove that Bobbi had died because she zigged instead of zagged when a drunk in the wrong lane bore down on her. Wrong was right, up was down, the guilty were innocent, and the innocent were guilty.

The judge listened diligently, asking questions, taking notes, and recording the entire proceedings on TDK tape and a miniature unit the size of a paperback book. When he rendered his decision, six to eight weeks hence, the worst they could do was take away McGuire's right to drive—instead of his right to live.

I was first to leave after the hearing. Bruce Springsteen on the secretary's portable was shouting about the joys of being "Born in the U.S.A."

I had my doubts.

---

Virginia wore a dress I'd never seen before, a tangerine and lemon-yellow polka-dot creation that clung to her like a second skin. And tangerine shoes. Her hair was loose and lustrous. She'd cut down to half a pack a day and it showed in the fullness of her face. She'd acquired a fantastic tan in the backyard on a beach chair while watching me plant my garden. Observing her apply lipstick, I knew my father was in for a major surprise.

Nat stepped out of the motel as if he'd come ashore from his yacht. He was dressed like some gentleman skipper in a dark blue blazer, light blue Bill Blass sport shirt, white ducks, and white canvas shoes. His hair sparkled from a dab too much of Brylcream, and his tan matched Virginia's, except her nose had peeled to a brownish-pink.

"Virginia, Nat. Nat, Virginia," I said. My father's teeth were perfectly aligned chiclets when he smiled. I noticed Virginia's chipped tooth for the first time in months. Still, she was very lovely.

We were seated at a restaurant in Freeport along the dock where Guy Lombardo once owned a home, before Nat said anything significant. He'd been content so far to study Virginia from the backseat of the car. Our table was so near the ocean I could see the red buoy lights near the docks bobbing up and down, and farther out on the ocean the blinking of passing ships, as though stars had fallen from the night sky.

"You really amaze me, both of you," said Nat.

"We surprised a lot of people," I told him. "But be careful what you say. I know you, and I can tolerate your nonsense most of the time. But Virginia doesn't and doesn't have to and won't."

"Virginia can speak for herself should the need arise," she said, lighting her first cigarette of the evening, tossing her head and blowing the smoke away from us.

"I have no intention of saying anything derogatory about either of you. Just that my son's made quite a readjustment in his life, and you, young lady, are not what I was led to believe. Why, you're beautiful. A work of art."

I could feel Virginia's early-warning system snap to attention. She knew that behind some of the fanciest compliments lurked the deadliest insults. Trojan horses. With one like Nat, I'm sure she'd figured out, she'd have to stay permanently alert.

"A work of art." She laughed. "I've been called many things. Never that."

"Well, let me tell you, Virginia—or is it Ginny? You look like you could be called Ginny. I've been around the fair sex for a long time—maybe Mark told you—and I know the genuine from the ersatz. You're the real thing."

"It's Virginia," she said. "That's all it's ever been."

A sort of groundwork had been established and I felt secure enough to leave them alone and go to the men's room. I had to wait my turn at one of the three stalls. I came back to a changed climate, judging from Nat's end of the conversation. He was carrying on in that free-style manner of his about the weather in Florida ("it's the heat *and* the humidity"), the best eating places in Dade County, the large influx of Cubans that had transformed downtown Miami into Havana West, the reputation south Florida had earned as the money-laundering capital of the United States.

I preferred it this way: bloodless and benign. Virginia was not here for Nat's inspection and approval. I'd never sought his approval for anything. His blessings, to me, had always been the kiss of death.

All trussed up in quilted white bibs, we went to work on the two-pound lobsters, claw crackers at our sides. We stopped talking or sparring or whatever it was we were doing, as separating the white meat from the exoskeleton took all our attention. I have to admit I fell into an especially forgiving mood, with Irving's death and all. This could be the last time I'd see my father and I wanted at least one decent memory to carry around awhile, with all the indecent ones.

We dawdled awhile longer over coffee, then Nat made a dash for the john. He'd seen the waiter approaching with the bill;

therefore, his customary disappearing act, the one he performed every time we got together and ate out. After all, I was a millionaire's son-in-law.

To keep our record intact, I paid the bill and left the tip.

I dropped Virginia off at the bungalow and took Nat back to the motel. We were on the turnpike heading north and I could almost hear the wheels turning in his head.

"That's quite a comedown, Sonny."

I thought he was referring to Virginia. "What the hell is it now?"

"The shack you're living in. It's not exactly the mansion you had. But that wasn't yours anyway, so it doesn't matter. About your lady friend—that's a different story. I like her. She's tough. She's honest. She's good to look at. Built like a Doberman, but no skinny minny. Earthy, wouldn't you say?"

"If you're asking if she's all right in bed, the answer's yes. Does that satisfy your curiosity?"

"I didn't ask that question. It just so happens I know the answer. I can tell those things."

We were in the motel parking lot. It was the end of a long and terrible day. Tomorrow we'd go to Laura's and pay our respects. I'd put him on the nine P.M. flight to Lauderdale, then probably never see him again. If I didn't get it off my chest now, I might never have the chance.

"I'm sure you can," I said. "You're a real expert. You've had lots of practice. For as long as I can remember, and I've got a good memory."

Nat said nothing.

"That's what really killed Mom: your womanizing. Not the drugs she turned to. Not the penny-pinching with us, but the spending on all those high-class hookers."

Nat's fingers curled around the door handle. He was about to get out and I could sense his struggle between staying and leaving.

"You know, Sonny," he said, removing his fingers from the door handle and falling back against the seat. "You were always a great source of aggravation to me. Not that you were a bad kid or a discipline problem. But you always automatically took her side. Without ever even trying to consider mine." Nat lit a cigarillo. He'd smoked them years before they became popular. In a brief flash of light, I could see his hands cupping the match as if we were standing in a wind. His hands were steady.

"In a way, I couldn't blame you, and maybe I could have been a better father, but your mother and I had the kind of problem you don't solve around the dinner table and you never involve a child in, especially your kind, one that's hard to understand, freaky and secretive, who lives in a dreamworld where everything's white and black. Your mother was no saint. I've said that before."

"So you have. But that's no reason—"

"Let me finish. I'll only say it once. I've never told this to a living soul, except maybe a few times to a woman, and I didn't tell the whole truth. Maybe now that you've taken your lumps with Laura, you've finally learned what every married man knows. That you alternate between love and hate with a wife, even the best of them. If it's an okay marriage, there's more on the love side. If it's a lousy one, there's more hate. That's the kind I had. In spades. Maybe you wouldn't have believed me before, but you might now. Who knows?"

Nat took a long, pensive drag on his cigarillo and leaned against the headrest. The aroma filled the car, rich and nutlike and masculine. Our faces were hidden from one another, though the parking lot was brightly lit by closely spaced imitation Japanese lanterns on metal poles. Cars kept entering and leaving the motel, their headlights suddenly in our faces, then turning away. I'd see Nat, then not see him.

"I was a healthy young buck of twenty-five back when I married your mother. She was a nurse I'd met at a YMHA dance. She had your disposition, a real change from the floozies and hot numbers I was dating. Well, we hit it off and got married and it was fine for a while until she became pregnant. Then after you came along, she announced that now that she was a mother and had fulfilled her duty to God and husband, we were to forget about sex between us. It had always been a detestable act to her. Her very words.

"Well, I wasn't the sort of bloke to take no for an answer. So I badgered her and wooed her with flowers and candlelight dinners at the finest restaurants. While men my age were selling apples on street corners, I was throwing away a small fortune trying to earn what I'd already paid for. The result was zilch, *nada,* zip. Nothing would melt her frozen heart. In fact, all my attentions only turned her more against me.

"It was embarrassing, but I told her I'd never masturbated before and I had no intention of starting now. She said it was no longer her concern, but if I really insisted, she'd consider once a month. I told her that was worse than no sex at all.

"For the first five or six months I actually jerked off in the shower at night, hoping she'd eventually miss good old conjugal relations and change her mind. But as God is my judge, she never made the slightest move in that direction. So what was I to do? Bottle the stuff? Let it accumulate and choke me to death? I took the only healthy way out. I became a damned Frenchman with a wife at home and a mistress on the outside. Lots of mistresses. And one-night stands. And short engagements."

"Plenty of fathers cheated," I told Nat. "But they were still able to maintain a relationship with their sons. We had *nothing.* Whatever you had—or didn't have—with my mother shouldn't have affected us."

" 'Shouldn't have.' Idealistic words. Put yourself in my shoes. This woman doesn't want me but she does want my son and has him all to herself. She's made a real solid ally at my expense, and yours. So I never became a model father. And I spent too much on the broads, then came home to see the hate in your eyes. Sorry, that's the way it worked out. I'm a passionate man. I needed what they had to offer and I paid the price. For what it's worth, I'm sorry about it now, seeing what we haven't become to each other.

"Another thing," my father said, then changed his mind, as if believing he'd already said too much. He got out of the car, rubbed his cigarillo out on the ground, and leaned in through the open window. "I've got a few things to do tomorrow during the day. Pick me up at six and we'll go visit Laura."

"Okay," I said.

Nat looked at me as if expecting a summary.

I gave him one. "Nothing's changed, you know."

"That's how I see it, too." Straight-backed, he walked into the motel.

---

Virginia was up waiting for me when I got home. Her dress was draped over a kitchen chair, her shoes on the table. She was barefoot, in bra and panties.

"I was getting worried," she said. "I thought you two guys were having a shoot-out at the OK Corral."

"Not quite. I had to get a few things off my chest. Then he told me a few things I wasn't overjoyed to hear, if he was telling the truth. By the way, there was the definite scent of playacting in the restaurant after I got back from the john. Care to divulge what happened?"

"Are you sure you want to hear it? It's not pretty."

"What the hell's the difference? It won't change anything between us. Too many years, not enough battles."

Virginia was having a cup of tea. While she prepared one for me, I could see where the sun had missed her cleavage and the white stripes across her back.

"Well, he told me that I reminded him of a cheetah. Fluid motion, fine body lines, and all that shit. Then he leaned across the table and I could feel his hand on my thigh. I told him to please remove his hand or I'd show him all the cheetah he'd ever want to see. Which he did. Then, as you came out of the john and were walking toward us, he said if I ever got to Lauderdale, alone, to look him up. He'd be happy to save me the cost of a motel room. He'd also show me the sights. So friendly, your old man. I told him to go fuck himself. He said he'd consider it since it was the only form of sex he'd never tried."

"Leopards never change their spots, speaking of felines," I said. "Nor old goats their randy ways. He once made a pass at Laura. On our wedding night, no less."

"I imagine she must have almost fainted."

"No, as a matter of fact she put him in his place at once, the way you did. Though she wasn't that explicit."

Virginia placed the empty cups in the sink and we went to bed. "Laura told him off in a most refined manner, I'm sure. Not like me," she said when we were near sleep.

"The effect was the same. He avoided her like the tax collector all our married life."

"I think I'm getting to like your Laura. Should I act more refined, too?"

"She's not 'my' Laura and I wouldn't want you to act like anyone but yourself." I kissed her shoulder.

"I meant it joshingly."

"Remind me sometime tomorrow to laugh."

## *sixteen*

FTER LUNCH at the villa, I packed a picnic basket, some beach accessories, and the army blanket I'd bought the day before in the flea market behind the church of São Vincente de Fora. We divided the cargo and walked hand in hand along the beach between Cascais and Guincho, a wild sandy stretch of coastline usually deserted any time of day but ideal for swimming and sunning.

I wore a two-piece purple and white bathing suit that seemed almost puritanical compared to what the French and German tourists paraded the more populated beaches in. Bruno had on a black tight-fitting bikini that compressed his genitals. He could have been from anywhere. I could only have been an American.

"Isn't the beach in front of the villa good anymore, Bruno? It was good enough for Magda Lupescu."

Magda Lupescu was the mistress of King Carol of pre–World War II Rumania. We were told by the rental agent that our villa, though ridiculously inexpensive, had been their favorite love nest. Bruno and I, two hopeless nouveau romantics, adored the idea of a vacation base with such a lurid past.

"We're not going for a long hike, are we? After the tour of the harbor this morning I'm not in the mood for long hikes."

"Actually, love, we're going on a very short hike," said Bruno, taking the lead, me in tow behind. "To this special place I found while you were sunbathing one afternoon last week. A very private, primitive niche behind a rampart of rocks sculpted by wind and water. I'm told it was a rendezvous point for European refugees without legitimate passports. Portugal tolerated them for a short while and they used the time to arrange passage to South America with ship captains who had no objection to supplementing their incomes. The rowboats would pick them up here and ferry them to the ships waiting offshore, and on to freedom."

"The Danes did the same thing as an entire *nation* and without the profit motive," I told Bruno. "I once saw the beach where they took almost every Danish Jew across the water to Sweden."

"Wonderful people, the Scandinavians. Maybe next year we'll pay them a visit."

We soon arrived at a semicircle of beach, deserted except for a mass of coves and rock formations that sat on the far rim like huge tan sponges.

There wasn't a ship or a sailboat along the entire panoramic horizon. No jet above excreting white trails in the sky. Not a swimmer or a jogger or his footprints or the thrum-thrum of a motorbike. Only the limitless sea before us, the unspoiled sand under an inverted blue bowl of clean, crisp heaven, and a pair of sea gulls that materialized from nowhere and cruised overhead, crying out to one another.

"They're gossiping about us," said Bruno.

"You understand gull talk? In Portuguese yet?"

"Certainly. I took the Berlitz course before we left the States."

"And what are they saying, your friends, the gulls?"

"They're saying, 'Now, there's a very happy pair of tourists. Let's entertain them with some tricks of derring-do.' "

"If they only knew how well we entertain ourselves, they'd stop wasting their time."

The heat from the sand rose to meet the heat from the sun beating down. Both were tolerable, since Portuguese temperatures seldom leave the seventies in summer. With a relieved sigh, we dropped our bundles. Bruno spread out the blanket, then began rolling down his swimsuit.

"What are you doing, Bruno? This is a public beach."

"A public beach but a very private one. I've checked. No one ever comes here, love. Loosen up and undress. We're free of friends, family, and those who may know us. If someone should come by—but no one will—they'll say 'those ugly Americans' and quickly pass on."

"Are you sure, Bruno? I wouldn't want to end up in some Portuguese jail."

"The law in Portugal is interested only in political crimes. Skinny-dipping will never cause a revolution, except maybe in the swim-wear business. Bare-assing it will never bring down the government in power."

First I looked up and down the small horseshoe of beach, then inland beyond the giant sponges to the lime-green groves of trees behind which lay the road and rails leading to Lisbon. The air over the sand trembled slightly in early August warmth. Bruno stood nude before me, a thick, wiry nest of black hair sheltering his penis, shrunken and truncated in disuse. He'd never been circumcised, but that had proved less of a distraction in our lovemaking than I'd anticipated. If anything, it added novelty, but with only one previous lover all my life, any variation would.

"It'll be fine, Laura. Trust me."

I did. Wholly. Completely, as a child would a parent. I undid my bra and dropped my bottoms. We stood facing each other as we often did in our bedroom, without shame or sham, a latter-day Adam and Eve, though hardly innocents. Smiling.

I sang out a few nervous notes, then made a dash for the water.

Bruno echoed my scale and chased me. He dove in first. I followed a second later, filling the hole he'd made in the waves. We rose up together, inches apart in neck-high water pure enough to drink, except for the salt. Laughing uninhibitedly, we cavorted like the kinds of rowdies I'd always warned my daughters to avoid on the beaches of Nassau County.

Bruno splashed me. I threw clumps of seaweed at him, which he draped over his bald head like a Roman senator. Then he dove under my legs and flipped me over his shoulders. Oh, the welcome release to act so childish. So inelegant—but so refreshing.

"Shark in the water," he sang out as I savored being nude this side of the Atlantic. I was the shark and he caught and held me until I stopped struggling. This uniting of our bodies toned down the hijinks. Our swim together became part water ballet, part foreplay.

I was content being transported by Bruno, my back nestled in his front, my arms raised over his neck, circling his head. Bruno began fondling me. My breasts remained firm on the water's surface, demonstrating enough integrity not to bob, enough compactness not to sag. We would have had sex in the ocean or on the beach blanket if I'd allowed Bruno. But that would have been too much despite my newfound audacity.

I was first out of the water. I shook myself like a dog, then stomped on one foot then the other to get the Atlantic out of my ears. I fell on the blanket and covered my middle third with a towel. "Jelly me, Bruno," I commanded indolently, turning on my stomach.

Bruno got on his knees beside me, squeezed an inch of lotion into his palms, and worked it into a thin film over his fingers. He began at my heels.

"Not there," I said, chiding him gently. "No one ever gets sunburned heels."

"I'm nothing if not thorough. The mark of the serious artist is attention to the smallest detail. Remember Rodin's *The Burghers of Calais?* The minute folds in their capes? The creases in their faces?"

Bruno droned on about Rodin, making an elaborate production of applying the suntan jelly. Rodin, his role model, his mentor, his god. Bruno knew every event in the great man's life: successes, failures, illnesses, rejections, and scandals.

I let Bruno lecture while working over me. He lingered at my toes, especially between them. He buttered the soles of my feet, then swathed the muscles of my calves, working his way north to the soft insides of my thighs, kneading them as though they were dough.

"Ouch, that hurts."

"Sorry. I got carried away. I'll stop."

"Don't you dare. Just act less enthusiastic."

"An impossibility given the subject matter, but I'll try."

Bruno's fingers grew less insistent, only the tips massaging my back and shoulders. I drowsed and may have snored a bit. Bruno stopped, capped the tube of jelly, and wiped his hands on a towel. For the next hour he faced the ocean and sketched from memory the faces we'd seen during our month in Lisbon and Cascais.

While he sketched, my mind drifted back to June when Bruno and I had planned the vacation. I told Phil Coolidge I intended taking off the entire summer and would he please find a replacement to introduce the speaker each Wednesday morning for the Before the Beach series. Behind the thick facade of his meaty face, I could see that he would be delighted to do so, hoping as well that this defection was the beginning of a shift in interest that would end with my resignation.

I was leaving little behind me. The girls hadn't come around as yet, though a month had passed since the funeral. Mark's promise that they would was as worthless as the many meaningless words he'd uttered all his life.

Bruno was also free. He'd turned *The Flutist* over to a gallery in Manhattan that promised a quick and profitable sale.

I spent a few days taking care of loose ends with the post office, the police, the phone company, and the house-watching outfit that would send someone around each day to rattle the windows and test the doors.

One of those loose ends was Bruno's pride.

When I first suggested summer in Portugal—an idea he'd introduced at the Compassionate Friends meeting—Bruno was hesitant. "I honestly can't afford even my part of the tab, Laura. Maybe in the fall, if I sell *The Flutist*." He'd seemed so dispirited and ashamed.

"Bruno. Listen. It just so happens that I have the money. I don't need it, and since we're two halves of the same loving relationship, what difference does it make, really, which half pays?"

At the travel agency, we chose the village of Cascais on the coast and east of Lisbon, which fit Bruno's off-the-cuff description. But I didn't care for the rest of it: a room above a store or a tavern. That kind of accommodation might be fine for a young honeymoon couple just starting out, but not for us. The agent suggested the oceanfront villa that may or may not have been the vacation retreat of royalty. While Bruno stood in contemplative silence, I wrote out the check.

He protested vehemently, but finally accepted the ten thousand dollars in escudos I gave him to cover our two months abroad. I told him to take charge of everything, and that made him feel better.

Everything: beginning in the mornings when we rose very early in the large ornate bed that Carol and Magda may have made love in. We had breakfast in a small café in Cascais on the docks. We'd watch the local fishermen in their boats, painted splashily in reds, yellows, and blues, leave for their workday on the ocean. By eight, we'd be on the train to Lisbon, in the workingman's compartment where no one spoke English and everyone pretended not to notice the two foreigners. Twenty minutes and twenty-nine kilometers later we were at the Cais do Sodre, the central terminal in Lisbon. On the streets, policemen in three-cornered hats carried rifles that resembled old muskets, a scene out of *Carmen*. On the walls facing the terminal we saw advertising posters for Campo Pequeño, Lisbon's wildly popular bullfight arena.

"We should go," said Bruno. "Not to worry. The Portuguese

don't kill their bulls. They wear them out, instead, with their fancy footwork."

"Yes, we'll do that. Whatever you say."

We'd begin our walking tour at the Alfama, the Moorish barrio in the older waterfront section of town. Bruno had done his homework and knew where to go. We delighted in the narrow winding streets that ended in tiny public squares, most with monuments to some local hero, and the whitewashed houses, each holding centuries of history within its stone walls. And flowers, profusions of them everywhere, in windows, on stoops, lining steps, around monuments, even between the legs of those heroes in bronze.

Meandering, we'd stop for coffee at one of the workingman's cafés. How isolated we felt among those strangers. Here, Bruno's talent and my money meant nothing. We were stripped to essentials and our love had its best chance to thrive, unadorned and unfettered by who we'd become. Like lost children, we wandered, wholly dependent on one another.

Gradually, we wandered close to the center of Lisbon and the main boulevards. Up and down streets that rose steeply at forty-five-degree angles, then abruptly ended, only to begin again three blocks away.

On the Rua das Verdes Janelas we found the Museum of Ancient Art. Inside were many of the best paintings by Portuguese artists, and entire sections of foreign masterpieces. There was more sculpture at the Gulbenkian Foundation Museum across the city but Bruno decided against spending much time there or in any of the host of tourist attractions Lisbon had to offer.

"No, love, we're more interested in the faces and figures of the people of Lisbon. This is a wonderful city, not at all like Manhattan, which has too much for the mind to absorb. Here, the mixture, the admixture, the blend of faces is perfection. They're living history, an entire city of models."

Occasionally we felt the need to escape the *Lisboetos*. Bruno rented a Renault, and we'd drive up the coast past Cabo da Rocha, the westernmost point on the European continent. The wind off the ocean would carry the spume and we had to shut the windows until we turned inland to the towns off the regular tourist routes. Invariably, the choice of site, restaurant, and wine had been Bruno's. Invariably I was not disappointed.

All my married life Mark had depended on me to make many important decisions. I'd done the family banking and bookkeeping. I bought the CDs and clipped the coupons. I dealt with the tradespeople, called the phone company when there was static on the line, knew the plumber by his first name. Mark had supreme confidence in my judgment. Jokingly he said he was preparing me for widowhood. He was really running away from involvement and responsibility.

Frankly, I was tired of all that freedom and equality. I was sick of being capable. So far this summer Bruno, my benevolent despot, had done it better. I loved when he toasted me each evening with wine and brought fresh flowers into the bedroom the next morning. I was wanted, treasured, and fussed over. I could live the rest of my life this way.

This, of course, was the fantasy part of my nature responding. Analytical me had a few doubts. The odds weren't very good for long-range success. I was older, with money. He was poor, unappreciated, struggling. Alter any of his givens and the balance could be upset. I especially watched for the intangible: Bruno growing tired of me. The women of Lisbon were especially beautiful, some with faces so startling even other women turned around to stare. Yet Bruno didn't, not at the beautiful ones. Character lines interested him far more.

For love's sake or money's Bruno should have pushed for a commitment. We never spoke of the future. We were doing fine with only a present that renewed itself each morning. There was no urgency in considering a divorce.

During the month in Portugal, I'd gained the objectivity to consider my position with the girls. And discuss it with Bruno. For a bachelor he was quite sensible and sensitive about the entire subject.

"They weren't perfect, growing up," I told him one morning in front of the Statue of Neptune near Rua Doña Estefania. "Even if their father thinks otherwise. Bruno, they were wonderful children to raise but now they're very much adults and I'll have to deal with them on that basis when we get back. I won't stand on ceremony. I'll take the first steps. I can't have them not speaking to me. You know, I send them postcards every week. Without a return address. I want them to know I haven't forgotten them and that there'll be a showdown coming soon. That's another reason I took this vacation. We all needed a cooling-off period."

"And suppose, love, in September, when we get back and you go the two-thirds or three-quarters of the way, then find they refuse to go the balance?"

"I'll decide then."

"After all, love, I'm the worm in the apple. Suppose one of the conditions for making up is that you get rid of me?"

"Well, then, if they're that pigheaded and selfish, we won't make up. I love you, Bruno. I won't give you up for anyone or anything. Do you believe me?"

"I do. I have to. There's no other way."

---

Bruno's hand on my bare thigh stirred me from semisleep. I thought I was in our historic and opulent bed at the villa, and turned to receive him. Then I saw the sky, the water, the beach. The thought of losing Bruno had made me want him more. "Let's go home and make love until sundown. Keep it going for hours. You know how, Bruno."

We dined that night in a popular restaurant near the Botanic Gardens. Stuffed spider crab and *Frango na Pucara,* which was chicken baked in an earthen dish. For dessert, I shared with Bruno *Touchinho do ceu,* a pudding made of eggs and custard. Superb.

"Let's walk off all those calories," said Bruno when we were on Avenida da Liberdade, one of Lisbon's main boulevards.

"We'll have to walk to Paris for that," I said.

Lisbon nights are chilly, even in August. I wore a light sweater, Bruno an Irish slipover. Yes, I told myself, Portugal was working. The entire evening had gone by and I'd forgotten about the world back home, my father, my unforgiving daughters, Bobbi. For a short while, she'd left her permanent home in my soul, offering the kind of peace that could only be temporary. Over the month at the beach, on the streets of Lisbon or up in the hills in some fairy-tale palace, she'd suddenly stir inside and I'd fall into the saddest of despairs. Bruno would pick up on it at once and wait until the moment had passed and I could rejoin him again. He was the very model of patience and I loved him for it.

Through a series of twists and turns we found ourselves on the Rua Aurea, the gold and silver merchants' street. We paused in front of one jewelry shop, the window of which glowed from the glittering displays of bracelets, rings, and earrings, as though a burst of sunshine had struck it.

A man of about fifty stood in the doorway. He was tall, stocky, and prosperous looking, with rich, abundant black hair that had a wide swath of silver running up the center, large, soulful black eyes, and a prominent nose with flared nostrils. He could have been one of those Portuguese kings whose portraits hung in the Gulbenkian Museum or who sat astride a horse in the square between the railroad terminal and the Alfama.

"Shalom," he said to me, then at Bruno.

"Shalom," I said back. "How did you guess?"

"Something about you. A feeling. Intuition, perhaps. I am correct, am I not?"

"Very much so, about me. Not at all about my friend."

The man examined Bruno as if wondering why, then introduced himself. "I am David Silva. I own this store."

Bruno and I introduced ourselves, first and last names. We told him we were in Cascais for the summer.

"I am closing for the evening and I wonder if you'd care to be my guests for coffee or a glass of wine. My favorite *fado* house is nearby."

Bruno and I had heard about the *fado* houses, that they were yawning tourists traps. For that reason we'd stayed away.

Probably reading my mind, David Silva said, "It's not in any guidebook of Lisbon. Strictly for the natives and quite authentic. I'm sure you'll like it."

"We'd love to," I said.

"Very much," said Bruno.

David Silva closed his store and led us two or three blocks to a small, unpretentious café called the Kaverna. Inside, a dark, crowded room made smaller by clouds of cigarette smoke, with tables the size of handkerchiefs, we sat and listened to a single *fado* singer who accompanied himself on a Portuguese guitar the shape of a lollipop.

David Silva ordered fruit and a bottle of Mondego wine. "If you haven't been told, *fado* is an ancient Portuguese word for fate or destiny. That is one of the music's major themes. Others are love, its complications, women, and Lisbon."

As the guitarist played and sang, David Silva translated. "Lisbon is a girl, barefoot and light. A sudden and bright wind on her hair. Some thin wrinkles peeping from her eyes. The open loneliness on her lips and fingers going downstairs."

"Lovely," I said.

"Lovely," echoed Bruno, helping himself to a cube of pineapple.

We stayed for hours and finished a second bottle of Mondego. David Silva wouldn't hear of our paying or even sharing the bill.

From that night, David became woven into our lives, the part of it we spent in Lisbon. Each evening we'd meet at his store at eightish, then go dine at a restaurant he recommended. He'd do all the ordering and we'd talk continuously and endlessly through the meal. David did the most, Bruno the least. David had lived a fascinating life. His father's house—now his—had been a stop on the underground railroad, helping Jews to escape to the Americas, and aiding U.S. and RAF fliers to get back to their bases. In a secret room behind the wine cellar in his basement, David had met with poets, writers, scientists, and ordinary citizens of every land that Hitler had conquered, as well as Americans from Duluth and Tampa, Englishmen from Sheffield and Cornwall.

Bruno and I had listened with rapt amazement, Bruno with some mistrust as well, I'm afraid. Why, I couldn't comprehend: Portugal had been a hotbed of intrigue during World War II. He himself had mentioned the beach as a meeting point for refugees. And the places David took us cost less than our previous choices and half the time he paid the entire bill. He never made the slightest intrustion into our private lives. What he knew of us was what we told him.

David had also been to Russia, to China, to New York, and to Morocco, where he met the very liberal sultan. He'd visited the Vatican and met with the pope as part of a delegation of Portuguese Jewry urging papal recognition of Israel.

In his spare time, David wrote poetry and painted. None of these accomplishments did he volunteer. All came out in the course of our evening conversations, some of which lasted late into the night, almost until dawn.

---

Each time we met with David, we learned something new and interesting about him. I was intrigued and captivated by the man and the world he described. I thought that despite Bruno's vague and unstated misgivings, he was as well. Until one afternoon in the middle of August.

It was too cool for the beach. Thick-quilted clouds scudded across an indecisive sky, emitting only the briefest leakage of sun. We relaxed in the villa's garden, Bruno applying the final touches to his sketch of the young girl who came to the villa twice a week to clean and change the sheets. She was no more than fifteen, with sad, almond eyes and hair so black and thick it absorbed light without giving any back. With a few short strokes, he'd caught her essence. I was reading a work by Galdos from David's extensive library.

"What time are we leaving for Lisbon?" I asked, turning a page.

"I thought we'd go to Sintra. There's a monastery built by the Capucho monks I'd like to see. Some of the rooms are lined with cork. And there are penitence cells where the monks sat in silence for days for their small sins."

I looked up from the book. "You mean David is going to leave his beloved Lisbon to come along with us?"

"David's not coming."

"You didn't tell me he called."

"He didn't. I called him. I told him we had only a short time left in Portugal and we wanted to see more of the surrounding countryside. I said good-bye and wished him well from the both of us.''

"Without talking it over with me first? How could you, Bruno? David's a lovely person. How could you *do* that to him? Even if I felt that way, which I don't."

Bruno put down his sketch pad. With an almost studied slowness, he laid his pencil on top of it. "But darling, he was monopolizing all our time. We were getting too friendly. We were sinking into his world, becoming smothered by it."

"Bruno, you had no right to do that to me or to David. I feel terrible. Go call him right away and tell him it was all a misunderstanding and that we'd rather spend the rest of the summer with him instead of traipsing through monasteries. Now, before it's too late."

"I can't do that, Laura. What's said can't be unsaid. It was an honest attempt to keep us—to keep you—from becoming too dependent on David, from letting him control us. That was *my* assignment in Portugal, remember?"

Without waiting for an answer, Bruno picked up his pad and pencil and began sketching again.

I seethed. What gall! Taking charge of everything didn't mean ruling my mind. Or acting rude to a new and delightful friend. My wish to be free of decision had been granted with a vengeance. Beware of making wishes, a wise man once said.

"Bruno, why?" I asked, not satisfied with his answer.

"To be quite honest, I felt unhappy in our entire relationship with David. Any minute, I thought, he was going to ask for a donation to his temple, or to smuggle gold out of the country for him. Why else all his free time, all those colorful tales of intrigue?"

I got up so abruptly it startled Bruno. My book fell to the floor. I crossed the garden to our bedroom and slammed the door. In the room, I sat in a three-legged leather chair and stared out the window at the ocean. Never in my life had I been so humiliated. Even when I'd done something foolish, Mark had always backed me. He never went over my head.

Not at once, but half an hour later, Bruno came into the bedroom so quietly that before I knew it, he was on the floor beside me, contrite, almost in tears.

"Forgive me, Laura. I did a terrible thing." He tried to touch me, but when I flinched he withdrew his hand. "I've always been in supreme control of myself. Unassailable. Triumphant. Now, suddenly, I'm as jealous as some Sicilian who sees seduction in every man's glance at his wife. Certainly I was enchanted by his stories, but I saw—I thought I saw—a hidden meaning in them. A sort of subliminal mating call."

Bruno laid his head in my lap. My fingers, independent agents, stroked the soft fur of his beard. "That's silly, Bruno. There's only you. I wish you had told me earlier how you felt about David. We would have talked it through."

We stayed that way for some time longer. My anger cooled to a sympathy for Bruno, though I knew that later I'd think about what he'd done and feel heartsick over it.

"The truth also is," he said, turning his head and resting his other cheek in my lap, "that I'm getting bored with all this inactivity and indolence. You see, for weeks now, months, actually, an idea has been gestating in my head that excites me to my fingertips. A grand, noble idea."

Bruno raised his head and spoke to my eyes.

"I want to do a sculpting of Bobbi. The crowning achievement of my life."

The room became so quiet I could hear the waves running up the beach a hundred yards away. My heart stopped like an unplugged motor and I grew faint. "Bobbi?"

"Yes, a bust of her or a full figure. If you agree to it, that is."

At once I forgot about David and Bruno's cruel severing of our friendship and all the nights and days in Portugal. The idea took root in me and began growing like the trick photography of an opening flower. "Oh, Bruno, that would be wonderful—glorious—fabulous! I never dreamed of such a thing."

"But I did, love, from the first moment I saw her photos on your den wall. The seed was planted then, and even as I worked on *The Flutist* and sketched those fine Lisbon faces, it was her image I kept in my head. At home in the garage, I have about twenty different poses of her that I made while you were at work. Devious of me, but I knew you wouldn't object."

"A full-length piece, absolutely," I said. "So much of her specialness was in the way she carried herself and moved. Yes, that's what I'd like. Oh, if you could only capture that, sweetheart." I held Bruno's head in my hands and fervently kissed his mouth. "I'll want the finest marble—you must let me pay for it. And we'll need skylights in the garage. And better indoor lighting for the winter. Don't rush it. Take your time. I'll help you."

I got up and began pacing the room. "I've hundreds of photos of Bobbi. *Thousands* of images in my head, which, by the way, is reeling. When we get back, I'll call in a plumber. We'll install heat and a small bathroom."

Bruno waited patiently until I'd talked myself out. He got up and moved to the bed. I joined him there, quivering with excitement.

"Yes, yes," he said, holding me. "We'll do all those things." He held me tighter to slow me down.

But I was unstoppable, an unleashed fury. I continued on about the color of the marble, a stereo system in the garage to play his favorite music, and a telephone so that he wouldn't have to leave his work.

Bruno put his finger to my lips and I stopped babbling. The same finger he wagged in front of my face. "Sculpting is the one part of my life I must do alone. This statue of Bobbi cannot be a joint effort. Understand that now. In the sketching stage, the planning stage, the preparatory stage, I want your opinion, your help, your special knowledge of Bobbi, your *nourishment*. But the moment I take mallet and chisel in hand, you must back off completely and entirely. There is no other way. Is that agreed?"

I hesitated. Bruno in the driver's seat was merciless and uncompromising. He'd throw me out of the garage and bolt the door if he had to.

"Agreed?" he asked once more.

"Agreed."

Bruno was pleased, the way all men are when their will has prevailed. He held my chin as if positioning me for a sketch. "Besides, you really should be doing more creative things."

"Such as?"

"Such as composing. I've heard you now and then tinkering away. You have creative talent. Takes one to know one. Forget the library work; it's so demeaning. Pearls before swine. Create your own music instead of playing another's."

How did he guess that old secret of mine? Before we'd left for Europe, melodies had been crowding my head, spilling over into my playing. Crystal seeds that might grow, given the opportunity.

It was equally true that the library had lost its importance in my life. I no longer cared to enlighten and uplift my fellow Five Towners. Or fight Phil Coolidge. The girls surely didn't need me. When we patched up, I could only function as a glorified baby-sitter or the place to run to after a domestic squabble.

What better way to spend my silver and gold years than creating with Bruno? A marriage of music and sculpting. Perhaps I'd compose only a few sheets of decent music, but Bruno would create a Bobbi in creamy marble to match the Bobbi forever in my heart.

"That's probably what I'll do, darling," I told Bruno. He began undressing. Talk of his work had been more stimulating to him than foreplay. He was already primed for penetration.

But I wasn't interested in sex, not yet, not with so much on my mind.

"Composing can't be a full-time job for me, Bruno."

The shades were up and I could see the clouds beginning to disperse, combining and recombining into various shapes: a horse's head, a snail, a skinny girl walking on stilts.

"That's so. It's impossible to keep the flow for more than four or five hours a day and do good work. Maybe you ought to consider something more rewarding than the library. Move to a higher plane. The Consortium. You have the intelligence, the dedication, the sensitivity, the organizing skills. You could be a tremendous force for good. I can see you eventually sharing the leadership with Violet."

I felt a rapid de-escalation; a sinking. "I turned her down a dozen times."

"That was then. Things have changed for you these past few months. You're not the same unsure person. You've arrived. You can handle Violet. Between you and me, she needs handling, polishing."

I left Bruno and went to the window. A sailboat with a blue triangular sail moved effortlessly across the ocean halfway to the horizon. The sail united the blue of the Atlantic with the blue of the sky above. It was as though one were flowing into the other.

Bruno joined me at the window. I was held from behind. I could feel his bulge lessen and go flat until we formed a seamless weld.

"You were a pitiful sight at the cemetery, a broken shell. Brought to your knees—I must say it—by children who should have revered you. But here in Cascais, you've mended nicely. As strong as only the reborn can be. You should at least consider helping other women who have suffered similar painful losses. So Violet's not exactly your cup of tea, but the Consortium's the best game in town. At least consider it."

"I will," I promised, meaning it. "Maybe she'll seem less opportunistic, less a scheming manipulator oncc I get back. Maybe I *have* changed."

My mind now at rest, I pulled down the blinds, undressed, and welcomed Bruno into my bed. When I raised the blinds again, the sun was well on its way to America.

I felt a terrible longing to follow that sun. "Let's go home," I told Bruno. "It's time."

"Yes," he said, lifting himself, resting on one elbow. "Home is where the heart is, where the work is. I'll make reservations first thing in the morning." He leaped out of bed.

"Where are you going?"

"To phone David. Tell him we're leaving and that we'd like to see him one last time. I'll make my apologies when we get together, and you can return his book. This way, we can quit Portugal with no regrets and no hard feelings."

"That would be wonderful."

Bruno returned, laughing. "He was delighted to hear from us and that we'd changed our minds. We're to meet at 8:30 for a super-special send-off. And you're to keep the Galdos book as a memento."

"Thank you, my love," I told Bruno. I wondered if Magda Lupescu ever said that to Carol for some favor. If he'd been as charming as Bruno. If Magda had been as forgiving as me.

"No, thank *you,* darling, for a grand summer." He snuggled in beside me and we thanked each other again, but in a more expressive way.

*seventeen*

T̲HE HOTTEST, DRIEST sum-
mer in memory descended on the Five Towns like a biblical vis-
itation. Many of my customers and former neighbors had fled to
the south of France, the Hamptons, or those little-known islands
in the Caribbean that took over from Cancun and Cozumel as
the latest in-places. Rarely did any Five Towner venture out on
the Avenue during the middle of the day, since from eleven A.M.
to four P.M. a white-hot sun, like a glaring spotlight, hung im-
mobile in a translucent sky and impartially and unmercifully
baked both sides of the business thoroughfare.

I'd come to feel that summer was the price you paid for the
other three seasons and spent as little of it as possible outdoors.

During this especially arid one, I did my gardening in the late afternoon. Each day I noted with pride how the great Healy desert was changing to a shady preserve teeming with nature's bounty. Even Virginia stood with me in the early evenings before leaving for work, admiring what I'd created from nothing.

"You're a goddamn Luther Burbank," she said.

In spite of everything, Virginia taught me to enjoy the summer, one of the many things I learned from her. To be with my love, I took off Wednesdays and helped myself to occasional three-day weekends, conforming to her schedule.

"Sorry," she'd said in June. "I can't take my two weeks all in a string. Can't afford it. They just raised prices at Lawrence's institution. But we can still do a lot. For example, I'd like to go backpacking. I know this really primitive area in the Catskills. Near Roscoe. Mountains and forests and lakes and Indian trails you won't believe. We'll sleep in canvas bags, eat over an open fire, and make love under a canopy of stars."

"'Under a canopy of stars.' I'd like that," I said.

One Friday morning, we packed the Volvo and drove upstate. For three glorious days Virginia and I traversed in hip boots. We trooped. We trekked. We marched. We forded streams. We suffered mosquito bites, sore muscles, and rashes from toting our backpacks. But we also stood hush and enchanted by the sight of a small lake with the morning mist lifting to reveal a family of deer at the water's edge, drinking. A mountaintop at dusk. An open field strewn with buttercups and dotted with bushes of huckleberries at the peak of ripeness.

Evening brought contentment. A steak for two sizzled on an open grill. Tied to a tree with a sturdy cord, a six-pack of Tuborg cooled in a nearby lake. Safe in my arms against the chill of a Catskill evening, Virginia found and named the first stars. Then she pointed out things about herself I'd only guessed at. The general subject was mistakes.

She'd married Rob Alston while both were teaching in the same school. A case of throwing two complete amateurs at maturity together and hoping for the best. Before their first anniversary, it was all over. She got a divorce and lived by herself for a year or two. Her next was a drunk. Infused with missionary zeal, she would reform him. He was forty. She was twenty-five. He taught American literature at Queens College, where she went at night for a master's. She became pregnant. "How, I'll never know, since he was sloshed half the time and impotent the rest. I got rid of it; we needed both salaries. A few months later I walked out on him.

"About Healy, I won't say much. You've heard it all from John Tierney, our local Rona Barrett. Except to mention this: in order not to become a three-time loser, I tried awfully hard with that man. It didn't work, but I didn't stick my head in an oven over it. I'm pretty sound and secure, as you probably have noticed. Few things rock my boat. The secret of my success is I'm a failure. Being a loser has taught me a lot, Gerber. You don't learn anything from winning. Only how wonderful you are. And we all know that there's nothing really wonderful in life except ice cream, babies, and multiple orgasm."

We were into August, the month I dreaded. It was time again for her monthly journey to Albany to visit Lawrence.

"If you're doing nothing this weekend and want a few days out of the county, maybe you'd like to drive up to Greenbrier."

"Sure, I'd love to."

"It won't be a fun trip like backpacking. You'll be chauffeuring me up to the motel, then from the motel to the institution. I won't let you come inside, so you'll have to entertain yourself all day, both days."

"I'll go visit the governor. He loves to meet the people."

"Then it's chauffeuring me back to the motel in the evening. The same story on Sunday."

"Fine. No problem."

"After a day with Lawrence, don't expect much from me at night."

"I'll manage."

"The point is, Gerber, there's nothing in it for you."

"The point is, are you sure you want me along? It seems to me you said it and now you're sorry you did and you'd like to back out. But I won't let you back out. An offer is an offer."

"Maybe you're right. But if you really don't mind . . ."

What I'd heard was a small cry for help. Being with her these months in cramped quarters had taught me to listen with what Theodore Reik called "the third ear," a new piece of anatomy for me. I'd learned to sense when she was in pain or trouble. With Laura, I'd assumed that she could work out her own day-to-day problems as I could mine.

Instead of merely an overnight bag, Virginia packed a suitcase and a garment holder. "Maybe it won't be that bleak after all, Gerber. We'll be in restaurants three nights. Maybe a movie or summer stock, if I'm not too wiped out."

We left on a blisteringly hot Friday, a day that threatened to shatter all records. I drove away with a hard rock in my stomach. The day before had been Caryn's birthday, and all week I'd waited for her to return my phone calls, to at least acknowledge the card I'd sent. Inside I'd placed a note. "You're too old for presents, so how about dinner instead?"

No response. When I called her office on Thursday, I was told by her secretary that she'd already left on vacation. Wouldn't return until after Labor Day.

Sara and Steven had been gone since the beginning of July, counselors at a summer camp for diabetic children. Not a word from them all summer.

We took the thruway north. For the next few hours we chatted like sitcom sweethearts while Beethoven's Third, Fifth, and Seventh played on the tape deck. Virginia talked more than usual to mask her anxiety.

At Kingston, we got off the highway for coffee. In the diner she said, "You'll have to forgive me about not permitting you into the institution. Lawrence is hard enough to cope with when I'm alone with him, and I try to be alone with him for the entire day. It's a terrible ordeal. I'm almost sorry you're coming along."

"It'll be all right," I said. "You take care of business and I'll take care of me."

The village of Greenbrier (population 3,609 according to the marker on the edge of town) had been laid out by sensible and devout Dutch farmers almost three hundred years ago. In the shape of a cross, it had one street running north/south, the other east/west. They must have been fair and equitable, these farmers and their descendants, since Greenbrier contained two of everything, one on each street. Two pharmacies, two restaurants, two gas stations, two hardware stores, two supermarkets, and two doctors and lawyers.

We registered at the Dutch Maid, where Virginia was well known, then unpacked. After showering, we made love because she wanted it that way. "I won't be much good all weekend, so you better get me while you can."

Dinner was in the Bird in the Bush on Main Street, where they featured home-style cooking and local produce. Virginia swore she never got ptomaine poisoning in the nine years she'd eaten there. Afterward, we went for a drive along the Hudson. She sat close to me, her head on my shoulder.

At a red light, she said, "Do you have anything left for another toss in the sack?"

I made a sharp U-turn and headed back to the motel.

---

"Rise and shine, you old lecher."

I raised my head at the source of that jarring command. Virginia was emerging from the bathroom, the steam following her like a mugger. She was nude, wet as a fish pulled from the sea, and all fluid motion. She dried herself with a large white fluffy towel.

"We have to get up and get ourselves moving now, pronto."

"What time is it?"

"Six-thirty. We're late. Move it if you want a nice, unhurried breakfast. I want to be on the road by quarter of eight."

Virginia wore a white dress, high on top, low at the hemline, a pair of white flats, and a touch of Chantilly cologne. Prim and proper as a high-school girl going to her first prom.

We had breakfast at the motel. Virginia ate her eggs slowly, chewing assiduously, the look on her lovely face of a condemned prisoner resigned to his fate.

The low stone fence, open wooden gate, and tar road leading to the mansion on the hill gave no indication of the kind of services performed at the Lang Institute. Not even the townspeople knew, according to Virginia. "They think it's health-related, a sanitarium of sorts, but they're not sure. It's better this way. Fewer snooping Dutchmen to come peek at the freaks. This isn't Transylvania and the castle of Dr. Frankenstein. It's a fine facility trying to perform miracles."

I was ready to drive Virginia up the road to the main building but she asked to be let out at the gate. "I'd rather walk the rest of the way. I need the transition time. Have a nice day and pick me up at six."

I turned to give her a kiss of support, but she was already out of the car. She stood for an instant, facing the triple-storied brick-and-ivied structure as though estimating its worth, then threw back her shoulders and strode up the hill.

I waited until that moving apparition in white vanished into the mass of brown brick, then drove back to town.

Eight-thirty and the birds were still dozing in the trees. In Nassau County the birds woke earlier, life there being more competitive. I walked along the row of stores on Commerce Street. Little had changed here in four decades. The same green and white diagonally striped awning over the hardware store. The same, though faded, Ex-Lax sign hung across the top of the pharmacy whose windows displayed old-fashioned apothecary jars labeled in Latin. The streets were deserted, though lit by the sun lifting over the eastern hills along the Hudson, plowing a phosphorescent path up the sidewalk. At the end of Commerce I turned off to the residential area.

After a short walk, I found the perfect street to match my mood, which was sad and elegiac over the sight of Virginia bravely marching up the hill to the institute. Set back from lawns remarkably green despite the heat wave were the houses I'd come to see, that I'd known would somehow be there. Old, very old, each one was double-storied, turreted, gabled, and topped with spires and weather vanes that pointed the Dutch Reformed way to God. I halted before each house, absorbing it through my pores.

One house in particular reached out to hold me. It had a wide front, brown and white trim on the windows, and white crisscross lattice under a generous front porch. Towering over the frame were two front turrens, with a pair of attic windows between them, that gazed out at the Hudson like the eyes of a dragon.

Something about me loves old houses. The solidity, the security, the long association with a time, a place, an attitude. Whatever it was hadn't died when I'd left Woodsburgh.

The woman on the porch was completely disguised in a magenta terrycloth bathrobe and flowered bouffant shower cap. In her fist, a dry mop gave the impression of some equestrian knight about to do battle. She ran the mop across the low ceiling, then up and down the porch pillars. "Morning," she said in a sharp, forthright manner, more to dismiss than greet me.

I approached the house along a path of irregular flagstones. "Good morning," I returned. "My name is Gerber. I'm staying the weekend at the Dutch Maid."

"You don't look like an antiquer, so it must be the Lang Institute."

"Yes."

"Used to work there. In the kitchen. One of yours a patient?"

"No. The son of a friend is."

"Tell your friend to save her money and take him home. They're all hopeless cases out there."

"It's her money."

"Well, she must have plenty of it."

"I've been admiring your house," I said. "It's a very impressive house."

"Nicer than some. Not as nice as others." She dipped the mop into a bucket of water on the porch steps, wrung out the excess by hand, then painted long, even strokes across the width.

"Can I ask a kindness of you?" I asked.

"Depends on the kindness."

"I'd like to have a look at your house inside."

The woman suspended mopping. "Whatever for?"

"Well, that's hard to explain. I used to live in a fine old house like this. A long time ago."

The woman chewed on her cheek, part, I guessed, of her thinking process. "Darnedest thing I ever heard. I suppose it'll be all right, though."

The first-floor rooms were large, musty, and poorly furnished with items no one would consider collectible. More like the junk in Virginia's living room, and not at all similar to Laura's tasteful decor, each room as perfect and balanced as the movements of a Mozart symphony.

I was led up to the second floor. There were four bedrooms, in each a fireplace, a four-poster covered with a white frilly dust ruffle, a tiny mirrored dresser, and bare tongue-and-groove on the floor. From the unlived, museumlike quality of the rooms, I couldn't tell which were presently occupied.

"Should have sold out a long time ago," said the woman. We were having coffee in the kitchen, sitting at a wooden, hand-carved kitchen table in front of a Dutch oven that took up the entire back wall. "Got a son in the oil business in Saudi Arabia. Hell of a place for a Hudson Valley boy. Once in a blue moon I get a picture postcard from him of a camel in the desert. Then there's my daughter in Philadelphia, secretary to a bank president. She phones on my birthday and at Christmastime. Twice a year. Regular as clockwork. A second son somewhere in Alaska. Haven't heard from him since Jimmy Carter left the White House. Been a widow twenty years."

I left and the woman went back to her cleaning chores. I was sorry I'd asked to see her house. I'd come looking for fond memories, signs of a loving family built around a bastion of wood and stone. I'd found only the misery and bitterness of an abandoned parent. My country cousin.

The rest of the day I drove around, as far west as Schoharie, with its two-hundred-year-old buildings, churches, and watermills. As far east across the Hudson as Kinderhook and the home of Martin Van Buren, the first president born in the United States.

The broken and battered creature I picked up at six sharp bore little resemblance to the vision of beauty I'd deposited at the institute a few hours earlier. Her dress hung wrinkled and disheveled. There were dark stains all over it, as if a passing car on a rainy street had splattered her. Her hair had lost its sheen and body, hanging lank over her face.

Virginia got in the car and said nothing until we reached the motel. Then in a voice to match her trampled appearance, she said, "If you don't mind, I'll skip dinner. You go by yourself, then take in a movie. There's a drive-in a few miles south."

"We'll see."

Inside the room, she stripped, her back to me, suddenly modest, and left her clothes in a heap. She emerged from the shower and disappeared under the covers of her bed.

On my bed, I lay, waiting for her to speak. Whatever she needed, I would supply. All she had to do was ask or give a sign. It would take only a look, a word, for me to wade in.

"Get me a pack of Marlboros," she said about seven. "There's a machine in the lobby." Her back was to me, the covers still over her head.

I walked to the front desk, changed a couple of bills for coins, and came back with the cigarettes. I opened the pack and lit one, my first ever. She sat up, her back against the headboard, spread her legs, covered them with the blanket, and took the cigarette from me. Her eyes were puffy, and though there was little light in the room, she squinted.

"Move over, kid," I said, taking a chance.

Warily, Virginia ceded me half the bed. We sat together, shoulder touching shoulder while she smoked with deliberation and care, as if it were some intellectual endeavor.

For hours we sat that way, Virginia lighting a fresh cigarette with the glowing tip of the one she was smoking.

"Get me a refill. Please," she said with a dry, dead voice when the Marlboro box was empty.

The desk clerk was out of change. I had to walk to the Bird in the Bush. They were serving roast turkey with chestnut stuffing, candied yams, and fresh stringbeans. I'd lost my appetite.

When I returned ten minutes later, she'd already traveled a few more light-years away from me. I lay on my bed waiting for her to return.

Between nine and ten, judging by the number of cigarettes she smoked, she got up to go to the bathroom. In deathly darkness I heard the toilet flush, then the faucet run.

She came back and resumed her position. Then, "If this is less than thrilling for you, Gerber, you can leave first thing in the morning. I'll catch the bus tomorrow night and take a taxi from the Port Authority."

"When you finally say something, it's dumb," I said. "Must be from all that nicotine in your brain. Actually, I'm having a dandy time sopping up all that countryside, mucking through old barns."

"You son of a bitch," she said, and began crying.

I took the cigarette from between her fingers and snuffed it out in the glass ashtray on her night table already filled beyond capacity. She turned and held me as if she'd suddenly grown dizzy. "Mark, oh God, it's bad, bad, bad. They won't let me feed him anymore. He spits out everything I put in his mouth. I thought we were communicating during the meal. That's not too much to ask for, is it? A few hours, two days a month? They tell me he could live to be ninety or go next week. I could come up here for the next ninety fucking years and wash mashed carrots out of my ears every time. I'd do that gladly if I knew he knew who I was. If there was a spark of recognition."

Then Virginia broke away from me as though ashamed of her outburst. She reached for the Marlboro box. Failing to find it, she returned. I put one hand on the small of her back. The other held her head against my chest. She felt terribly warm, as if full of fever.

"Tell me about Bobbi," she said.

I didn't know if I could. I hadn't spoken to anyone about her since the crash. A kind of selfishness, Laura would say, an unwillingness to share. But in the motel room, in the safety of darkness, with a fellow sufferer I cared very much about, I told Virginia.

I held back nothing. Bobbi as a child, our unbelievable good fortune in conceiving her after years of specialists and medication, the rewards she brought us for waiting so long. My daughter at each stage of her life, anecdotes, bright sayings, and precious,

precious acts of kindness and generosity only she was capable of. Bobbi interacting with us, her sisters, the world at large, conquering all with the force of her goodness.

"I'm sorry I never knew her," said Virginia.

Then—it must have been three in the morning—I related the circumstances of Bobbi's death. That afternoon last August, almost an anniversary. Each searing detail. Telling her, I cried without shame.

Virginia put her arm around my head and held me, as she probably wanted to hold Lawrence. She rocked me until I fell asleep.

---

"It's seven o'clock," she said in my ear, her hand lightly on my shoulder. I'd conked out fully clothed, on the softest pillow I'd ever known.

She was up, showered, dressed in pink, and fresh as clean laundry. Her hair was dried, falling lovingly around her shoulders.

"I'm going to the institute with you today," I said firmly.

"Like fucking hell you are."

I began brushing my teeth. I rinsed and came out of the bathroom. "I'm going. I want to be with you on this. You can't take me part of the way and then leave me. I should have insisted yesterday morning."

"It's no day at the seashore."

"No fooling. But if we stand here playing tennis with it, we'll be late."

I dressed speedily, prepared for further displays of rejection from Virginia. There were none. "You must be starved," I said, sending up a trial balloon.

"Famished," she said. "Let's get to a restaurant and I'll show you how a healthy Irish colleen eats when she puts her mind to it. If I really let myself go, you know, I could look like Nell Carter."

---

Dr. Peter C. Kolbrun, the chief administrator of the Lang Institute, showed me around himself. First the grounds, baronial rather than institutional, with many randomly strewn shady weeping willows and flower beds, and more varieties of roses than I dreamed existed. I saw nurses sitting with patients on back lawns or strolling along threadlike paths. Therapists and patients together on benches, one to one. I gleaned honest concern and saw spotless cleanliness, modern private rooms, and state-of-the-art equipment when Dr. Kolbrun took me indoors. I was duly impressed, and told the gray-bearded, sad-eyed, sixtyish administrator. I said that if anything could help Lawrence, it was this oasis of kindness and skill.

Then I met Virginia's son and realized that all the restful grounds and hi-tech methodology didn't mean a thing as far as he was concerned.

My first impression of Lawrence Healy was of a very large, very old baby. He had the vacant, innocent eyes of the blind, but like a newborn, nothing about him was coordinated. In his wheelchair he sat, arms and legs dangling like those of a puppet at rest. His voice, when he cried out with some inner distress, was feral and inhuman, the only provocation being our entrance into the room. Then he threw himself and jerked his arms and legs, and would have fallen from the wheelchair if not held around the middle with a restraining strap.

At Lawrence's side, a pretty young girl of twenty-five named Molly Cardin, touched and talked to him, calming his internal storms. She was almost beautiful, with a rag mop of curly red hair, button nose, and a smile potent enough to dissolve an iceberg.

Despite Lawrence's contortions, I could detect a definite similarity between mother and son. The same long, shapely face, strong chin, brown eyes, and chestnut hair. Except that in a millisecond during his early fetal life, a gene so small it could only be seen through an electron microscope, had gone awry, wrecking at least three lives.

We sat in a room so pleasant and airy it could be offered as a prescription against depression. There were so many windows we seemed to be at the bottom of an ocean of light. Molly Cardin remained close to Lawrence's side as if fearful that we'd come to spirit him away.

For the next half hour I remained close by, observing Virginia trying to make herself known to her son. Each time she touched him, he howled. Each time it took Molly minutes to quiet him down. It seemed to be a Theater of the Absurd drama for three players. Virginia would put her hand on Lawrence. Lawrence would bay at an invisible moon. Molly Cardin would take his hands in hers and press them together, sending vibrations of assurance up his arms to an infantile brain.

"He does that with everybody," Molly explained.

"I'm not everybody. I'm his mother."

"I know that, Mrs. Healy, but he doesn't. His mind is at the development level of a two-year-old."

"He knew me once. Before we came here and for a little while after. But it's less and less each time I come."

"That's because then you were with him night and day," said Molly.

"That's impossible now. I have to work to pay the bill."

"I know that," said Molly, releasing Lawrence's hands, then sitting on the arm of his wheelchair, her fingers brushing the hair from his sightless eyes. "What's happened to Lawrence eventually happens to all our patients. We become the only parent they acknowledge. Everyone else they repel. Violently, in Lawrence's case."

"So all my efforts to reach him are meaningless."

"As far as he's concerned, yes. For you, that's another story. Mrs. Healy, if you feel the need, keep coming back. You're most welcome, of course. As long as it doesn't distress him so badly that he becomes . . . impossible."

"Like yesterday."

"Like yesterday," agreed Molly.

"So you're really telling me not to visit anymore and make your job more difficult."

Molly thought for a long moment. She tapped Lawrence's earlobe, a playful gesture he instantly recognized and responded to with an idiot's grin. "I'm officially telling you to do as your heart and conscience dictate. Unofficially, as one human being to another, I have to say you're only wasting your time. And you're probably doing him some harm. Each time, after you leave, we have to give him a tranquilizer, otherwise he keeps the entire dormitory floor awake with his cries. Considering the rudimentary nature of his nervous system, we'd rather not medicate him. I hope you understand."

"I do. Honestly. That's the problem. I know I shouldn't be here, but I also know I must. I have to tell you, Molly, that there are times I wish he'd die and end all this misery. For a few moments I'm happy thinking about being free of him. Only a few moments, though."

Throughout this tormenting scene, I could only act as spectator, remaining at arm's length and offering Virginia no more than the shadow I'd cast in that brilliant room. I sensed she'd gained strength from that shadow. I was beginning to believe in the power of a loving presence.

For the remainder of the day, Virginia made no attempt to touch her son. Indoors and out, over the spacious grounds, we stayed a few feet behind Molly, like an entourage, as she pushed his wheelchair and sang Beatles' songs and crooned Irish lullabies.

"'Danny Boy' seems to be his favorite," said Molly. We'd halted before a natural pond behind a second building where many of the staff lived. Virginia picked up a pebble and tossed it into the pond. "That's the song my mother used to sing at his crib when she'd visit," she said.

———————

For enduring such punishment all weekend, Virginia was strangely talkative on the way back to the City late Sunday afternoon. Almost lighthearted. "Well, Gerber, you've gone to the bottom of the barrel with me and I'm grateful you insisted on it. Thank you. You've seen my darkest moment, my deepest secret."

She wasn't kidding.

"I'm glad I insisted."

"I guess you've lost any illusion you may have had of me as a tough old broad."

"You *are* a tough broad to everyone, but underneath that veneer is your real strength, the kind that brings you up to Greenbrier every month and sends you home knowing that a month later you'll be doing it all over again. I admire you for that."

"Enough to buy me a very expensive dinner in a very French restaurant?"

"That much, yes."

"I know a place near Newburgh that serves frogs' legs you'd have an orgasm over."

"I could use another one this weekend. Let's go, *ma chérie.*"

––––––––––

We arrived home after midnight. There was a message on the machine I'd recently installed in the living room. From Calvin Spotswood, the assistant DA handling Bobbi's case.

"Mark, this is Friday afternoon. Four P.M. I'm calling to tell you that the trial will start for sure Tuesday, October eleventh, nine-thirty A.M., at the usual place. It'll run about six weeks, from the way McGuire's attorney is talking. Fortify yourself and try and be there as much as possible."

The next morning I told Chuck Eisenberg, my manager, to help me out. I'd make it up to him as soon as the trial was over.

He told me to do what I had to do and he'd cover the bases.

I told him all I had to do was show up and sit there.

He said that should be easy enough.

I told him it would probably be the hardest thing I'd ever have to do.

# *eighteen*

**H**OW ARE YOU, dear lady? So very nice to see you again. It's been *ever* so long, and may I say you're looking splendid. Sensational. Retirement fits you like a glove."

Phil Coolidge gave me the warmest greeting of my life, now that I was no longer a threat to him, real or imagined. This pleasant October morning I was merely a patron, come to the library to return the new Hilma Wolitzer novel.

I'd spent a few moments with Stella and Margarite, then headed for the Current Fiction shelves. Phil had blocked the way, then showered me with compliments.

"What are you doing, now that you're a lady of leisure?"

"Quite a bit. Music takes up most of my time. I'm trying my hand at composing." I tried to be indefinite without being deceitful about my new vocation. Phil was no longer the enemy but he hadn't become a friend.

Besides this new demeanor, Phil had also changed physically. He'd lost a few pounds and discarded his thick glasses in favor of contacts. There was a new devil-may-care ambience about him, as though he'd spent his summer viewing Cary Grant movies.

"I'm on my way to your successor's office. Care to join me? If, of course, the trauma won't be too severe."

"There is no trauma, Phil. I resigned, remember? I wasn't fired."

What hadn't changed was his condescending manner and the contempt beneath it. But now it was Suzy Gordon's problem. She'd volunteered to introduce the Before the Beach speakers after I'd left for Europe. Evidently she'd done a satisfactory job. When I got back and quit, Phil had asked her to take over my other duties. The first week in September I cleaned out my desk, took the few odds and ends that were mine, and left. My replacement, I subsequently learned, was in divorce court that very day, shedding Paul. I did leave a handwritten note wishing her well. For the library's sake and despite our disaffection, I'd meant it.

Suzy Gordon had always been a very handsome woman. Full-bodied, with a face no one could ever find fault in. More than ample breasts, the answers to most men's deepest needs. Her crowning glory of wheat-colored, shoulder-length hair had never been abused in a beauty parlor, the envy of all her tinted and bleached friends. So I was surprised at how much she'd changed since I'd last seen her on the streets of Cedarhurst. A slimmed-down version of my once-best friend rose to take my hand. Her hair had been cut and frosted. Someone clever had rerouted her eyebrows and shown her how to apply makeup. She'd gone from bovine to vulpine while I'd sunned myself on the beach at Cascais. Now she resembled three-quarters of the overforty females in the Five Towns.

"The world takes funny bounces, doesn't it," she said. "Thank you, by the way, for such a neat, clean, lovely office. Everything was so orderly. Knowing you, it shouldn't have come as a big surprise. The few problems I did have, Phil came to my rescue."

A spark flashed between them that I'd have to be legally blind to miss. It lit up the dark corners I'd been wondering about, such as why the change in Phil's appearance and in Suzy's. Evidently they'd found one another and made the necessary alterations to suit.

"I should have come before to wish you well in person instead of that note. But it's the old story: since I've retired, I'm busier than ever."

At what, Suzy didn't ask. I wasn't at all peeved when Phil cut in. "Now that you are here, Laura, perhaps you'd like to sit in— elder statesman–like—on a meeting. A short one, I pray. Do you recall the much-publicized Martha Haymarket trial?"

"Vaguely," I said. "Isn't she the battered wife who stabbed her husband to death on her birthday."

"One hundred and twenty-eight times, and with an ice pick," contributed Suzy. "She certainly made her point—literally and figuratively."

Phil beamed as though Suzy was his precocious daughter who'd uttered a gem. "Anyway, she was acquitted in July with the aid of the Women's Consortium and their world-class battery of lawyers. Well, the notorious Mrs. Haymarket is now working for the Consortium. In what capacity, we'll soon learn. She's due at any moment."

With that, Suzy's phone lit up. She answered, nodded, hung up. "Mrs. Haymarket is as punctual as she is thorough," she said.

Phil left the room but returned at once with a woman in her middle sixties. Her short white hair she wore in a carefree, crown-of-laurels style, with a thin hawklike face and the deep-set hollow eyes of a heroin addict.

Martha Haymarket entered the room ahead of Phil radiating sweetness and light. "Good morning," she said, fake-cheery. "I didn't know I was to meet with a full committee."

"This is not a full committee, I can assure you, madam," said Phil, falling naturally into his officious mode. "We are Susan Gordon, the new director of activities, Laura Gerber, our former director of activities who came by serendipitously, and who, I'm sure, can only add to our discussion, and I am Phillip Coolidge, the director of the Cedarhurst Library, the one your most able Mrs. Fleming spoke to originally. I'm present because any representative from the Consortium merits my hands-on attention."

Martha Haymarket nodded her acceptance of the three-to-one ratio, though I could see mistrust flickering in her eyes. She had small, thick hands and stubby fingers. I could see them wielding an ice pick.

"You're busy people, so I'll get down to cases," said Martha Haymarket. "As you know I was recently acquitted in a murder case that received quite a bit of attention from the media. But of course they only played up the lurid details. They hardly touched on the broader issues, those of the battered wife and very often her abused children. How the law mistreats us. We'd like to hold a public forum, here at the library, about this entire range of subjects. Actually we'd like a series of town hall–like meetings for the month of November. We've put together twelve informative sessions of an hour lecture by various authorities with a second hour for questions and answers. We'll provide the coffee and cake."

Phil was sitting tensed on the new fake-leather couch brought in for the new assistant director. His eyes floated immediately to the ceiling and beyond, in what I knew from past experience was a form of communication with the deity as well as an expression of disgust. Suzy listened diligently, lending a kind of seriousness and authority to a proposal I would have declined since that meant bumping the entire November program on very short notice.

"My dear woman," said Phil. "I'll have you know that I'm quite sympathetic toward your cause. I support ERA. I'm pro-choice. But I cannot, even in the cause of justice, permit the Women's Consortium to destroy our already overburdened schedule. Why don't you try the high school?"

Martha Haymarket blinked but refused to budge, obviously no stranger to resistance. Her deep-set eyes found a spot in the center of Phil's head and latched on like suction cups. She said, "Does that mean you won't cooperate, because the library prefers to show a movie or entertain a bunch of seniors who are really removed from what's truly happening in this world? Where are your priorities, Mr. Coolidge? Do you realize how much influence we have in this community?"

Phil excused himself and called Suzy to his office for a conference. I was left alone with Martha Haymarket. Till this moment I'd been no more than furniture to her. She examined me now as though I was at the other end of a rifle scope. Knowing Phil, I smelled surrender in the air.

Martha Haymarket smirked. "So you're Laura Gerber. The eighth wonder of the world, according to Violet. Any day you're going to join us, they said. As though you were the Messiah and we were waiting for the dead to rise out of the grave. Well, let me tell you that in spite of your money and good looks and background, you don't seem much like salvation to me. You look more like a snooty Five Towns dame."

"Looks can be deceiving," I told her, unshaken. "I'd never have thought that after having the guts to ventilate a man one hundred and twenty-eight times, you'd surrender your brains to a manipulator like Violet Fleming. And you needn't worry. There'll be no Second Coming at the Consortium. The only Messiah I'm interested in is the one by Handel."

There was a moment of rest between us, a regrouping of forces. I rarely engage in swapping insults, but she'd cut too deep to be allowed to get away with it. Phil and Suzy returned, Suzy out front like a stalking horse. She took her seat while Phil found a position by the window overlooking the back garden. Without me, that island of serenity had reverted to a weed patch. I tried not to think about it.

"In the interest of fairness, this is what we propose. We'll serve as host for your series. But only once a week, not three times. You can use the premises for the next three months, however. You'll have your twelve sessions but at our convenience. I—we— think that's a very generous contribution to your cause."

Slowly, Martha Haymarket stood up, savoring the taste of victory, the hard lines of her face melting. "I'll bring it back to the board for consideration. But I think we have a deal." She walked up to Phil at the window and stuck out her hand. Queasily, as if grasping a live electric wire, Phil took it.

"Done," he said without enthusiasm, and left the room. I understood his haste. The French generals must have left that railroad car at Compiègne just as speedily after caving in to Hitler.

The victor was waiting for me in the parking lot by my car. I set myself for confrontation.

"I did damned well in there with those nonworldly types," she confided. "My first outing for the WC. I told Violet I could do it. They wanted *you* to tackle the libraries but I told her we needed someone with a backbone."

"They?"

"Violet and that pint-size Italian you're keeping."

I got in my car and drove off, not because I was afraid of what else she might say, but because I had a lunch appointment with Mark. I'd phoned the day before. We'd talked about how my summer went and what it was like at the trial for him. He wasn't the least surprised that I'd stayed away. Calvin Spotswood had sent a formal letter announcing the start, with a handwritten footnote asking me to attend. "It has psychological value in influencing the judge," he'd scrawled.

"To what end?" I'd said to Mark. "Whatever they do to McGuire can't be enough. I won't go through it all again."

I switched tracks. "Have you heard from the girls yet?"

"No."

"I have. That's why I'm calling. But I'd rather not discuss it over the phone."

"How about over lunch? At the Garden Spot. We can still have a civilized meeting to discuss common problems. Children make strange bedfellows. And bedfellows make strange children."

"Do you want to put us on display at the Spot? Start the whole town buzzing again?"

Mark thought awhile. "We're meatless old bones to them, Laura. I'm sure they've got plenty of fresh kills to tear apart."

---

During the short ride to the restaurant, I reminded myself that if mishandled, the lunch would end abruptly and badly, with one of us getting up and walking out. I wanted peace between us and in my new life. I no longer hated him for what he was, and wasn't—which didn't mean I forgave him his inconsiderate behavior and shortcomings. Only that I'd adjusted to them and put it all behind me.

I sat in the parking lot behind the Spot and went over the things not to do, such as flay him for past errors or make fun of the woman he lived with, or the house he lived in. After all, I wasn't entirely free from ridicule, as Martha Haymarket had demonstrated. And we really did have family business to kick around, not one another.

I was late a forgivable five minutes only because I sat trying to imagine some of the dialogues Violet and Bruno may have had about me. If Bruno had truly betrayed me, then what was I to do?

Mark was waiting, on time as always, though he'd never confused punctuality with integrity. An awkward moment arose when each of us wondered whether to kiss or shake hands, but Mark solved the problem by taking my topcoat and hanging it in the coatroom. I wore a black skirt and white blouse without realizing that they were Mark's favorite colors for me. My hair, unusually long, still contained pieces of the Portuguese sun.

Seeing Mark after so long had no effect on me, even though he looked better than I'd seen him in years. Better even than at my father's funeral. No longer the dry, foggy academic or the lethargic businessman he'd oscillated between. How much of this rebirth could Virginia Healy take credit for? Was it frequent and vigorous sex? For a man, sex is always the major life force. For a woman, for me, it was only a contributing factor. Bruno's care and concern had been the instruments of my resurrection.

We sat far enough away from our usual table to remove it as a topic of conversation. George, the waiter, had grown slower over the summer, his shuffling gait more painful to watch.

"Parkinson's," said Mark, as if I hadn't been in the Spot since our last time together, hadn't noticed the man deteriorate week by week.

"It's good to see you two together again," said George. Neither of us tried to disabuse him of the notion that we'd reconciled. He seemed confused enough.

"Small chef salad. Diet Coke," I told him.

"The same," said Mark.

Never one for useless words or the long way around, Mark said, "You haven't cashed any of the checks I sent you. Didn't you get them?"

"Yes, every one. I tore them up. I don't need the money. Daddy left enough for quintuplets."

"That's good to know. It would have been better if you'd told me sooner. There was a time, when Eric first opened his new store last spring, that I was living hand to mouth. But I made sure your checks would clear. Anyway, I'm in pretty good shape now financially."

"I never knew. Why didn't you tell me?"

"Too much pride, I guess. I didn't want to be lumped with all those unsavory characters Violet and her bloodhounds track down. Those deadbeats."

"I'm sorry, Mark. I really am."

"That's history," said Mark. "Tell me about the girls. I guess you've made up with them. The last time we saw each other at the cemetery things looked pretty bleak."

"Nightmarish. You predicted they'd soon come to their senses and come back to me begging forgiveness. You were wrong about the timetable but right about the results. I feel you should know about it and what to expect from them."

The waiter returned with two retsinas and one huge salad for two instead of separate orders. "It's what you always have," explained George. "And the wine is on the house in honor of this occasion."

We didn't fight him; it would have been foolish to try and explain. We knew we were apart forever, our only living ties Sara and Caryn. They may have been fortune's hostages, but we were theirs whether we liked it or not.

"May I serve you, madam?" said George.

"Yes," I said resignedly. "Please do."

When George left, I said, "We've made up. I think they came to realize what an enormous injustice they were doing to Bobbi's memory and to us."

At the mention of her name a cloud passed over Mark's face. He sighed. "She would have loved this fine fall weather," he said.

"She was a fall person," I agreed. "Though she made the best of whatever came along. Any season or situation. Let me tell you how we finally got together, Mark."

Mark put down his knife and fork to listen.

"It happened last week. For over a month the phone would ring. I'd pick it up and there'd be no one there. At first I thought it was you, but indecision was never your problem. It wasn't a pervert—no heavy breathing or dirty words. Once, I heard lots of children in the background and a school bell. Anyway, a kind of mother's intuition—I still believe in such fictions—told me it was time to act.

"The next afternoon, I went to Sara's apartment. I got there at five. Plenty of time for her to have gotten home and unwound. After a day in the classroom, Sara always needed lots of foraging time. Steven would be at his second job at the yeshiva in Far Rockaway. We could talk undisturbed for hours.

"Well, Sara didn't get home until six. A departmental conference. I sat waiting on the bench in front of her door almost regretting I'd come. She greeted me with raised eyebrows. You know how Sara can manipulate her eyebrows. 'Mother,' she said in that pseudo-sophisticated attitude she assumes when she's confused."

"My father's an eyebrow lifter," said Mark. "She got it from him."

"Well, she fumbled for her keys. Her knees were shaking, poor dear. She opened the door and entered first. I hadn't seen the apartment in months but it was Sara to a tee: books neatly stacked all over the place, Jackson Pollack on the walls, along with her conservationist posters. Order within chaos. You know at once that Sara's involved in a dozen worthwhile projects."

"And no food in the refrigerator," said Mark.

I laughed. It had been nearly a year since I'd done that in his presence and I wondered how its sound registered in his brain. "Exactly," I said. "She did make me some chamomile tea, though. I tell you, Mark, I wanted so to hold that child. After I'd punched her face a few times.

"We small-talked. Imagine Sara small-talking? She asked how I felt, how I was doing. The loving daughter in her was winning out over the strict Calvinist. She asked about Portugal, how the people live, about the bullfights in Lisbon.

"Anyway, Sara, being Sara, didn't beat around the bush for long. She said, 'That day at Grandpa's funeral I was heartless, rude, insufferable, and about ten other deplorable things. But I wasn't entirely wrong. Caryn feels the same way. We talk about it constantly. God, we were vicious shits. But we were right, you know.'

"'Maybe a little, at the time,' I told Sara. I was being conciliatory to keep her going. Later I'd whack her around when the bridge had a firm footing."

This time, Mark laughed. The last time I'd heard him do that was over a year ago, in July, at Caryn's birthday party. Our last and final family gathering in Camelot, in a world so glorious and shiny we thought ourselves exempt from the woes of mortals.

"Then I told Sara, 'I don't know how much serious thinking you and Caryn have done about that afternoon. It was unforgivable, really, but I've forgiven you both. But only because what you did came from a love for Grandpa and not because of any real malice toward your father and me.'

"Sara was about to speak, but I had months of bottled-up feelings to get out of my system. 'Hear me out first,' I said. We were in that tiny kitchen of hers. It seemed even smaller because of the notes hanging from magnets on her refrigerator and a giant corkboard on one entire wall covered with fliers of all sorts.

"I told Sara that we didn't kill her grandfather. Heart disease killed him. His genetic makeup killed him. I said, 'You of all people, with your scientific training, should know that. I won't deny that I contributed in some way—in some slight way. But so had Bobbi's death and your grandmother's many years before. And losing two of his own children. Love kills, Sara. It's as simple as that. Love cures and love kills and there's no way to have one without the other.'

"Mark, she winced and almost cried. Then I told her that you and I had our problems, and some of the ways we chose to solve them were costly and risky but had to be taken. In the process, the whole family took it on the chin. It couldn't be helped. I said, 'Now that I've had a whole summer and a continent away to think about it, you and Caryn were really expressing anger that we'd broken up. Selfish anger. Blind anger. You were terribly hurt and disillusioned. But didn't we have the right to rebuild our lives? If your father and I can accept the changes we've made, shouldn't you? If you can't, you and Caryn, then your love for us doesn't amount to very much.'

" 'However,' Sara started, but I wasn't through. 'Tell me honestly,' I said. 'How much of your righteous indignation came from thinking about me and Bruno sharing the bedroom? How much from running into your father's girlfriend in her home? In both cases, from having sex with other people?'

"Sara swirled her tea bag in the mug she'd gotten from MADD, Mothers Against Drunk Driving, the group she became active in after the crash. Then she said, 'Caryn and I talked about that very subject before Steven and I left for camp. We decided that it had to be the sex thing, with all that heat expended at the grave. You see, as enlightened as we were—thanks to you and Daddy— we still couldn't accept you two as active sexual beings. Only as neutered parents. I don't know why—you're both young and attractive. I guess it was because we always saw you and Daddy very much in control of yourselves, never losing your temper, never passionate about anything. We'd figured we were produced by cell division instead of the usual way. Then you took up with the Italian and Daddy moved in with his Irish sexpot. And it shook us. In an instant, our parents had become characters from "Santa Barbara." ' "

"Is that what we seemed to them?" asked Mark. "Tight-assed WASPS?"

"Let me tell you, Mark. That did it for us. Seconds later we were both bawling away. She couldn't stop apologizing, telling me how ashamed of themselves they were. They felt we hated them for causing such a ruckus and we'd refuse even to talk to them again."

Mark said, "I tried all of July and August to speak to Caryn, but she'd have none of it."

"That was childish and stupid of her. She told me that. But you know how hard it is for Caryn to apologize. We spoke the day after I saw Sara. She wants to call you but she's afraid you'll hang up on her."

"I won't. You know that. I'll give her a hard time for ignoring me, but I won't hang up."

"And Sara's burning for you to come for supper one night. You and Virginia. She wants to meet her again under less tense conditions."

"We'll see about that," said Mark. "Dessert? If you remember, they served a damned good rice pudding."

"Sure, why not?"

It was only after we'd finished eating and gotten up to leave that Mark said, "How are you getting along with Bruno?"

"Wonderful. I'm very happy. And you with Virginia?"

"Fine. She's not at all what you and the girls think she is."

Mark helped me on with my coat. I told him, "Sara came away loathing her that time, but the more she thought about it, the more she realized that Virginia had treated her the way she deserved to be treated and that Virginia must be pretty okay to have defended herself so well on such short notice. On the other hand, she wasn't too crazy about the house, especially that Norman Bates living room, or dead room, according to Sara."

Mark chuckled. "She's not a slob or an eccentric. She just doesn't get all worked up over clutter and current fashion. She's an essentialist."

I knew he was contrasting us, and before it might lead to harsh words, I asked if he'd spoken to Jason Fiedler about any legal action they might be contemplating.

"No, nothing on the boards. And with you?"

"Nothing."

"Good," said Mark, anxious to get back to the store. "For the time being, let's let sleeping dogs and overeager lawyers lie."

---

I didn't go straight home but drove around, wondering if Martha Haymarket had been telling the truth. Had Bruno and Violet been grooming me for an assault on the library? Was he a sort of recruiting agent for the Women's Consortium? Was I being duped?

At the edge of the golf course, with the Atlantic Beach Bridge like some child's toy in the background, I turned around and made for home. I wanted answers only Bruno could provide. I wanted them at once.

I parked on the apron of the driveway and went directly to Bruno's studio, once our garage. In the six weeks we'd been home, I'd poured over twenty thousand dollars into the transformation, all the improvements I'd rattled off that last wondrous day at the villa. What once held three cars and a wall of garden implements now contained two skylights, a solid wall with a tiny door instead of remote-control garage doors, a workroom blessed in all kinds of weather with baseboard heating and track lighting, a phone, a cot, and even an electric stove to heat his Progresso soup on cold wintry days. The pegboarded tool wall now supported an armory of mallets, hammers, and chisels of all sizes and shapes.

On days when the work was going well, he'd remain sunup to sundown, communing with his chosen gods. On days when it wasn't, he'd do his best to placate those same fickle deities until, disgusted, he'd hang up his tools and leave for parts unknown. In either case, he was unreachable. I understood. When I was composing in my own prison cell, the world would also fade from sight and any phone call or disturbance would bring out the savage beast in me.

The slab of marble we chose for Bobbi's statue came from a dealer in Hoboken, New Jersey. We drove down in a rented van the second morning after arriving back in the States, to pick it out and haul it back. It was, according to Bruno, the finest piece of marble he'd ever seen. "The skin tone of a Swedish blond and as hard as Swedish steel."

The next morning Bruno had taken out his sketches and we'd pored over all his preparatory work. Bobbi playful, serious, pensive, joyous, sad. Combinations and varieties of those moods.

Hours later we'd made our decision; Bobbi captured as long as the marble would last in a pose of eager anticipation, which was mainly how she attacked life. For whatever museum accepted the piece—we decided not to sell to an individual collector but to offer it for the widest audience—we would call the work *Youth Triumphant*. Between us, however, it was, of course, "Bobbi."

"With such a conducive atmosphere," Bruno had said, surveying the completed studio, "I'm going to do the entire piece indoors. No risk of chipping the marble schlepping it back and forth from the garden."

In the five weeks since, Bruno had let me look in only once. "I'm just ensuring your promise not to interfere. What you can't see, you can't criticize." As further protection, he bought a lock for the studio door and kept the key around his neck like some religious symbol. During sex, he'd shift the key around to his back so as not to remind me of the barrier between us.

That one time I was allowed in I understood that in spite of Bruno's idiosyncrasies—or perhaps because of them—he was a great artist. Just the barest outline, yet he'd caught her essence, her very soul. She was almost alive in the inchoate form, and it frightened me. This was Bobbi at the end of one of our early-morning joggings, her face flush and full of promise. Could I handle the finished product?

The stroking I gave him in awe of this future masterpiece was effusive and spontaneous. Unrelenting about his order, he'd said, "Remember, not again until I say so. Then, as often as you like." To reinforce his decree, Bruno hung curtains on the studio windows and kept them permanently drawn. He said it was in case any of the tradespeople who came to the back of the house might disturb his concentration. He meant me, of course, knowing that my love for Bobbi far outweighed any promise to him.

Bruno was finishing up for the day as I got out of the car. He hurriedly locked the studio door, and we kissed without touching, since he was coated with the Vaseline and the hard roseate chips of Carrara marble.

After showering, Bruno poured himself a glass of Mondego wine, the one David Silva had introduced us to in the *fado* house in Lisbon. Bruno had developed a taste for the stuff and I'd had a case sent over from the local liquor store.

"I met Martha Haymarket today," I said. "She's working for the Consortium, doing Violet's dirty work."

"Oh, yes. The ice-pick lady," he said, holding the glass of Mondego up to the fading light in the kitchen.

"She may have given up that weapon but her tongue is just as deadly. She got what she came for from Phil."

"You were at the meeting with her?"

"By accident. She hasn't a high regard for you. She seems to know quite a lot about me, about us, down to the car I drive. I wish you wouldn't tell Violet any of our business."

"I didn't. I don't. I've seen her only once since we've gotten back. To pick up some money she owed me for the sale of a statuette I'd left on the premises. We didn't discuss you. I'd never discuss you with her. Or anyone."

I knew Bruno was lying. I'd come to recognize his body signs. First a twitch of his lips as if to crank up the machinery of deceit, then a slight shift of the shoulders, followed by a pointed concentration of the eyes, and finally an openness of expression, the better with which to disarm the recipient of all that belaboring. However ugly, the truth would have been so much less complicated.

I wasn't prepared to thrash it out with Bruno. I was every bit as cowardly to accept the lie as he was in offering it. Instead, I chose a substitute to strike out at. "Well, at any rate, I'm thankful I didn't go to work for her or with her."

A twitch, a shift of shoulders, the pointed eyes, then that look of innocence. "Really? When I met Martha Haymarket in the office that one time, I told Violet she was hardly the person to send out to twist Phil Coolidge's arm, whatever the assignment, not knowing the assignment, of course."

Did you tell her that *I* was? I wanted to say, but changed my mind at the last second. Martha Haymarket would have spoken up. She was truly far better suited for Violet's purpose than I was.

# *nineteen*

O<small>N A BRIGHT</small> and brisk late October morning, in less time than it took to feed him breakfast, Lawrence died. I came home from a day in court and found Virginia sitting on the kitchen steps. She'd been crying. "He got up at eight, took a vitamin with his juice, ate his oatmeal without fuss, gave Molly Cardin a big goofy smile, then closed those sightless eyes. And that was that. Over. Ended. Finis."

The Friday before, I'd absented myself from the trial to go upstate with Virginia on what had become our regular monthly sojourn. For me, this particular weekend in Greenbrier and at the institute had been less a grinding obligation than usual because I'd welcomed a Friday away from the trial, which had been in progress for two weeks and even more harrowing than I'd imagined.

"I have to go back there to sign some papers and claim the body," she said, washing her hands in the sink, then starting my dinner.

"I'll go with you."

"No, not this time, Gerber," she said, and though I tried to talk her out of going alone, I knew her mind was made up. "You take care of your business in court and I'll take care of mine in Greenbrier."

Lawrence was buried in Holy Rood Cemetery in East Meadow in a corner away from the rush of traffic and the din of horns. The procession of mourners had been led by Father Gregory, a youngish man of forty with a thatch of black hair that never seemed combed. I'd noticed him at many of our ball games, cheering us on, but never knew he was a priest, as he always wore Bermudas and a Madonna T-shirt. Suddenly I knew which Madonna.

Among the mourners were Tim O'Hara, Dennis, the Devils, John Tierney, and some of the neighbors I'd met while working in the garden. All were in black except Virginia. She wore blue. The night before she'd said that black was for Dracula, tuxedos, and the Mafia.

The grave-site service was brief and simple, matching the one at St. Brigid's, where most Devonites worshiped. Virginia had requested only the bare necessities from Father Gregory as befitted the unadorned life of her son. No flowers, no wake at the bungalow before the funeral, no gathering after to wash down the dust from the cemetery.

At home, she went directly to bed. I followed her upstairs to offer whatever I could, but she was already under the covers. I put my knee against her. Virginia sat up and made a backrest of her pillow. "Listen to me, Gerber. Please don't feel offended, but this is something I have to get through by myself. Go back to the trial or the store. I have to straighten out a few things in my mind. Then we'll do some serious talking. Until then, give me a lot of time and space," she said, as if time and space were my possessions to give.

I didn't return to the courtroom or the store that day. I changed my clothes and went out to the garden. I'd had a bumper crop of everything I'd planted, and all summer and fall we'd eaten as much homegrown produce as we could and gave the rest to friends and neighbors, most of the excess going to John Tierney. He claimed that his daily walks and conversations with the vegetables had made them thrive.

Two weeks earlier I'd met with Assistant DA Calvin Spotswood in his office an hour before the trial's opening. Again, I thought of taking a gun along in case of a severe miscarriage of justice.

"No more delaying tactics, no more extensions for every little bit of nitpicking the size and weight of a fly's ass. It's show-and-tell time, and Mr. Ira Golub has nothing to show—but I'm sure a lot to tell."

We'd shared bagels and coffee over a small desk in a small room on the second floor. Spotswood carefully went over the ground rules once more.

"Mark, as I told you at the beginning, there's been no offer to plea-bargain from either side. We are shooting for vehicular manslaughter, second degree, which is a class-D felony and carries with it a two-and-a-third-to-seven-year price tag. Vehicular manslaughter is composed of two separate offenses—driving while intoxicated and criminally negligent homicide. I have to prove both. The problem in all these DWI cases is that the act of getting behind a wheel soused is not considered by most judges and trial lawyers to be a criminally negligent act. There is a bill in Albany to eliminate the criminally negligent requirement so we can nail these sons of bitches, but the pols in all their Solomonic wisdom have kept it bottled up in committee—would you believe—since the 1970's. Every year the bill comes up to bat and every year it strikes out.

"I'm pretty sure, though, I can prove both charges. But as I told you, jury trials are iffy affairs. I sure wish he'd pleaded guilty."

I'd hardly touched my bagel and took only a sip of the coffee. "Is that what we call our American system of justice, Cal?" It was mostly a rhetorical question.

"Heaven is the place for justice, not the courtroom," he'd said, almost afraid to smile.

"I can't wait that long," I'd told him.

For the trial we were given the same judge—Adolph Cameron—but a larger courtroom. The big leagues after a year in the minors.

Up front, on a raised dais, Judge Cameron's bench loomed majestically between the flags of Nassau County and the United States. To the right, the jurors' boxes were also elevated, like the tiers of a high-school gym. Twelve good and true citizens entered and took their seats, seven men and five women. Of the dozen, two were blacks and one was a Latin, an Argentinian who Cal had told me originally came from Tierra del Fuego, as far south in South America as Montauk Point was east on Long Island.

Cal had also informed me that the selection of the jury had been one of the less obvious judicial battles between himself and Ira Golub and might determine the war. Many a case was won or lost by how the jury had been chosen.

"Oh, he was cute, Mark, our Mr. Golub. He tried to exclude every parent, everyone with a Jewish-sounding name, everyone upper-middle-class. He wanted blacks, Latins, WASPS, and Irishmen—all those good taxpayers traditionally more tolerant of alcohol and who might sympathize with McGuire."

"Put me on the stand, Cal, and I'll quickly disabuse them of that notion. I'll tell them about the kind of person Bobbi was, then they'll see this bastard knucklewalker for the animal he is."

"And blow the whole case? The one I've been sweating out for over a year? Not a chance, Mark. His lawyer will show you to be only a vengeful, overwrought parent, and all your good intentions will backfire. He'll make an idiot of you and a martyr of McGuire. You'll be made to seem unstable and maybe someone on the jury will conclude like father like daughter. You've got to keep a tight lid on for the next few weeks, no matter what Golub says or does. You've got a million pills in your store. Take a handful with you every morning. If it's any consolation, Golub doesn't personally believe a word of what he'll say. He's only conducting a defense, doing his job. What takes place in a court-room between lawyers and judges is a lot like Kabuki."

I promised to behave, though over the next few weeks I re-gretted giving Cal my word. For the trial he'd gotten a new suit, an eggshell white gabardine with curled strands of red, green, and blue, like the textured material used to make dollar bills. Golub wore an off-the-rack dark blue serge and an equally blue tie. If I were on the jury, I'd guess that of the two, Spotswood was the more prosperous and successful. Perhaps my sympathy would go to the apparent underdog, the poor soul in the Sears Roebuck suit who'd gallantly taken on the full might and majesty of the state.

McGuire was the constant in the sartorial equation, dressed in his usual courtroom suit. His mother wore no makeup, looked ten years older, and had on a very matronly black dress with a plain white collar. Ira Golub, I decided, was a master of stage costuming. From the sparse audience, a man in his late sixties, pink-faced, with short, nappy white hair, introduced himself to me.

"I'm Bill Curtis. I'm monitoring the trial for MADD. Your daughter, Sara, gave us the authorization. We like to keep abreast of these proceedings as a public service. The legal establishment needs a spotlight turned on them. It holds down the wheeling and dealing between the good old boys."

Since the judge hadn't entered the courtroom yet, Bill Curtis filled me in on his organization. "MADD began in 1980 when Candy Lightner lost a daughter to a hit-and-run drunk driver who'd been out on bail only two days from another hit-and-run crash. Since then we've grown to over four hundred chapters nationwide. We have two offices on Long Island and a new sat-ellite in the Five Towns. Your daughter, Sara, is the coordinator of that one."

"Sara?"

"She's a fantastic kid."

Sara hadn't said a word about it when we'd sat down to dinner, just she and I, at her apartment a week after my meeting with Laura. It wasn't time yet to bring Virginia; we'd talked it over at the bungalow. "Maybe next time, Gerber. You go break bread and ice first. Then we'll see."

Steven was off at his second job and Sara had prepared baked chicken, a tremendous concession for her since she was a vegetarian. Before we'd gotten through the salad, she brought up Virginia. "I thought the whole situation over, Daddy, and I behaved very badly to you and her. I acted like all those terrible kids in town I used to make fun of."

I forgave her, of course. What are parents for but to forgive and forget? I patted her curly hair and kissed her forehead, and we talked of old times over chamomile tea and oatmeal cookies. We even included Bobbi and Laura in those reminiscences.

"Did you know," continued Bill Curtis, "that there were two million arrests last year nationwide for DWI? Five thousand alone in Nassau County. Every year twenty-five thousand die in DWI-related crashes, twenty times that many injured."

"What else does MADD do besides attend trials and compile statistics?" I asked. I was one of the few liberals I knew who mistrusted statistics.

"Let me tell you about monitoring trials. In this state, before we made it a big issue, rarely did a DWI serve time. Even in cases where there was death or injury. Sentences were usually a few months in a county jail, which was like attending military school, or else probation with the promise to go for therapy. But since MADD got into the act, we've had a few laws passed with teeth in them. The court isn't as much of a judge's private fiefdom as it used to be. It's not perfect, but we're on the right road.

"We're also active in victim assistance and in education. We go into the public schools to try and teach kids that self-esteem isn't a matter of getting drunk. We're always looking for a few good men and women to help us in our work, Mr. Gerber."

"Like the marines," I said.

Bill Curtis had an answer but saved it, as we rose for the judge. Florid-faced as usual, Judge Cameron took his seat and the court officer read the charges against Christopher John McGuire.

Spotswood stood up and made his opening statement. In less than five minutes he told the jury about the life of my child in all its promise and beauty. In more than ten, he dwelled on the day of her death. For that eternity, I suffered once more my own version of the day and the still-impossible-to-accept fact that in a few seconds she'd been wiped forever from the face of the earth like some ketchup spill on a waxed table. My child. My beautiful child.

Laura, I knew, had been the infinitely wiser one not to attend what could only be a reopening of unhealed wounds and a vulgar mockery of justice.

And the trial hadn't even begun.

The defense attorney offered his statement. Ira Golub kept it short so as not to bore the jury. He stressed two points of law—that it was the state's obligation to prove beyond a reasonable doubt that Christopher John McGuire was guilty of vehicular manslaughter, which he then defined in layman's terms, and that his client was innocent until proven guilty. "I'd like to state for the record that Chris McGuire has never been in trouble with the law, has never had as much as a parking ticket."

I can still hear Golub sanitizing, sanctifying his fair-haired angel. I still see McGuire lowering his head modestly.

". . . a fine young man, who since the age of fourteen has supported his widowed mother."

All eyes fell on the woman in black in the first row, who, I'm sure, was as helpless as a killer shark.

Each attorney had his first at bat, and the trial that followed became one long night in purgatory for me, during which every aspect of the case was handled and rehandled by both sides like coins in a miser's fingers. Debated and fought over as though the two attorneys were rabbinical scholars engaged in *pilpul*.

Officer Joe Pagano, then his partner, were called to the stand to testify. Both, veterans of courtroom procedure, stated only the facts as they'd been entered in their notebooks. Carefully they refrained from making suppositions and drawing conclusions. Ira Golub had little to erode in their description of McGuire's physical condition, though he did suggest that shock had made his client stagger and stumble and rave incoherently at the scene of the accident. The two policemen spent a full day in the box.

The testimony of Officer Nestor Quinones took infinitely longer. He was the policeman who'd administered the Breathalyzer test to McGuire. For four days the policeman was grilled to a turn by Golub, who treated him as if he were some sleazy informer whose very word, period, and comma couldn't be trusted. Hours, while I groaned and twisted in my seat, Golub picked and probed at the officer's qualifications to administer the test. Where had he received his training? How many hours of instruction? How many tests had he given? How many convictions as a result?

The Breathalyzer itself came under Golub's minute scrutiny. When was it serviced last? By whom? How precisely did it work, part by part? Dials, gauges, galvanometer, comparison ampoule. What was the temperature of the room at test time? Was the machine permitted to warm up properly before use? At what time was the first sample taken? The second sample? At what time was first test concluded? The second? Was the subject under direct observation and for how long prior to obtaining the breath sample? Did Mr. McGuire have anything to eat, drink, or smoke during the test periods? Did he vomit or belch?

If this hadn't been the trial of my daughter's murderer, I couldn't have sat through it. Bill Curtis, with an acquired taste for such courtroom gamesmanship, explained why he found the trial fascinating. "Don't you see, if he can create any doubt at all in the Breathalyzer or the cop, he's won a big point. Spotswood's major piece of evidence is that test. Invalidate it and it's good-bye voluntary manslaughter."

Ira Golub continued hammering away, but Officer Quinones didn't flinch or back down a hair. I could see the jury grow restless. The man from Tierra del Fuego nodded off once or twice during the Breathalyzer testimony. In his country, men such as Christopher McGuire were given ten minutes before a judge, then sent to the wall.

During the first two weeks of the trial, I'd go back to the store after the final recess and work the late shift. Later, at home, I'd tell Virginia what had happened in court and present Bill Curtis's informed comments. After Labor Day, Virginia changed to the day shift so we could spend more time together. We'd sit in the kitchen dawdling over melted-cheese sandwiches and fresh corn from the garden. I'd tell her about the defense attorney, who was always on the attack, a classy dancer and expert jabber. Virginia had shown a good deal of interest in the trial those two weeks.

Then Lawrence died the day Golub had finished his cross examination of Phillip Lopata, the toy salesman who'd witnessed the crash (I remembered him and his evidence from the Department of Motor Vehicle hearing in May.) After the funeral, Virginia tumbled into a deep pit of depression. I know I could have done more to help her, but the trial had dumped me back into the same pit by resurrecting all that hell again. The point was, I'd learned that the time and space she requested only worked against you in the grieving process, if you utilize them alone, unaided. But I wasn't out of the woods yet myself. At night, I'd come home too seething and self-contained to help Virginia. We lay side by side in bed for hours, mummies in separate sarcophagi, rehashing our separate torments, incapable of reaching outside ourselves.

I could have tried harder. The way Laura failed me, I failed Virginia. The way I failed Laura, I failed Virginia. Laura had a good reason. I didn't: Lawrence was somebody else's child.

The second witness to the crash, the kid with the Mohawk haircut and the ring in his ear, proved to be a bonanza for the defense. After the first ten minutes of cross-examination, Ira Golub had him jumping through hoops and doing other obedience tricks.

"Mr. Brubaker, how fast do you think the defendant was going?"

"The blue Chevy?"

"Yes. Mr. McGuire and the blue Chevrolet."

"Not too fast."

"And what in your estimation is not too fast?"

"Oh, thirty, forty, fifty."

"In this case, would forty be a reasonable estimate, forty being the legal speed limit for that area?"

"Yeah, sure.

"And do you have occasion, Mr. Brubaker, while in traffic, to judge the speed of other cars?"

"Yeah. All the time. I'm doin' like fifty and I pass a guy and I say to myself he's doin' forty. Or he passes me and I figure he's doing sixty."

"And how fast were you going last August twenty-seventh at two P.M. on Woodmere Boulevard?"

"No more than thirty-five."

"And when Mr. McGuire pulled out in front of you, is it your testimony that he was going about forty?"

Of course Cal objected to this patent leading of the witness who was, after all, the state's witness. The judge agreed and refused to allow Brubaker to respond, but the damage had been done.

The only bright moments at the trial were those I spent with my daughters. Sara came with pad and pen, taking notes for MADD or just to hold my hand. "We're winning, Daddy. We're definitely winning," she'd tell me whenever Cal would lay a damning piece of evidence before the jurors.

"Winning what, Sara?" I said. "The best we can hope for is not to have Bobbi convicted of her own death, the way Golub is running this show."

The trial dragged on for five weeks. Only now, in retrospect, do I realize how in that time the gap between Virginia and me widened. Only now do I see that she was grieving exactly as I'd grieved. Never once after that first time on the kitchen steps did I see her cry. It was as if she'd gone into a bunker and sealed the door.

A few times I did reach out. Once I said, "Are any of his things still in Greenbrier? We could take a ride up there on Saturday. Sleep over. Say hello to Molly Cardin."

"Everything's been attended to. Everything. Understand?"

I understood. I heard myself with Laura in that clipped manner and gave Virginia plenty of leeway. But where I'd retreated from work, she threw herself into it, often taking double shifts. Very late at night she'd return home, unwilling or unable to talk to me, offering her weariness as excuse. Neither of us was getting much sleep then, despite her long hours at the diner and mine in court and the store. I dreaded sleep because when I did drift off, Bobbi would come sit by my side and talk to me. "Well, how did it go today? Are they going to throw the book at Christopher John McGuire? Anything new and exciting at the store? Who's driving the van these days? What about my sisters? Any of them mothers yet?"

When I was able to shift focus to the woman lying next to me, lighting up the dark like a firefly with her glowing cigarette tip, I wondered who she was trying to escape—Lawrence, herself, or me? I could understand the first two possibilities. I couldn't accept the last. Until Lawrence's death, we'd made wonderful progress. Broken down the double walls between us. Reached across the impossible barriers of age, religion, and background to build a loving relationship. Once the trial was over, I was going to ask her to marry me. We'd track down the long-gone and shadowy Mr. Healy and get her sprung. I'd sit down with Laura and the lawyers and work things out. Virginia and I would live here or any other place by the ocean. We'd continue building our new lives, giving each the freedom and understanding necessary. We could even have a child; it wasn't too late.

I tried broaching the subject of the near future for starters. She was sitting at the pianola picking out the melody to "Yes Sir, That's My Baby," a peanut butter on rye at one end of the pianola, a tall glass of Kool-Aid next to it.

"When all this is over, let's go away for a month. The Caribbean. Blue skies, white sand, cool green water. Scuba diving, sunning ourselves like lizards, lobsters for dinner every day. Love-making every night."

" 'No sir, I don't mean maybe,' " she sang in a low talk-sing growl.

"We owe it to ourselves, Virginia."

" 'Yes sir, that's my baby, now.' "

"Or China. We could go visit a whole new world. Exotic places, interesting people. Before Burger King and Coca-Cola take over."

" 'By the way. By the way. When we meet the preacher I'll say—' "

"There's life after death, Virginia. I know that now. Mine after Bobbi's. Yours after Lawrence's."

Her voice rose to blot me out. " 'Yes sir, that's my baby.' "

I was sitting on the mohair couch, reading the Travel section of the Sunday *Times*. I carefully folded the paper, stood up, and walked over to the pianola. Virginia looked up at me defiantly and set herself as if to receive my blow. I spun her around in her seat and slammed the lid on the piano keys.

"Not a music lover, I take it," she said, rising. I made a move to grab her but she eluded my arms.

She went upstairs and into the shower. I waited for her to come down so I might try again in another way. But my eyes scanned the lead story in the Sports section. A star athlete had wrecked his career and the lives of two innocent bystanders in his Porsche during a drunken spree. That washed me out for the rest of the day. I went for a walk along the beach instead.

---

The end of the trial drew near. Surprisingly, I'd muddled through all Golub's attempts to discredit our witnesses and lend credibility to his. An independent auto mechanic was brought in to swear that the Ram could have used a new set of brakes. Then there was the gas jockey at the Esso station in town who testified that Bobbi had the reputation as a fast-lane driver, which Golub further tried to prove by inserting her two traffic tickets into the record.

Spotswood countered by showing that alleged reputation and citations notwithstanding, Bobbi had put over seventy-five thousand miles on the van without as much as a dent. As far as the brakes were concerned, they'd passed inspection at that same auto mechanic's service station.

Sensing my dismay and disgust at Golub's attempt to malign

Bobbi, my eldest invited me to breakfast. At eight the next morning, refreshed somewhat by seeing her so poised and lovely, I escorted Caryn to a table at a diner near the court building where opposing lawyers sat with each other to cut deals and make offers.

That morning, she was lovelier than usual. At once I knew something was afoot. She'd never been able to keep a secret for long. Her hands would weave patterns in the air. She'd run her fingers through her hair.

"What is it, kid?" I said, inspecting the menu. "A new promotion? A nice fat Christmas bonus?"

"Both, sort of," she said, ordering scrambled eggs, pancakes, two slices of buttered toast, and Sanka.

I ordered my usual juice, bran flakes, coffee.

"I'm going to have a baby." Almost embarrassed, she turned away.

"Are you certain? You sure as hell don't have morning sickness, from the way you ordered."

"That should have been a clue. I haven't stopped eating since we got the results of the test."

"That's absolutely wonderful. I'm very happy for you both. Does your mother know?"

"I saw her last night. She's ecstatic. She wants to take me to buy a crib and carriage."

"That's Laura all right. Are you going to do the Lamaze thing?"

"Are you for real, Daddy? I want to be out cold when it happens. I want Warren at home, out of harm's way. Not standing around with ten other kibitzers, telling me to take deep breaths and push down. You know how I hate to take orders."

Later that morning in court, Ira Golub showed himself to be a master of fiction as well as an expert costumer. He tried to prove that his client was a good person despite his predicament by calling eight witnesses—friends and family—to attest to Christopher McGuire's profound humanity. Then Golub wound up his list of yea-sayers with an alcohol therapist.

Dr. Marvin Brodsky took the stand, swore on the Bible, then they began the dreadful alchemy of turning garbage into gold.

"Isn't it true, Dr. Brodsky, that you've been treating the defendant, Christopher McGuire, for almost ten months?"

The bald, spidery man said, "Since January third he's been seeing me on a twice-a-week basis. He hasn't missed a single appointment."

"Would you say he's made progress?"

"Absolutely. As remarkable as I've ever seen in twenty-three years of practice."

"And isn't it true, Dr. Brodsky, that we as a society should be more interested in rehabilitation than in seeking revenge, the Babylonian eye for an eye, if you will?"

"Absolutely."

Not once did the doctor cast his eye in my direction. If he had, he would have seen another absolute—complete and total loathing for what he was trying to do.

The next day, Golub made a daring and dangerous move. He put Christopher McGuire on the stand. I don't remember much of his testimony or Spotswood's cross. Only that he'd tried to get back into his lane and found Bobbi there. I also remember bits and pieces of McGuire's apology to me, phrases such as "I pray for her soul" and "I didn't mean to harm nobody" (purposely double-negatived, no doubt, by Golub, the author of the script). I remember vividly how he faced me, feigning repentance. "I know all the apologies in the world won't bring her back, but from the depths of my being, I'm sorry."

I hated Christopher John McGuire for this pretense of remorse and Ira Golub for writing the words. If I were the judge, I'd tack on a few more years for his cynical abuse of the English language.

Not much of the closing summaries remain in my head. Calvin Spotswood told the wearied jury that he'd proved what he set out to prove and was confident they'd do their duty, as well as send out a powerful message to all those who would drink and drive, then expect the law to look the other way.

Golub, of course, sang a different swan song. He conceded the charge of driving while intoxicated. As to criminal negligence, he claimed that his "very able opponent had failed to prove *beyond a reasonable doubt* that Chris McGuire is guilty. It is our contention that—hard as it may be for some to accept—Roberta Gerber was partially to blame in this tragic accident. There was, ladies and gentlemen of the jury, no intent to harm Roberta Gerber. In that terrible moment, Roberta Gerber collided as much with my client as he collided with her."

That evening I threw up the dinner Virginia had indifferently prepared and spent the night trying to force hot tea down to halt my churning stomach.

The morning of the verdict had begun in a cold and chilly rain. I opened my eyes at dawn and saw the outline in the sheets where Virginia should have been. I checked the bathroom, then ran downstairs naked, fearing for her safety. She'd been unreachable for days.

Virginia was pedaling up the front walkway when I saw her, wearing only a light sweater and thin jeans. Barefoot and hatless. I watched her hoist the bicycle into the minibus and slam the door.

"Jesus, you scarcd the shit out of me," she said at the screen door. "You're naked as a newborn baby. Suppose I was the mailman or the Avon lady?"

"Never mind me. What's with you out there in this kind of weather?"

"What are you? My mother? I'll pedal my ass wherever I please. When I please. Anytime I please."

She looked down at my penis and scoffed harshly, as if that part of my anatomy had failed to pass inspection. Then she went upstairs to bed. I thought of staying home and joining her so as not to face the verdict, so as to force a breakthrough with her. It was only a passing thought.

The jury had been out since the morning before. By evening they'd notified the judge that their decision would come the next day, rain or shine.

After I showered, dressed, and forced down a glass of cold water, I went back upstairs to Virginia.

Either she was sleeping or feigning it. I kissed her shoulder, the only exposed part of her in bed, and left.

I arrived early in Mineola and waited alone in the large, cavernous hall of the courthouse. Two days before, Caryn had left on a buying trip to Singapore. Bill was on vacation and Sara couldn't leave her classes.

I guess it was the old idealist in me that turned a hopeful face to the foreman of the jury when, around noon, he and his fellow jurors filed back into the courtroom.

I closed my eyes and held my breath.

"We find the defendant, Christopher John McGuire, guilty of driving while intoxicated on two counts. We also find the defendant, Christopher John McGuire, innocent of voluntary manslaughter in the second degree."

McGuire let out a whoop and embraced his attorney the way men do at ball games and in war movies. Judge Adolph Cameron, passive and evenhanded all through the trial, shook his head in disbelief and ran his hand over his face, crumpling it as though it were a handkerchief.

I turned to Spotswood; he turned to me. Between us were yards of dead space slowly filling with electrical charges. I made a move to cross the wooden gate between myself and McGuire. Cal reached across his side of the fence and held me back.

"You son of a bitch," I shouted at Cal. "Get your goddamn hands off me. I want to fix him good. The way you were supposed to, you incompetent imbecile. You ought to be doing mortgages instead of trying criminals."

"Sorry," he said without relaxing his hold. "I did my best. I warned you about juries. He'll be doing time, though. Cameron will see to it."

"Not as much as I've done," I said, as everyone began leaving the room. Over Spotswood's shoulder I could see all three of them in a huddle, McGuire's mother having joined in. They broke up and Golub led the way to the door.

"I hope you get cancer soon and suffer a long time with it," I told McGuire only a foot from me.

McGuire waited until he was at the threshold. "Fuck you, creep," he shouted over his left shoulder, and disappeared.

Spotswood held on a moment longer, then let go. "It's a lousy system, Mark," he said. He tucked the six-inch file on the McGuire case under his arm and left.

---

I sat in the empty courtroom for a long while. A black porter came in and began sweeping up. He whistled "Sweet Georgia Brown" through his teeth as he emptied the wastebaskets. As I got up to leave, I noticed the clock above the jurors' box. It read one o'clock even though it was half-past three. Even that they couldn't get right.

I left the courthouse and walked through the maze of governmental buildings. The rain hadn't let up since I'd seen Virginia cycling through it this morning (was it only this morning?). Everyone held an umbrella except me. I was too locked up inside to feel a thing.

By five, it had grown dark. Still, I wandered through those stone canyons because I had no place to go, no sheltered harbor. The Isle of Devon had lost its atavistic power over me. Once more I was rudderless.

I found my car and drove for hours. The rain grew heavier, and some primitive part of me began plotting revenge. I'd find McGuire at home and burn it down. Blast him to shreds as he fled the smoke and flames. Then go after Golub.

Another part of me saw that blue Chevy bearing down on Bobbi. For the thousandth time I heard the screech of brakes, felt the impact, saw Bobbi fly out the door, watched her life flicker like a candle in the wind on that road. Saw her body lying there, not a drop of blood spilled, yet all the life drained from it. She could have been asleep except for the tangle of her body.

As Bobbi's life ebbed away, so did mine. I felt a tightening in my chest and a burning stream of lava course down my left arm. My vision blurred as if the windshield wipers had stopped. My breath came in short, urgent gulps.

If I was going to die, Woodburgh was the place I wanted to be. In my own house. With Laura—hers was the last face I wanted to see before I closed my eyes forever. Or if this wasn't a fatal heart attack, to tell her that for the second time they'd ravaged our daughter—first her body, then her spirit in that hall of terrors.

I plowed up the old familiar driveway along the sentry line of yews. They seemed thinner than I remembered, less protective. It was already as dark as it was going to get. There were no lights on anywhere in the house, but they were home. Their cars were parked at opposite ends of the garage like watchdogs. It wasn't a garage anymore, however, but a small cottage.

I got out of the car, hesitant, suspicious. The rain was so steady it might have been a fixed condition on Earth, like gravity or daylight. I made a wide circle of the garage like a dog sniffing out a stranger. Curtains on the windows kept me from seeing inside. A wall and a small entrance had replaced the overhead double door. A glistening on the roof came from twin skylights.

I walked around the garage again, pausing momentarily at the left wall alongside which the only tomatoes in Woodsburgh once grew. It was bare and had probably lain fallow all year. "A waste, a terrible waste," I muttered, meaning more than the absence of tomatoes.

The lock on the side window had always been defective, the top half never quite meshing with the bottom, like inept lovers. I alone knew this. When the electric doors had failed to operate mechanically, I could still get in the garage and hand-raise the door.

Hesitating at the window, I strained to listen just in case the garage had become a love nest and they were nesting. I heard nothing, only the plop of rain on the plastic skylights.

A bit of pressure, a little jiggling, and the window lifted—slowly at first, then almost by itself. Parting the curtains, I put one foot inside, then the other, with the cold-blooded agility of a tightrope walker.

A slick gloss coated the overhead bubbles but little light filtered in. I took a moment for my eyes to adjust and memory to make the room familiar. Both failed me and I stumbled around searching for the light switch. Then I found it and a blaze of light like an atomic mushroom blinded me. I covered my eyes and cursed.

After I lowered my hand, the room's lesser objects came into focus: a cot, a string of baseboard heating units, a gas range, a wall of hammers and chisels.

Then I saw it—her. Bobbi. She stood before me as alive and vibrant as she was in my heart. I cried out and ran to her in the center of the room under the skylights. Her head was turned at that pert, inquisitive angle that so characteristically defined her. Her mouth was about to offer something funny and original, those expressive hands uplifted in concert with her words.

But this Bobbi was cold, cold as the rain that had fallen on me for hours. This was a Bobbi carved in stone, and though it drew me at first, the fascination quickly ended and a powerful revulsion took its place. It was grossly wrong what Laura and Bruno had done, monstrously evil to have made an idol of her. An image to be revered and worshiped! That wasn't how it must be done. Memory was the only way, our hearts the only acceptable location.

Revulsion soon gave way to a rage even greater than I'd felt hearing the verdict. There was no Spotswood to restrain me and I ran to the wall and seized the heaviest mallet I could find. Half-metal, half-wood, it felt heavy as a brick. I smashed it against the statue's hands. They fell off and lay on the floor, a pair of birds shot out of the sky. I raised the mallet again, this time with both arms and swung it like a baseball bat against the torso. A sharp stab of current shot up my arm and through my chest, charging my entire being with a burst of energy. Suddenly the mallet felt lighter than a child's plastic toy.

I continued slamming away until the statue cracked midcenter. The upper half of the torso split diagonally across the hips and slid to the floor like a torpedoed vessel sinking into the ocean. The sound it made meeting the floor was almost inaudible because of the blood pounding in my ears.

I stood panting over the fallen half, scanning its face for signs of life, of suffering. Nothing had changed. The stone Bobbi, like the Bobbi I'd fathered, kept its optimistic and generous smile.

Instead of assuaging my anger, the sight of the bisected figure only inflamed it. I tightened my grip on the mallet and continued to hammer away. I didn't stop until that abomination in marble had turned to rubble. Only then did I relent for a moment, my tongue stinging with the tangy saline taste of blood. It *was* blood, I realized, putting my hand to my mouth, from a cut on my lower lip. A flake of marble had chipped off and struck me. Warm and invigorating, the taste of blood only made me flail away again all the harder. The rubble was rapidly reduced to small rocks, shards, and dust.

Only the head, the most offensive part, remained whole and unscathed. Sweat poured from me and made wet rags of my clothes under a light raincoat. In my hand the mallet felt hot, on fire, as though all the heat in my body had collected there like a solar panel.

I lifted the mallet with both hands and brought it crashing down on the statue's face. Again and again. Yet that gorgeous smile refused to go away. I ran to the wall and took a second mallet, heavier than the first. With alternate blows, I split the skull from the right eye to the left side of the chin, then into eight or nine parts.

At last the face was gone, obliterated from sight and restored once more inside of me where it belonged. Still I wasn't satisfied. I was furious with Laura for allowing such a travesty to take place, for trying to duplicate in stone what in love and hope we'd created from ourselves.

Hundreds of broken pieces of the statue lay flung across the garage floor. I gathered up a handful and began hurling them one at a time at the windows. With demonlike accuracy I broke every one of them, delighting in the melodic tinkle each direct hit made, like the high notes on Laura's flute.

When all the windows in the garage had been knocked out, I loaded my pockets with rocks and ran outside.

I was shivering with what could only be fever. The rain cooled me and I drew a baseball-size rock from my pocket, took a long slow windup, kicked high, then sent it speeding toward the kitchen window. Strike one as the window blew apart.

All the lights in the house and over the grounds were on. I ignored them and started on the upstairs. After a few misses I hit Sara's old bedroom window dead center. Hit it a second time, then a third—a whole symphony of breaking glass.

I went back to the garage for more ammunition, and coming out, I saw a flashing yellow circle of light. My old friend Joe Pagano was heading toward me as if he were Lou Piniella come to the mound to settle down a wild pitcher.

"Shit, you're no burglar," he said. "He's no burglar," he shouted toward the house. "Doc," he said, "you shouldn't be doing things like this." He peered beyond me at the garage all lit up and windowless. Then he surveyed the direct hits on the kitchen and upper-story windows.

In pajamas and bathrobes, first Laura, then Bruno came out onto the patio. Together they advanced toward me, Bruno tip-toeing not to get his slippers wet, Laura running. I was shaking and sweaty, drained by the release of violence but feeling cleansed and elated and light-headed.

Bruno minced by me to the garage, where he stood in the doorway facing in, his head bowed as if in prayer.

"Oh Mark," said Laura. Her arms were straight at their sides as if she was carrying shopping bags. Her hands were clasping and unclasping.

"He's going to be free as a bird in a few months," I said. "McGuire." I think I was crying. "She's dead forever and he's going to walk away as though nothing happened. I came here to tell you and found some fucking pagan idol of her in the garage!"

Joe Pagano, who was watching from twenty feet away, muttered, "I don't think I'm needed here."

"No, I don't think so either," said Laura. "Thank you for coming anyway."

I watched him leave, feeling nothing. The circle of yellow on top of his car grew smaller, fading until I faded as well. My feet turned to pudding, then soon after my head wound up in Laura's lap, the rest of me sprawled out on the wet lawn. I remember Laura and Bruno lifting me, hauling me up the steps and into the house like a drunk with two friends. Then being vaguely undressed and bathed and towel-dried. Then a period of floating in and out of the world as in some Ingmar Bergman movie. Between bouts of sleep I recall being ordered by Laura to swallow and drink and turn over.

I remember that the whole of it was not an unpleasant experience.

# *twenty*

ARK HAD NEVER been physically ill before, not even a cold, even during those long isolated winter months when he'd dared the worst weather. At the time, I'd thought he truly wanted to come down with a serious condition: You took her; now take me. But he'd been an impregnable fortress, unreachable to me, unreachable as well to the powerful unseen world of viruses and bacteria.

So when Mark collapsed at my feet that evening, a small part of me welcomed its perhaps deeper significance: a wall breached, the battery of self-destructive weapons silenced.

I considered it a minor miracle that his mind hadn't snapped as well under the load he'd carried for over a year. Perhaps he had his father to thank, the early years of neglect immunizing Mark somehow against the external world. Or maybe the credit should go to Virginia Healy for what she did for him while he was living with her. I've come to believe that the months spent under her roof had saved his sanity, maybe even his life.

Mark left skid marks on the lawn as we dragged him up the steps of the patio, then tracks across the kitchen and over the stairs of the bathroom. He was running a high fever, so I undressed him and dunked him in cold water. Even after that, he was flushed and hot and incoherent.

I sent Bruno downstairs to prepare orange juice and hot tea and brandy while I bathed Mark. Bruno had offered to help but I wanted to be alone with Mark. I had to scrutinize his body, to touch its parts again, and see for myself if his leanness was due to muscular tightening or neglect. From the fullness of his penis, I tried to estimate how many times a week he and Virginia made love. I touched his scrotum, shriveled and purple from the cold water. In his semiconscious state he smiled. I wondered about his visions.

Bruno had had the good sense not to come back upstairs until I called him. I'd dried Mark in the tub, helped him into bed, and got him into one of the sweatshirts he'd left behind and a pair of my jogging pants. Together we set up a small hospital on a folding table near the bed.

Bruno took away the second pillow, the one he'd slept on, as if trying to conceal the fact that we shared the same bed. Did he think that Mark believed we only held hands? Or that Mark was in any position to do anything about it?

It was senseless to take Mark's temperature. He had a fever high enough to ignite paper. I tried calling Rudy Frank. The housekeeper told me he was at the theater and wasn't expected back until long after midnight. I left a message to call me as soon as he came in. In the meantime, I knew enough as a pharmacist's wife to give Mark two ampicillin five hundred milligrams and two aspirins. Docilely he swallowed all four with a half glass of juice.

Bruno stood by in case I needed help. But every mother is part nurse and I hadn't forgotten.

"I'd like to sit here, alone. Just in case," I told Bruno.

"Of course. I'll be downstairs. Call if you need me."

It was a rusty but experienced angel of mercy who snapped back into action, and for hours I remained at Mark's bedside, mopping his forehead and holding his juice cup steady. I sat for an eternity hoping he'd show some sign of recognizing me. But he eventually fell into a deep sleep and began to snore like the low rumble of a tuba.

For an hour longer I remained by the bed, studying the lines in Mark's face. The old ones I remembered. The new ones came as a mild shock, those roadways through virgin land. His eyebrows had become flecked with gray. Silver slivers appeared in the hard-to-shave recesses under his chin. Occasionally he muttered disjointed phrases that I tried to stitch together. It would have helped my speculation about his recent life. Then, when the only sounds escaping him were those of a well-oiled machine, I got up and left.

The phone started ringing as I got to the last step on the bottom landing. Dr. Frank had just gotten home. I explained Mark's condition and how I'd medicated him.

"Good girl," he said, though I felt like neither. "I'll be by the second thing in the morning. First I have to look in on Paul Gordon. He had a mild heart attack last week—too much Chinese food, if you know what I mean—and I have him in St. Joseph's for a few days."

Bruno was waiting for me in the living room, a large silver pot of tea and two cups on the coffee table. One was empty, and I thought of Elijah's cup when we'd go to Suzy and Paul's for Passover seder: the unseen guest. Suzy was now firmly implanted at the library and as Phil's lover. Paul was living with his Oriental sweetheart and had already paid the price. How easy it was for everything to go wrong. So hard to go right, as though life had become a labyrinth with only one exit.

"How is he?" asked Bruno, standing up smartly as though I was his superior officer.

"Sleeping soundly. He's stopped rambling on about the trial. The young man involved was given a ridiculously light sentence.

Mark had been counting on a public beheading or at least two years behind bars. I'm sorry now I wasn't there, at least when they read the verdict. He shouldn't have faced it alone."

During the night a strong west wind had chased the rain out to sea, then remained to rattle the windows and sing in the eaves. I could feel the day coming in cold and wintry. Before the sun would burn it off there'd be a sugarcoating of frost on the front lawn. A cold autumn after the hottest summer in forty years. Nature had a way of equalizing things, fairer in the long run than life.

Nodding, as though I'd uttered the most sage profundity, Bruno poured my tea. He'd changed not into work jeans but street clothes. The entire atmosphere of the room seemed to be that of a Broadway drama, the last act of the play. We weren't given the script, hadn't rehearsed our parts, but I think we both knew the lines.

"It's over, isn't it?" he said.

Before I could reply, he left his seat on the couch opposite me to listen to the wind outside the front door. For a brief second I listened, too.

"How did you know?"

"How could I not know? The moment I saw your face when you realized it was Mark in the garden stoning the house as if we were biblical adulterers, I knew. Then watching you cradle his head after he collapsed. Your fingers brushing away the hair in his face spoke volumes, as they say in cheap novels. And even if I were congenitally dense, how could I miss the way you tenderly nursed him and gave him medication? If I could have only captured that moment in marble."

"I'm afraid I love him after all."

"Don't be afraid, Laura."

"But we had such a beautiful affair going, Bruno. Love and lust and the start of a fine friendship."

"Illusions, Laura. What we had really, honestly, truly, was a dovetailing of interests, a marriage of convenience and necessity. And we served each other well. We had a very simpatico quid pro quo."

"I never looked at it that way."

Bruno left his listening post at the door and returned to the couch. He poured some tea but didn't lift his cup. "Come, come, Laura. Now that it's over, you must have realized, surely you must have suspected that it wasn't fate or accident that threw us together."

"Violet Fleming," I said without emotion. "Suspected, not realized. The truth is I'm neither shocked nor angry to hear it from you. The truth also is I didn't want to know, not consciously. Maybe we would have gone on like this for a long time if Mark hadn't burst in and pulverized the statue. But his moment of insanity jarred me loose, made me see clearly that it was wrong, terribly wrong, what I'd encouraged you to do. Whether it was wrong for you to suggest and create the statue is something you have to decide. Probably not—the piece was beautiful and art is seldom wrong. And yet, when I saw you bent over in the garage and guessed where the rocks had come from, I knew, Bruno, I knew that the statue symbolized everything wrong between us."

"I offer no apology for my action or my statue."

"None required. I'm not as naive or gullible as you may think. Your mother warned me. My own instincts warned me later on. Violet didn't exactly pull the wool over my eyes either. Actually, I took as much advantage of you as you took of me. You were there when I desperately needed a dear friend. I thank my stars it was you, the absolutely perfect, gentle, and considerate companion to hold my life together." I stopped, wondering if I wasn't being too analytical, too condescending, but above all much too calculating. "Of course I knew that the hand of fate was attached to Violet but I didn't care, not in my condition. You were very gallant, Bruno."

Bruno had been trying to speak, to offer a few thoughts to offset mine. I gave him the opportunity. "Don't think it was a carefully hatched scheme, Laura, a trick to bilk you in any way. Though Violet and I are fully capable of deception and have deceived before in ways not even my dear suspicious mother can guess. In your case, it was different. We were sitting around her office—summer before last—and I speculated on how wonderful it would be to enjoy the patronage of some wealthy intellectual woman who loves art more than middle-class mores.

" 'The only one fitting that formula in this cultural moonscape,' said Violet, 'is Laura Gerber. But even more than her money and her appreciation of art is her intelligence, and ability to get things done.' Then I said thoughtlessly, 'Fine. Let's share this Laura Gerber. I'll take her patronage and you her organizational skills.' Never dreaming that anything would come of it."

"That sounds more like jackals dividing a kill."

"Yes, I suppose it does now, in retrospect. Though it was only idle speculation then. Until I got the chance to exhibit those three pieces in the library garden. Then Bobbi died and I dipped my toe in the water and found it warm and inviting. How could I resist? Then things blossomed."

"I guess I should despise Violet instead of merely disliking her."

"Don't, Laura. She's not a bad person. She's like so many decent manipulators who do God's work yet use Satan's methods. It's the path of all those who do great things. Roosevelt packed the Supreme Court to get his New Deal through. Lyndon Johnson twisted arms in Congress to complete John Kennedy's agenda. Only the ruthless can make significant progress."

"And Violet Fleming used Bruno Coletti to try and snooker me into the Women's Consortium. It's a pretty pale comparison."

"At the moment of conception it made sense."

"Like most moments of conceptions."

I left him sitting on the couch to see how Mark was getting along. The sun rose cold and red. It met me on the top landing as I made my way up the steps. I hurried to close the curtains in the bedroom.

Mark had turned on his left side facing the center of the bed, his usual sleeping position. I got in next to him. He sighed in his sleep and I hoped he'd recognized my being there. He was resting so peacefully that I decided not to feed him any more antibiotics or aspirins. Soon, because there was unfinished business between myself and Bruno, I got up and went downstairs, refreshed from having lain next to Mark.

Bruno had packed, his three suitcases side by side on the

kitchen patio. Lying in bed with Mark, I'd missed the thin coat of white on the lawn. The melting frost glistened like fields of diamonds. Standing in a thin, narrow beam of sunlight, I watched him load his car.

He came inside to say good-bye and caught me in my near trance. "That's a lovely last impression to take with me. If you're not immersed in sunshine, you're radiating your own. Don't be concerned about my tools in the garage. In a few days I'll be back for them."

How could I send him off that way as if he were some employee caught stealing the family silver? I still had a great deal of affection for him. I do to this day, more than a year later. "Please have some breakfast before you go."

Bruno accepted and I began cracking eggs for an omelet. The activity invigorated me.

"I'm sorry you had to spend a fortune on the garage. You know, I'd have been perfectly happy to work my old ways out of doors when it was feasible, indoors with a light hanging from an extension cord. I would have paid for the marble myself somehow."

"But I wouldn't have been happy. It was my fault, not yours. Don't give it a second thought."

"Oh, but I will. More than twice. I was very happy here. The happiest. But artists have no right to think of happiness or permanence or creature comforts. Our happiness, our salvation, is our work. If we're lucky, permanence is in what we create. Comfort comes in knowing we've made something from nothing. Those of us who forget these things become either lapdogs or poseurs. We pose our subjects. Why not ourselves? Survival is the reason. You know all about survival, Laura. You've learned, I've noticed. Artistic survival is a special kind. Failure surrounds us all the time in most of what we do. In the world's eye and in ours. Even the strongest of us has occasional doubts."

Bruno cut his omelet into uneven portions and diligently spread them apart. They resembled the continents dividing from the solidified, primordial ooze. He proceeded to eat each continent, the smallest first. Australia, then Africa.

"Very often we're overcome with frustration, buried by it. The aftermath of failure. Did you know that when Rodin finished his *Orpheus* he deliberately broke off three of its fingers as an expression of his frustrations, a kind of self-mutilation?"

Bruno started on North America in combination with a piece of rye toast. "So much of my work is derivative of his. I took his strengths and added, I think, a delicacy, a subtlety missing in the master. I love contrasts, shadings, light, curves, sharp angles."

California and Mexico vanished in the scoop of his fork. "I'm not a failure, am I?"

"No, Bruno, you're not."

"Did you know that for a long time Rodin was an abysmal failure? To eat, to endure, he worked on embellishments for fireplaces. So I didn't feel the least guilty or embarrassed in taking from you. I didn't relish it either," he added, dispatching the entire Midwest, leaving only the eastern seaboard. "You have to know that, Laura. You also mustn't think I agonized over living here with you. I knew I was helping you to cope even as I was helping myself. I hoped that someday, when we parted, you'd feel a certain amount of gratitude for having nurtured a famous and talented sculptor whose works grace every major museum in the world." Bruno laughed at himself. "You see what childish bourgeois illusions I entertain, thinking you'd feel grand and noble for having contributed to my well-being. A Medici to Michelangelo, a Baronness von Meck to Tchaikovsky."

South America went, then half of Europe, up to the Iron Curtain. Only partially listening to Bruno now, I felt his apology or explanation or whatever, to be slightly ridiculous. But I was also moved by his admission of doubt and fear.

"It was more than looking to advance art, for me," I told him, touching his hand, momentarily delaying the dismemberment of China.

"For me it was more than that, too," he said. "But I can't allow myself to think that way. Bad art comes from such sentimentalities."

When the omelet world had been completely obliterated, as

though Bruno were a vengeful Jehovah dissatisfied with his handiwork, he pushed out from the table and stood up straight.

We kissed good-bye. Why not? We hadn't quarreled, only come to the end. All things die—civilizations, people, relationships. Ours ended better than most—with a warm hug and a cold kiss.

I walked Bruno to his car, arm in arm. I could see the missiles of last night all over the lawn and on the patio where they'd struck the house and fallen. Squares, triangles, and needles of glass from the broken windows sparkled in the sunlight, taking the place of the evaporating dew.

"We had a lot of good things going for us, Laura, but we didn't have love. Not really. I'm not capable of love in the usual sense. It's all channeled in one direction. And yours was temporarily misplaced. You'll want to remember that in the coming days. It'll help rebuild your marriage. You'll also want to know that never once while we were together did I lie to you."

This, of course, was a lie. But I didn't tell that to Bruno. There was no good reason soiling such a lovely ending. Mark had already destroyed one of his creations.

Dr. Rudy Frank came about 9:30 that morning and declared Mark a very sick man, but a healthy one who in short time would conquer the severe case of pneumonia. "Forget the hospital. You can really get sick in a hospital. He'll sweat it out at home, Lorri, just give it time. In my business, time works as well as antibiotics and aspirin, but keep it under your hat. We wouldn't want the public to know, not with Cedarhurst Chemists' rent to pay and my wife's expensive tastes. Just continue with the medicine, the juices, and the soup. But make sure *you* do the feeding."

"Why?"

"Because I want him to see you at the other end of the spoon. That's another medical trick of mine I wouldn't want the public to know."

For the next week, Mark floated in and out of consciousness. When coherent, he was often confused and I had to assure him that he was home, in his own bed, and that the statue of Bobbi no longer existed. He didn't once call out Virginia Healy's name or inquire about Bruno.

Rudy made two more house calls a week apart and each time said Mark was getting better though still terribly weak and subject to other viruses that lurked in the bushes.

House calls were also made by Sara and Caryn, Sara after school, Caryn on weekends. One brought him a book on Woodrow Wilson and the League of Nations, the other Eugene Maleska's collection of Sunday *Times* crossword puzzles. I forget who brought which but not the pleasure Mark showed in receiving both visitors and their gifts. They stayed for longer than the hour Rudy Frank had allotted them.

There was plenty of time for Mark and me to be alone. I read to him from the Wilson book and was his scribe doing the crossword puzzles, as well as his secretary, calling the store twice a day, and his courier between home and Cedarhurst Chemists for signed checks and the daily checkout sheets. At this request, I played some of the music I'd composed. He said that it touched him the way "Clair de Lune" did.

That first week, Virginia Healy called and asked if she could come by.

I wasn't sure whose benefit I had in mind when I answered, "The doctor wants no visitors for at least another ten days. He's very weak."

"It's you I want to see," she said.

---

The morning of Virginia Healy's visit I watched the road and driveway between trips to the bedroom. The cough medicine shimmered on the spoon as I fed it to Mark, thinking about what she might say. Meticulously, I'd prepared myself for the meeting: not too overdressed, yet not a slob. Beige slacks, a green pullover, Reeboks, and a dab of color on my lips, my hair brushed to sleekness and tied Indian-style behind.

I'd finished Mark's daily alcohol sponging and gotten him back into the pair of pajamas bought in honor of his pneumonia. I didn't hear the crush of shale as her car climbed up the driveway. The kitchen bell startled me.

She'd parked where the driveway ended, close to the patio, and stood at the screen door. With Bruno gone and Mark so sick, we hadn't changed to storms. The afternoon sunlight broke against her back, wisps of it curling around her body and setting fire to her hair.

Virginia Healy was nothing I'd imagined, yet everything I feared: tall, willowy, overflowing with life and sexuality, with a face that had retained a large measure of beauty despite obvious indications of a hard life.

"Would you help me?" she asked.

"Help you?"

"Yes. It's not that much but I'm in an awful hurry."

I followed her springy, toes-only stride to the car, a late-model red Honda with rally wheels and a sun roof. All the windows of the house and the garage had been repaired but the back lawn still held fragments of the statue, overlooked by the gardener. Like mushrooms, they dotted the still-green grass. I wondered if Virginia Healy noticed the pieces, if she suspected how they got there.

The rear seat of the car was covered with suitcases, newly bought and fresh smelling. Two garment bags hung in the back. The two old suitcases on the front seat and one of the garment bags, I recognized.

"I'm on my way to Phoenix and I thought the best thing was to bring his stuff myself. I know that he's been pretty sick but that he's recovering nicely, so I won't disturb him. Actually, I wanted to see you before I left town. I think I indicated that in my phone call."

We each took one of Mark's suitcases and she carried the garment bag over her shoulder. I let her go first so I could see her weighed down with the luggage, imagine her at work in the diner, guess how she might be in bed supporting herself under Mark's body.

Inside the kitchen, she lowered the suitcase and slung the garment bag over a chair.

"Do you have time for lunch?" I asked.

"Coffee would be fine," she answered at once and with certainty. "Nothing more. I'd like to be in North Carolina by sundown."

"Would you care to look around the house?" She was intelligent, that was for sure, and intelligent people are usually curious. She must have wondered about Mark's home for twenty-five years.

"No, thank you. Houses are only wood, stone, and glass in differing combinations. I'm seldom interested in physical objects, things. People, yes. That's why I wanted to meet you. I wanted you to know from *me* that he's back home where he belongs for good."

I usually take forever to get used to people. Longer if they're different from me. But at once I felt a kinship with Virginia that was more than her going-away present of my husband.

"I don't know if *he's* pleased about it," I told Virginia. "We haven't discussed the subject. He's not strong enough for serious things."

"Believe me, Laura—is Laura okay?"

I nodded.

"Believe me, this is where he wants to be. Oh, he made a valiant stab at another kind of life. You should have seen him puttering around the house with his caulking gun and paintbrush and hammer, getting everything shipshape like any other blue-collar worker on weekends. And making like Farmer Brown. Then there was that bit of silliness with the softball team. They were younger and tougher, my hard-drinking, hard-playing roughnecks. But he became one of them, a hero almost. To please me, I think," she said, first testing my coffee, then drinking half the cup. "The truth is, though, he never fit in. My people in Devon are decent people by any standards, with the same mix of good and bad as any group, but they weren't his kind and that's the whole of it."

In another rapid swallow, Virginia finished her coffee. "I saw them last night at the place Mark and I would often visit. To say good-bye and good luck. I didn't explain about Mark because I didn't have to. They knew. The Irish and the Jews are both very intuitive people. Anyhow, when Mark's up and around, tell him that O'Hara's irregulars were asking for him and that he's welcome there anytime. Also tell him that they're keeping shortstop open until the first of May. This may not seem like much to you but it's the highest compliment they could pay an outsider."

"I'll tell him."

"Tell him also that wherever I put down roots, I'll start a garden. I loved the way he made things grow."

"Yes."

"Can I have another cup of coffee?"

I hurried to pour for her and offered a piece of chocolate pound cake. When she accepted I felt grateful. She ate the cake slowly and I thought she'd have more to say. But she broke off only a corner and hardly touched the refill before getting up. "I think I'd better get started now. I'd like to beat the rush-hour traffic."

I walked her to the Honda.

"I hope you do well wherever you touch down," I told Virginia, meaning it. "Mark was very lucky to have found a person as decent as you."

Virginia laughed, and I noticed she had a crooked front tooth. "You wouldn't say that if you knew how seriously I'd thought of asking him to come with me. But the truth is I don't love him. I can't handle that emotion, but that's my problem. I cared a great deal for Mark, but it's no effort at all to care a great deal for him. I think he might have packed up and left, too. We'd have been happy for a while, maybe a long while. Except for one small detail. He doesn't love me. Eventually he'd find out and leave. I don't need another rejection from a man."

Virginia pulled up alongside me. She rolled down her window. "I don't usually give advice. But since I'll probably never see you again, or Mark, I'll offer it anyhow. Don't be so strong and self-reliant. Bend a little and let him into your real life. He's a rarity, our mutual friend; a good and decent man. The best I've ever known."

Before I could agree with her, she gunned her engine, raced down the driveway, and turned into the road on two wheels. I waited until the dust had settled before going back into the house. The coffee cups were still on the table, the coffee cold, the nibbled slice of cake lying flat on the plate. I sat for some time opposite her chair, finishing my cup and offering Virginia better responses than I'd given the first time.

---

From his sickbed, Mark emerged shakily to take charge in the store of the Christmas preparations. The season had already begun, making his task all the harder.

The first few days he came home late every night and we didn't talk much. I gave him supper, asked if he'd taken his medication during the day. He told me of his progress in the store. He asked about the girls. Caryn was growing more balloonlike and crotchety by the day. Sara was growing more sisterly, calling Caryn each morning to take soundings.

I waited patiently for Mark to make the first move. I tried priming him with the blandly expressed statement that Virginia had stopped by on her way out of town to drop off his things. That we'd talked and I'd found her kind and generous.

All of which he accepted with unuttered equanimity and nothing more. What was he thinking? I felt frustrated, but I was there for him every night, no matter how late he came home.

I enrolled at Hofstra for a course in folk music and joined Sara at MADD. Composing filled my mornings. I was almost content.

By the second week in December, Mark was caught up in the store. He decided to rest at home that Sunday. Totally. Not a scrap of paperwork in his attaché case.

That morning we were up early. We slept in the same bed but he'd studiously avoided touching me, fondly or otherwise, all the days of his recovery, and nights after his return to the store.

Breakfast had been a homey, friendly affair, pleasantries swapped, domestic questions bandied about. Outside, a light-as-dust snow was falling, the first of the year. All the shades in the kitchen had been raised, the back door opened to greet the wintry scene. The morning before, Mark had replaced the screens with storms. I'd observed him as he'd worked, remembering how Virginia had described his "puttering around." He'd seemed miles away, perhaps as far as Phoenix, though he enjoyed the chore.

Mark looked up from his cream-cheesed bagel. "When we're done, can we sit in the living room together? I'll build a fire and we'll talk."

The cups rattled their saucers like kettledrums as I removed them from the table. I must have seemed like a new bride serving her first breakfast. Mark offered to help me but I sent him on ahead to start the fire.

I expected and dreaded the worst. After all, he'd so deliberately shunned me. In the store, he could have used the phone to trace down Virginia. They could have made plans long-distance.

The living-room setting was a perfect Currier and Ives print. The snow bleached the lawn and evergreens outside. There was a busy fire on the hearth, which tossed playful shadows on the walls and ceilings. Mark was seated before the fire, some of the shadows performing on him.

I pulled up a companion chair but sat a few yards away. We watched the drama of the flames until he was ready to begin.

"I've changed some, Laura. I've learned a little about sharing and reaching outside myself. But maybe not that much. Maybe not enough for you. I don't know." He looked at me. "I just don't know."

"I've changed, too, Mark. And learned a lot. Maybe not enough either. I'll never know—we'll never know—if we don't try. We're not exactly the same people anymore. Let's begin with that and see where it takes us."

To be honest, I expected one of those melodramatic pauses, music rising to a crescendo, then for Mark to sweep me in his arms. A neatly choreographed climax. Instead, he put his head in his hands and cried through his fingers.

"Oh, Laura, I miss her so."

At first I thought he was carrying on about Virginia, his lost love. Then I knew that it was for Bobbi, and everything he'd kept inside those fifteen months began pouring out. I went to comfort him and found him willing to be comforted. He had changed, more than a little. But coming to his rescue, I found myself trapped in his tears. And mine.

The snow grew heavier, keeping pace with the unloading of his terrible burden. Unattended, the fire gradually died out, but we didn't know it, sealed in each other's arms.

When we both could speak, Mark said, "I was such a fool to believe I could escape heartache, that decency and hard work would protect us. But I was a bigger fool to think, when it came, that I could handle it alone as though it were my private possession. I expected you to understand everything without my saying a word. When that didn't happen, I ran away like some spoiled child. I should have stayed and fought back. I should have helped you. I should have helped us."

We were sitting together on the floor. I don't know how we got there. I moved out of Mark's arms. "I did the same thing, Mark. I ran away, too. In my own way, looking for answers. It didn't work. But I never stopped loving you. Then you destroyed the statue and that made everything clear again or maybe for the first time."

"I can't make any promises, Laura."

"I won't either, except to say that we're talking and sharing. We've begun well."

Mark stood first, then lifted me. I felt the pressure of his hands leading me into him. I didn't need directions. His kiss was the sweetest, longest one of our lives.

"That was . . . nice," I said, nearly wordless.

"Now, shall we walk to Cedarhurst in the snow for dinner or stay in?"

"Stay in. We have a lot of homework to catch up on," I said bravely, hopefully.

Mark ran his hands down my back and over my buttocks. "What a lovely idea. Next problem. Shall we do our homework before dinner or after?"

"After," I breathed. "Awhile after. We have all day."

"We have lots of days. Weeks of days, years of days. Centuries, if we do it right."

"This time we will," I promised.

"This time," he agreed.

# *epilogue*

I's AUTUMN AGAIN, when life should be golden and bountiful, and is—most of the time. We've gotten through our first summer in Greenport, far out on the North Fork of the Island. We sold the house and the store after Christmas and moved out here during a January thaw. One day over lunch, we suddenly decided that the old barn was too big for us, that it held too many memories, good and bad. The good we treasured but they'd become harder to deal with than the bad.

I've gotten a job at one of the local pharmacies and put in three days a week behind the prescription counter. Laura works part-time for the town library, developing new programs that don't cost too much, her old specialty. We haven't entirely abandoned our old ways, you see, just enough to allow for change.

Together we've embarked upon a fine new life. We live mainly for each other and ourselves in the smaller house on the Sound, down a narrow one-lane dirt road, half a mile from the nearest neighbor.

We're fifty feet off the shoreline, with enough land for me to grow a variety of vegetables and for Laura to raise marigolds, zinnias, and mums in all colors of the spectrum. My crops have been tomatoes, of course, and bell peppers and stringbeans on a low wall of chicken wire, and corn taller than me, with tassles that bow gracefully to the ocean breezes. For the first time I've tried eggplant and have gotten the most erotic-looking purple fruit that hang heavy as the breasts of African women. Also cucumber and squash, pumpkins which we've found can be cooked and eaten and not used solely for jack-o'-lanterns.

We read a lot. We go to concerts and plays at the high school. We eat out three times a week. We swim in the Sound.

Last summer we bought one-speed bicycles and traveled the entire North Fork back roads with our lunches strapped over the rear wheels.

This fall we picked apples, three dollars a bushel, and stored them in our pantry room.

Part of the property is a thick woods where we're hard at work cultivating a bird sanctuary with feeding stations, watering troughs, and warning posters.

In the winter we plan to spend our free mornings laying down fresh prints in the snow.

Caryn has a child now, a fine healthy son they've named Samuel. In the spring Sara will give birth to twins, according to Rudy Frank, who should know.

Laura has made the adjustment better than I imagined. She doesn't jog at midnight or spend excessive hours locked in a room playing the flute, though she's continued composing. In March she hopes to give a one-woman recital of her own works, with Vivaldi and Ravel thrown in for variety. She no longer gets up during the night to go out on the redwood deck and read the Sound.

Without concerted effort, we've grown closer together. Brave and funny and optimistic, our new marriage has knit more strongly than the old. Some mornings when we're home and it's raining or too nasty for bird-watching or beach walking, we lie in bed for hours and make love.

Bundling together under the blankets, we talk about the hell we've been put through and put each other through. I think of Virginia then, fondly and with gratitude. That part of my life has become a blur. I suspect that Laura thinks about Bruno now and then as well. Any day now we'll laugh about our brief excursions away from one another, the funny as well as the unfunny parts.

We've even begun to talk about Bobbi without completely breaking up. The wonderful and foolish things she did. After all, she was no angel. She was the child we loved and lost and still love as strongly as ever. Once a month we drive across the Island to visit her grave. Those are the best and worst of times for us, and we are always happy to get back home.

We have no real fears about the future or getting old, with dewlaps and abdominal overhang. We've survived the worst of all tragedies and have gained inner peace, a reward granted very few despite payments made in full.

Of course none of this means we've gotten used to a world without Bobbi. In our hearts and minds, though, she's gained a kind of immortality, and that's all we can truly expect of life and death. But a day fails to pass that I don't stop and recall the time she . . . Should the memory become too vivid, too overpowering, I call up Laura wherever she is and share it with her. (Often she calls me first with a similar thought.) Laura adds her own version, then slowly the pain subsides and we go about our business again.

---

We're getting better, we tell ourselves, and someday we'll be adjusted to the one supreme fact of our lives and we won't have to make those emergency calls.

But for now, when we think of her, it hurts.

God, does it hurt.